Secrets of a 100ft BOY

A Partially-Fictionalized
But Mostly-True
Semi-Autobiographical
Coming-of-Age
'70's Murder Mystery

**JULIEN CHARLES LEIGH
LÖWENFELS**

PALMETTO
PUBLISHING
Charleston, SC
www.PalmettoPublishing.com

Copyright © 2024 by Julien Charles Leigh Löwenfels

All rights reserved

No portion of this book may be reproduced, stored in a retrieval system, or transmitted in any form by any means—electronic, mechanical, photocopy, recording, or other—except for brief quotations in printed reviews, without prior permission of the author.

Hardcover ISBN: 9798822959910
Paperback ISBN: 9798822959927
eBook ISBN: 9798822959934

Contents

Music List.. vii

Preface xi

Chapter 1 — *The Move* 1

Chapter 2 — *The Hotel* 13

Chapter 3 — *The Villa* 22

Chapter 4 — *The Record Booth* 33

Chapter 5 — *The Parents* 37

Chapter 6 — *The Grandmother* 53

Chapter 7 — *The Bigger* 61

Chapter 8 — *The Abandoned Cottages* 78

Chapter 9 — *The Bus* 92

Chapter 10 — *The Zombie Kitten* 96

Chapter 11 — *The Brogues* 116

Chapter 12 — *The Smell* 132

Chapter 13 — *The Investigation* 142

Chapter 14 — *The Waitress* 155

Chapter 15 — *The Tortoise* 162

Chapter 16 — *The Plague* 165

Chapter 17 — *The Wok* 174

Chapter 18 — *The Slapstick Gene* 183

Chapter 19 — *The Owner* 187

Chapter 20 — *The Restaurant*. *203*

Chapter 21 — *The Capture*. *213*

Chapter 22 — *The Murder*. *221*

Chapter 23 — *The Showing of Hers* *228*

Chapter 24 — *The Winter (of our discontent)* *239*

Chapter 25 — *The Check Out* *252*

Footnote — *The Guests* *259*

Epilogue 1 — *That Pic by the Pool* *261*

Epilogue 2 — *Murder – A Family Affair* *263*

Epilogue 3 — *A Return To The El Encanto*. *282*

Epilogue 4 — *How Scott Camp Became Julien Charles Leigh Löwenfels* *292*

Music List

Chapter 1: "Band on the Run" *by Paul McCartney and Wings*

Chapter 2: "In the Hall of the Mountain King" *by Will Bradley & Ray McKinley*

Chapter 3: "I Ain't Got Nothing but The Blues" *by Ella Fitzgerald & Duke Ellington*

Chapter 4: "Magical Mystery Tour" *by The Beatles*

Chapter 5: "Bei Mir Bist Du Shein" *by The Andrews Sisters*

Chapter 6: "Falling in Love Again" *by Marlene Dietrich*

Chapter 7: "Rock On" *by David Essex*

Chapter 8: "Time in a Bottle" *by Jim Croce*

Chapter 9: "I've Got to Use My Imagination" *by Gladys Knight & The Pips*

Chapter 10: "The Exorcist Theme" *by Michael Oldfield*

Chapter 11: "Lucy in the Sky with Diamonds" *by The Beatles*

Chapter 12: "The Air That I Breathe" *by The Hollies*

Chapter 13: "Rikki Don't Lose That Number" *by Steely Dan*

Chapter 14: "Sundown" *by Gordon Lightfoot*

Chapter 15: "Wish You Were Here" *by Pink Floyd*

Chapter 16: "Midnight at the Oasis" *by Maria Muldaur*

Chapter 17: "Fire" *by Ohio Players*

Chapter 18: "Pineapple Rag/Gladiolus Rag" *from "The Sting" Soundtrack*

Chapter 19: "Love Hurts" *by Nazareth*

Chapter 20: "Nothing from Nothing" *by Billy Preston*

Chapter 21: "Billy Don't Be A Hero" *by Bo Donaldson and The Heywoods*

Chapter 22: "Earache My Eye" *by Cheech & Chong*

Chapter 23: "Crocodile Rock" *by Elton John*

Chapter 24: "Sunshine on My Shoulders" *by John Denver*

Chapter 25: "Seasons in The Sun" *by Terry Jacks*

Dedicated to my parents,

who paid a high price

for a good sense of humor.

0051
Date 6/24 1974
Dollars $
RECEIPT
Date May 21 1974
Received From
Address
For
Dollars $
0029
By
0072
Dollars $
By A. Camp
0342

Preface

NOVEMBER 1ST, 2022

Most families have interesting stories to tell and I, therefore, don't feel particularly special, which was one of my many counter-inspirational blocks. After literally decades of processing my own issues, I finally realized that the events and people that this story addresses are unique to me, and after all, I am one of many unique voices in the world, and only I have this particular story to tell. In fact, I'm the only person left to tell it, as my mother, father and sister are all deceased, my oldest brother Randal has been estranged and disinherited since 1978, and my other brother, Casey, has other pursuits, and is, by his own admission, traumatized by our childhood.

The story involves things that do standout a bit from what friends and acquaintances have told me about their families – things like the combination of an extremely dysfunctional old Hollywood family involved in a murder, while living in a hotel, I have found are somewhat rare within my sphere of understanding; there is also a later murder, within the family itself, which is the ultimate designer piece in the dysfunctional style, an "accessory to murder," so to speak. For these reasons, while this has been a story I have always wanted to write, it has taken me about thirty years to face this project; I have in the meantime received a gold medal in procrastination, a silver in avoidance, and a bronze in distraction.

Almost forty years ago, I was just beginning to find enjoyment in writing stories – mostly autobiographical – and the habit began when I left home for the last time at nineteen and took to sending letters back home about my exploits. I didn't know how much my parents enjoyed them until they told me that they were reading my letters to anyone who would listen – their doctors, the postman, the veterinarian – who were all surprised I wasn't a real writer, and my parents were very encouraging themselves, often telling me to consider becoming a writer professionally, way back then. But those were the encouragements of parents and their friends, pleasant but nothing I would count on to pay my rent; now the question is, can I really do this writing thing?

I've avoided what felt like a "true calling" for as long as I could, instead pursuing mediocre success in excitingly mundane careers in the food service, television, legal and sales industries, occasionally sitting down to write about my struggles within these contexts – and there have been many – and also coming up against a personal belief and wall of resistance, which goes something like: So many crazy things have happened, how is anyone ever going to believe that this has all happened within this one family? And to me? As the saying goes, you can't make this shit up – so I hope that my commitment to writing this book will open the flood gates of confidence for me, and I'll be able to continue to share my actually rather fucked-up journey with the world – or with at least anyone who graces my stories by reading them; this is but one story of many I could tell. And, if my story can provide any healing or support for someone else out there in a tricky family situation or recovering from one, then and only then will I consider my efforts a success. My only hope is that it reaches those who need to hear it, and that it helps them somehow. Complex childhood trauma and post traumatic stress disorder are sticky wickets to sort out, and my recovery continues minute by minute as I rocket toward sixty-years old as of this writing.

Inspired by what they saw in my letters home, my parents kept telling me that I should especially write "that" story about the El Encanto Hotel – or furthermore, they would ask me the question, "When are you going to write that story?" The answer turned out to be right around the time I receive a frightening medical diagnosis of severe coronary artery disease, that's when.

This story in particular was one that felt exceedingly overwhelming to write, as it takes place over a year that my family spent living at the El Encanto Hotel in Santa Barbara in 1974-75. A variety of different and strange events happened in that year, and the years prior and after, to the point it felt exhausting just to think about jotting it all down; I've been literally getting up the nerve to do this, so thanks for your patience. The El Encanto story seems to me to be the black hole at the center of my family's wobbly galaxy, so I'll start here and see where it leads, hopefully avoiding the event horizon for fear of being pulled down into its dark core to never emerge again.

So, yes, it's now or never for me to write this thing – perfect timing with a doctor-encouraged medical retirement after nearly forty-four years of various jobs and careers, last one being a real estate broker; it seems that stress has now become my kryptonite, and my heart and nervous system simply can't handle the stress of another real estate transaction – and I refuse to die at a septic tank inspection.

Prior to receiving my diagnosis in August of 2022, I had already decided to take June and July off from work to get married (a destination wedding no less) and begin this book; in retrospect, it was so cute of me to decide that the best time to begin this lengthy process, which requires deep levels of concentration, was right before planning and preparing for a destination wedding.

On top of that, our beloved sixteen-year old dog, Upton O' Goode, began his final journey to the other side of the rainbow at the end of

June, so the fact that I was able to get anything down on paper afterward, given the wedding and his death, is a personal miracle.

So, despite the distraction of planning a wedding, I stuck to the commitment I had made to myself, and on my 58th birthday, June 1st, I found myself with a mug of coffee and a blank screen, ready to begin, with a whirlpool of the stuff of life swirling around me. Like a lot of writers whom I've heard about, the screen remained blank for the greater portion of that first day, until finally, I decided to make a request to my parents hoping they could provide some details to help me begin; the only obstacle was the fact that they're dead.

With a mind as blank as my screen, I walked up to the altar I have set up in a corner of our bedroom, hoping to use it as some kind of cosmic cell phone. The altar includes various family artifacts and knick-knacks, along with feathers, crystals, shells, (plastic) skulls, porcelain Chinese figurines, with a larger Chinese figure set in the center, which sits on top of an old and heavy iron water meter cover I found in the backyard of the first house I purchased.

Suffice to say, it's not what many spiritualists might see as a proper altar, and I can't say whether or not it actually does anything, other than gather dust - it just feels better somehow to approach this altar and those figurines, which belonged to my father, and talk to them when I'm working on manifesting something.

Under the larger statue in the center, there are the four smaller porcelain Chinese figures, and my father used to repeatedly tell me who each figure represented - my two older siblings, my mother and himself. The one he indicated represented himself was the poor fellow with the large yoke over his shoulders and a hangdog expression, fitting for the erstwhile provider of the family.

So far unable to write a single word, I approached the altar with high hopes, and lighting a stick of Palo Santo, I used a hawk feather to spread the smoke around the figures, and spoke the following request:

"Okay, Mom and Dad, you "In-Search-Of"-watching, ghost-believing, bigfoot-obsessed, UFO-loving freaks – I need details! Please, come to me in a dream or whatever and tell me some things about the El Encanto, so I can finally write that damn book. If you're really listening, if you're really there, then prove it! This is your chance!" I know, quite the sacred, respectful spell, wasn't it?

After my moment in front of the altar, nothing came to me the rest of that day, nor overnight – no dreams, no visions – zippo – so, on the morning of June 2nd, with a heavy sigh and an over-the-mystical shrug, I sat down to begin the book anyway.

Within a short time, the words were coming, although I wasn't feeling jazzed by them, but after about twenty minutes I hit a wall, which for me was wanting to know the square footage of the cottage at the hotel into which we had moved in 1974. You see, part of the difficulty at that time was the fact we had been evicted from a large, Queen Anne-style farmhouse we were renting, and I always have wondered how the hell we fit into that little cottage – what was the square footage of it anyway? Blame it on a realtor's innate desire to know such details, but I couldn't get past this lack of necessary information, so I leaned back in my chair and sulked for about five more minutes, nursing a really good chunk of writer's block.

More questions began bubbling up, such as, when exactly had we moved in – what date? I panicked a bit realizing that I was only ten-years old at the time, so how much could I really remember of the details? I certainly could construct somewhat of a story, but I was attempting in my amateurish way to write a good book – and "good" is in the details, or something like that.

Oddly, just then, this little voice floated down to me while I was stewing in the chair, and asked, "I wonder if you have anything in your old paper files about the hotel?"

Like many of us in the personal computer era, I haven't used paper files in a long time, and I certainly had not found any reason to look in my old filing cabinet for at least ten years or so. I was inspired by the little voice's question enough to begrudgingly rise from my chair, walk with annoyance into the other room, and I opened the lower drawer of the cabinet. I had the same feeling I used to get when kid me asked my mother where something was, and she would impatiently answer, "Just look." "Okay, Mother, I'm just looking," I said to myself.

Opening it made clear how much time had gone by since I last looked in there; dust bunnies, or more like dust bears, comprised of the old dog hair of my other departed canine, Wookie, were inside the cabinet, and he'd been dead for nearly ten years. Like something out of a horror movie, the files were not only covered with his fur, but also cobwebs and a thick layer of dust; I was surprised that a colony of bats didn't explode from the drawer, and also a little disappointed. Turns out, the cabinet is open at the bottom and has no backing, which accounts for the interior dirt, and while I have vacuumed in the last ten years around it, who vacuums the insides of their filing drawers? Not me.

Sneezing and thumbing through the files, I did have a couple of nostalgic "Oh ya, that!" reactions to certain items and near the end of the alphabetical order, I came to the "W" section, and there was a manila folder with the word "Writing" scribbled on it. It was overstuffed with old attempts – some of my handwritten poems and other items leftover from when I first joined my writing group nearly seventeen years ago and used to print everything out to read to the group.

There was also a manuscript from the early '90's entitled, "Fred Mertz is a Gay Alien," with a large post-it stuck to the front that said in my usual all-caps handwriting, "This is a first draft and it's no good!" - which speaks greatly to the confidence I have in my own abilities.

Just behind that document though, was a rather tattered, business-sized mailing envelope shoved way down in the folder, with my mother's unmistakable handwriting in a combination of ballpoint pen and felt tip, "Please choose what you need for the story – & PLEASE BURN THE REST!" and I could hear her saying the last section in all caps in her usual theatrical delivery, which was always meant to be funny, so I giggled nostalgically, feeling instantly close to her again. And beneath that statement, "El Encanto Hotel (Receipts), Rental Agreement + pay schedule." Eureka! Just the sort of time capsule of information I needed to start the book.

I have no recollection of how this envelope ended up in my files, but she must have given this to me some thirty-years ago during one of my parents' urgings that I needed to write "that" story.

As you can imagine, chills went up and down my body – I couldn't believe what I was holding. As I opened the envelope and investigated the contents, the goosebumps and tingles rose even more sharply; not only were the items she mentioned inside, but also there was a schematic of the cottage, with all wall measurements, expertly drawn by my father – I now had the square footage and the layout!

In addition to that, I made another startling discovery: We moved into the cottage at the hotel on June 1st, 1974, my tenth birthday, a fact I never knew – an amazing coincidence. And lastly, there was an old fax print-out, on the kind of paper that just disintegrates, with my mother's notes about what she could remember about our year at the hotel; unbelievable!

I was absolutely astonished and began to yell excitedly at my husband about what I had just found. It was as though my request at the altar the night before had been heard, and because I'm always hunting for any motivational sign that I should be writing "that" story, this discovery is what made me sit down and get to work.

A final note: Selected music choices are suggested at the beginning of each chapter with the thought that listening to each before reading the related chapter will set the mood for you – an interactive experience, the reason for this becoming clear by Chapter 4. The music was chosen based on what I was directly listening to or overheard during the year at the hotel.

I hope you will enjoy this.

~ Julien Löwenfels.

Please choose what you need for the story – & PLEASE BURN THE REST!
El Encanto Hotel
(Receipts)
Rental agreement + pay schedule

Chapter 1 — The Move

RECORD BOOTH SUGGESTED SONG: "BAND ON THE RUN,"
PAUL MCCARTNEY AND WINGS

"Oh, Arthur, there's no dead body over there in the bushes!" Mother yelled. We could all smell something, though.

It was June 1st, 1974, and we had just moved into Villa 100 at the El Encanto Hotel in Santa Barbara. I quietly picked at my sunburned nose early that first morning as I contemplated the upper-crusty sound of the included weekly maid service that came with our rental cottage in the hotel's upper gardens. Mother had ordered some scrambled eggs and orange juice for me from the front desk, and I also liked the sound of "from the front desk" just a little bit too much. As far as I was concerned, we had finally made the grade. I was part of a dire family financial situation, but I still wanted to become accustomed to a life I actually wanted to be accustomed to. I was playing with pretentiousness.

We had just been forced out of our beloved two-story, vintage home on Chapala Street, by an evil Santa Barbara attorney; our former home would forever be known by my family as the "Big House on Chapala" or simply the "Big House." I think we all were somewhat in a state of shock as we faced our fate in Villa 100, where we were surrounded by seemingly endless cardboard boxes, antique furniture stacked to the ceilings in every available room, a sea of strewn clothing, and my father's many artworks and paintings covered with blankets, which were leaning against the walls all around us - we barely had room to move.

Our furniture and other belongings were in no discernable arrangement of any kind, since we had rushed-moved from the five-bedroom Big House. We were now going to full-time occupy a tiny cottage that was really just a weekend bungalow for the El Encanto's guests. In looking around, I realized it wasn't much of a "Villa," a worldly title that in my mind suggested it should be much grander than it actually was. Once again, a feeling of crushing disappointment flooded through my body. I yearned so greatly to be to the manor born, but the imagined silver spoon in my mouth tasted more like pewter.

Along with the other difficulties of residing in such a small building, given the amount of furniture and belongings we had, the move would require the unspeakable truth that I would be sharing a bedroom with my brother, Casey, something I had not had to do since I was in a crib. My assessment of him was that he was mean, violent, scary, and that he smelled – he rarely bathed. I had been developing my own witch's spell for a couple of years to compel him to brush his teeth. And besides, his being fourteen-years old meant that he was well on his way through puberty; he was getting taller, hairier, smellier and meaner than ever before. My only escape from all of this "him-ness" had been my own bedroom at the Big House, and, well, now, I had no idea what I was going to do if I inadvertently pissed him off and needed to run; if he caught me, I knew he would pin me down and breathe on me.

I stopped thinking about this for a moment and returned my thoughts to the upside of living in a hotel, with all of its included amenities. In addition to the weekly maid service, which included linens, and cleaning, there were other perks, like having food sent up from the kitchen and about five acres of hotel grounds where I could roam, play and explore, and which also included the most exciting thing for me – a swimming pool. I continued to sit quietly while assessing the pros and cons of our new situation, and decided to focus on the pros, which remains to this day a deeply-embedded coping strategy.

In our parents' opinion, this all was the fault of Mrs. Zimdin, owner of the Big House on Chapala, and her attorney, the pestilence-tongued thug-at-law, Mr. Rosenberg. My mother had long ago dropped the "Mrs." simply referring to her as "Zimdin," a name befitting an evil Disney villain. Zimdin and her flying monkey in a three-piece suit had all but thrown us out of the Big House with their own spiteful claws.

Squeezing through the Villa, packed with our household dishevelment, I mournfully thought about our lost Big House; it was unassuming in its grandeur; a rather plain but imposing 1906 two-story farm-style residence on a large corner lot. The home was built by and had once belonged to the Hunt Family, who owned a locally well-known china and flatware store at 12 East Carrillo Street, in downtown Santa Barbara. To a physically small boy such as myself, the rooms, hallways and yard surrounding the Big House were the stuff of fantasies, and it had all loomed large from my perspective, like a castle.

I had lived there from ages five to ten, so half of my life thus far. It felt like it was our home, and it is still hard for me to think about the Big House as merely a rental. The concepts of landlord and tenant, ownership and leases were of no meaning to my young mind at the time of the eviction – all I knew was that our home had been taken away from us. For the first time in my life, I felt the exquisite pain of being a Santa Barbara family that could not afford to buy a home of their own, and the feelings of being less than my contemporaries sunk deeply into my soul, the evidence of our low status being that we could be so unceremoniously kicked-out of the Big House; I didn't want any of my friends to know.

I was already missing the front and side yards, and the little orange trees that produced so much fruit that even the raccoons could eat no more. The home also had a hidden rear patio, and a mysterious basement with a crumbling sandstone block foundation. The rumor was that this sandstone had been taken from the Chumash Indian dwellings (built by their Spanish oppressors), which were several little sandstone houses on the Santa Barbara Mission's original grounds. There were still some of these one room sandstone hovels up by the Mission with no roofs but relatively intact, and the stones of the Big House's foundation did indeed look very similar to the sandstone building blocks of the Chumash dwellings; I thought this was really cool.

We had really settled into the Big House over our five years of residency and added features to it as well. I especially had enjoyed the tree houses that Father and our older brother, Randal, had helped us to construct – we had two; one in the large Pepper tree next to the driveway and another in a small oak near the sidewalk – great for spying on passersby.

It was sad to realize that I would never be in the large country kitchen with the service porch again, where my parents had hooked up an antique, wrought-iron gas stove for me, supporting my desire to learn how to cook. The service porch was a long, narrow space with many windows, making it almost feel like a greenhouse.

I was spoiled by the hallway between the kitchen and the dining room where my parents had installed our own soda fountain, so we were able to make banana splits and hot fudge sundaes for ourselves (with permission) – a fairly substantial childhood fantasy made real and the stuff of legend with our friends.

We'd had so many great holidays in the Big House, with stunning, giant Christmas trees lighting up the large entry hall, trees which reached to the bottom of the landing, eleven feet above; large, sumptuous Thanksgiving dinners in the expansive dining room, and theatrical Halloween nights, when the Big House was transformed into a haunted mansion by my father, who had once been involved in the art and set design for the original Disneyland.

I would miss the days that my father taught art classes in the large study, his students sitting with their easels around him, listening intently; he looked so impressive to me. I'll never forget the day our gardener interrupted an art class to ask my father how to operate a shovel – a short anecdote that was legendary for my parents.

Most of all, I was going to miss my room and the door I used to shut out the insanity that was my family and my childhood. My mother and father were the sort of couple who would have nearly a daily argument, if not several, and we had a variety of other family members that had stayed with us over the duration of our calling the Big House our home, who all enjoyed a good fight. My eldest brother, Randal, his wife Sylvia, who suffered from schizophrenia, as well as my older sister Andrea, and her husband Michael, and my baby nephew Lindsay, had once lived in the house with us for a couple of months until they were settled elsewhere. When Grandfather died, Grandmother moved-in and was cared for by Mother in the home as well until Grandmother moved into her own home up the street from us. They all took turns verbally sparring with each other any time the opportunity presented itself.

There were a lot of comings and goings of visitors and other guests, and being from Hollywood, my parents enjoyed colorful, eccentric people; lovers of music and drinking, witty banter, and the unfortunate shadow side to these qualities – dysfunction, addiction, narcissism, and more arguments. We had become known in the neighborhood as the "Crazy Camps," a title I was learning little by little was not entirely inaccurate.

Mother had been urging Father for years to figure out a way to buy the Big House; we all really loved it and as I said, it felt like our forever home. There was an elegance and stability in its presence, things that we almost genetically yearned for as a family, and often failed to obtain, despite all of the positive things to which all of us children were exposed – such as endless history and art books, an extensive music collection, original artworks, foreign films – all the trappings of sophistication with none of the substantial resources to make these interests sustainable; it had the reverse effect of making us unsatisfied by the status quo and the financial struggles all the more frustrating. We had champagne taste on a tap water budget.

Lack of money was an ever-present issue, and there was a baseline frequency of insecurity in our family – this made it hard to enjoy and honor the family's gifts and talents. Intellectual, artistic, and musical gifts were quietly resented unless they produced income to medicate our deprivation anxiety, particularly when it came to Mother's feelings and attitude toward our father.

We'd moved into the Big House in 1970 from another house in the Samarkand area, which was an ugly duckling of a stucco suburban home and was our first landing place in Santa Barbara. My older siblings had explained to me that before I was born, our family had moved many times in Los Angeles as well, so being in the Big House for five years straight was the new family consistency record.

Unfortunately, Father had waited too long and was unsuccessful in putting together a viable plan to purchase the home, and even further, he was falling behind on the rent as well. It was inevitable that Zimdin would eventually come swooping down from her roost of judgment above the Montecito Country Club to root out the Crazy Camps from her property.

She had arrived unexpectedly one day, knocking loudly on the door. As Mother opened it, Zimdin pushed her way past and began to walk through our home like a drill sergeant conducting an inspection in a barracks, dragging her white-gloved fingertips on every surface, peeking in closets, all the while ignoring Mother's protesting of the intrusion. It appeared that Zimdin had obtained some insider information, or had heard some neighborhood gossip about us, because it felt like more than a simple look-see; she seemed to be seeking something – maybe a cache of weapons or illegal drugs – it felt less like a landlord's visit and more like a police raid.

Making her way outside, Zimdin had literally turned up her nose in disgust at the sight of our tree houses, while also citing the clauses in our lease, which stated "no pets," casting sideways glances at our dog, our cats, our doves, and our tortoise during her investigation. She finally stopped, turned to face Mother, who had been following behind her. Zimdin folded her arms across her belly and gave the look that the well-to-do will often give to whom they perceive as inferior. We rarely saw Mother beg in any situation, but she pleaded with intense sincerity with Zimdin to let us stay, promising to remove the tree houses, and asking her to continue the talks with our father regarding our purchase of the home, and explaining that we had adopted pets with the assumption that we would soon be the Big House's owners.

Instead of commiserating with a mother who was trying to protect and care for her children's wellbeing, the old witch turned and stomped across the lawn, heading for the limousine waiting for her at the curb, stepping into the rear seat and slamming the door, making no further eye contact with Mother; Zimdin's large automobile purged away with a surprisingly dramatic flourish of rumbling engine noise and exhaust.

A few days later, the flying-monkey attorney, Rosenberg, appeared on the porch, handing Mother an eviction notice, citing lease violations, and stating that the talks about the purchase were utter rubbish; Mother found out at that very moment that there had been no mention of such a plan and that Father had been leading us all on. Father was at work when Rosenberg arrived, and overhearing this, I preloaded my anxiety about the upcoming fight my parents were now going to have when Father returned home.

The eviction notice provided only three days in which to vacate, a monumental task. All five bedrooms and any other spaces were fully furnished, a mixture of our parents and their parents' antiques, books, art – all the furnishings of a large household. Since Grandmother had already moved out and into her own townhouse, which was not large enough for all of her belongings, we had a lot of her stuff too. There was also a basement full of the accumulation of twenty-nine years of marriage and children: Piles of "I may need that someday" stuff, locking trunks, leftover classic automobile parts, Randal's childhood toys, Father's childhood toys, portfolios of old college artwork and a stunning collection of Christmas tree decorations. Father was the docent of our museum of junk, and he liked to foster the family mythology that there were "valuable" items in the accumulation as a way to prevent anything from being discarded.

There was also a detached garage full of more stuff, not to mention my father's art studio with cases, easels, tools and all of his art supplies. The night following the Rosenberg visit, the despair in our parents faces as they discussed the move caused a visceral sympathetic feeling for my brother and me - and I was finding it hard to breathe just listening to them.

Another factor was my parents' utter feeling of humiliation. The Big House on Chapala had become a symbol of long-sought success for them and to lose it meant being the people their judgmental parents had said they were – unstable, flakey, artistic Hollywood types, and a big joke to all; here we were again, the Crazy Camps, back on the road for another circus-like "adventure" to an unknown destination, they'd probably say.

A volcanic argument ensued about what Rosenberg had said about the alleged purchase of the Big House. The fight became so heated, that my mother began hurtling lamps and other possessions at my father, so Randal (who had been called immediately, at his new home in Los Angeles, to come help with emergency packing) had taken my brother and I out of the house for safety and sat us in his car. As we hid in Randal's car crying, we could still hear our parents screaming at one another inside the Big House, and finally the police arrived, likely called by a neighbor; the officers didn't need the address – they'd been to our house before.

The police left after helping our parents to calm down, and Father left for about three hours. I guessed that he must be out looking for a place to move. Despite what might be viewed as his failings, Father was a charming and bright man, and although I was in the throes of grief and panic, I knew he would succeed in finding a place for us to go. His powers of charm were so strong, that I had witnessed Father driving away with a car from a used car lot, more than once, without spending a penny. He was so successful at doing this that Mother nicknamed him "Boris Car-lot." By the end of his life, Father would own over one-hundred automobiles.

Father failed to tell us where we were going – there was too much to do. All he said was the often-heard battle cry of "Get packing!" - so that's what we did. It took us every second of all three days to pack the Big House's contents, between the crying, blame-assigning, rebuttals and anxiety-driven screaming fights. Despite every effort to expedite our preparations with all of the harsh, rushed work, we still ended up moving in the middle of the third and final night, with Randal's help, by loading a rented moving truck. There was a lot of bickering going on during the process between Randal and our parents. Old wounds were ripped open as fast as boxes were sealed, and after moving night, Randal would disappear from our lives for the next three years.

I had been sent to bed earlier than everyone else, my mother having sensed the overwhelm and struggle of her high-functioning autistic child. My room now consisted of a sleeping bag and a bare mattress on the floor of my otherwise empty bedroom. I wept uneasily amid the chaos and sounds of the crisis unfolding downstairs. I was in and out of sleep, occasionally awakened by the sounds of my parents and Randal as they were packing by the light of the uncovered bulb of the last remaining lamp. The sound of exhaustion in their voices, heard over the sounds of tape screeching off of rolls, the crunching sounds of breakables being wrapped in newspaper, and chaotic footsteps echoing up and down the rear steps, as they were carrying items out to the truck parked in the driveway, was demoralizing.

The doors of the Big House were open downstairs, making it easier to move items out, but given the early hour, the chill of the morning crept all the way up to my bedroom, adding to the discomfort of what was once a cozy bedroom for me, turning it into a cold and dark place. The shadowy, hollow feeling of my room was the perfect live metaphor for our situation, and I felt as though I was now trying to sleep inside the death of our dreams.

It was indeed like a terrible nightmare and after only a few hours of off-and-on sleep, waking a few times hoping it actually wasn't true, and discovering it was, Mother awakened me for the last time, whispering to me that it was time to go. I decided the best thing to do was to open my eyes as little as possible as we exited the Big House, the psychological pain making it impossible to take my last looks at the space to which I was so completely emotionally attached. Our home had been like large, comforting arms to me, and I was being thrust-out, removed from all of the little places I had discovered around the house over the years, the places that I went to hide when the adults were out of control with anger and/or alcohol; all of my safe places where I had developed my largest, personal safety mechanisms, were about to become something of the past.

I barely remember arriving at the El Encanto Hotel, other than the musty smell of the place when we entered, so I awakened bewildered in an unfamiliar place a couple hours after the sun rose the next morning, in a sleeping bag on my bare twin-bed mattress, among the disorder of boxes piled high to the ceiling of the "new" bedroom I was going to share with my brother. I stood, then began stumbling and meandering my way toward the voices in another room.

My parents had somehow crammed most of the contents of that five-bedroom turn-of-the-century farmhouse into this weekend cottage at a hotel, and after groggily making my way through the labyrinth of our belongings, I found them at last, deep within the maze. They were clearly spent, depressed and traumatized, and hungry too, which were four of the lighter sensations we all were feeling on that first morning. Living at the hotel was already promising to be a tricky adjustment, and we had not even spent an entire night.

It also happened to be my tenth birthday.

RENTAL AGREEMENT
(MONTH - TO - MONTH TENANCY)

THIS AGREEMENT, entered into this __1st__ day of __JUNE__, 19__74__, by and between __EL ENCANTO HOTEL__ and __ARTHUR AND ELISE CAMP__, hereinafter called respectively lessor and lessee.

WITNESSETH: That for and in consideration of the payment of the rents and the performance of the covenants contained on the part of lessee, said lessor does hereby demise and let unto the lessee, and lessee hires from lessor for use as a residence those certain premises described as __VILLA #100, EL ENCANTO HOTEL__ located at __1900 LASUEN__ Street, __SANTA BARBARA__, California, for a tenancy from month-to-month commencing on the __1st__ day of __JUNE__, 19__74__, and at a monthly rental of __FOUR HUNDRED FIFTY AND NO/100B__ ($ __450.00__) Dollars per month, payable monthly in advance on the __1st__ day of each and every month.

It is further mutually agreed between the parties as follows:

(1) Said premises shall be occupied by no more than __2__ adults and _____ children.
(2) Lessee shall not keep or permit to be kept in said premises any dog, cat, parrot, or other bird or animal.
(3) Lessee shall not violate any city ordinance or state law in or about said premises.
(4) That all alterations, additions, or improvements made in and to said premises shall, unless otherwise provided by written agreement between the parties hereto, be the property of Lessor and shall remain upon and be surrendered with the premises.
(5) Lessee shall not sub-let the demised premises, or any part thereof, or assign this agreement without the lessor's written consent.
(6) Any failure by lessee to pay rent or other charges promptly when due, or to comply with any other term or condition hereof, shall at the option of the lessor forthwith terminate this tenancy.
(7) Lessee shall keep and maintain the premises in a clean and sanitary condition at all times, and upon the termination of the tenancy shall surrender the premises to the lessor in as good condition as when received, ordinary wear and damage by the elements excepted.
(8) Except as to any condition which makes the premises untenantable, lessee hereby waives all right to make repairs at the expense of lessor as provided in Section 1942 of the Civil Code of the State of California, and all rights provided in Section 1941 of said Civil Code.
(9) The __LESSOR__ agrees to properly cultivate, care for, and adequately water the lawn, shrubbery, trees and grounds.
(10) The __LESSOR__ shall pay for all water supplied to the said premises. The lessee shall pay for all gas, heat, light, power, telephone service, and all other services, except as herein provided, supplied to the said premises.
(11) Nothing contained in this agreement shall be construed as waiving any of lessor's rights under the laws of the State of California.
(12) This agreement and the tenancy hereby granted may be terminated at any time by either party hereto by giving to the other party not less than __THIRTY__ (__30__) days prior notice in writing.
(13) If an action be brought for the recovery of rent or other moneys due or to become due under this lease or by reason of a breach of any covenant herein contained or for the recovery of the possession of said premises, or to compel the performance of anything agreed to be done by Lessee, or to recover for damages to said property, or to enjoin any act contrary to the provisions hereof, Lessee will pay to Lessor all of the costs in connection therewith, including, but not by way of limitation, reasonable attorney's fees, whether or not the action proceed to judgment.
(14) Remarks: __CLEAN LINEN AND MAID SERVICE ONCE A WEEK__

IN WITNESS WHEREOF the parties hereto have executed this agreement in duplicate the day and year first above written.

_____ _____
Lessor   Lessee

Chapter 2 — The Hotel

RECORD BOOTH SUGGESTED SONG: "IN THE HALL OF THE MOUNTAIN KING," *WILL BRADLEY & RAY MCKINLEY*

We would now be residing in an area of the city that felt like being far from town, up on Alameda Padre Serra, or "APS" as the locals called it. This part of the city was also known as the "Riviera," because of its intertwined, curving roads that dipped and rose, twisted and separated, often lined or divided with sandstone walls topped with beautiful balustrades, traffic lanes traversing a series of foothills, in a region with flowers, trees, vines, cacti and succulents, spilling down the hillside like a fecund waterfall of greenery, all far above and a world away, with a view of downtown Santa Barbara, the ocean, and the Channel Islands.

The drive to the hotel was spectacular, taking you first past the Old Mission, "Queen" of California's missions. Next, the road turned passed a lighted sign that said, "El Encanto Hotel," with an arrow, and went up the hillside, cutting through the native peoples' ruins, with the remains of the sandstone houses on the right and a reservoir and aqueduct on the left, then continuing, driving beneath the Riviera Theater and the Brooks Institute Photography School. That's where you veered left, passing above Orpet Park until you saw another grand old sign; in a stylish, 1920's style, white lettering on a green background read "The El Encanto Hotel."

The lettering of the sign was typical for Santa Barbara, a style my mother referred to as "stuffy white people attempting to appear ethnic." Nonetheless, there was a vintage grandeur to the sign, and it made you feel like you had really arrived at an important, historic destination.

The El Encanto Hotel had catered to celebrities and world travelers for nearly sixty years and, up until the late fifties and early sixties, had been a favorite and rather exclusive resort. By the time we arrived, it had fallen into disrepair, like a west coast version of the infamous Grey Gardens in East Hampton. Short of the normal traffic of weekend guests and unable to compete with new, better seaside hotels downtown, the El Encanto had long since opened up its cottages to long-term residents, luckily for my family.

As I would soon discover, the grounds of the El Encanto included a maze of dilapidated brick pathways; rolling, bumpy, cracked, with damage by tree roots and soil settlement. Spread out in this maze of pathways and overgrowth, were separate cottages and some long, rectangular multi-guestroom buildings. The villas were a mixture of craftsman-style structures, which were some of the first buildings on the property, along with some Spanish stucco bungalows, with red roof tiles, built sometime after the earthquake in 1925, when Santa Barbara was nearly leveled, and the City's chiefs decided that any rebuilding or new construction would be aligned with a Spanish theme, a tone-deaf nod to the Spanish "founders" of the town.

Some of the cottages and bungalows were practically invisible here and there among the gardens of the El Encanto, which had become really more of an overgrown jungle with the little structures appearing in the clearings throughout; the jungle ruled the land and the dwellings were subordinate. Vegetation was growing very close to or on all of the bungalows, with some nearly covered in ivy. All exterior walls of the buildings were in need of a new paint job. Screens on windows and doors were rusted and worn – all springs on these doors were loud and squeaky. Walkways, driveways, stairs and patios were all cracked, with the unstoppable growth of vegetation appearing everywhere through the asphalt, brick pavers and cement. What had once been merely decorative landscaping had become a force of nature, and nature was doing its best to eat the El Encanto.

This exotic vegetation had been planted nearly fifty years before, chosen for aesthetic reasons to provide allure, with no real research as to what these families of plants would do given frequent irrigation and plenty of sun for a half century. It was probably something of a wonderland when they were first placed in the ground, but without appropriate pruning and cutting back, or really any knowledgeable care, these beasts had done what tropical plants do, and the jungle that was generated was, by the time we moved in, busy squeezing the hotel's guest suites to death like a hungry python.

Permeating the lush landscape was a tangible "vacationing adult" energy, even though children stayed at the hotel, too; it was definitely a place where many couples would escape from Los Angeles for a romantic weekend. Even with its crumbling appearance, the place still earned its name, and calling it "enchanted" wasn't far from the truth. There are "good" enchantments, and "bad" enchantments in legends, and the hotel fell somewhere in between. And just like any primeval jungle, there was something wild and erotic in the air, and the place beckoned every visitor to explore their own hedonistic pleasures.

Being the seventies, there was a cultural trend of celebrating the "funky," especially when it was a formerly stylish backdrop rooted in another time. The El Encanto looked like a location for a movie or book, and in that way, it was like stepping into a story already in progress, so people still loved it. Nobody was overtly complaining about the condition in the easygoing roll-with-it zeitgeist of the time, nor noticing the El Encanto's staff's languid approach to maintenance – rather than making big, restorative repairs, the crew merely pampered the hotel as if it were just another guest recovering from one hell of a hangover.

The guests who stayed there and the staff were comfortable with the squalor and it actually made the place a little more appealing, because it wasn't "uptight." It's very difficult in general to find the combination of stylish and sloppy in a vacation destination, and the hotel was just the ticket for anyone looking for an environment that was as fashionable as it was forgiving. As for the clientele and how they fit into these surroundings, it was a lucky coincidence that the clothing styles of the 1970's often mimicked the styles of the 1930's, so the El Encanto was the perfect setting for a fun, fling-y weekend for every wannabe femme fatale and man about town, and as Mother said, anyone who was "putting on the fritz."

With all of its faded charms, the El Encanto was going to be an amazing place for me to explore; magical, eerie, with its overgrown vines, and caretaking that only seemed to be embracing its beautiful state of disarray in the manner of a nurse providing affection to a mental patient. In a way, even with its choking hug, the jungle may have actually been holding the hotel together, with the way its vines were deeply in the process of replacing walls and foundations, creeping toward doors, swallowing the pathways and proliferating everywhere almost unchecked. As far as the brick walkways themselves, even if they were cleared of plants, they would still seem to have no discernable plan to them, and one could become easily lost, especially at night, in the dense maze of broken paths and overgrowth.

The centerpiece of the gardens, in my youthful opinion, was the lily pond and pergola area – a rectangular brick pool about twenty-five feet long, which was surrounded by a crumbling brick columned and wood trellised arbor, both of which seemed to be held aloft only by the wisteria vines themselves. There were the remnants of little wood benches between the square columns of the arbor, but most of them were unusable due to the overgrowth that was in the process of claiming them. It was darker under the old trellises and thick vines of wisteria, even in full sunlight, and at night, the darkness would be nearly impenetrable. Plus, there were always unidentified creatures scuttling about in the gloom there, kicking through the layers of leaves covering the dirt, their tiny footsteps echoing and often accompanied by unnerving scratching sounds.

In an area just north of the pond and trellises, there were abandoned concrete flumes running down the slight slope, which once must have functioned as man-made water features for the gardens, likely installed in an effort to create make-believe jungle streams. At the end of these channels, upside-down giant clam shells had been cemented in, which likely made interesting waterfalls when there was flowing water, with each loop of the upturned shells' edges creating its own separate flow. These concrete flumes had once been painted a bright sky blue, and one could see the remains of electrical lighting, some pointed at these artificial streams, some integrated into the flumes themselves, which probably casted a reflective splattering of light on the gardens at night, a further nod to creating an atmosphere of romance and the feeling of an exotic, tropical retreat. These flumes were now bone dry, the blue paint was chipped and sun-faded or completely missing in some places, and it was obvious that water had not flowed in these artificial streams for quite some time; most of them were clogged with leaves and other garden debris. None of the former lights were working.

South of the lily pond was the aforementioned huge perk of the hotel for me; the swimming pool, which had not changed much since its installation in the 1950s. It was surrounded by a rather simple pinkish cinderblock wall comprised of glass panes, alternating between the block columns. The pool area was incongruous with the style of the rest of the hotel – it looked more like a something you'd see at a roadside motel, the difference being that this "motel" pool had the amazing view of most of the city below, including Stearns Wharf and beyond, all the way out to the islands, weather permitting.

The pool itself was small, a classic rectangle with semi-elliptical ends, complete with a sun-damaged diving board and rusty chrome pool ladder. The cement areas surrounding the pool were furnished with the typical and fairly old metal lounges, the kind with rubber straps that always managed somehow to pinch unsuspecting bare thighs between them, with the added benefit of becoming exceedingly hot when warmed in direct sunlight. There were a few patio tables with faded umbrellas rising from their centers, over the beveled-glass table tops. For us, the kids, none of this mattered – and the thought of having a pool was very exciting indeed, regardless of its condition or size. The pool also had the ubiquitous yellowing plastic pool signs, noting in particular that there was no lifeguard. The pool was surrounded by overgrown bushes and trees, that were once small when planted in the '50s.

The truth was, I loved swimming more than most activities, and here I would have the opportunity nearly at any time. Knowing this, Father and Mother were playing up the El Encanto's pool quite a bit in an effort to ease my agony of leaving the beloved Big House behind.

Surrounding the pool on all sides was a large, sloping area of lawn, and beneath the lawn to the south was a strip of dirt with various cacti growing happily in the heat. Below this, a sandstone wall, then the sidewalk, and then below again, Lasuen Road.

From the looks of things, the hotel and grounds had clearly been here for a long time and in fact, by 1974, just over sixty years had passed since the El Encanto started its life in 1913.

The land now occupied by the El Encanto was first purchased in the 1870's by a man named Charles Storke, whose son would one day start the Santa Barbara News Press. Because the area was devoid of trees, full of large boulders, couldn't be planted, and far from town, it was originally referred to as "Storke's Folly" by the locals of the time, suggesting that he was a fool for purchasing it in the first place.

Then, in 1913, six bungalows were built under the direction of the new owner, James Warren, as housing for the students and faculty of the adjacent and new State Normal School (predecessor to the University of California, Santa Barbara), which had relocated from its original downtown campus to the site next to where the El Encanto now stood. Along with many other speculators who were busy buying land in the area, Warren's plan was to build these units as rental housing for the school, foreseeing a campus neighborhood, an up-and-coming area which had also been recently linked to downtown by a streetcar line.

By 1916, Warren's plan for student and faculty housing failed because only three of the units had actually rented – hardly anyone wanted to live full-time on that hillside. In the following years, Warren's property turned inadvertently into an artist's colony, whose residents included William Otte and Clarence Mattei.

To save his investment, Warren hired an architect to design a new main building for what he called a "cottage hotel" and refurbished all of the existing structures to include steam heat and telephones. More cottages and the landscaping were added as well; it must have been splendid then. We later heard that guests of the time were even treated to their own private stenographer, who would transcribe postcards and letters home for them during that early era. Fancy stuff.

When we moved in on my tenth birthday, there was still a sense of that earlier heyday, floating like an invisible, ethereal mist across the grounds and, if one listened closely, one could almost hear the echoes of the bygone parties of the '20s, '30s and '40s; haunted laughter, New Year's Eve horns and the sounds of old fancy big-fender cars were easy to imagine. In the coming months, I would find myself sometimes "listening" to the hotel, as if hearing the ocean in a seashell, by pressing my ears to the cracked, brick pathways.

Mrs. E. L. Shonley
804 Klemp St.
Leavenworth
Kansas

Secrets of a 100 ft. Boy | 21

Chapter 3 — The Villa

RECORD BOOTH SUGGESTED SONG: "I AIN'T GOT NOTHING BUT THE BLUES," *ELLA FITZGERALD & DUKE ELLINGTON*

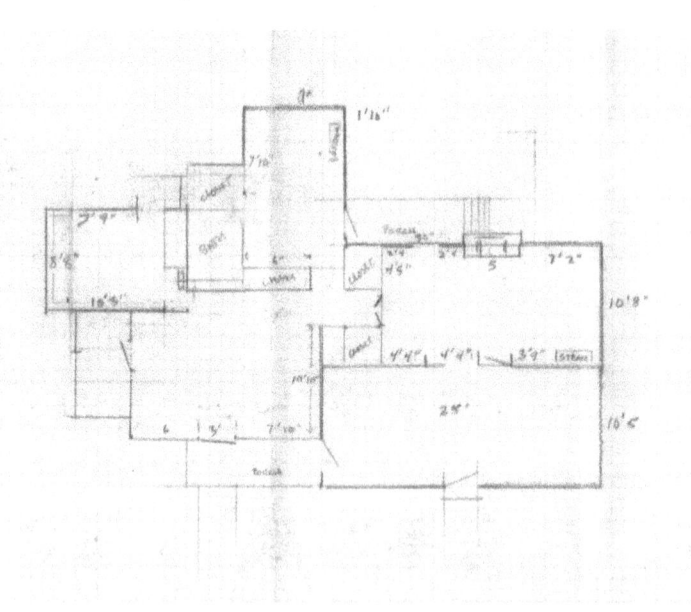

The El Encanto in 1974 looked like one would expect after decades of visitors, parties and holidays – the current guests were still soaking in that residual glamor, the sense of abandonment, and the echoing sights and sounds of several decades of entitled debauchery, including the counterculture feelings of the early, erstwhile artist colony - the essences of all these stories clinging to the walls of every structure like the yellowing wallpaper in our kitchen.

Even for the time, the monthly costs seemed expensive, which made the rundown nature of the place all the more frustrating. My parents were already stressing about the $450 per month rent for the small cottage, and that utilities and maintenance of the immediate grounds surrounding Villa 100 were also going to be their responsibility. It seemed like a lot for what we got, but after having to give up a home we were hoping to purchase, we focused on the element of adventure and intrigue about moving into a hotel. We just had to go with it – there was no other choice. My father must have been in a crazed rush during those three days of the eviction process to find us some place to land. I'm sure my mother was consulted – and looking back, I think they were trying to cover up the disappointment and truth behind why we had to move in the first place.

Father had seen the advertisement for the hotel in the paper while looking anxiously to find us a home, and on a whim, made an inquiry. I have no doubt that his charm and powers of persuasion came into play, and the diagram of the cottage was drawn in a nod toward future expansion – had my father promised some sort of renovation?

Whatever had sealed the deal, my parents had been doing a mediocre job of hiding their desperation and embarrassment, and I could only imagine their difficult machinations during the process of trying to determine where we were going to land as a family, given the issues of income, children and pets. In a way, the hotel was the perfect solution, requiring no first nor last deposits, and because it was existing in a state of stately shabbiness, was also okay with pets, and I bet our parents looked at it as simply a place to rest for a bit until they could locate a more viable solution.

The accommodations, our little Villa 100, like the rest of the hotel, were also in a semi-state of decay and neglect but were still completely functional; referencing her own depression, Mother referred to our cottage as existing in a state of depreciation.

It was one of the original first set of bungalows built for the State Normal School in the craftsman-style, and it was still charming, but maybe only for a weekend - it had clearly seen better days. The walls, the creaking floors and the roof were still in relatively good shape, but the infrastructure was beginning to fail. Villa 100 was somewhat set apart from the other cottages, perched on the northeast corner of Alvarado Road and Mission Ridge, with a commanding view of the El Encanto's main hotel building down on the slope below. There was a strangely long and surprisingly straight and comparatively well-maintained brick pathway leading up from the hotel's circular driveway to Villa 100, which gave this bungalow a sort of inadvertent grandness, as though the cottage itself was an administrative office or watchtower.

On entering the Villa through what functioned as the front door, you first stepped up to a small exterior row of stairs, and then found yourself inside a screened-in porch, which was fairly large and would be essential in the hot summers up on the Riviera in Santa Barbara, since air conditioning was unheard of. Up two more steps and you entered what would become my parents' bedroom. The original function of this room was to be the living room for the cottage - it was approximately two-hundred and twenty square feet, which was not a lot of space for my parents, their four-poster bed, antique hutches, giant dressers, end tables and colonial secretary cabinet, many of which they had easily kept in their large bedroom at the Big House.

Continuing to the left from their "bedroom," and through a tiny hallway with two closets on both sides, you were led into another room, which was like a sitting room, and it had a small porch through a door to the west, and another porch through a door to the north; the room was lined with built-in shelving for books. Off of the sitting room to the east was the bedroom to be shared by myself and my brother, which had its own entrance from the outside via a porch that faced the hotel's main building below. Through a door on the north wall of our room was the only bathroom in the cottage, and it contained a clawfoot tub, complete with circular metal shower curtain frame with a showerhead, balancing delicately at the top of a large metal pipe. There was also an old pedestal sink and a beveled-glass mirror. It was a fairly basic, old hotel bathroom that was certainly never intended for a family of four. The walls were painted a dusty mauve, and it only had one small, frosted-glass window, set nearly to the ceiling and blocked by overgrowth on the outside, which made the bathroom quite dark, even during the day, and especially when the light was turned off.

Returning through our interior bedroom door and through the sitting room and to the north wall was another doorway, which led to the kitchen. The kitchen had not been updated since the 1930's, and it had a small dining area and an old-fashioned wall fan embedded into the wall to the left side of the classic O'Keefe & Merritt stove's burners. There were a lot of windows in the northwest corner of the kitchen, making it feel similar to a sunroom, so the kitchen was generally the brightest room in the house. The kitchen had its own doorway to the east, which was a six-pane glass door with a screen; outside this door, you then stepped down two steps to an outside area that was surrounded by small sandstone boulders.

In total, Villa 100 had five porches and five entrances from the outside, which was probably due to the fact that it was meant to be a dorm room and later a vacation spot, giving all of its visitors and residents their own porch on which to relax - and perhaps to provide all occupants with a private exit to head out for any number of nefarious activities in the El Encanto's enchanted jungle.

What we all had to keep remembering was that technically, we were going to be living in what was supposed to function as a vacation accommodation. To us, it just looked like a very small house, and somehow into this space we had crammed two adults, two children, two cats, a dog, two doves and a tortoise, and the aforementioned furnishings.

Keeping with its overall style, the carpeting throughout Villa 100 was old and worn, and of a variety that was popular in the '50s. Mother referred to it as "high-low carpeting," to match her moods, she'd say.

There were ridges and valleys that were part of the weave of the carpet, the ridges making it plush underfoot (the "high"), while the valleys notoriously pooled dirt and debris (the "low").

Everything else, such as all windows, screens, doors, glass doorknobs and other features were true to 1913 when it was built; the glass of the windows had the telltale distortions and unevenness of the old way of making glass panes. What was apparently hardwood floor underneath the carpeting creaked in every room, making stealthy late-night behavior nearly impossible, and the interior and exterior of the cottage needed a fresh coat of paint, or maybe three, after a furious sanding of course.

There was also the fact that, unlike traditional homes, this "house" had entertained a persistently transient population of humans, and the essence of the uncountable comings and goings over the decades was easily felt; the structure of the cottage felt stewed in a likely, albeit occasional, scandalous history. Regular homes would only have so many occupants over the years – but a hotel room or cottage of this age must have housed thousands of individuals by the point we arrived, and as I surmised, if one increases the amount of people in any situation, the amount of drama and decadence will scale up proportionately. I wondered what had happened in a place like this? One could feel the deeply embedded grime from multitudes of indiscretions; it was the housing equivalent of threadbare party shoes.

The afternoon light on that corner of Mission Ridge was generally a beautiful liquid amber nearly every afternoon, which just added to the odd romance of the location. Vertically enormous eucalyptus trees lined Alvarado Road, and their scent in the warm, summer air, was intoxicating. We soon discovered that down Mission Ridge Road behind the Brooks Institute and around the corner, was a huge, vacant lot with giant stones that remained warm from the sun's heat far into the early morning hours, where we could play Frisbee and exercise our dog; it would have to do.

As small as Villa 100 was, it did possess a casual elegance, and despite the fact it had become mostly shabby and less chic, long before "shabby chic" became a recognized style, it still emanated a sense of better days gone by. It provided easily accessible denial for us, and we could pretend as though we, too, were on vacation, delightfully taking in the sites of Santa Barbara's Riviera, and not at all in some desperate family situation. The hotel's atmosphere somewhat sheltered us from knowing we had nowhere else to go and made it easy to practice avoidance of feelings in a way that a regular home couldn't do. Although, we would soon find out that our stay at the hotel would be everything but a vacation.

Not only was Villa 100 one of the originals, it was one of the largest and most desirable spaces available to the public in the complex, according to the front desk. All agreed that despite its meager size, there was some kind of questionable grandness about it – the way that this Villa sat away from the other cottages. That single, lengthy brick walkway to the front door from the hotel's main driveway and entry gave it the feeling that you were really arriving somewhere, and it was easy for me to pretend we were on a long, fashion show catwalk when we made use of it. The pathway was lined with small olive trees, and even though its bricks were slightly rough and uneven, I could see the opportunity for future dramatic entrances, when we could be witnessed as we approached the main building's dining room from what I gathered was an envied perch.

Despite the discomforts and in retrospect, all of these attributes caused us to actually sort of fall in love with our Villa from that first day, helped by its sordid, residual glamor, even including the signature musty smell that only an older home can produce; a mixture of mildew, old carpet, a variety of carpet shampoos, a little cigarette smoke, spilled cocktails and the essence of human dander thoroughly embedded in this overused nest - this was simply a part of the full experience. We felt as though we were now weaving ourselves into a larger history and our part in that history was still unclear; there was a sense of adventure in the moldy air. We were becoming part of a large mythical tapestry, albeit one that needed a good dry cleaning.

Underpinning the entire emotional and esoteric vibration of our new home was something far more tangible and firmly available in this dimension; the odor of a sewer or refuse nearby, with a dash of necrosis, would intermittently waft by our noses, but none of us knew the source, its smell certainly more present when we were outside of the cottage. Mother joked and said it was her new perfume, "Evening at the Morgue."

But back on that first day, my birthday, when every last bit of furniture and boxes had been packed into the cottage, things were still feeling very grim, further enhanced by the memory of the last three horrendous days of doing it all ourselves.

The first challenge was to figure out how to unpack and make it work somehow. Our father started by placing the biggest furniture first – the cream white radio-phonograph and TV console with turquoise speaker fabric was placed along the south wall of my parents' bedroom, and the two hutches, one painted gray, one maple, were placed in the sitting room, with the twin loveseats covered in white fabric that had a repeating pattern depicting the United States American Eagle coat of arms, which matched the two wicker and wood armchairs.

Getting set up in the new bedroom with my brother was the worst for me. For years I had enjoyed that private large bedroom with a door upon which I often hung a misspelled sign that read, "Keep Out! That's an Oder!" The main person I wanted to keep out was Casey, and now I would be sharing a small, dark, narrow, rectangular bedroom with him, an arrangement whose time should have never come.

The only place his captain-style bunk bed would fit was the west wall of the room, between the bedroom's door and the north wall, behind which was the bathroom; Casey would be sleeping in the path to the only toilet.

My bed was placed perpendicular to and underneath the large east window, placing my head directly under the old glass panes with a rusty screen that wouldn't close, which immediately made me feel a bit insecure.

A plus for me as a covert rebel was that single bathroom only accessible through our room, so shutting our bedroom's door would not only be an act of defiance, it would be war. Going into my calculations was the fact that Mother and Father would need to use the bathroom and would be traipsing through our bedroom at any given time; because I possessed a detailed visual imagination, I was not looking forward to hearing my parents do their business.

Put directly, our room sucked. The more I rolled the sound of "our room" in my head over and over, the more I moaned. Sharing with him was going to be like joining my mugger in his cell for the prison sentence.

I had taken great pride in my bedrooms of the past – as soon as I could walk, I was decorating – organizing my toys and books "just so," and already my propensity for creating spaces I thought beautiful was a hobby of sorts. Once unpacked, my brother's aesthetic was entirely different from mine, which was not exactly a surprise. His bed had louvered cupboards below his mattress platform, and drawers like a dresser, which would be essential now for storage, but he was already outgrowing the mattress, and his feet tended to dangle over the edge of the bed while he slept. There were two closets, so at least Casey and I each had one for ourselves.

Casey was getting the shorter end of the stick bedroom-wise as there was very little room for him to "decorate" or to make his own zone at all. So, there we were – beds at one end of the room to the other, but it would have to do because we knew there was no other choice, and I don't think either of us was very excited by the proposition. Our age difference of four years was a gap that now occupied a significant part of our separate development; technically, I was still a child, but Casey was nearly fourteen, and the rages of puberty already had a tight grip on my brother. My mother would stare at him sometimes and say, "Sex has reared its ugly head."

In the kitchen, our parents crammed our large round oak pedestal dining table in the kitchenette area and the cupboards and drawers managed to absorb most of the utensils and gadgets. It was a hot afternoon while we settled-in by the end of that first day, so Mother switched on the wall fan in the kitchen, which turned-out to be exceedingly loud, being a whirring, rattling device from the late '30s.

This kitchen was wallpapered with a soft, yellow pattern. The cupboards and drawers had white porcelain knobs. The floor had sea-foam green and gray linoleum tiles set on the diagonal. The kitchen had a tiny old refrigerator, perpetually equipped with its own free-flowing glacier that looked ready to engulf any innocent leftovers sitting on the upper wire shelf below it.

That northwest corner of the kitchen with the bank of windows was the best feature, but my mother had pulled the curtains to block the view into the kitchen from Mission Ridge Road – it was a bit of a fishbowl, and our stacks of boxes made it clear that we weren't just staying for the weekend. Even though my mother was doing her best to keep the mood light, I could see in that space between her eyebrows that a small line had dug itself into her flesh from frowning – as she herself would put it, her forehead was "creased with worry." I could see in that small line in between her brows all of what she was feeling – the shock, the embarrassment, the strain – it was as though the line functioned as an arrow pointing to her smile below exposing its falseness. I felt her pain, too, but like her, I chose to focus with her on the task of unpacking our boxes.

The sun was starting its plummet to the horizon, and rays were shining through the dingy, yellow, ruffled kitchen curtains. Something about the illumination of the kitchen and the heat further revealed where we really were in high detail – in an old, forgotten bungalow, reclining like a hungover flapper still reeling from yesteryear's soiree. Some sort of twisted Great Gatsby-style story had already taken place and we were in the remains. Some other story was also about to begin – we could feel it.

The light in the kitchen coming from those windows would provide a lot of peace over the next few months. The space would often be filled with that golden twilight amber light, filtered through the towering eucalyptus and messy olive trees surrounding the cottage. It was comforting somehow. Unfortunately, the light would soon be outdone by the foul smell from somewhere outside that we had not realized yet would begin to overpower all other scents.

Mother ordered pizza delivered for that first night to try to make my birthday "fun" I think. We were all pretty depressed, each of us quietly lamenting the loss of the grand house we had left downtown. We were unpacking furiously all day not just to get settled, but to create more space in the cottage; it was small enough without being packed with boxes, and the more we unpacked, the more it felt like a viable living space, rather than some sort of storage purgatory for deadbeat renters.

As we sat eating our pizza, we could see that it was going to take more than one day to completely unpack. In fact, we lived for those first days by making tunnels through our boxes, and very slowly worked our way toward the sense of organization that we had lost in such a hurried move.

Within a few days, we were able to move some things (not needed in this era of our lives) to the storage that came with our single garage space, and then Villa 100 wasn't all that bad. Something the cottage had in spades were those many doors that could be closed – many places to be alone in such a small space. Porches all around the outside, not to mention the hotel and all its surrounding property. Plus, there was the park nearby, and the entire school complex across the street.

After a week or so, our place was officially workable, and we also confirmed that we were indeed in an enviable spot on the hotel's property, affording more privacy than any other unit. From our position, we also had a pretty clear view across the street and could look at the beautiful architecture of that State Normal School complex that housed the photography institute, the Riviera Theater and a wing of the building that contained a Montessori School.

The roads around us were not as heavily trafficked as Chapala Street in front of the Big House, so there was a lot more of the rare substance called "quiet," and almost a country feel to our surroundings, both helping to ease our nerves.

While appreciating the gardens, Mother seemed a bit nervous too, because outside our doors, there was indeed a hotel in operation. Even though we were going to be considered "long-term guests" by the hotel's staff, there would be regular, short-term guests checking in and out and enjoying the hotel, walking the paths in bathing suits, partying, and parking their cars in the large multiple single-car garage building just to the east of our cottage. People on vacation behave differently than while at home and could therefore be unpredictable, Mother instructed us. She pleaded with us not to forget that there were a lot of strangers, some from out of town, and whether they were guests or staff – walking around, everywhere, hidden in the overgrowth of the garden and the pathways, we should "Keep eyes in the back of your heads," she cautioned, repeatedly.

Chapter 4 — The Record Booth

RECORD BOOTH SUGGESTED SONG: "MAGICAL MYSTERY TOUR,"
THE BEATLES

Villa 100 was indeed going to be a hot little box that summer. Thankfully, we had the pool to jump in when it was a particularly scorching day. Mother was pretty much always home, at least when she wasn't taking Grandmother to a hair appointment or a doctor. The isolation and confinement in our small crowded bungalow were tough on her, especially with two arguing brothers at her feet. She liked it when we were away from the cottage exploring our surroundings.

The truth was, we couldn't always be outside though, and we also wanted to just hangout inside the bungalow most of time. There were all these other people outside – the guests wandering the gardens or down at the pool, the maids and rest of the staff, people coming and going from the restaurant, and just other curious folks from the neighborhood at large. The El Encanto's mystique pulled in all sorts, and for a place that was mostly a wistful reminder of a bygone era, it still could sway its charm and pull people in; it was busy.

To go outside meant to be in public. We didn't really have a proper yard, just the dirt and cacti around our cottage. We could sit on our porches, but this usually required waving or saying hello to some random person, and my family wasn't big on the usual inane discourse that people share when they are strangers while in a shared space; we weren't great at small talk, and loosely quoting Bette Davis' character in "All About Eve," we detested cheap sentiment. We grew tired of the courtesy waves, so to speak, so we were less inclined to sit on the porches after just a couple of weeks.

Particularly on the weekends when Father was home, there were sequences where we were all inside, in the heat, together, and being together too long in our family took about twenty minutes. All of us were becoming tired of finding "something to do" and exploring the hotel had even become even more daunting with the increasing number of summer guests.

Seeing the need for some place in the house to get away from each other, Father decided to convert one of the closets in the hallway leading from their bedroom to the sitting room. The closet had an electrical outlet inside, which was perfect for plugging in a receiver and a turntable. Father had a large collection of albums, which included a fairly rare collection of old '78's – thick, vintage jazz records he had collected in the '30s and '40s. According to Father, there was the expected malt shop on the corner down from where he lived in Hollywood as a pre-teen and teenager, equipped with the requisite juke box. The juke box was regularly updated with new records once per month, and Father found out which day the "juke box man" would come and change out "old" tunes with newly-released hits. One day, my father, casually sipping a malt, waited for the juke box man, and watched while the man pulled out old LP's and replaced them with new ones. When the man was nearly finished, Father approached him and asked what he was going to do with the old ones. To my father's astonishment, the man said he was going to throw them away! My father instantly struck a deal with the man and offered to take the old records off of his hands and would dispose of the ones he didn't like. The juke box man was fine with this, and so began my father's vintage jazz record collection.

We loved these old records; they were so captivating to us – the music of an era from thirty to forty years ago was something we thought was really cool and suited the backdrop of Villa 100 perfectly. In addition to this collection, both of my parents, being music lovers, had amassed quite a collection of other music as well.

Also thrown into the mix were the records that my teenage brother was beginning to collect. Casey was adding contemporary music of the time – rock n' roll and "stoner music" – to the collection.

My father took all of these albums and put them on the shelves in the closet – and there were so many that every shelf was full to capacity. He then put a comfy, padded chair he had snagged from work in the closet and purchased a nice pair of headphones. My father could sit in the chair, close the door, slip on the 'phones – and get away from his family for an album or three. Of course, we boys were completely in love with the "Record Booth," and both of us would sometimes argue over who got to use it next.

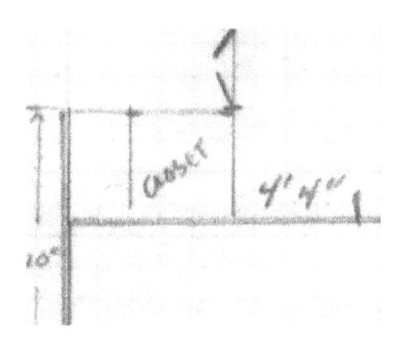

Even Mother got into the act, and sometimes there was the need for a schedule, so everyone could enjoy the Booth. It seemed like such a simple thing to do, but it was actually a stroke of genius on my father's part. A purposeful and clever use of space as well as a new zone to "check out" from our somewhat challenging reality. In addition, the closet was cool in temperature terms – with no external wall – it stayed fifteen degrees colder than the rooms of the thinly-walled holiday cottage. We could even switch-off the closet light and take a private journey with each album in complete darkness, covering the lights from the receiver with a black towel.

This simple addition to Villa 100 changed everything. We were all avid users of the Record Booth and having it as an amenity made the place better. With this isolation and focus on music, time in the Booth became a true meditation. I fell deeply into the magic of each album I listened to; these sonic journeys became a source of therapy to me.

Of course, it was also a great place for my brother and I to escape all of the arguing of the parents, so we were in the Record Booth a lot. I mean, a lot a lot. We'd have to select our music very carefully if there was a melee in progress; hard rock was really great to drown out the din of their incessant bickering. When my mother reached the upper registers of her screaming, she could actually sound like a lead guitar riffing. My father's voice was like a bass guitar in overdrive, very boomy, so he was easy to cover with the music in the headphones; anything to distract us from the fighting, and what we called the "AC/DC" show.

The Record Booth was our haven – a safe beach within our cottage where we could land during the most ferocious of parental verbal hurricanes. The bands and musicians we listened to became like trusted aunts and uncles, who would provide a caring, melodic hug just when we needed it. It empowered me, being in a place where I could be in control of the volume when our household became too loud, or as I said as a toddler, "too woud."

Chapter 5 — The Parents

RECORD BOOTH SUGGESTED SONG: "BEI MIR BIST DU SHEIN,"
THE ANDREWS SISTERS

When our parents were first married, they got a kick out of calling themselves "AC/DC," because these were their initials. Of course, in their young days, AC/DC brought to mind electrical power, not a rock band. My father was Arthur James Camp, Jr., so "AC." My mother, born Dorothy Elise Fyfe Hopton and becoming Dorothy Camp, was the "DC," and they said they came up with this because they were electric together – and in this rare moment of corny cuteness, they coined "AC/DC." After hearing this for the first time, I thought, "Blecch." They signed early artistic collaborations with "AD/DC," so I think most of the inspiration was less sentimental and little more like branding. With my parents, there was always a baseline in everything they did of creating a product, with less emphasis placed on being remotely romantic; to this day I still don't' know the date of my parents' anniversary – they never celebrated it, as far as I can recall.

They met in art school in Los Angeles, and I can only imagine what their early conversational exchanges may have sounded like. My mother was a vivacious and vibrant redhead – not the orange variety of red, but a deep red auburn with no brown – and she stood five feet tall, with an hourglass figure. My father reported seeing her sitting in the quad at school, early in that first fall semester of '45, and he was immediately enchanted by her appearance and demeanor. At that point, my mother was being courted by several young men, some chosen by her snobby parents, and rumor had it that she was actually engaged to someone else when she met our father, "Artie."

Whatever happened, it resulted in their elopement to Mexico City, just three short weeks after meeting, and then the staging of a mock wedding on a church set at Paramount Pictures about a month later.

By the time we arrived at the El Encanto, my parents had already been married thirty years, with me being born somewhat late in the game – my mother was thirty-eight years old and my father, forty-one when I arrived two weeks after my predicted birth date. Due to what was considered a late-in-life pregnancy at the time, I was born with some congenital anomalies, a fact that I think also weighed heavily on my mother.

Between the time they met and our time at the El Encanto, many difficult things had already happened. Our parents married at ages eighteen and twenty-one - they were simply two art students, except my father was also a vet of World War II with severe untreated, misunderstood post-traumatic stress disorder. In his day this was referred to as "shell shock," but it was so much more than that. He was discharged with a thirty-percent disability. The government believed that all he needed for rehabilitation was a degree, so they paid for his schooling while never addressing his true, underlying trauma. There was no counseling, no psychologist, no therapist - no one to talk to. There was only art and there was only school. And then Mother entered the picture, unwittingly starting a relationship with a man who had issues that were far beyond her skill level, with no resources nor support.

Father's genius had been confirmed through testing, and he was skilled at several disciplines, while specializing in art and art history – as well as possessing mind-boggling abilities such as being able to sum large columns of numbers with only a glance. Because of his rare talent and intelligence, there were full expectations all around that this man was destined for fame and wealth, but his underlying and unrecognized psychological issues, which continued without support, turned him into the consummate self-saboteur. In her desire to have his back, Mother quit art school and chose to stand fully beside our father; she didn't realize that she was entering a mine field.

The depth and cunning with which his self-sabotage appeared was impossible to track while it occurred and was only reflected in his track record – unable to hold down jobs, and constant loss of income with the resultant evictions from many rentals, including the foreclosure on their home that was underway while my mother was pregnant with me. Without a healthy and honest perspective throughout these challenges, my parents took to constantly blaming each other for their troubles, endlessly taking swings at each other in the pitch blackness that is ignorance.

At the time they were married and then through the '50s and '60s, there simply wasn't the vocabulary nor resources to discuss these issues in a way that would have helped them. They were isolated and trapped in a hand-to-mouth existence, shunned by most communities because of their dramatic struggles, and looked down upon by their parents and extended families as being too "artsy," and high drama. My parents were both outcasts of their families due to their eccentricities that were not considered "normal" especially by Mother's family. It was okay to be interested in things such as art, film, literature and theater, but odd to want to pursue these things as careers. These interests meant that our parents were sophisticated without the funds to support it, which added to the friction. My brother and I, as their last two children, had absolutely no idea that we were caught in the middle of a deadly assignment-of-blame struggle that had been going on for decades.

My parents were fighting constantly by the time 1974 was underway – at least that's what it felt like to me. I can't really say that I was like most children, who may believe their parents' unhappiness is somehow their fault. I honestly don't remember feeling that way – I didn't believe that it was my fault, but what I did feel was a deep dislike of my parents and a desire to be with a better family.

Mother and Father's acoustically aggressive arguments rained down inside of our home, like hellfire around us. A "cute" story from my mother was that at two-years old, during a melee, I would often assume a squatted position, cover my ears and say, "Toooo wwwoud!" To me, there was nothing cute about this anecdote.

The days leading up to our move from the Big House on Chapala to the El Encanto were different only in the intensity of my parents' arguments, which under the extra pressure, had escalated to near-volcanic proportions. They really had hung their dreams of safety and stability on the many coat hooks just inside the door of the Big House, and for some reason this arrangement, still loose and only verbal, and perhaps completely fabricated, felt real to them. They were definitely in a state of shock when that eviction notice arrived and during the packing and move. Whatever love remained and sense of team partnership they felt among themselves was already stretched thoroughly to the limit by the time the eviction notice arrived, and after wards, the gloves were metaphorically off, and they went for each other's jugulars.

We listened far too closely to their arguments, not that there was anywhere far enough away where we couldn't hear them. My mother would yell terrible things at my father, telling him he was a loser, and reminding him that her parents had referred to him as just a "Hollywood Creep." She blamed him for her societal placement, thoroughly entrenched in the "cheap seats," and would remind him (as if he needed reminding) that he was a poor provider and a liar, since none of his schemes or plans ever worked out or were discovered to be false. My father would often retort that she had "ruined him," and that he would have been better off not married to her, and he repeatedly stated he wished he had never met her. He believed that he would have been successful had he not married her and had children, to which my mother agreed that he was not the "type" to have children, which made me feel further like I didn't belong in this world. As a child of Hollywood, my father should have realized how hack and trite their script sounded.

Even as a kid, I would tell them to "just get a divorce," and again, unlike other children, I would fantasize about how great it would be if they could get away from one another. Forget "The Parent Trap" – how about "The Parent Catch and Release"? My mother's response to this was always the same – they were together for economic reasons – which made no sense to me whatsoever since they never had any money anyway.

It was hard for me to imagine that they were ever in love and to this day, it's a bit of a head scratcher. How was I conceived? Did they accidentally run into each other in the hallway going to the bathroom in the middle of the night?

They seemed like absolute enemies to one another in my estimation, and residing in even smaller accommodations at the hotel, there was nowhere to get away from them but outside or in the Record Booth.

Evenings with my parents would often devolve into something like the edited scenes from "Who's Afraid of Virginia Woolf?" – the 1956 film with Elizabeth Taylor and Richard Burton. I had watched the film once with my parents on television before, and it stuck with me, being so close to home. The biggest difference was that my parents weren't actors, paid to act this way – they were doing it all for free. My mother was extremely sensitive to the effects of even one beer, or their latest favorite, Cold Duck, and I would silently shudder in the anticipation of the horrors that would follow when I saw my parents sipping away. There was pretty much a ninety-nine percent chance that a simple reminiscent conversation of the past over drinks could spiral out of control if there was any slight disagreement about how some terrible event went down or whose fault it was. This would quickly lead into their angrily blaming each other for the problem, whatever it was, which would escalate to an all-out screaming brawl.

Later in life, my mother often asked me if I had felt abused by either of them as a child, and I would always reply that the abuse my parents hurtled at each other during their fights was the toxicity from which I actually needed to recover; even though there had been some definitely inappropriate anger and physical assaults that were directed toward me personally by both of them, the way they treated each other in my presence during these fights was far more damaging to me as a child. They were the worst role models when it came to love and partnership.

Along with the verbal shrapnel I suffered while witnessing their fights, there was the extended embarrassment I felt at the hotel knowing full well that we were living in a vacation cottage with very thin walls. Guests, staff and visitors were constantly wandering the grounds of the El Encanto, just outside of our windows. I felt certain that no matter what time of day or night my parents began their long winded and loud attacks on one another, someone would be somewhere outside listening to it. Their escalations into all out below-the-belt verbal punches were aided at the hotel by the Cold Duck. Perhaps the more festive atmosphere of the resort made them abandon the mundane likes of beer for something with more tra-la-la. My parents' drinking had increased since moving to the hotel; they were self-medicating at an alarming rate. Every week on the maid's day, there would be a case of empty Cold Duck bottles sitting in the original box, which was removed with the rest of the garbage. To me this meant that the staff at the hotel was also aware of my parents' alcoholism.

The shame and embarrassment I felt was monumental – I wanted to hide somewhere – out of the cottage – pretend to be a guest, somewhere else, anywhere else on the premises, during the brawls. The local police had a long list of domestic disturbances at our previous homes that had been reported by neighbors, so I always felt anxious that the police might arrive at any moment at our cottage's screened porch.

During the altercations, I got into the habit of exiting the building through the rear doors and cutting a wide swath through the grounds to the pool, so I couldn't be traced back to Villa 100, or sometimes, I would leave the grounds altogether. Often, during the fights, I would duck out the back door off of the kitchen, run up to Mission Ridge Road, walk to the west and then around the corner down on to Lasuen, and walk by the Villa, still hearing the argument inside. I would feign a look of astonishment in the event there were other people walking by on the road, to seem more uninvolved. A few times, I added a faint shake of my head and an eye roll, sharing a moment of bonding with complete strangers who shared my disbelief that people were inside of that cottage having such an audibly grisly argument. "Who are these horrible people?" I said with glances to the other witnesses if any were present. Having a connection with some of these strangers was healing for me, as I could pretend that I was absolutely not a part of such a vial family who, as far as we innocent bystanders knew, were merely guests at the hotel; who would have the audacity to present such a public display of vitriol while on vacation? What terrible people they must be! And we, the casual onlookers and listeners, could revel in the fact that no matter how disappointing our lives might be, at least we weren't part of that family!

I had no resources for myself in that situation, other than my own imagination. I was without the wonder of the internet, with no knowledge of PTSD, unresolved trauma, family dynamics – all of these concepts I would know well in the future were completely unavailable to me when we lived at the hotel. I was psychologically and emotionally isolated with my parents on their island of despair.

FATHER

My father, holding to his brushes like guns despite the financial strain, never gave up as an artist and worked as an art teacher and commuted to Pt. Magu every day for work (a one-hundred-mile round trip), operating on energetic fumes most of the time and doing his best to function with his undiagnosed and most importantly, unknown to himself, PTSD. His work with the Navy was visual in nature; creating displays for informational seminars, and visual aids for other presentations to the public. His title was "Commander of Visual Arts," which sounded very impressive to me.

Whatever he was doing, there was always the red, faint glow of trauma under his skin, secretly dictating his actions, without his knowledge. It was as if his emotional body was having secret meetings with his mind – meetings to which he wasn't invited. Changes would come down the pipe from his internal "upper management," at the worst of times, and instead of paying his bills or feeding his family, he would find himself purchasing a classic car.

EXCAVATION BLAMED

An excavation in the street at Fifty-fourth street and Fourth avenue was blamed for an accident in which Arthur Camp, 31, his wife, Maybelle, and 5-year-old son, Arthur, Jr., received injuries which may prove fatal. Each was reported to be suffering from a skull fracture when examined at Georgia-street Receiving Hospital, and the father, apparently was also injured internally.

They were returning to their home, 5315 Ruthelen street, after an automobile ride, Camp said, when the accident occurred. University police were assigned to investigate.

Camp was one of the victims of the explosion which occurred in front of the Orpheum Theater several weeks ago and had only recently been released from the hospital, where he was treated for a broken leg and other injuries.

Mrs. Camp Dies From Car Crash

Mrs. Mabel Camp, 31 years of age of 5311 Ruthellen street, died at the General Hospital yesterday as the result of injuries received on May 24 when an automobile in which she was riding with her husband, Arthur Camp, and their 5-year-old son overturned at Fifty-fourth street and Fifth avenue. Camp and the boy, seriously injured, are confined to the hospital.

Camp's machine was wrecked when he swerved to avoid hitting another car, according to spectators. Mrs. Camp was thrown from the machine. An inquest will be conducted at 1:30 p.m. today.

The car-related trauma act-out and resultant purchases were very deep-bucket-seated in an accident that occurred when he was nearly eight-years old. In Los Angeles, in 1930, his father, Arthur Camp Sr., was driving his family home, with Maybelle, my grandmother, in the passenger seat, and my father, "Junior," asleep behind the driver's seat, curled up in the footwell. The 1920's car, with its narrow wheels, hit a rut in the road in a construction zone, rolled several times, ejecting both my father and his mother from the vehicle, and the injuries sustained plunged both into comas. Arthur Sr. was also severely injured but remained conscious. Maybelle survived briefly in her coma, but ultimately passed. My father remained in his coma for nearly two weeks; the doctors and nurses were sure he would die, too. While the newspapers had reported Father's age incorrectly, they did not fail to mention that Arthur Sr. had already been involved in an infamous gas line explosion several weeks before the accident, the injuries from which may have interfered with his cognitive abilities.

Since the medical team believed my father would pass away too, his family gave his toys and clothing to his cousins while he was unconscious in the hospital. On top of that, according to my father, when he awakened from his coma, his first thought was of his mother and the attending medical team didn't have the heart to tell him that his mother was gone. They encouraged him to write letters rather than visiting her in person, telling him she wasn't well enough to see him. My father remained in the hospital for an additional month and wrote letters to his dead mother, and the nurses responded to his letters pretending to be his mother. Once my father learned she was, in fact, deceased, and that they had been lying to him, he spiraled into a deep depression from which I don't believe he ever really emerged, as evidenced by his addiction to purchasing classic automobiles; as the one marriage counselor said after my parents' one and only visit to any therapist, my father Arthur Jr. was always trying to "put the car back together."

He would tend to purchase fancy vintage automobiles at the worst possible financial times for us which, from a psychological perspective, made perfect sense. When things were at their worst, his preferred escape was behind the wheel of a newly-purchased automobile; it must have provided a dopamine rush for whatever the current issue was, along with a trickle-down effect, anesthetizing his age-old trauma related to the destruction of the car that killed his mother and nearly him too. The lifetime tally of one-hundred automobiles purchased led my mother to the comfort of her gallows humor, and she would often comment that she counted the cars, not sheep, when she had trouble falling asleep.

In 1941, eleven years after the deadly car accident, our father enlisted and went on to further suffer trauma serving his country in the South Pacific at the infamous Guadalcanal. We never really were told the full story of what he experienced, but whatever it was, it was so terrible that even a consummate storyteller such as Father couldn't even speak about it. His war trauma was layered on top of the automobile and death-of-mother trauma that was already unresolved. He had what I now know as compound trauma, and as a result, he was in a vicious whirlpool of unregulated emotions from which he could not escape. Not a single person in our household or any friend that I ever heard about really understood what my father was going through, so he was isolated and confused, as his pain was also a mystery to himself.

Potential success for him would still rear its head throughout his life. There were countless brushes with fame and fortune. A few years after graduating the Art Center School in Los Angeles, one of his first major art gigs was with Walt Disney before the opening of the new theme park under construction, Disneyland in Anaheim. My father was hired based on his ability to perfectly match Walt Disney's artistic style; he and Walt Disney became friends. Father was responsible for the murals and facades for the amusement park rides such as Mr. Toad's Wild Ride, Peter Pan and Alice in Wonderland. These murals were still in existence when we arrived at the El Encanto in 1974. Additionally, my father worked on many of the refreshment stand facades as well as the sets for the Mickey Mouse Club. I bet my parents believed at the time that this was just the beginning of an art career that would keep growing.

There were numerous other gigs including stints at ABC Television and local networks; Father was on the crew of the Lawrence Welk show during the KTLA years – 1951 through 1955 – and he completed set work and portraiture for feature films at Paramount Pictures, where Arthur Sr. had worked as a Property Master since 1917. Along with the odd jobs my father worked to make ends meet (such as valet parker), he completed many automobile designs for notables like Tony Curtis.

Throughout all of this, the low but growing hum of his trauma would cause him to lash out; he often went uncredited for his work – my father was a fan of handshake deals – many of which fell through or worse, he put a lot of time and effort into them without getting paid or acknowledged. In addition to therapy, what my father needed was an agent – someone to protect his interest. He was a visionary artist and skilled draftsman, but his business negotiation skills were lacking, and he would lose to the sharks who were swimming in the waters of '50s and '60s Hollywood. My father had the talents but not the ruthless savvy required to make it there.

By the time I was born in 1964, there had already been a series of disappointments, moves, firings and periods of starvation for the family. That foreclosure when my mother was carrying me, I think, was one of several final straws – it had become clear by then that my father was broken, evidenced by that unnamed and mysterious self-saboteur, always waiting in the wings to pull the rug of his self-confidence from underneath his follow-through. Despite all of his efforts, my father often lost to people of greater shrewdness and astonishing dishonesty.

MOTHER

Mother was a clever and talented young lady from Newport Beach, California. She was the younger daughter of the two in her family, her older sister Louise Jr. (Benny) was a dark tale of a person. My grandmother, Louise, was a somewhat spoiled girl from New York, who was married at age sixteen to a British man named Charlie, a veteran of World War I, who had served at the blood bath that was the Western Front in France, where he fought for four years as a sharpshooter.

Mother's family lived on Kings Road in Newport, overlooking the harbor and landings her family owned, and also where Charlie worked as a yacht salesman and harbormaster. My grandparents also owned the airport in Newport Beach, and Grandfather was also a pilot. Grandfather and Grandmother also had a keen interest in deep sea fishing and at one point, Grandmother had held the title as World Champion Lady Angler. Their home was full of silver fishing trophies, which were only outshined by their conservatism, racism and general disdain for others they deemed as less-than.

Into this family came the surprise redhead baby, my mother. She was a bit of a tomboy when she was a child, and even thought of as ugly, but she quickly blossomed into a beautiful woman with a killer figure and hair the color of deep red mahogany. Throughout her life, Mother was accused of dyeing her hair, so unusual was its color; her standard reply was to tell her detractors that only her gynecologist "knew for sure."

What made Mother stand-out further was her wicked, gallows humor and her artistic talents. While her contemporaries were only thinking about which young, rich pre-med student they would marry, my mother was devising a scheme to go to art school. When she expressed her interest to her parents, she was completely squelched – artists were considered to be of the unsavory sort – like show people – and her parents were therefore on the lookout for a nice conservative and boring young man for her to marry. Grandfather Charlie protested her choice by refusing to pay her tuition for art school, so my mother worked many extra jobs to raise the funds for herself. When it was time to go to the fall semester, her parents further refused to drive her to school in downtown Los Angeles, which was far away from Newport Beach. Without her own automobile – she didn't have a driver's license – she ended up having to leapfrog every day to school, riding nine different public conveyances that were available at that time in 1945 Los Angeles, including buses and streetcars.

Examining the context for a young woman at the time, this was a courageous undertaking, but that's how deep my mother's desire was to become an artist and escape the doldrums as another doctor's wife in Newport Beach. This was how my mother became the Red Sheep of her family; along with all her other differences, being a redhead was considered a flaw by the culture into which she was born, and her mother became the subject of the standard must-have-been-the-milkman jokes, which gave her dark-haired family further fuel for their disdain toward my mother. They all wrote her off and thought she was daffy and silly, and this very bold move of hers to follow her artistic dreams confirmed their belief that she was an embarrassment – and emboldened their ridicule of her.

Everything about her was subject to her family's disapproval – her hair, obviously – but also her clothing, decorating sense, way of thinking and in particular, the man she chose to marry.

She told us many times that no matter what she wore, her father had a problem with it. Mother had an artistic flair in everything she did, including her progressive way of dressing. She really was courageous in so many ways and way ahead of her time. Mother was the unsung intellect of the family, hidden in the shadows of a patriarchal societal structure that was not yet ready to recognize the genius in most women. Also, Mother often reported that her parents really did not understand her sense of humor, which was laced with irony and often dark paronomasia. She found her father rather humorless. Her mother was wittier but wasn't amused by her "bonehead" daughter.

THEY MEET

By the time my parents met in that quad of the Art Center School, they were both seeking something to release them from the torture of their lives up until that moment. I'm sure their first conversation was lively and humorous. I'm sure they bonded over their outlier status and differences. I can imagine what they saw in one another – two artists who were going to prove to their families and everyone else that they were wrong about them. My parents likely shared that confidence that is only shared between the people who have been abused and marginalized but suddenly see a light at the end of the tunnel through each other. They clung together and held on tight, taking those first early steps to build a life of their own design and to live and thrive in art and culture.

Off to Mexico City they were after only knowing one another for three weeks. Still so afraid of her dictatorial and judgmental parents, my mother returned home with various excuses for her absence (she was eighteen, after all), but did not tell her parents that she was married. Mother was terrified of letting her parents know that she had married the "Hollywood Creep" because she knew they would believe that she had thrown her life away because of her "silly" passion for art.

Mother remained at home for another month before adding another lie to the situation, which was that she was going to marry Arthur; little did her parents know that she was already married. Of course, her parents were vehemently against the marriage and, as predicted, wrote her off as a failure. Her marrying my father was all the proof they needed that she was just a red-headed idiot, a reject and a fool. For them, their embarrassment over their daughter would continue and, oh, what would their friends and neighbors think? My grandmother found humor in the situation and just used the situation to impress her friends with her own perceptiveness – "See, I told you she would never amount to anything." Her parents refused to attend the wedding.

My father's family was much more accommodating, and Arthur Sr. even arranged through his colleagues at Paramount Pictures for the wedding to be in a wedding chapel set for the movie, "The Bride Wore Boots" starring Barbara Stanwyck. Very apropos for my parents to be fake-married on a chapel set rather than in a real chapel, but the officiant and the secret first marriage were not an act, and it was all a part of the general sense of gaiety – and cemented my parents' belief that their way of life was to rebel against the uncreative and non-artistic forces.

I would really have loved to have known my parents then – when their love was strong, and they felt like they were going to conquer the world. They both believed that my father was destined for worldwide fame as an artist, and my mother had aspirations as a humorist and cartoonist. The world appeared to be made for them, which was part of the high of victory running through everyone post-World War II; it was all about the United States and its newly-established "superiority" in the world. They were part of what is called the "Greatest Generation," and my parents' confidence must have been overflowing. Damn their parents, damn the judgments and damn them all for their lack of vision – my parents were going to show everyone how it is done.

It was from this strong beginning that their story unfolded in a continuing spiral down rather than up. My place as the youngest child in the family always gave me the feeling of being extremely late to the party, which, given the ultimate nature of party, may have been the thing that saved me. I never lost the feeling of being baffled that my parents had remained together, and I pressed this point with both of them throughout the rest of their lives. My father would only respond that he did love my mother; my mother would respond with, "I paid a high price for a good sense of humor."

Chapter 6 — The Grandmother

RECORD BOOTH SUGGESTED SONG: "FALLING IN LOVE AGAIN,"
MARLENE DIETRICH

Another silver-plated character in our saga was the woman who quickly adopted the phrase "The Crazy Camps," used it frequently, and had plenty of money to help but rarely did; our grandmother, the self-exalted Louise Gertrude Craig Fyfe Hopton. But we need to cut her some slack; it isn't an easy journey from the Barnard School for Girls to World Champion Lady Angler, but somehow, Grandmother had pulled it off.

In our sitting room at the hotel, there was a picture of Grandmother from her Barnard phase; a pose in profile, which showed her remarkably lovely features, including her waist-length hair. She was indeed a beauty at sixteen-years old.

That was two years after Grandfather Charlie spotted her at a summer camp in upstate New York, shortly after he had crossed the pond after serving in King George V in World War I. Grandfather had been awarded many medals in his four years, first enlisting when he was merely sixteen-years old.

He hated England, well at least living there, and left with war-related health problems and a fully-inventoried trunk of belongings. Grandmother was merely fourteen-years old when they met, so he waited two years until she was sixteen to begin courting her. Of course, we were spared the details, but we understood it had been a passionate affair, which led to their marriage and subsequent move to the west coast at the urging of Louise's father, who was already living in Sierra Madre, a small town in the hills above Los Angeles.

Flash forward a few decades, and Grandfather was operating the yacht landing in Newport Beach, and they were both deeply involved in deep sea fishing. Over the years, Grandmother had become quite the party girl, even during the depression in the '30s, as their fortune was assured by her wealthy father and she was able to maintain a lively social life, which included going out dancing whenever possible. Even though she was aging rapidly and gaining weight as a result of her indulgence, she never lost her habit of flirtation, still thinking herself the ravishing beauty she once had been throughout the rest of her life – a good attitude, in my estimation.

This behavior irritated her youngest daughter, my mother, to no end, and when my mother would describe her childhood to us, she would include stories about her own mother that were quite embarrassing. My mother referred to Grandmother as the "Eternal Coquette" and Grandmother would constantly attack my mother's appearance, mainly due, again, to her red hair; Grandmother had delighted in repeating to Mother what a friend had said about her appearance, which went something like, "She [meaning my mother] would be beautiful if it weren't for that red hair!"

Our mother had never really dealt with her resentment of her mother, often repeating the terrible things that had been said to her to us, over and over. But worst of all, for all of us, was Grandmother's excessive drinking, a habit she had developed over the years, during all of the parties and the fishing trips. So, after Grandfather had died, and Grandmother moved into the Big House with us, there was a thick layer of animosity spread between them, that could turn into a quagmire if I happened to ask just the perfect and inadvertently wrong question about times before I was born.

Luckily, Grandmother had moved from the Big House into that townhome up the street before the eviction had occurred, and she was actually fairly delighted that we had landed in something as glamourous as a hotel on the Riviera. She expressed the belief that it would be "fun" for us and chuckled unashamedly in front of my parents about their predicament. In sharp contrast, Mother believed that all of Grandmother's excitement was really about the availability of a bar on the premises, and the chances of flirting with various staff members; nothing could stop Grandmother from being the Eternal Coquette – not weight gain, not her double-radical mastectomy, nor the fact that she was seventy-years old. Grandmother continued to carry on as though she were an Edwardian period, flirtatious pre-debutante, and this drove my mother crazy.

Grandmother enjoyed the multiple opportunities to visit us at the hotel and take us to the restaurant, treating us to dinner, and playing the matriarch of an imagined dynasty. I can't say that I minded at all – I enjoyed my grandmother, and her generosity, I only wished it extended to helping us purchase a home somewhere. I couldn't understand why she just didn't help with this, but even as a kid, this sort of conflict I already knew was something to avoid.

Rudely, Grandmother would occasionally dangle the carrot of a possible purchase in front of us, and we even went out occasionally to look at houses with her. If she were to purchase one, this would mean that she would be living with us again, and my mother would be her full-time staff, a role in which she had been cast early in her childhood. It would have been better if the idea of our grandmother purchasing a home for us was a flat-out "no," but instead, it was this nebulous possibility, which doubled-down the pain of our continuing impoverishment and evictions. Each time we went out to look at homes with Grandmother, my hopes would go up, only to come crashing down when she would suddenly turn on us, call "our" plan Quixotic, at best. It was confusing to me that we could be in such dire straits quite often, while also knowing that Grandmother was wealthy enough to be living off merely the monthly interest of her estate, quite comfortably.

For years, Mother had tried to care for Grandmother, all the while being disrespected through stories my grandmother would tell her bridge cronies, but Mother was committed to helping her mother, despite the taunts, teases and occasional insults.

Sometimes while at the El Encanto's pool, Grandmother would ask Mother to fetch things for her and my mother would remind her that there was a full-time hotel staff at her beck and call, at that she herself was on her "day off." Witnessing their dynamics was somewhat entertaining to me, but I really just wanted everyone to get along; there wasn't a tiny corner in any of the relationships in my family where "getting along" was common or sustainable, and I continued to feel incredible shame about my family, particularly when we were in public and an altercation of some sort was about to break out at any moment.

It all seemed to come down to the fact that Mother was an error to her family. My mother had broken the sacred code of knowing her place in the world by seeking out something more unique to do with herself, and then finding another artist to marry rather that the medical school student her parents had picked out for her. It wasn't so much that my mother had made a mistake, although that was the conclusion discussed at length by Grandmother, it was also that Mother was such an alien being to my grandmother, and I think she resented my mother for not following her advice; this made Mother fair game for a lack of understanding and the resulting ridicule. So, when Grandmother came to visit us at the hotel, she did so with one hand holding a cocktail glass, a cigarette dangling from her lip, and an I-told-you-so look firmly fixed on my mother.

My direct relationship with my grandmother was good. Good, not great. There was a contradiction for me in the way my mother described her, and how I experienced my grandmother; I didn't think my grandmother was as bad as I had been told. Instead, she was quite loving toward me and seemed genuinely interested in my life and goings on, not that I let her into my private world. I kept my conversation with Grandmother relatively vague and traditional; I trusted no adults, not even her. I had been made fully aware of Grandmother's drinking issue for as long as I could remember, and I learned firsthand what it looked like.

Grandmother's alcoholism was made clear to me, arriving in in a Trojan Horse named "Baking Cookies." While we were still living at the Big House, it was decided that I would spend every Wednesday afternoon at Grandmother's baking cookies after school. This was another example of my family trying to act like regular people, and it all sounded rather quaint and special to the casual observer. This sweet-sounding idea, like all positive plans put into practice in the Camp Family, was short lived. At least we did manage to have about a dozen afternoons together before it stopped.

The visits were about two to three hours long, the main focus being that I was going to learn how to bake cookies with instruction by Grandmother. During these times together, we would be interspersing baking with lessons at her piano, as she also wanted to teach me how to play. Grandmother had once been a concert pianist in her day, among her other accomplishments, so I was eager to learn from a master.

The cookie making went fine in the beginning, and I soon learned the wonders of eating raw cookie dough and having hot, freshly-made chocolate chip cookies to dunk into glasses of cold milk. After baking, we would sit and watch television together, play piano or talk. The first half a dozen visits or so were very wholesome. As Grandmother grew more comfortable, it seemed she had the desire to be even more comfortable, and she began to ask me to make cocktails for her while I was in the kitchen baking. Grandmother wanted to get baked, too, and realized she had a willing bartender trainee on her hands, as I was always eager to learn something new.

I enjoyed making the cocktails for her, her favorite being screwdrivers. I believed it was okay to do this because my grandmother thought it was okay. She first taught me how to mix this drink, and once satisfied with my bartending ability, suggested we played "Bartender" in addition to baking cookies. As I became better at mixing screwdrivers and also taking full-charge of the cookie baking, Grandmother was inclined to lounge in her regular spot, smoke cigarettes, and tell me fishing adventure stories, ice cubes in her glass clinking away with each gesticulation.

It became habitual at the beginning of every cookie session for her to say, "Oh sweetheart, could you fetch Grandmother another screwdriver?" I would dutifully pull the highball glass from the cupboard, snap the ice tray and drop three cubes into the glass, add "two fingers" of vodka, fill the rest with orange juice, stir it gently (as to not "bruise" the vodka), and deliver the drink to Grandmother, who would always remind me to use a coaster before setting the glass down on her coffee table. This process would be repeated at least three times during my visits on Wednesday afternoons, which always ended with my dipping cookies in cold milk (my cocktail), and Grandmother getting screwed up.

My mother was always asking how it was going with Grandmother when I returned home – I think she wondered if something like our cocktail hour was going on, but I didn't want to tell my mother about the screwdrivers because Grandmother was confessing all sorts of family secrets to me as she became more intoxicated. I started to learn things about my mother from a perspective I had never heard before; about how my mother was extremely rebellious, hard to control, and had multiple boyfriends and love interests to the point that my grandparents couldn't keep up with all the suitors. These were halcyon days for me; unmonitored cookie consumption with juicy family gossip for entertainment.

As the weekly Wednesday Afternoon Cookies n' Cocktails Truth-Telling Hour™ continued, it became less and less important to Grandmother that cookies were involved, so pretty soon, it was just me making drinks for Grandmother as she told me stories. I missed the cookies and I started to see what my mother had been talking about. Grandmother was beginning to get really quite drunk with me watching on the final few afternoons, and I was feeling very uncomfortable, as she was divulging secrets no child should hear.

By what turned out to be my final "cookie baking" visit, the cocktail process had completely devolved into something untenable. When I first arrived that last Wednesday afternoon, Grandmother asked me to mix her a screwdriver as usual, so I did this first, and then went to the kitchen believing I could get things back on track by starting up a cookie-baking process, which was the original intent of these afternoons with Grandmother, after all. So, I got out the ingredients, and before I could reach for the bowls, Grandmother said from the living room, "Sweetheart, Grandmother is ready for another." I made and delivered it, following all bartending courtesy and coaster protocols.

By the time I had the dough ready, she asked for another. While the cookies were in the oven, she asked for another; she was now on her fourth.

As I took what would be the last tray of cookies I would be making at Grandmother's townhouse from the oven, she slurred from the living room, "Grandmother is ready for another, but this time, sweetie, very little ice."

Then, after we had a couple of cookies, the request for the next drink, "Perhaps sweetheart, I don't really need the orange juice."

Next, "Now, Sweetie-pie, now this time, you can skip the ice this time."

Followed ten minutes later by, "Dear Boy, you may just give Grandmother the bottle of vodka now – no need for a glass. It's just easier, isn't it?"

I packed up the last dozen or so cookies, and while leaving I noticed that Grandmother had passed-out; it was 4 in the afternoon.

As I walked the short distance back to the Big House, I felt very confused. When I opened the front door and Mother saw my face, she knew exactly what had happened. I had just lived an afternoon in my mother's childhood, and Mother did not want that for me. So, with that, a good try by all to provide some wholesome normalcy and routine in my life came to an abrupt end. I'll give it a "B" for effort, and an "A" for alcohol.

Even though I had no intention to continue the Wednesday afternoon visits with Grandmother, the move to the hotel was the perfect excuse to say "no" anytime Grandmother suggested we do it again, since we were no longer living just a block away; I bet she believed that was the reason.

Chapter 7 — The Bigger

RECORD BOOTH SUGGESTED SONG: "ROCK ON,"
DAVID ESSEX

As time passed, it became clearer that whatever humor and adventure there was to be had in living at the El Encanto, it could not eclipse the darkness in my family, and I had the nasty habit of comparing us to other parents and kids I saw around me, especially while I was at the pool. I tried to focus on the relaxed vacationers around me, pushing endless dark thoughts in the form of questions as best I could from my mind. It's hard to pick one, but likely one of the biggest questions gnawing at me was: Where will we go if the parents can't pay the rent here? I calculated that living in a hotel was one step removed from living in our car, or worse, living on the streets. Like many of my concerns, this thought was the result of doing the math; my parents were unbelievably only paying $375 per month for the Big House, and the hotel was $450 per month, so how was this more sustainable?

I would stare at the distant ocean from my chaise, looking at it through the perpetually dirty glass partitions between the pool's cinderblock columns, and think about the hugeness of my problems versus the size of the sky above, and how, beyond that blue sky, I knew the expanse of never-ending space was there, and I hoped that I was just living out some story, and none of it mattered. The enormity of space above and the life ahead of me, and what that life would look like if I were able to survive childhood, seemed to have the same largeness that was impossible to absorb. I was angry that I was being forced to grow up so soon, to have thoughts like these to ponder. I knew that my knowing I was growing up too fast was a result of the family's issues. The other kids around the pool seemed blissfully unaware of how terrible life really could be. I had become hypervigilant about making the right decisions now, and worried about the decisions to come as I grew older; I did not want to turn out like my parents. I must strive for perfection, in all things. A simple error could be deadly. I was petrified of making a mistake.

These musings would persist quite often beyond bedtime. I would sneak out and wander around the El Encanto's gardens, sometimes lying down on any of several benches to ponder for a moment, looking at the city's lights below. This should have been the true luxury of the hotel – these times with nothing else to do but relax; instead, I was searching for solutions and a plan – I was unable to relax. Even though I may have lost my own bedroom in the move, I had gained an extensive outdoor "room" in the form of these gardens, where I could sit or wander, away from my family, and ruminate.

Pacing around the grounds, I would visit the little forgotten areas – at least what I perceived as places on the grounds that the adults had forgotten. I believed that the spaces themselves now recognized me and were relieved somehow by my presence – reassured that at least someone was noticing them, closely, including the abandoned garden statues face down in the soil, and the crooked benches lost in the jungle. They mirrored my feelings of being abandoned by the adults in my life, so I wanted the inanimate objects to know that I cared about them – we had something in common. I also believed the garden places longed to be found again; I wondered if that was my role, if that's why I was here – so the lost corners of the El Encanto at least had the attention of an also-lost little kid, someone to mourn their decay.

Other evenings, I might try lying on my back on the cool lawn by the pool, smelling the grass, wondering which bugs were crawling underneath me, a little society and civilization of other creatures that had their own story none of us would understand. On my back, I would look at the night sky – full of stars, or clouds, or the occasional passing airplane. I appreciated the El Encanto's unique, lofty spot up on these hills above Santa Barbara proper, and if one waited until early in the morning, even more stars were visible as lights dimmed and the majority of traffic tucked-in for the night.

In these early hours, having successfully navigated the squeaky floors and being able to sneak-out of the Villa, all alone while the hotel and its guests slept, I would reach my arms out to the expanse of space, as if to embrace it all and pull it toward me, the feeling of the earth and grass beneath, as if my arms could envelope my dreams of being something more than who I was, and pull it toward me. When alone, it was as though I entered my largeness, where I could discuss things openly, only with myself. A deep, internal life had formed over the last few years, and I felt a sharp separation from everyone else and everything around me. I may have begun withdrawing from the world, but to me, it felt like expansion – in a direction away from the world of other people that I found as uninteresting as it was troubling.

Thinking alone in my imagined, huge internal space, I understood that I would have to be larger if I were going to be able to contain the immensity of life, regardless of successes or failures. My family's situation, history, and the dynamic between our parents had forced me to grow up swiftly, as a mode of survival, and I had become a very tactical and strategic thinker – and a big dreamer – so here it is, I thought to myself, taking a big, psychic yawn. With no one to trust nor count on, I had made the conscious decision to only trust myself, but this decision wasn't new to me.

It wasn't as though I had developed something that might be called a spiritual practice; it was a necessity for self-preservation to be thinking about the total picture, to be asking for higher guidance, waiting for something to show me or tell me how to improve my life. I deeply desired that better story. I believed I had to be a completely self-contained unit, partitioned from my family, and for that matter, pretty much everyone else. I needed a larger me wherein I could innovate new techniques to navigate this family situation, and this world that I could already tell did not care about me.

In my childhood, I clearly understood that remaining dependent on my undependable parents was not logical. With my back on the moist grass, its post-watering cooling wetness soothing my sunburned legs on a particularly warm summer's midnight, I considered who I had to become to overcome my circumstances; the journey ahead of me seemed immense.

Years ago, prior to living at the hotel, I was existing in some sort of vacuum, wherein I had become so accustomed to the daily drama of my family that I believed all other families must be the same. But that was when I was a child of six or seven – I was ten now and had snapped-out of the vacuum and was thoroughly in a strategy mode. The various family units that had come and gone from the hotel provided an excellent basis of comparison. I was sure there were some conflicts hidden behind the scenes of these families; it was pretty clear to me, at least, that there wasn't a lot of the deep resentment between parents and children that I saw in my family – at least I was unable to detect any such tension.

No one else's children talked about evictions and foreclosures. No other kids I met talked about dodging lamps as they flew through the air during their parents' arguments. No one ever spoke of police involvement to subdue their parents' brawls, or anything similar to the terrible and personal insults I had heard tossed about in fights without any thought as to their impact on my feelings of safety. There was no hint of alcohol, drugs or schizophrenia in the other kids' conversations. I knew, because I asked, which likely made me seem pretty strange to them. Perhaps it wasn't an in-depth study, but as far as I could tell, we were the worst family that I knew, which was made even more poignant by the fact that I loved my parents, separately, so intensely. I knew that I was too young to be wrestling with such a conflict.

I didn't think my mother and father were great parents – but, I did also like them, as friends – and sometimes "like" is more important than love. It was in this spirit that I had one day approached my mother when we were still living at the Big House to tell her how things were really going to be.

In 1973, the year before we had to move to the hotel, I had been gradually finishing up some steps I had been taking for a couple of years, in the effort to figure out a way to live independently within my family, not knowing about any legal or other avenues I could take to remove myself from the situation. Even back then, I knew my family was sick – no matter how I may have responded to the dynamics on the surface – I knew it was sick because of how it felt to be a part of the family, and I was afraid to tell anyone. I may not have articulated it this way to myself at that age, but I couldn't deny how I felt in general as my family moved through their day-to-day existence, and this continuous unhappiness of my parents was something all of us could feel, viscerally, down to our bones, which made us profoundly unhappy, too. So, the child I was supposed to be was instead held in safety and protected by the larger me who could handle the bruises I might receive, protecting a softer version of myself, hidden from the world.

So, back at the Big House late one night when I was seven-years old, I was awake, far into the wee hours, thinking about stuff, when "the math" dawned on me that I had to find a way to survive this for another eleven years! By that time, I would be eighteen, and could legally leave my family behind. Horrible thoughts went through my head that night – images of my entire family dead and queued up on the landing, so I could be free – that's just how desperately I wanted to be away from them – it would just be so much easier if they all died. I knew immediately that thinking of my family being dead was a horrific thought (I didn't have the emotional tools yet to understand this was really about freedom – I just wanted them all to STOP), so I shuddered, and shoved this worst of thoughts away and started, instead, to strategically plan how I could begin "Operation Survival," from this time in my life until I was an adult, when I could finally just get away.

That thought gave birth to a voice in my head I called "The Sergeant" - a voice of authority, who from then on always kept me moving and motivated whenever I was in danger or something needed to change or if something dangerous was getting too close to the sensitive me-child that I was protecting. It was the voice that urged me to run faster than any bully at school and he was the reason I was able to do it. The Sergeant also helped me stick to my Operation Survival plans whenever I became distracted by a loving act of my parents. I'm not sure who the voice was, but it was almost as though I asked for him, conjured him, and he had simply materialized. His voice was deep and masculine, with just a hint of underlying compassion, and I was glad to not be alone anymore.

The Sergeant suggested that I start stockpiling personal supplies in my room, instead of sharing with the rest, as a way I could begin to assert my separateness, to stop a useless and dangerous fraternization with the family. He summarized by saying the more that I interacted with my family (and other people at large), the more danger I was in; the most important thing was to live in the margins of this family successfully for the next eleven years, sort of like a roommate. So, the next morning, I asked my mother to purchase on my behalf my own towels, my own soap and shampoos, and a tidy pajama, robe and slipper set. To the outside observer, this could be seen as a child playing some sort of game, but it was very serious to me.

To her credit, Mother supplied all of the requested items and needs within a few days, including throwing in a small basket for me to carry the travel-sized bottles to and from the upstairs bathroom. Every morning,

I would emerge from my room, opening my door that had the "Keep Out, That's An Oder" sign, and I would glide down the landing holding my neatly folded towel, with my toiletry basket perched on top. This is when Mother decided on a nickname for me, "The Boarder," and while she didn't understand completely why I had requested all of this, or was acting this way, she slipped easily into just being amused rather than questioning my motives and supported me without needing to understand. Perhaps deep down she knew that this was some sort of coping strategy and in her sadness and desperation, she just let me have it – 'Poor kid', she may have thought.

So, in the mornings, The Boarder would walk with his toiletries to the bathroom to start his day because, naturally, he had important things to do and think about and no time for the petty squabbles around him. He was bigger than his circumstances and trained to visualize himself this way. After all, The Boarder was me, and in this way, I found even a larger safety within myself; growing bigger added more room and reduced the danger to a workable amount.

The issues in the household – the fights; the constant dives into financial holes; the weekend short trips to intoxication that only took about two beers; Father's addiction to buying automobiles – he had six cars at that time - which generally facilitated the first two issues along with the resultant hysteria; the parade of older, drug-addled dysfunctional siblings sometimes living in the house, then suddenly moving out; and whatever was going on with my parents' unknown and therefore under-supported psychological issues – all of these things were just more reasons for me to do my best to rise above and away, and grow, most importantly, grow bigger. It was as if the pressure of these family sideshows were squeezing me so tightly that I was popping-out the top of my skull.

This led to this conceptual practice about growing big, like really big, one-hundred feet tall or more; then, I could look down on the Big House and see it as small, like a dollhouse with little porcelain people that could do me no harm. It was a mental state that I worked hard at staying in – no matter what was happening, I wanted to be bigger than it. I would clench my fists and teeth as hard as I could and try to physically grow behind the closed door of my bedroom, while yet another fight or some other melodramatic mayhem ensued downstairs. I would imagine myself towering over the streets of Santa Barbara, seeing all of the rooftops and trees and in this fantasy in my mind's eye, I would feel relieved and safe. After using this technique with success a few times, I dubbed it "The Bigger," since it was even bigger than the Big House, and I worked on it constantly, improving my ability to grow quickly and taller each time.

The Bigger not only functioned as the headquarters for The Sergeant, as well as a resting place for my outside persona, The Boarder, it was also a warehouse to hold the current problems as well as the terrible stories of the past shared with me at such a young age. To me, it was both my giant self and a large bubble-like immensity, where big troubles became small, a bit like a hangar for a Spruce Goose full of worries.

One of the worst truths sequestered in The Bigger was the story of my birth, the original horrible tale. Like other stories I had been told, my parents and siblings never held back or tried to protect me by perhaps being gentle with the facts or, I don't know, how about not telling me at all? For as long as I could remember, they spoke to me as if I were an adult, so I also had to hold emotional space for their suffering created by my birth. I was told by nearly all that my birth was a mistake. My siblings and my mother had told the story independently to me, and their versions matched, which was enough confirmation for me; it must be true then, I thought.

The story went that my mother had a miscarriage before my birth – a little girl – and my parents were told by the doctor that there could be no other pregnancies. At that point, Casey was the youngest of three:

There was Randal, fourteen years older than Casey, then Andrea (Andy), our sister, three years younger than Randal and eleven years older than Casey. In some ways, I think Casey's birth in 1960 was a bit of a surprise as well, but it didn't cause any immediate panic.

When Casey was born, the family was on a relative upswing, though they still wouldn't qualify as "happy;" our paternal grandfather, Arthur Sr., or "Pappy," the retired prop manager at Paramount, had a stroke and required care, so it was thought the best thing to do was to find a house together, so Mother could care for him.

Pappy had a bit of savings, so the family purchased a home on Laurel Canyon Boulevard in Los Angeles. Everyone felt very relieved that they finally owned a home, so when Casey was born, there was some sense of stability. Our eldest brother and sister had not turned into the surly, acid-dropping teenagers yet that they would soon become. Apparently, Pappy was a bit verbally abusive toward my mother, and had made inappropriate advances as well, but she was handling it. Two years later, at sixty-two in '62, Pappy died, and one stream of income (his pension) died with him, putting the entire weight of keeping the home on our father's shoulders, which was never a good idea.

They scraped by with the help of some inheritance for a year or so and then, the worst possible thing happened – my mother became pregnant again, but then had the miscarriage, and Randal, Andrea and to some extent the toddler, Casey (because he was also not spared from hearing the issues), were relieved there wouldn't be another kid because that would have tipped the financial scales disastrously for all.

The legend continued that Casey liked it when things were settled and was not a big fan of change, even at his tender age, so in late 1963, when my mother announced she was pregnant again with me, in spite of what she was told after having the miscarriage, it wasn't happy news for everyone. They all had felt momentarily safe when it was thought that another mouth to feed was impossible; my parents were being taunted by "friends" about having so many kids that they clearly couldn't afford. By the time I was forming in my mother's uterus, my family was also facing foreclosure on their home because my father could not make enough money as an artist – in other words, they were broke, again.

Our mother's latest pregnancy (me) was not affordable – how could they feed another when they were barely able to feed the first three and themselves, or make their mortgage payment? This was all happening concurrently with Randal and Andy discovering acid and marijuana, and there were still more problems brewing as a result, including that Randal had impregnated his teenage girlfriend as well.

So, in June of 1964, I was born into a huge mess with an unstable family that did not really want me, did not know how to afford me, and saw me as something that was only going to increase their financial peril - rather than excitement, my existence was met with consternation – this is what I was told. That said, once I made my entrance into this world, my father and mother of course embraced me and loved me. Being two weeks late, I was a large baby (nearly 10 pounds), bald except for oddly bushy eyebrows. Based on my appearance, the family doctor, Dr. Linett, who had delivered all four of us, said to my mother, "Congratulations, it's Uncle Fester." The Addams Family was complete.

When I arrived at home from the hospital, four-year-old Casey's first reaction to me was to say, "Take that baby back where you got it!" Understandably, because he had been told and/or overheard all of the pregnancy-stressing around him. Still, it's hard to resist a baby, so I think I won over Randal and Andy; I don't think I ever won over Casey.

Sadly, the medical expenses related to my birth did indeed exceed the available household funds, and the house on Laurel Canyon was foreclosed upon.

Father did manage to rent another place in Los Angeles, but in 1967, the family decided to move to Santa Barbara. I was told the motivation in leaving L.A. was the increase of ongoing ridicule and judgment by so-called friends of my parents, who saw my birth and the foreclosure as just another failing of the Crazy Camps; the rumor mills were at full-steam. My mother especially wanted a new story – to get away from all of these unkind judgments - and after the move to Santa Barbara, she cut-off all contact with these former friends, refusing to answer the phone or respond to letters.

By the time I was nine-years old, I had heard this story many times from everyone, together and independently, except Father. In particular, Casey often told me how I had "ruined everything." I had also heard that everyone "got along" better before me. It wasn't who I was, what I did, or what I said that was the problem – it was my very existence that was an issue. It was a hard thing to hear as a child from family members, and I could not know that this "story" and the connected resentment would keep appearing in one form or another throughout the rest of my life.

I was overwhelmed by this information, and it was, of course, too much for my young mind to process, and I wasn't even aware that I was not processing it. I didn't know if I was supposed to apologize or what. The only person who never took this angle was Father, which was very ironic because it was on his shoulders to make the ends meet; he never blamed me, though.

All the moves, all of the evictions, all of the transitions and housing struggles from then on were framed as a direct result of my birth. What else could I do with such a huge burden, but to create somewhere inside myself that was big enough to hold it? Because these people so close to me were unhappy with my actuality, my heart perceived them as enemies. I didn't feel loved – I felt, at best, tolerated. This is the very seed that grew into The Bigger and why I needed a place from where I could look down upon it all, objectively. This worked so well with this core problem, that everything else that happened afterward was also then stored within the one-hundred foot bigger me-space.

These concepts and fantasies bulged from my brain and into existence due to lack of processing space in my head; I simply did not have the room, in my original form to hold this much sorrow – my own, and the sorrow of them all – and it also made me think that keeping to myself as much as possible, for my own protection, and also not to bother them, was the best thing to do.

The Sergeant continued to remind me, with his voice echoing in The Bigger, to keep my eyes on the goal of turning eighteen and doing everything to protect myself from this family as much as possible in the interim. The Sergeant kept reminding me to draw as little attention as I could to myself and to tread carefully.

Returning to the projected cuteness of having my own separate toiletries, it was just the tip of the iceberg in my journey of learning how to be self-sufficient, and this learning became one of my top priorities. Each time I performed this bathing ritual, my confidence grew stronger and I became more determined to achieve complete autonomy.

One morning, my mother interrupted The Boarder's walk to the bathroom and finally asked why I was going to all this trouble when there were perfectly good toiletries already available to me in the bathroom. According to her, I turned and replied, "So, I understand that you are my parents and that you gave birth to me, but I don't feel like that was my choice. Just because someone creates another person doesn't mean that they own them. Nobody owns me, and I don't really see why I have to do what you tell me to do. I don't really need you to help me, and in turn, I won't ask for anything. Please just ignore me." She was a bit astonished but simply replied, "Well, okay, Sir!" not realizing The Sergeant returned her salute from The Bigger.

During 1973, I was also quite aware that I was still dependent on them financially, so I began scheming ways to earn my own money; having my own toiletries wasn't enough – I required more independence. So, at school, I had created a grifting operation I called a "Gallery," which was a simple but nearly unwinnable marble game that cost one quarter to play. During recess at Wilson Elementary School, I would sit with my legs fanned out, and place a marble at my crotch, and at each ankle. When another kid handed me a quarter, I placed it on one knee, and handed the player one free first marble, even if they had their own. I would have the player sit a couple of feet back and shoot their marble. If the marble hit one of my marbles, the player got to keep the marble and their twenty-five cents, so they would essentially win a marble; only the first marble was free though.

If the player missed all my marbles, I kept the quarter bet and their marble. It seemed fair to the casual observer, but I found that I quickly had a big collection of marbles and quarters. The concept caught on, and soon there was a large group of children playing this game at one end of the playground. It was like our own miniature gambling casino, and it was serious business for all involved. Many would sit down next to me and yell, "Gallery!" becoming their own sideshow barkers.

It was very successful and fun for all, and I amassed a tidy sum of winnings. Some of the money I earned was spent on candy, but some I stashed away and would use it to buy the travel-sized toiletry bottles from the dime store. Eventually, the Yard Duties saw what was going on, in particular that the game involved real money, so they shut our casino down.

All of those times I hid out in my bedroom behind the 'Oder' door, seeking some sort of shelter from the storm that was my family, I quietly stepped into The Bigger and consulted with The Sergeant, while I sat cross-legged on the floor counting my riches.

Luckily during the long weeks as I secretly strategized, there were the breaks in the storm – the holidays, the fun road trips, the quiet evenings, the trips to the beaches, parks and museums, when they happened – there were plenty of non-melodramatic days and nights to make my wait until the day of liberation a little more tolerable, so I can't honestly say that every day was a misery; I was glad for this.

The Bigger filled the space between the domino-like days as they fell, and I continued with my visualizations of largeness, and developed a deeper sense of independence, and I grew even more interested in avoiding complications between people that I found so unnecessary and, in my opinion, actually mostly just interfered with progress. I observed and noted the fallacies of too much closeness. Again, my young mind may not have framed nor described these feelings in this exact way, but I had a very strong sense that the histrionics and all the things "they were doing" were just another form of running in circles. I needed somewhere to think in peace, which was me, secretly in The Bigger, behind my closed door. My mother must have noticed my deep sessions, sitting and pondering things; at one point a concerned neighbor, who noticed my anemic blue skin and commented to Mother that I needed "more time outside doing something," infuriated my mother and she responded angrily, "He is doing something – he's thinking!" If she only had known what I was "thinking."

Sadly, even though I felt I could separate myself mentally from "all of them," The Bigger didn't include the awareness that my internal, intellectual separateness did not necessarily equal complete safety, and the emotional harm that came along with being in the crossfire of a family in perpetual crisis was still taking its toll, even if I didn't know it.

Looking back on it, I was a deeply depressed child, without the tools nor resources to make a change for myself. Inventing and imagining these things – The Sergeant, The Bigger, a one-hundred-foot-tall me – and even owning my mother's nickname for me, The Boarder, became ways to self-medicate, cope and survive. My hope came in the form of a plan, and that kept me going.

A year after the formation of The Bigger and The Sergeant, we were in Villa 100, where it was more challenging to live separately and be alone with my thoughts. I had lost my private room and now my brother was in all of my stuff and in my face all of the time. He was just starting his travels through juvenile delinquency, so at least some of his criminal behavior kept him preoccupied and away from our room. I had to hide my money in increasingly clever and unpredictable places in the room, and I was constantly worrying about him finding it.

Also, as a result of the lack of storage space, there was greater access to family archival files, kept in boxes here and there, filling the closets, and given the chance, I dug desperately through box after box trying to find some new way out of this family. I'm not sure what I was looking for exactly, and I could only do it when I was the only one home alone, which was rare. During my digs, what I mostly found were endless bank statements and receipts, and old tax files; mostly not items that were too exciting, but it was during one of these archival searches that I came across a copy of my own birth certificate and was absolutely mortified to see my parents' names listed. Despite the terrible birth story I had been told, I had been nursing the fantasy that I was actually adopted somehow and that all I had heard about my birth was a lie. Realizing that I was truly their child deepened my resolve to become something different. I liked my parents, and thought they were interesting characters, but I didn't want to be like them; no way.

I continued to spend my days at the hotel, vanishing occasionally in the gardens and growing into The Bigger, always trying to figure out my next moves, while gazing down from the magnificent heights that it could provide. At the pool, or in the jungle, I was actually a giant boy, even though I appeared to be a small one.

The Bigger was invisible, so nobody at the hotel ever realized that I was actually one-hundred feet tall. I took pity on them and decided I would tolerate these silly mortals as long as I had to. I became a great observer and when anyone was talking to me, I would secretly analyze them from my lofty height and process what I was being told, who was saying it, what their motivations might be, and how actually mentally ill they could be. No one else could see how large I was, but then again, being so big, I didn't need them to.

My largeness gave me the room to handle the fact of how on display my family and I were at the El Encanto. We were an anomaly – the longest-staying long-term guests, and not a family of wallflowers by any estimation. People would make silly, teasing comments about how all of us were "crammed" in tiny Villa 100 with our "zoo," with supercilious giggles. In reaction, Mother once uttered, "All the world is a stooge, and the people merely preyers."

Many of the family arguments were indeed overheard, due to the thin walls and often opened windows, and those combined with Father's natural humorous charm and stories of art and movie stars, which given any chance he would recite, made us something of a dark joke; after all, if he had done so many amazing things – he had designed cars, worked with Walt Disney himself, and at Paramount and ABC - then how the hell did we find ourselves living in a rundown hotel? Mother would tell Father to stop being "Mr. Showbiz" because she knew how it sounded. While people generally liked my father, he had no idea that many of them were also snickering a bit. The unfortunate part of it all was that Father really had done all of the things he talked about, but his circumstances belied these prior achievements.

Even though I could retreat into The Bigger at will, being his son around the El Encanto was never easy. When I would encounter adults, whether staff or guests, they would mostly speak to me in the way adults speak to children in almost a baby talk, in a way that told me they felt sorry for me. I would then view the person as a moron because they were so easily fooled. I would play-act with them – give them back the innocent little-boy-speak – it was an excellent cover. Alternatively, I was concerned about someone discovering The Bigger because then they would know what I was capable of and might interfere with my plans to get away, or they might make fun of The Bigger, only seeing it as the fantasy of a strange little boy. In reality, I was on a secret mission, so I developed the persona of a child. Mother knew there was more somehow and would often refer to me as "ten going on sixty-five."

The weeks rolled on at the hotel, the story there continued to unfold, and I bided my time. I was watched by the hotel's staff as I traveled to and from the pool, or when I walked around the gardens. Other than hiding out in the Record Booth, I was always in view and monitored at home; it was suffocating. I could rarely escape the presence of other people, so I continued to employ The Bigger, creating space within myself to hold all of the happenings at the El Encanto that I was experiencing. I played within the fantasy of my true stature, imagining myself walking around the hotel's gardens with my Bigger Feet, smashing everyone – guests, gardeners, housekeepers, parents, brothers and the owner too. And I remember thinking about what Casey had said on my first day home, and I wished they had taken that baby back where they got it.

Chapter 8 — The Abandoned Cottages

RECORD BOOTH SUGGESTED SONG: "TIME IN A BOTTLE," JIM CROCE

Not every cottage was invited to the El Encanto's party anymore. Whether because of costs, exhaustion or just dismissive laziness, the hotel's owner and her staff had decided at some point to just to ignore a group of four cottages on the far east side of the property. They were locked tight, some with curtains drawn, but occasionally I would see workers going in and out of them, being the spy that I was.

For some reason, that section of the property seemed hotter, dryer and more exposed; its own desert-like microclimate. The cottages showed signs of severe sun damage, and all had an advanced case of paint leprosy, the chips and shreds hanging in lengthy pieces, barely clinging to the wood.

From outside of the cottages, especially on the hotter days, I could also smell the mustiness coming from within. Since these cottages were sealed, there was no airflow, and the thin walls were no protection against the heat of the summer on the Riviera. Whatever was inside of these cottages was being cooked, every day, and the fumes of the roasting permeated the walls.

Set away from the other buildings, and with no activity, these cottages and this section of the El Encanto were closer to the truth of the place; just looking at them and being in the quiet and stillness which surrounded this "neighborhood" of the grounds, I could really feel the hotel's loneliness and abandonment. There was something very sad about being over on the far east side - it felt like a graveyard. Having only seen them once (at my urging), Mother called them an "embarrassment of wretches."

The creepy void of these structures didn't stop us from trying to figure out how to break into them. Casey and I climbed all around and even under them in their crawlspaces, trying to find a way, somehow, to pry our way in to delight in the potential treasures inside.

One day as I explored by myself, at last, I discovered a window on one of the large duplex cottages that was actually missing its lock and brace mechanism – somehow we had missed it - it was just kept shut to have the appearance of being locked, but it was easily pried open with an old, rusty butter knife I had found, expertly wielded by my tiny, inquisitive hands. This window was quite high off the ground, and I had to stand on my very tiptoes to get it open. Once ajar, I then had to strain and pull my body up, gripping tightly to the paint-chipped window sill, and was able to stick my head and upper torso through the window first, resting on my stomach. Because there was so much sun damage to the paint, my t-shirt was quickly covered with a fine, white powder dust, and my stomach became red and scraped underneath as I slid over the sill and dropped to the floor inside. I noticed that I had also cut and abraded my skinny legs, which jutted out from my still semi-damp swimming trunks. I sat for a moment assessing the damage to my legs and clothing, and already considering how I was going to explain it to Mother.

I started looking around the bedroom I was in – it was full of old furniture. The air was stale, and it felt as if I had breached some sort of time membrane. Brass lamps, mirrors, chairs, dressers and desks, a vanity or two, and a somewhat out-of-place rusty wheelbarrow; must be a place for indefinite storage, I supposed. Some of the items were partially covered with old sheets, but most were exposed and coated with a thick layer of dust. It was so hot inside that I could hear the wood frame of the cottage creaking and popping as it expanded, and the room smelled like baking old maple and wood stains and polishes, since all of this furniture was sitting essentially in an oven and off-gassing.

I was a little nervous, of course, not only because I was breaking into the place – therefore, doing something I shouldn't be doing – but also because I had no idea who or what else might be inside; the idea of being inside one of these cottages was much more exciting when I had been outside. I may have gone too far with my exploring this time; maybe the entire idea was a bad one from the start. The room felt smaller, hotter, dirtier – I had the feeling of being squashed in some big monster's sweaty fist. I looked up at the window I had just climbed through and considered climbing right back out. My reluctance to explore further wasn't really a result of worrying about being discovered - I wasn't too concerned with a hotel worker showing up because it appeared, at least from this first room, that no one had been inside of this cottage in some time. It was more of a feeling – like I was intruding on someone's space, and I had the uncanny feeling that I was being watched, as though I was some anomaly in the space – a living, breathing child – a rare and potentially delicious offering – or sacrifice.

Soon my lust for excitement overrode my fears, and I stood up and walked from that room, into a tiny hall, and this felt a bit better. There was another bedroom behind me and to the right, also filled with old furnishings, and off of the hall, there was the entrance to the bathroom. I was especially interested in the bathroom, since ours in Villa 100 was so small and dingy. This bathroom was tiled in an amazing way – black and yellow jagged designs and borders, nothing like our dull and dreary bathroom at all. This one also had a large window and tub, and a vintage pedestal sink. There were pretty severe rust stains near the drain in the old tub, but all in all, it wasn't too bad of a place. I turned on the cold-water faucet over the sink and to my surprise, rusty water poured out. This made me curious about electricity, so I flipped-on the bathroom light switch but nothing happened. I couldn't tell if the bulb was burned out or if the power just wasn't working.

I noticed then that the ceilings in this cottage were higher also than those in our cottage, and the wood floors were still exposed with no carpeting. Even though this place was clearly abandoned, for now, it also was evident that it was, originally, far grander than the one we were staying in. I had a feeling of envy, and again, the wannabe social climber in me took over and I felt dejected once again.

I stepped out of the bathroom and continued down the narrow hallway. There were two doors to either side of me, both leading to separate bedrooms, meaning that this cottage had a total of four bedrooms. If we lived here, I could have my own bedroom again! I felt the flash of possibility pour over me, and I started conceiving a plot where I could encourage my parents to convince the powers that be to allow us to move to this cottage. With a renewed positivity, I peeked my head into through each bedroom door and said, in my best Bugs Bunny voice, "Ah, yes, this will do nicely."

Adding to my delight, these two bedrooms were filled with old mattresses – on the floor, leaning up against the walls, nearly taking up every square inch of the room; my first thought was to host a jump-a-thon with friends. I continued down the hallway into the main living area, which was also full of mattresses! So, this was the hotel's secret mattress graveyard, sort of like what elephants do by hauling their dead to an undisclosed location. Mattresses lined the floors and walls in three rooms – pretty intriguing – but I continued through into the kitchen, which was large and finished with bright yellow tiles. I realized while standing there that this cottage was not a duplex at all, but a large single structure with two entrances – it must have been one of the original units for student housing for the State Normal School. I was already in love with this cottage and my body vibrated with opportunity to make the switch from Villa 100, which, it turned out, was not the largest cottage on the property.

I had completed my tour, so I peeked out the windows to make sure the coast was clear, and I left via the front door, leaving it unlocked behind me.

When I returned to Villa 100, I telephoned my friend Anthony to tell him the good news and whispered into the receiver I had found the ultimate fort for us. His hunger for adventure overcoming him, he decided to head up right away and hopped on the bus.

Anthony was my best friend; we had met in third grade and became inseparable. Anthony was Filipino and dealt with racism from all of the other kids, whether they were Mexican or Caucasian; even in an elementary school full of diversity, he was still an outsider.

It was a really tough town if you were something different, economically or otherwise. I think Anthony and I bonded so deeply because we were both fringe kids, myself less so, after all, I was only poor. Plus, he was as silly and cartoon-addicted as I, so we had a lot in common, including our interest in exploring places in the community that we were told were strictly forbidden. We had climbed fences, walls, through deep brush, and sneaked in through open doors and even been under the city through the accessible areas of the sewer system. We were two stealth little shinobis, getting into everyone's business with nobody knowing. This is why I called him first once I had made the discovery of what I viewed as the ultimate bouncy house.

I watched from the screen porch with anticipation, waiting to see Anthony's form walking up Alvarado Place. This, of course, piqued my mother's interest, and she had a sixth sense for my mischievous behavior. Mother poked her head into the porch and asked, "What are you doing?"

I replied that Anthony was "coming up" for a swim in the pool, as he already had a dozen times before. Mother said, "Oh, okay, but you should have asked me first." I assured her that he wouldn't stay that long, wheedling my way to some sort of retroactive permission from her. I think I oversold it a bit in a way that made it obvious that something was up; I said, "Yep, we're just going for a swim!" in a loud, out-of-character enthusiastic tone. She looked at me for a second and said, "I think I'll go with you, down to the pool." "Curses," I thought to myself, "foiled again!"

Just then, I saw Anthony walking up the road, so I burst out the screen door and ran the short distance down to meet him. I quietly let him know that we were going to have to distract my mother for a bit. He had his usual blue backpack on, something that he always carried, and he was dressed in his best Catholic Sunday School attire.

Anthony had a particular style, that was far more formal than I. His mother, Catalina, was an avid shopper at J.C. Penney's, and Anthony was always clothed in a way that I admired greatly. He generally had on a polyester no-iron short-sleeved dress shirt, worn over a crisp, white undershirt, a nice pair of pants or shorts, bright white socks and little black shoes. This was very different than my impoverished surfer boy look; hand-me-down Hang Ten t-shirts and swimming trunks, most of the time. This day was no exception for either of us, and Anthony had his swimsuit and his own towel in his backpack. He didn't like to use the hotel's towels at the pool; it grossed him out that so many people had used them, despite the fact that they were taken away and cleaned by Mission Linen Service daily. Anthony could somehow still smell the stench of other bodies even in the clean hotel's towels, as he put it.

Anthony walked back up to Villa 100 with me, while I explained my mother's suspicions and how she had horned in on our plans. After all, going for a swim and perhaps some treats from the bar wasn't such a bad thing, so we agreed we would check out the cottage with the mattresses in secret, afterward, once we had thrown my mother off our trail.

As we walked up the rickety front steps and into the screened porch, we could hear my mother talking to my brother. He had been listening to music in the Record Booth for a couple of hours and had overheard some talking. Now, he was going to the pool, too, and while I felt confident that Anthony and I could lose Mother somehow before we headed to the abandoned cottage, my brother would be so much harder to fake out. He also had a keen intuitive power to detect shenanigans, and both my mother and my brother knew that when Anthony and I were together, there could be some trouble. As Anthony and I walked up to my mother and brother standing in the hallway, outside of the Record Booth, they both turned to us with very suspicious glances.

Mother asked, "So, are we all ready for the ... uh ... pool?" with a little sideways grin. I stammered a bit, and said, "Yes ... what's wrong?" "Nothing yet," she replied.

Mother pulled her yellow terrycloth bikini out of a dresser in her room, and a white cotton pullover dress with yellow embroidery – her go-to pool outfit. She walked out the room and into the bathroom to change. Anthony and I stood there fidgeting a bit, because it was something of a rush for us to even be under suspicion. My brother was just wearing his trunks, as usual, so he stood there looking at us with his arms folded. "What the fuck are you two up to?" he asked.

Anthony and I tried really hard not to glance at each other suspiciously, but there must have been a little eye contact. Casey said, "Uh. Oh."

Mother returned to the room in her pool wear and asked again if everyone was ready. We all said "yes" at the same time, forming an accidental harmony with our voices.

We took the long brick pathway in front of Villa 100, all of us walking single file with my mother at the rear. We crossed the main driveway of the hotel, and the site of us made the bellhops smile and wave. My mother, brother and Anthony waved back, but I was lost in thoughts inside The Bigger, taking a moment to savor this little moment that felt so entirely "normal." Receiving this brand of warm, simple waves and greetings were such a luxury item in my life, while so regular and mundane for others. My heart and mind just wanted to seize and hold that feeling – from the outside, we looked like a happy family, merrily on their way to enjoy the pool; I didn't just want to project this illusion, I wanted to be the illusion, but knew deep down that we weren't. By the time I processed all of this, I had to turn and wave as we had already passed the entrance; but my wave wasn't received – the bellhops had moved on, and the fact that my wave was a misfire sent me deeper into my ruminations of feeling disenfranchised from the world and I wondered if I would ever truly feel part of it.

As Mother opened the pool gate, my mood had shifted, and I was feeling very introverted, so my usual "resort posture and stride" was rather more of a depressed march to a chaise, where I plopped down. Mother asked if something was wrong, but I didn't answer – I was too overwhelmed with the prospect of trying to describe it to her. On some level, she knew she had a sad little boy on her hands, even if she didn't completely understand why; I think she cared, I just didn't believe that she had the ability to really understand how I felt.

I didn't have the capacity to discuss my feelings – they were just really big and complicated to the point that I could not figure them out for myself; there was no way I'd be able to express them to anyone – so my go-to coping strategy externally was just to become really quiet, while on the inside, I huddled in The Bigger. Mother knew that my silence was a sign that I was troubled and to distract me, she asked if she had ever shown me her custom swimming strokes. "No," I replied, in a very bored and downtrodden voice. She slipped off her cotton pullover dress and there she was in her yellow bikini. At forty-eight years old, Mother was a knockout and I noticed a few men who were sitting on the other side of the pool look up from their newspapers and attempt to suppress grins.

Mother was also an expert swimmer. Being raised in Newport Beach, she was a member of a few swimming and diving clubs. As a result of her prowess in the water, Grandfather used to ask her to do terrifying (to me) things like diving to the bottom of the harbor to free fouled anchors of yachts and fishing boats. Watching Mother swim had always been something to behold – she cut through the water like a greased seal. Her diving was elegant and precise, her pointed hands and feet slicing into the water with hardly a splash. When she was about to swim, her walk changed to one of confidence and elegance. It was the one time she exhibited dominion over her surroundings, so she knew that I would enjoy seeing her invented swim strokes.

She walked with perfect posture and in her full beauty to the pool ladder, swung a leg gracefully over the top, and lowered herself into the water. She did maybe two or three strokes and was immediately at the far end of the pool, like magic. I stood up and walked over to the water's edge. Mother looked up at me asked, "Are you ready?" Boy was I!

Mother completed one lap with her usual expert back stroke and then stopped halfway in the pool and said, "I call this The Hollywood Backstroke," her voice echoing off the walls of the pool and catching the attention of the other guests. She demonstrated a stroke that consisted of dragging her hands across her face and up to her forehead, and then stopping for a moment in a glamourous pose, chin straight up, with a dramatic expression, hand held for a second, resting palm face down on her forehead, which then moved on to appear as if she were smoothing her hair. She repeated the pose with each stroke – it was hilarious. A couple of other adults sitting next to the pool laughed. Mother stood up in the shallow end and took a little bow. She then slid back into the water and did essentially a regular forward freestyle stroke, but as each hand met the water, she mimed the brushing away of imaginary debris. She did this a few times, then popped her head up and said, "That one's called The Sewer Crawl!"- everyone laughed at that one. It was all I could stand, so I cannonballed into the pool, followed in short order by Anthony. Casey dove in, too, and we all practiced The Hollywood Backstroke and The Sewer Crawl with my mother. We splashed and yelled, and took turns demonstrating these new strokes. At one point, Casey challenged Mother to a swimming race, and she easily trounced him. She was lightning in the water, and she was very clever. I had completely forgotten my earlier sadness – we were, for that afternoon, a normal family – for real.

After about two hours or so, the sun began to set, and we were all feeling tired and hungry. Mother ordered burgers for everyone from the pool phone, and they appeared about twenty-five minutes later on a tray, with Coca-Cola's over ice in fancy glasses, decorated with little paper umbrellas piercing two cherries for each. There was a general sense of pleasure and happiness even from the waiter – the staff knew who we were, and they could easily see the pool from the restaurant's upper deck at the rear of the hotel; we had been being watched and appreciated, and they had put a little extra panache in the food presentation just for us. Working at a venue in such a state of overall disrepair, I'm sure that seeing us enjoying ourselves with our mother at the pool must have been a much-needed time of regularity for the staff who worked there and knew us, perhaps a little too intimately.

There was no "hungry" like the after-swimming hungry I could feel, and we all ate our burgers and fries with enthusiasm. We were sitting at one of the pool tables with a sun-bleached and just-about-to-tatter umbrella, sipping our Cokes, and talking about my mother's swimming strokes. Anthony and I had completely forgotten about exploring the abandoned cottage, and the sun was starting its nearly-final decline to the horizon. The sky was a deep blue with swirling apricot-colored wispy clouds. The pool area was catching the reflective glow of the sky, and we were all bathed in the orangish amber light. Our skin looked tan, our teeth looked white, and the contrast of my mother's yellow bikini, her tan skin and her crimson red hair made her white smile all the more radiant. It was one of the few moments at the hotel that I had seen her look truly happy, and I knew that this image would be tattooed in my memory forever.

The waiter returned and cleared our plates and glasses, so Mother decided it was time to go. She asked Anthony if he needed a ride home and he declined, saying he would just walk. One of the many amazing things about Santa Barbara is that it is an easily walkable city, so my mother was fine with this offer and knew he would be safe. We all arose, and my mother and brother began to walk back to Villa 100, and I said that I would escort Anthony to the bus stop. When my mother had asked Anthony about the ride, it had triggered my memory about his reason for coming to visit in the first place, and I was already scheming to sneak away with him to the abandoned cottage before darkness truly fell.

Once Casey and Mother were out of view, I said in an excited whisper to Anthony, "Wanna go to the abandoned cottage?" He replied, "Well, of course my dear Watson."

We left the pool area using the east gate and ran up the grass hill to the first pathway. We took the path behind the building that housed the multiple guest quarters facing the lily pond. As we got closer to the abandoned cottage area, we became more excited and shifted into high gear. My rubber sandals were making a loud slapping sound, and Anthony told me to slow down, worried my brother would hear us – we weren't entirely sure where he was. Our best guess was he was back at home – but you never knew – he was prone to snooping and keeping an eye on me. Anthony completely stopped for a minute and listened for any footsteps or sign that we were being followed, which was difficult in the fading light and overgrowth. When we felt confident that we were alone, we continued along the path that twisted around a couple more occupied cottages and finally came up to the blighted bungalow's area.

Anthony was excited when I told him which cottage it was, and I motioned to the front door, which I had left unlocked. When I turned the knob, though, the door was locked again. I shrugged and motioned to Anthony to follow me to the rear of the cottage. Once in place under the window I had crawled through earlier, he made a hammock with his hands, and I stepped up easily with his assistance to grab the sill and opened the window until it was fully extended. I pulled myself up and through, then put my towel from the pool over the rough sill and ledge, and leaning-out with both hands I helped Anthony up, while he used his feet to scale the wall. When he got close, he grabbed the sill, now covered with my towel, and pulled himself through the window, too.

    The air inside remained hot from the day, and the cottage still smelled like old mattresses and dust. It was slightly stifling inside, so we left the window open. Nighttime was now advancing swiftly, and inside the cottage was extremely dim and extra sinister in the twilight. Some of the corners of the room were in complete shadow, and the random sheets being used as a dust covers were taking on the appearance of classic ghosts. Anthony and I both loved the thrill of what we were doing – the danger and intrigue – so we pressed on and entered the hallway.

    I gave Anthony a tour of the place as if I were a guide in a historic mansion, with my most affected accent – pointing out the fine details of the tile in the bathroom, the hardwood floors, the classic lavender crystal glass doorknobs, even though much of it was hard to see. I switched on the light in the bathroom, not expecting it to work, like last time. To my surprise, the light flashed on! I immediately shut it off, realizing it would draw attention. So, the place still had power after all, I pondered, making me feel more assured that I could talk everyone into our switching residences.

    The two bedrooms full of old mattresses were getting simply too dark to enter, so we headed to the main living area. Mesmerized by his surroundings, Anthony dropped his back pack by letting it slide slowly off of his shoulders and down his back and legs to the ground. He walked to the middle of one of the mattresses on the floor and began jumping up and down, creating a hellish dust cloud almost immediately. I joined in shortly thereafter and very soon, we were bounding from mattress to mattress, colliding with one another, and also shoving one another into the mattresses leaning on the walls. The light was nearly gone, but there was still just enough coming through the front windows of the cottage for us to see one another. We had created quite a dust cloud, so it was exceedingly unhealthy but nonetheless a blast, and we were both sweating profusely from the effort and the uncomfortable stale heat of the room.

An electric light switched on suddenly from outside and for a moment we thought that our activity had attracted someone's attention. I stopped jumping for a minute and pushed the old draperies aside and peered out one of the front windows. An old metal pseudo-colonial style path light outside was now on with the rest automatically for the evening, as some of the pathways were illuminated by these lights at night. I relaxed and returned to jumping.

In spite of the pathway light outside, the main room of the cottage was becoming prohibitively dark, so I realized it was probably already time to go, and therefore gave Anthony the hardest farewell shove I could. This caused him to lose his footing completely, and he tripped backward, falling into a far corner of the room. He slammed into a mattress that was leaning there and that had partially slid down the wall; Anthony let out a playful yell, and then we heard a lower octave grunt come from somewhere in the room.

It is often described in horror stories – the chill that runs down one's spine in these moments, which I had always believed to this point was more of a metaphorical description as opposed to a true visceral sensation; I was wrong. A freezing chill rocketed through my entire body and I was unable to move. Anthony was standing somewhere in front of me, but it was so dark in the room now, I could only see his silhouette and the glow reflecting off the moisture in his eyes. Once again came a grunt, and we could also hear some movement. I strained to see in the darkness, but it looked as though something was moving behind the mattress leaning against the wall. I tried to swallow but I couldn't. Anthony screamed, "Where's my backpack!" and started crawling on the ground to find it. I spun around on my heel and took one large and bouncy step toward the front door, and began struggling, in classic horror fashion, with the door lock, trying to open it. I think I locked and unlocked a few times before I actually tried the knob – and Anthony was already on my heels, trying to grab the knob, too. We both pulled open the door together, and darted from the cottage, barely touching the front steps, and ran with our full force away in two separate directions.

    I guessed that Anthony had run all the way home because he wasn't back at Villa 100 when I got there. When I stepped off the porch into the bedroom, I had the realization that it was probably Casey hiding under the mattress back at the old cottage, and I relaxed – and was also kind of pissed. Mother walked into my room and asked, "Where have you been?" I responded by asking, "Where is Casey?" She replied, "He's been in the record booth since we got back from the pool."

Chapter 9 — The Bus

RECORD BOOTH SUGGESTED SONG: "I'VE GOT TO USE MY IMAGINATION," *GLADYS KNIGHT & THE PIPS*

The hotel was funky, but I liked it. I also liked the Riviera area, seeing it as "above and away" from the "vulgaris" (my new favorite word of 1974) of downtown Santa Barbara. It's not that I wanted to be another privileged Santa Barbara snob, it's just that I was so tired of being in the cheap seats all of the time. Other kids were on family vacations to Mexico - everyone was asking, "Have you been to Cabo?", which made me embarrassed for them - or they were seeing Europe, and everything I heard seemed better than the inside of a little, dingy cottage. My brother's friends had new surfboards, new swim trunks, new bicycles – and some of them were being gifted mopeds, which was the ultimate cool at the time for a Santa Barbara teenager. My brother and I were dealing with hand-me-down bicycles, ill-fitting clothing, food stamps and everything else that was perfectly designed to make a kid feel less than. Had it just been the material things we were lacking, it would have been easier. Instead, this surface issue only doubled down on all of the insanity.

We were both often overcome by that somewhat trite and common interest of many kids – the desire to fit in. It was even more extreme given that we were living in a town that was home to many rich and famous people, seldom seen, but who were known to be hidden on their vast estates in Montecito, the affluent little suburb to the south of Santa Barbara. The irony for us was that a branch of our ancestors had settled in Montecito, but that wasn't the sort of clout one could cash in at the bank.

Even the city buses were a cut above in Montecito. The Metropolitan Transit District had purchased a fleet of miniature Mercedes buses, like the kind I had seen in movies that were set in Europe. They were tall buses with large windows tinted a warm yellow, and their engines were diesel, and had that distinctive rattle that I only had heard in foreign films as well.

There were still the standard city buses, too, but for the shorter routes or routes with winding or narrow roads, the City employed the stylish German buses. To that little climber in me, the Mercedes buses gave the Riviera this intercontinental flair, and I practically wet my underprivileged shorts every time one drove by. I would purposely take routes around town that I knew were traveled by these special buses, even if I had nowhere to go; riding on these, I could adequately fantasize about being on the other Riviera, the one in Santa Barbara's sister city, Cannes, France. I was that hungry for a different life – something elevated – something away from the truth of our household. Logic dictated that we would be just as miserable in a mansion, but at least we would have enough resources and space to completely avoid one another.

When we first moved in to Villa 100, I had about three weeks of fourth grade to complete before summer vacation, so imagine my glee when I found out that the route from Alameda Padre Serra to my downtown elementary school was serviced by a Mercedes bus. I would be taking one every day from home to school and back again, and I was absolutely giddy about this.

As an introverted child, it never occurred to me that anyone would even notice my comings and goings to the bus stop or give a damn about my troubled life. I often slumped along when I walked, hoping no one would notice me, feeling downtrodden most of the time.

Childhood depression was a difficult thing, and I remember reading and hearing quotes from older people about "enjoying your childhood" while you can. I had no idea what they meant by "enjoying," as I was just trying to get through it, survive it. While riding that fancy little German bus to school, I would sometimes recalculate how many years, months, days and hours it was at that moment until I could get away.

Also, walking down to catch the bus to school on Alvarado in the morning, I was sometimes preoccupied in The Bigger with new information I had just heard that morning in some new and terrifying parental torrential downpour of an argument that I had not heard before; a reference to their past before I was born, or something of that nature. There was so much about their lives before my birth that I didn't know. Or, perhaps, I might be lost in thought considering what I was about to face at school after a somewhat blissful twenty-five-minute bus ride - what new torments would the bullies at Wilson School have devised for me this day? How fast would I have to run? Those last few weeks before summer vacation, I was also calculating how many days were left until I was out of the fire (school) and only in the frying pan (home). The only refuges I had were the pool, the grounds and the Record Booth.

It was on the fourth or fifth time when I was walking to the bus one morning, headed for school, when I heard a voice saying "Yo!" from somewhere in the main hotel building as I passed it. I was extremely shy and quite embarrassed to be noticed, plus Mother had ingrained in me to never respond to strangers who were motioning for me to approach them (and I used to think, "There are people who are stranger than my family?"), so I ignored the voice and walked a little faster - there was about half a block left to the intersection and stop where I caught the bus.

When I arrived at the stop, I looked back to see a person running toward me in an all-white kitchen staff outfit. I stayed perfectly still and prepared myself for whatever was about to happen – was I in trouble somehow?

As he approached, I could see it was one of the cooks from the kitchen and when he walked up to me, he handed me a white, paper sack and he said, "Here you go – for your bus ride."

I looked in the sack, and there was a freshly-baked blueberry muffin with a pad of butter, a plastic knife, and a paper napkin. I was so unaccustomed to this sort of kindness, I barely mustered a very quiet, "Thank you," and the cook smiled and replied, "Sure."

My private fantasy of riding a Mercedes bus on the French Riviera just bumped up a huge notch.

When I boarded the bus that morning, as I always did, I sat in the very front seat, close to the driver, so I could see the view from the large windshield of the bus. I had decided this was the best seat in the house, so this is where I positioned myself. The entire bus was quickly filled with the smell of my hot blueberry muffin, and the bus driver looked over his shoulder and said, "I normally don't allow eating on my bus, but if you promise to be careful, please, dig in."

I wasn't sure if it was real or imagined, but I got the feeling that other adults were somehow aware of my plight and were doing their best to provide some comfort and normalcy.

No muffin has ever nor ever will taste better than the first blueberry muffin delivered by that cook, that morning. Little did I know that he would continue to give me a muffin, every school morning that I walked by, for the rest of my stay at the El Encanto. Even into my little unstable life, a muffin-shaped shooting star had fallen.

Chapter 10 — The Zombie Kitten

RECORD BOOTH SUGGESTED SONG: "THE EXORCIST THEME,"
MICHAEL OLDFIELD

I had further developed my own special route to the pool. Rather than go down the long brick path that required me to cut-across the El Encanto's circular entry driveway, which would have been the shortest way but very public, when on my own, I liked to exit the door to the south from my bedroom and head east along the brick pathway that curved up and then down, and ran along the abandoned flume to the lily pond. Once there, I would run the length of the pond to another pathway, the one that ran along the front of a row of attached guest rooms, a building also in the 1913 Craftsman style, where I would end up at the top of the sloping lawn, next to the row of park benches perfectly placed for guests to enjoy the view.

On this one particular day, I rushed down the grassy expanse once again with my flip-flop sandals smacking my feet underneath me and entered through the east entrance of the pool area. Once inside the enclosure, I collected myself, controlled my breathing so no one would suspect that I had been running like a child or something, and quickly adopted an air of celebrity, draping my towel with a flourish on a chaise lounge. There were no other guests at the pool, so I played my performance to an empty house, staying in character regardless, reminding myself of the importance of dress rehearsals.

Sitting down, I made sure not to sit too far from the pool phone, in case I wanted to order any refreshments. As we all had learned, the pool phone was hit or miss – depending on the busy-ness of the bar or if anyone felt like picking up on the other end. About fifty percent of the time, they would answer, and my orange juice or 7-Up would be delivered by a waiter; alternatively, I sometimes had to climb up the sloping lawn and into the hotel's main building to order a drink directly if someone failed in the bar to answer the call from the pool phone. Either way, I enjoyed the hotel's coin-free economy and being able to say, "Please bill Villa 100" no matter where I placed an order.

A word or two about my state of mind during this time: Of course, it was quite clear that my messed-up family was in a serious financial jam, and more than just that, by being a Southern Californian native born, I innately knew how to adopt an air of false luxury and importance – it was bred into me, as a flipside to the state of perpetual crisis that was part of my family's DNA. I perceived that everyone in my city was fronting, a little bit, and I was quite adept at emulating the behavior of the adults around me. I had studied completely broke hippy adults, who could walk into and crash the Santa Barbara Art Museum for a members-only function, and still not be questioned as to whether or not they were on the guest list, because they simply succeeded in comporting themselves with entitlement and authority. I saw that it was all about appearance, attitude and posture.

What I wasn't emotionally intelligent enough to understand, though, was that this was also a coping strategy and a shield for me from the truth of myself; behaving this way, I didn't have to face the fact of the economic emergency that was my parents' continuous operating mode throughout my childhood - our baseline was struggle. So, while at the hotel, and particularly while at the pool, I would often pretend to be a rich kid on vacation, or whatever it took to not be recognized for what I actually was; a poor kid, from a severely dysfunctional family, in a very tough situation. My projected importance was a salve for the burn of my pauper status and my feelings of irrelevance.

So, that June of '74, it was very quickly my daily routine to sleep as late as possible, as though I had been at some "affair" the night before, then eat a quick breakfast in our "hotel room's" kitchen, and then off to the pool, as if I had time for only a quick swim before I had to be on the set at "Metro."

While all of this glamorizing was going on inside, my external appearance told a different story. I had no clue then about sunscreen or SPF, nor did my parents or anyone else, so my pale skin took the full brunt of the sun's fury, generally all day long. Since Mother was a redhead, and I was somewhat similar, leaning a bit more perhaps to the strawberry blonde spectrum, I was at great risk of burning. My natural skin tone was an anemic parchment with delightful hints of grey and blue, and by the end of June, I would be a painful toasted red color with only aspirations of an actual tan appearing in areas that had been burned repeatedly, such as my shoulders, stomach and legs.

Unhappily, the sun also enraged my melanin, so I was a sea of freckles, too. To top everything off, the occasional blistering of my shoulders and nose resulted in an inordinate amount of constant peeling. Not a single adult of the time had an issue with my appearance, and only Mother would occasionally suggest that I wear a t-shirt while in the pool.

As far as the water goes, the pool was a gamble as to cleanliness. It varied from shades of blue to green, depending on the week. There was a certain shade of light green that I considered acceptable enough, and I would swim in the pool if The Sergeant and I determined the water was "survivable." This resulted often in my blonde-ish hair turning a bit green, alternately stained by the algae, if the pool turned green, or by the copper in the algaecide, when it was dumped into the water in copious amounts to clear the algae – I couldn't win.

Of course, there were guests checking in and out all of the time, and the pool was the center of the daytime social scene at the hotel. Nearly everyone who stayed long enough complained about the pool to no avail; things happened in their due time and no sooner at the El Encanto, and complaints were swatted off like the mosquitos that generally grouped together at dusk over the lily pond.

Back to the day in question, after I arrived at the pool, assuming my spot and attitude, I finally noticed Hiya Boy, our maintenance man with a nickname I'll describe later, in the middle of the northside of the pool, on his knees, scrubbing the algae buildup on the perimeter tiles. I did not want to disturb him as his cleaning of the pool was a rare occurrence. Regardless, I was determined to get in the pool anyway, so I decided to lounge on the chaise until he was finished. As I leaned my head back, so it was resting on my hands, and crossed my legs as I had seen the stars in movies do it, something black, floating in the pool, caught my attention. I jumped up from my chaise, and slipping on my sandals, I casually flip-flopped my way over to where the mass was floating, and to my horror, there was a drowned black kitten, lifelessly bobbing on the surface of the water. Hiya Boy glanced up at me and said with his typical aloof grumpiness, "I'll get to that soon. Don't touch it." Then he added, "You're the little boy whose parents have too much quack-quack." I guessed he meant the Cold Duck; this is the most he would ever say to me.

Before he could finish his sentence, I was reaching down to lift the lifeless kitten out of the pool. Its poor little pink tongue was hanging out of its mouth, its eyes were half opened, and while very small, it felt heavy due to the saturation of its fur. A living cat wet is certainly a pathetic sight, let alone a dead kitten that's saturated. I put it down gently on the cement and studied it for a bit, squatting down with my elbows resting on my knees. If I had been alone, I would have allowed myself to cry, but I held back as I did not want Hiya Boy to see my sensitivity.

I remembered something I had seen on television – a resuscitation of a drowning victim – and even though the event on the T.V. was fictional, I did learn a few things about how to deal with this sort of emergency. So, I lifted the kitten up and gently held it upside down; pool water drained from its mouth and splattered on the cement. I carried the kitten back to my chaise and wrapped it in my towel. I held the kitten to my chest and started to cry a bit, making sure my long hair was over my face as a privacy screen.

At first, I thought I was imagining it, but I began to feel the kitten squirming under the towel. I looked at its face, and its eyes were still at half-mast and its mouth was open, too, with the tongue hanging out; it looked really quite dead.

I held it tighter with more care, and close to my heart and gave it another hug, feeling something like a love energy emanating from within me. This was not my pet, I had no clue how this kitten had fallen in the pool or where it came from, but I still loved it, somehow, as I did with all animals I came across.

Feeling this love more intensely, I gently rocked the kitten back and forth as though it were a baby, with an occasional glance full of judgment from Hiya Boy. That's when it began to squirm – there was no doubt about it. I held the bundle up and in front of my eyes, staring into the kitten's face, and I watched as its eyes rolled back in its head for a moment, and when they returned to center, the eyes fully opened. It retracted its tongue and sneezed, spraying a mist of pool water onto my face. I could barely believe my eyes. Then, it really squirmed and with a few loud vomiting sounds, began to cry loudly. This really got the attention of Hiya Boy, and he looked up from his pool brush and gasped, dropping the tool. He put his hand over his mouth and shrieked something, muffled by his hand. He walked over to me and looked at the kitten, and said, "This is not good."

I didn't understand what he meant by this – I was so happy to see the kitten alive, who was now yowling as loudly as possible. I felt very nervous – as if the maintenance man were going to take the kitten away or harm it somehow – so, I stood up, slipped on my sandals, grabbed my other towel and walked quickly away from the pool, carrying the kitten. Hiya Boy just stood and watched me, glaring a bit. I hurried back to the cottage, glancing behind me all the way to make sure that he wasn't following me.

I was often referred to as a "special" child, and with that often came a shadow of doubt with the tales that I told. No one openly questioned my stories, but often when I recounted my tales, they were met with silence, which made me feel insecure and as though I wasn't being believed. My mother had this very look of doubt on her face when I walked in with the kitten, and when I told her what had happened, it seemed to me that she thought it was all a clever ruse to elicit sympathy, so I could simply adopt this cat I had found somewhere wandering the gardens. She asked, "Are you sure that's what happened?"

In response, I handed the kitten to her, and on closer inspection, my mother did note that the kitten was wet and smelled like the pool, so this added validity to my story. She glanced into my face and held my gaze for a few seconds, searching me for any clues that my story was false. She didn't press the issue, most likely due to the look of anguish and surprise on my face, so she helped me dry the kitten. Our dog, Sheila, and our cats, Nip and Tuck, watched with intense curiosity, having been provoked by the sound of the kitten's cries. All three took turns sniffing the little, damp creature, but all of them seemed to disappear in a hurry once they had completed their own personal inspections.

Mother did make it clear that we simply could not have another pet and explained we would need to find a home for the kitten. I felt a bit sad when I heard this because I felt a very special bond with this creature already, believing I had somehow brought it back from the dead with my special animal love powers. I was holding the squirming and crying kitten while pondering many questions, including whether or not I should approach Hiya Boy and ask him how long the kitten had been in the pool. Had he been there when it was swimming desperately while trying to free itself from the water? Had he watched it struggle, trying to climb out? Had he cruelly watched it drown, not caring? Or worse – had he put the kitten in the pool to drown it?

I walked with the tiny cat to the kitchen, setting it down on the floor. It wobbled a bit as it tried to walk – it was very small and very young. Its fur was beginning to dry, and I could see that it was the offspring of a short-haired cat. Mother followed me into the kitchen and pulled out a little bowl, which she filled with milk. She set it on the floor next to the kitten, which began to lap up the milk ferociously. We both noted that the kitten was quite thin and undernourished and was going to need some rehabilitation.

Father was at work and my brother was out with his friends, so it was just my mother and me tending to the kitten until the magical afternoon light began to come through the kitchen windows, creating the now familiar warmth of the room, and I had big feelings of safety and comfort for a moment.

Mother had pulled a hot dog from the refrigerator, smashed it with a fork, and heated it slightly in a pan, making sure it was not too hot. She put the mashed meat into the kitten's bowl, and it ate quickly. "Well, he seems to be alright – look at the appetite! This is one hungry little guy!" even though the kitten was clearly a female. I could see that Mother's love of animals and the delicacy of the situation coming to bear in her demeanor, and now that the kitten was dry and fluffy again, its cuteness returned, and made it all the more appealing.

Mother repeated again that we really couldn't keep it (perhaps reminding herself), so she began speaking aloud our options: We could put up posters in laundromats, and also let them know at the El Encanto's front desk about the rescue, and perhaps they could help find a home, after all, it was on "their property." I didn't like this last idea because I was worried Hiya Boy would suspect I had said something about him, and he frightened me.

I piped up and said, "What about Grandmother? Does she want a cat to keep her company?"

Mother looked at me for a moment, and said, "That's a good idea, Steve." The "Steve" response was a classic of Mother's, and only she knew why she called us "Steve" when we had a good idea. What I did know was that it was a high compliment coming from her, so I smiled back.

Mother called Grandmother and first suggested that she mention the kitten at the next bridge game down at the Senior Center. My grandmother became very excited about the story and decided to adopt the kitten herself. I was so relieved.

Grandmother's favorite show was "Bewitched," which had an animated opening showing a black cat that turns into Elizabeth Montgomery's character, Samantha – so, Grandmother would be naming the cat "Samantha." Grandmother often adopted the mannerisms of and would pretend to be the character Samantha's mother, Endora, even occasionally referring to my father as "Harold" rather than "Arthur" in the way that Endora always got Samantha's husband's name wrong, to drive the point home. Come to think of it, my grandmother did carry herself like Endora as well, so it was not exactly a stretch for her.

Samantha the Kitten had scored. Grandmother was an amazing chef and known for lavishing handouts and treats on her pets. This also meant that there was a very good chance that Samantha would become a very rotund cat, so we would have to make sure Grandmother was feeding her appropriately.

Grandmother had pet cats and other animals before, and she didn't manage to kill any of them, so we were assuming everything would be okay. I remember one of Grandmother's cats pretty clearly - a particularly psychotic pure-bred Siamese named Tabasco, who would leap from the top of furniture, landing on guests' heads with claws unfurled, gripping tightly to ensure maximum insertion of nails into flesh. Tabasco had passed away during Grandmother's stay with us at the Big House and I can't say that any of us grieved for him – well, at least not that much.

Samantha was still a tiny kitten who we believed would be a breeze for Grandmother to manage and raise. Mother ended her call with Grandmother, and suggested we deliver Samantha right away to Grandmother's townhouse.

While holding Samantha on my lap in the car, I had enormous feelings of satisfaction and accomplishment. With her now-full belly, the kitten was sleeping peacefully and purring quietly. I was struggling to let the "good" in at that moment; I had a very difficult time believing that anything could work out. Yet, here I was, having saved this adorable kitten from death, on my way to deliver her to her new home – a home that was part of my family. I would get to visit Samantha all the time, so this was the best possible outcome. Within my subconscious, though, there were echoes of some as-to-yet unseen issue – some circumstance – something – those preemptive echoes were blocking my ability to release something good into my thoughts; it was as if something inside of me knew better, and my struggle to completely embrace the moment was weighing heavily on me as we arrived at a pet store to get some supplies for the care of Samantha.

When we arrived at Grandmother's place, we let ourselves in, which was what we always did, and there was Grandmother, lounging on her mohair fainting couch, with the ubiquitous cigarette dangling from the corner of her mouth, and a freshly made cocktail sitting on her coffee table. She was dressed in her customary lounging outfit, which was something like a kaftan, and she had her beaded slippers on, which were struggling to contain her gout. Grandmother's place always had a slightly sour smell – a combination of roasted meat and cigarettes, with notes of formaldehyde, likely due to some of the trophy fish, which were mounted and hanging from her walls.

"Well, dear, let me see the cat!" Grandmother said, scooting herself up to the edge of the sofa. I had tremendous reservations suddenly, and I looked down at the sleeping kitten in my arms, so warm and cuddly.

"She's sleeping right now." Grandmother smiled at mother when I said that, so Grandmother whispered, "Don't worry dear, Gran-ma-ma knows what to do," employing her finest Endora-ish impression. I walked around the coffee table and sat down, and slowly transferred the sleeping kitten from my lap to hers.

"Oh, what a dear little thing she is," Grandmother said, slowly stroking the kitten's head with her own relatively small hands. I felt a little better because I was sensing genuine love already from Grandmother.

My mother set down the bag of kitty supplies on the coffee table, and started listing the inventory – two bowls, some toys and some chow for kittens. "Okay, that's just fine … just fine … thank you," said Grandmother.

I left the sofa and walked into the kitchen while the two women continued speaking about the kitten. Grandmother had been used to having a butler, which was evidenced by the fact that the kitchen sink was full of dirty dishes. There were several full ashtrays sitting on the kitchen's countertop next to the sink, as well as spilled food. I started to wonder how she would take care of a cat when it didn't appear that she was so great at taking care of herself. The truth was, I needed to let it go and trust – the deed had been done; kitten, rescued, dried, fed and delivered. I did my best to silence the suspiciously negative thoughts running rampant in my mind.

Samantha began to yowl a bit, while Grandmother was busy petting her. I walked back into the sitting area and watched Grandmother stroking her. "You're petting her too hard," I chirped, and Grandmother and Mother looked at me. "Well, yes sir! I will be much gentler from now on," Grandmother replied with a wink at my mother.

I really just wanted to leave. Now that I really, for sure, couldn't have the kitten, this little creature that I had pulled from the pool ... well, then I just wanted out of my grandmother's place. I felt a little nauseated by the scene, so I walked past my mother and slumped myself down in the classic wing-backed chair by the window. Mother sensed my uneasiness, and said, "Well, Mother, you know – let us know if you need anything and call me if you need any help with Samantha. We need to go now so I can make the 10-year-old-boy-going-on-65 here some dinner – I can tell that he's starting to fade a bit. It's been a big day for him." I knew when Mother said this, she was attempting to be caring, but the way she spoke to me was almost as if I were a child, which I didn't appreciate in the least. I wasn't thinking about dinner or anything else – I was busy assessing Grandmother's skill level with the kitten and the environment into which Samantha had been delivered. Instead of expressing any of this, I groaned and then stared glumly at the floor; we left shortly thereafter.

Weeks went by, and all seemed well with the kitten and Grandmother. Mother and she would spend hours on the phone speaking about the kitten's antics, and it seemed that the addition of the little feline was a good thing for Grandmother. This eased my mind a little – I thought, well, she hasn't killed it yet, so that's good.

As time passed though, and Samantha grew, she became more and more aggressive. The initial innocence of kitten play seemed to be taking a dark turn, where what at first seemed like the spontaneous, playful behavior, turned into something that began to appear much more premeditated.

My grandmother began calls with, "You just won't believe what Samantha has done now!" Grandmother reported that Samantha would begin clawing at Grandmother when she tried to pet her, hissing when someone new entered my grandmother's home, darting from room to room yowling, seeming confused and appearing as though she was receiving commands from some unseen person. Grandmother noticed that Samantha would also sometimes move as though she were being petted by some invisible hand. The least concern with all of this was the fact that the cat had been refusing to use the litter box, and we couldn't tell if it was some aberrant behavior or just Grandmother's poor kitty training. Regardless, she really loved Samantha, but the strain of having what was pretty much an angry feral cat was beginning to weigh heavily on her, and the tone of the phone calls switched from the humorous anecdotal variety to something more like a story from the T.V. show Outer Limits.

Of course, with all of this cat drama, Mother and I decided we should go together to visit Grandmother and Samantha to see if we could help out somehow. During the regular course of errands and hair appointments, my mother had been inside Grandmother's home a few times in the past several weeks, and Samantha seemed fine. Mother patted and held the little cat without issue, so she was concerned by Grandmother's accounts, but also confused. I had been refusing to go because my reaction to the violence reports was to want to go and rescue Samantha again, believing that perhaps it was all due to the fact that Samantha really wanted to remain with me – at least that's what I told myself.

When we arrived to conduct our investigation, Grandmother was standing next to an ugly plaster dolphin fountain in the courtyard of the townhome complex, with her arms folded across her stomach. Apparently, Samantha had been out of control all of that morning, and Grandmother had attempted to corral the cat into the downstairs bathroom, so she could be locked within; Grandmother had been unable to accomplish this. She referred to Samantha as "black lightning," because she was so incredibly fast when she ran through the apartment. Grandmother said that Samantha would run from upstairs, bank her turn halfway up the wall and front door at the bottom of the stairs, and jump to the nearby curtains, where she would claw-climb her way to the top, finally sitting and glaring at Grandmother from the valance.

We walked together to my grandmother's front door – my mother first, then me, with Grandmother behind us, and my mother slowly turned the knob and stepped in; Samantha was sitting on the mohair fainting couch, casually licking her paws and cleaning her ears – she was even purring – making the complete presentation absolutely adorable. Grandmother said, "Now, wait a minute – she never does that."

The situation was tricky because Grandmother was known for her rather tall tales; being a lady angler, she had many a big fish story, which could sometimes include a sea monster or two. Though we said nothing out loud, both Mother and I were starting to wonder if Grandmother was the one in the duo who was losing her mind, not the cat.

I walked over to Samantha, who looked up at me sweetly, and picked her up. She was purring heavily and seemed completely relaxed. I glanced over at Mother and shrugged my shoulders. "But – but – she was just climbing the curtains a minute ago – look, you can see the snags from her claws!" Grandmother pointed to the curtains, so Mother stepped over and took a closer look; there were indeed snags in the drapes. Mother said, "Hmmm ... are you sure you wouldn't like us to find a different home for Samantha?"

"Oh, no, perhaps it's just a phase – maybe I just need to be patient and wait until she calms down a bit … you know, gets a bit older." Grandmother said this almost pleading for mercy.

With nothing really to be observed, Mother stepped into the bathroom and cleaned the cat box for Grandmother, as it had definitely been used. Perhaps Grandmother wasn't cleaning the box enough, and Samantha didn't want to step into a dirty box? That was a possibility.

Mother sensed that Grandmother was already drinking that day, so Mother leaned over and whispered in my ear, "Let's go before Grandmother reaches the pint of no return." I knew what this meant.

We bid farewell that day and went on about our business. After a few more days, Grandmother called to report that Samantha's attacks had escalated to all-out strategic and violent assaults.

From her own report, Grandmother's gout was getting worse and worse, which slowed her down quite a bit as she walked through her home. She also had already gone through a double-radical mastectomy, and a hysterectomy. She smoked as well and was a bit overweight. All of these added up to a formula that equaled a nearly complete lack of balance, graceful mobility and coordination. To add to this, as discussed, Grandmother was no stranger to alcohol, often ordering entire cases of Boon's Farm Strawberry Hill from a nearby liquor store for delivery, so by nearly every twilight, Grandmother would most likely be pretty schnockered – and it was as if Samantha knew this and would plan her attacks accordingly.

There were a series of attacks throughout the day (between meals). There were many hiding spots since my grandmother's townhouse was packed to the gills with antiques; she, too, had crammed the contents of an extensively furnished home into less square footage. There were many shadowy corners for a seemingly possessed black kitten to hide, and being very small, too, it was impossible to see Samantha coming.

Samantha's Daily Attack Schedule ™ went something like this: Upon awakening, Grandmother would take each step down from the second story on the carpeted stairs, one at a time, without knowing where Samantha might be. Grandmother would arrive on the first floor and gaze nervously around the room – where was the hellcat? The ground level would often be deathly quiet – a little too quiet, with just the sound of an old mantle clock ticking away.

Grandmother would take a deep breath and begin her twenty-foot trek to the kitchen to make coffee (she had counted the steps). Sometimes, the pounces came at about the midpoint of this short journey. Per Grandmother's description, she wouldn't even see Samantha do it, but all at once, searing pain would rise from one of Grandmother's ankles; looking down, Grandmother would see deep, bleeding scratches on her lower legs where none had been moments before. On the next pass, Grandmother would look down at her round and indelicate ankles and see Samantha in a full bear hug. Claws would be fully extended and piercing the flesh, and Samantha's teeth were bared during repeated deep bites into Grandmother's ankles, like a vampiric jackhammer, and once creating a fully-pulverized spot, the cat would clamp her jaws firmly, shaking her head back and forth while having her teeth still embedded, as if she were shaking a mouse to death. Blood would spurt and drip down, but due to Grandmother's lack of coordination and flexibility, she couldn't bend over to remove the kitten, nor could she balance well enough on one foot to shake the cursed cat off. Instead, Grandmother would continue limping to the kitchen with the cat attached to her leg. Usually, Samantha would let go once the walking started but only after two or three steps; she would leap from Grandmother's leg and run at full-speed into the darkness of the townhouse dripping blood from her mouth, to once again hide in the shadows in preparation for her next act of brutality.

The second part of the morning attacks mostly occurred when

Grandmother was at last standing at her sink washing dishes, with the ubiquitous cigarette dangling from the left corner of her mouth (it seemed the cat had decided that morning attacks were ideal, when Grandmother was at her most wobbly). As soon as she forgot about Samantha's first attack for the moment, perhaps distracted with the task at hand or lost in some thoughts, the second attack would come – sort of a drive-by clawing, which would leave red scratches on Grandmother's exposed and swollen calves. This would sometimes cause Grandmother to drop a plate and break it, and scream, dropping her cigarette to the floor as well. This is a big reason dishes were piled in her sink – Grandmother was too afraid to wash them.

As things continued to devolve, Samantha began biting Grandmother in her sleep – sometimes on her feet, through the covers, and eventually Samantha bit my grandmother on her cheek. Grandmother kept calling Mother asking for guidance, and although everything my mother suggested should have worked, it came down to my grandmother sneakily closing the door anytime Samantha was in the first-floor bathroom where her cat box was located, to trap her. These occasional imprisonments further enraged the kitten who, once let free, would go on a rampage, destroying upholstery with her claws, and performing more horrifying ambushes on Grandmother by suddenly running out from another hidden place repeatedly, latching onto Grandmother's ankles with her claws, and sinking her teeth deliciously once again into aging human flesh.

The violent behavior escalated to the point where we started to wonder if during the drowning, Samantha suffered some sort of brain damage or at least a possession, as she was now one-hundred percent a demon cat. Being the Camp Family, we were able to find humor in Grandmother's descriptions of the attacks to the point where even she laughed, albeit bleeding from her ankles while she did so. Our family had many pets, generally all the time, but Samantha was the standout; no other furry Camp had ever developed this sort of violent behavior, not even close. Many heads and chins were scratched in a more delicate way while pondering what could have happened to Samantha to make her this way. With all of this consideration going on, we were all trying to actively avoid the point, which was that Samantha had to go. I don't think anyone wanted to face that fact – my family was notably loyal to the animals in our care, and no matter what the costs, including money for vet bills over money for food, rent, heartache and suffering, nothing could pry one of our beloved animals from our loving arms – to do so was unthinkable. This is why everyone who heard the stories became mired in the riddle of Samantha's behavior, rather than doing something about it.

I, too, pondered some facts about the kitten, being the one who had pulled her from the swimming pool in the first place. Something that loomed large in my mind with regard to the cat were the hotel's grounds, where the cat had passed away and then was resuscitated: Early in the dawn of human habitation in the area, what we now all called the Riviera was once a rocky hillside, full of caves and large sandstone boulders, overgrown with various manzanita varieties, mountain mahogany and century plants, among many others, making up an almost impenetrable overgrowth. It must have been a steep, wild place, hard to navigate, and likely seen as a realm of the spirits, I imagined. For me, the story of Samantha's possession went something like this:

The hotel was in an area where historically the native people, the Chumash, were thought to roam for spiritual reasons, and some had created cave paintings in similar mountains nearby, above and to the northeast of the Riviera, which would make it one of many foothills of a sacred place. Shamans were believed to have used these cave paintings to influence supernatural beings, to appease them, or perhaps even summon them.

It wasn't until the late nineteenth century that white settlers began to see the Riviera area as a potential location for dwellings, partly due to its scenic terrain and views. When it was finally developed, most of the sandstone boulders were removed, cut into pieces, and repurposed for dwellings; that's perhaps how the Big House on Chapala got its sandstone foundation, and some were used to build some of the native people's sandstone dwellings that were next to the Mission. The Chumash had not chosen to be enslaved by the mission system in California, and often paid with their lives for their conversion to Catholicism and their "service," either through the spread of infectious diseases or all out murder – so, who knows what (rightly) angry spirits might be cursing the lands of the El Encanto? My mother referred to this in another dark play-on-words by saying the Chumash were victims of "a case of mistaken idolatry," clarifying that she was not a fan of the Catholic Church, and my father referred to the Bible as "Mother Goose for adults." In support of their anti-religion stance, not a single child in our family was baptized; we all were sympathetic to the plight of all native peoples and against organized religion of any kind.

Given all of this, and with my penchant for imagining things and tallying up information in the most ghastly way, I wondered what unhappy spirit might have been seeking a vessel when Samantha had gulped her last lungful of water and slipped into eternity – and being the child spiritualist that I was, I became convinced that an angry entity had entered the kitten and that I, in my innocence, had not revived the kitten, but assisted in a possession – and then unleashed the beast upon my grandmother! I was mortified but kept my feelings of responsibility hidden deep within The Bigger.

Fostering my active imagination regarding the subject of possession was the prior year's release of The Exorcist, which Anthony and I had snuck into when it played at the Arlington Theater. Not knowing that I was way too young to see it, and seeing it anyway, it naturally made a huge impression on me, but not in the way most people would think; Anthony and I laughed so hard during the movie that one of the usher's had discovered us and thrown us out – but we only snuck in again. I wasn't frightened by The Exorcist, I was intrigued by its concepts, even taking it as far as, during my leisure time, going to the Santa Barbara Mission and hissing at priests.

With all of this in my feverish head, I had the idea to exorcise Samantha at my next earliest convenience.

My exorcism plans were foiled because the final call came from Grandmother - my mother lowered her voice, and though she whispered, I knew it was about Samantha and that they were making the most awful decision that had to be made.

In the literally immortal words from Stephen King's Pet Sematary, "Sometimes, dead is better." Grandmother, not wanting to pass on the misery to someone else, felt that she had no other option but to put Samantha down, and no one was as upset by this as I. I felt personally responsible for the kitten's spirit possession, and even though she was evil incarnate, I still wanted her to live. I secretly comforted myself by acknowledging that Grandmother would no longer be harmed, even though she was very sad indeed. Despite all of the abuse, she still loved

Samantha, and had tried everything to help. My concern was that once the spirit was released from the kitten, where would it go? Would it come find me? Would it inhabit someone else at the El Encanto? Perhaps I would get to perform an exorcism after all.

But my grief, concerns and sadness were short-lived; as if knowing what was coming through her demonic telepathy, the morning of her final trip to the vet, Samantha had chewed a hole through Grandmother's kitchen window screen and escaped, once again proving that you can't keep a dead cat down. She's probably out there still to this day – immortal, vicious and preying on the elderly – it warms my broken, goth heart.

Chapter 11 — The Brogues

RECORD BOOTH SUGGESTED SONG: "LUCY IN THE SKY WITH DIAMONDS," *THE BEATLES*

The sounds of glass clinking, laughter, heeled shoes trip-scraping across the crumbling brick pathways, and cars arriving and leaving echoed through the enchanted gardens and bungalows. It was the 4th of July weekend for Santa Barbara, and the El Encanto was more populated than usual.

Locals and guests alike targeted the grand, sloping lawn above the pool as an optimal place to spread blankets and get a nearly-unobstructed view of the coastline and fireworks. I felt like we had the best seat in the entire town, and my heart was filled with excitement and joy at another perk that represented our high living on the Riviera.

Along with the fireworks later that evening, there was another annual event that coincided – the Fourth of July Sale at the Santa Barbara Mission. This was an opportunity for local craftspeople – potters, jewelry makers, macramé artists etc. – to display and sell their wares.

Andy and her husband, Michael, were absolutely quintessential young people of their time; they even lived in a converted bus (very de rigueur) on a bare, grassy knoll, south of Santa Barbara in a town called Summerland.

"Andy" was my very first word – at least that's what everyone told me. The age gap between us only made things more tender and interesting – my sister was also somewhat a second mother to me, being fifteen years older than I.

She was like the "cool" mom, where our mother, Elise, was more the enforcer of rules, therefore "uncool" to me in some ways. Plus, since my parents were always fighting, I saw Andy in a different light; we were united in our fear and dislike of our parents. During the parental screaming sessions, I was infamous for yelling "Andy save me!" with a large amount of dramatic desperation, hoping she would come whisk me away for some adventure.

Yet another weird thing is, no one ever thought to ask from what I needed saving; rather, my repeated cry for help became the stuff of legend and humor in the family instead of what would seemingly be an appropriate level of investigation as to what was causing my need for saving in the first place.

Andy would indeed often come to my rescue – if she could – and she was always a vision to me. Her style was beyond cool, her glorious and wavy deep auburn hair always smelled good, and her big brown Clara Bow eyes were generally accentuated with an impeccable makeup job, lashes carefully separated into symmetrical arrays, her brows and cheeks adorned with glue-on face gems in just the right places. She was a magical being to me.

Even my sister, my would-be savior, never directly asked me from what she might be saving me, and it wasn't until years later that I understood – she already knew because of her childhood with them. So, Andy often heeded the call (via telephone), and would pull up in front of the Big House in her groovy car, an old VW, and take me away to the beach, or a park, or a favorite place.

Sometime after she and her family came to stay with us in the Big House, I could see that something was shifting in her mood.

After we had moved to the El Encanto, I kept asking Mother where Andy was and how come we rarely saw her. Mother would often remind me that Andy had a child of her own now, who needed special attention, due to an issue with his legs that required he wear braces.

When Andy did visit us at the hotel, she didn't seem quite the same to me – darker, somehow, and a bit boozy, like the people in the bar in the main building. Andy's style had changed somewhat, too, going from what I would describe as a wholesome hippie earth-mama, a version of her that I would imagine dancing through a wildflower meadow, tossing handfuls of wheat germ to all the little people. She had taken to wearing more makeup, and her clothes had become skimpier, more daring – sexier – and I would see men leer at her when she did visit us at the hotel – and the thing was, I could see her leering back, or winking, even if she were with her husband.

Andy's visits generally meant she would stop by Villa 100 briefly to say hi, and then head down to the hotel's bar, with or without her husband. Mother also made it a point to not have Grandmother's and Andy's visits overlap – Mother felt they were too much the same, and when they were together, it was like watching two titans of sloshy coquettishness go head-to-head for attention – Mother couldn't stand being around it. Every waiter or bartender or any male guest would be like the last strip of zebra on the scorching Serengeti, surrounded by two hungry lionesses.

Throughout my early childhood, Andy had been like a magical, beautiful angel to me, and since I had been forced by circumstance to abandon my own childishness by the time we moved to the hotel, I could see her for what she was, or at least what she was becoming, in an honest and unfiltered light. It was another blow to my feelings of safety that my savior was no longer interested in whisking me away to somewhere safer, and it seemed that Andy herself was on her way for a bit of saving too.

To refer to Michael and Andy as just "hippies" would not have been fair to them as people. While they had many trappings of their generation, they were not just the stereotypical pot-smoking long hairs.

Michael was an incredible carpenter and craftsman, and he had converted the Melni Bus they lived in himself. The interior was off-the-charts;

all finished with fine woods, stained glass windows and even a pot belly stove. Their bus was an object of amazement and wonder in their community.

In addition to this, Michael also made leather sandals and brass jewelry, so he was present at the sale on the Mission's lawn that year, with a booth and his goods for sale.

So, well before the fireworks, around midday, I walked the ten minutes down Alameda Padre Serra to the sale to find my sister and Michael, and to just check things out. When I arrived, it was jam-packed with people, and it was difficult at first to locate Michael's booth, but eventually I did. Michael was sitting behind his display table, looking a bit bummed-out.

When Michael saw me, he smiled and welcomed me into his booth. He showed me the items he had for sale – comfortable looking leather sandals with arches and big toe straps, and his cool brass jewelry, hexagonally shaped and woven pattern rings and flat-pounded hair combs and pins. It was hard to concentrate on what Michael was explaining to me because loud rock music was coming from somewhere at the sale. I listened as closely as I could and after a few minutes I looked at Michael and asked, "Where's Andy?"

Michael's smile instantly disappeared, and I thought that I had hurt his feelings – I worried I had seemed uninterested in him as though I were only looking for my sister. Michael put his arm around my shoulder and gave me a squeeze, then pointed toward the direction of the loud music, without saying another word.

I left the booth and weaved my way through a huge crowd of adults who were all dressed in their hippie finest. Clouds of marijuana filled the air, and people were stumbling around with cups full of beer and wine. It was very hot on the Mission's lawn that day, and the sun was making the adults sweat profusely; the air was pungent with the smell of body odor, incense, marijuana, dirty hair and patchouli oil.

The closer I got to the music, the thicker the crowd, and the rowdier, too, and there were a couple of high girls along the way who tried to grab my hands to dance with me; but I wasn't interested. The last one who tried just smiled when I refused and sarcastically said, "Peace," making the appropriate hand sign without any enthusiasm.

I found my way to a row of folding chairs on the periphery of a large group of people dancing as hard as they could to some live band I couldn't see. The music was loud, but the packed circle of people dampened it a bit. I looked around the crowd, which was difficult because everyone was so much larger than I – I couldn't see my sister anywhere, so I decided to just sit down and watch the dancers for a while.

I found myself sandwiched between two dudes with long beards and leather cowboy hats. Each had a can of beer in his hand, and they were in the middle of what sounded like a very deep conversation. They barely noticed me sitting on the lawn chair between them as they continued to describe to each other what they were seeing.

The guy on my left was talking an awful lot about colors – he was seeing colors around people, trailing behind the dancers as they moved, patterns and forms in the air. The guy on my right said, "Ya, man, I see that, too, and the colors are like penetrating me, man ... and, OH SHIT! They're penetrating you, too, man!"

They continued from there, discussing the nature of reality and the universe, or rather, the illusion of reality, and that's when one of them said, "Hey, who's this little dude sitting here? Where'd he come from?" They both looked at me, and the guy on the right leaned in close to me and said, while exhaling potentially the worst breath I had ever smelled, "Do you understand the nature of reality little man?" I replied by folding my arms and rolling my eyes.

"Whoa, we've got a tough customer here!" he said to the guy on my left. He looked back at me and said, "Little dude, my friend here and I have just figured out the nature of the universe, man!"

I looked him in the eyes and replied, "Nah, that's just the drugs you took earlier."

Just then, a roar came from the crowd, shouting and whistles – something was going on within the circle of dancers. I forgot all about the two high guys I was sitting with and climbed the folding chair until I stood on the arms to get a better view. I was barely balancing, looking directly into the sun, so I shielded my eyes with my right hand. Being on the grass, the flimsy chair was wobbly, so I looked down and the two men next to me had each grabbed my chair to stabilize it. I looked back toward the crowd, and there she was, my sister; lifted by several men above the crowd, posed like Cleopatra reclining on her golden barge.

Andy was only wearing a purple knitted bikini, which looked amazing against her darkly-tanned glistening olive skin, one of her nipples poking out from the mesh of her bikini top. Her waist-length wavy auburn hair, moving in the light breeze, backlit by the sun, was shimmering with flecks of light and the embers of some cosmic distant fire; she was a goddess.

Before I could really process everything that I was seeing, Andy was lowered back into the crowd around her and disappeared from sight.

I jumped down from the chair and screamed at both of the high men, "That was my sister! That was my sister!" and I sprinted headlong into the dancing crowd without looking back.

It proved to be too impossible to find Andy in the large crowd of sweaty dancing bodies, and I became overwhelmed and claustrophobic. When I exited the crowd on the other side, I looked back and decided I would just walk home again; I knew that this was no place for me to be.

I walked slowly back up Alameda Padre Serra to the hotel, feeling very lonely and sad; now Andy wasn't even an option for me – a safe harbor – she seemed like someone else all of a sudden – someone I didn't know. I gave up relying on any adults ever again on that walk home.

PERGOLA, EL ENCANTO, SANTA BARBARA, CALIFORNIA

As darkness fell, I was with the crowds gathered on the large poolside lawns, and we all witnessed a fairly impressive display that evening. As the fireworks came to an end, there was an odd chilly breeze sweeping up from Mission Canyon and onto Alameda Padre Serra, pulling with it the foggy marine layer, and the adults began gathering belongings, pulling on sweaters and jackets, and many moved into the bar and hotel's lounge to continue their drinking and carousing.

As I walked back to Villa 100, there were many people walking just about every direction on the paths – it was odd to have so many people shifting around in the darkened gardens – and I was feeling a bit uncomfortable with all of these strangers lurking about. I abandoned my usual plans of skulking and observing other people from the shadows in the gardens – a favorite and often enjoyed evening hobby – and instead headed straight home, entering through the porch door off my brother's and my bedroom. Even though it was cooling-off outside, Villa 100 was still warm from the day's heat, and so I opened the window in my room – the one above my bed.

I imagined that my parents were still down at the bar, a bit tipsy and talking to visitors, doing the adult things that I found so trite and embarrassing. I pictured my father once again being Mr. Showbiz, and my mother was likely injuring her eye sockets with intense eye rolls while he spoke. I was glad for the peace inside the bungalow while, at the same time, I had a small feeling of trepidation, as though I were missing out on something.

I had no idea where Casey might be – probably in the pool – or maybe, with our parents, or out with friends and drinking down at one of the beaches, but I was all alone with the dog and cats when I crawled in my bed to lie down for a minute. The cool air from the window above me felt good on my burned skin, and the sounds of crickets and frogs slowly replaced the sounds of humans, and I drifted-off, still in my swimming trunks, and was soon in a very deep sleep.

I think I was slightly aware of my parents and my brother arriving home; the bathroom light switched on a few times, and I could hear Sheila panting and making excited I-want-to-go-out sounds. There were some screen doors squeaking open and closed, and some quiet muttering. I was aware that my family was aware that I was in bed, sleeping, but not aware enough to be completely awake. It felt like telepathic communication, where I transmitted "I'm trying to sleep" to them, so that they would keep it down and not disturb me. I started to drift off again pondering my imagined psychic powers, which I was convinced that I had, for several reasons.

In my mind, the most conclusive evidence of my psychic powers, as I called them to myself, was the fact that I had already seen several ghosts in my young life. I was still in that rush of youth where I was afraid of sharing my reports of ghosts and other entities, because I knew what I saw would be doubted. I kept most of my sightings to myself because I was so negatively affected by criticism and judgment; it was physically painful when someone didn't believe me, and due to this, I didn't speak much to anyone about what I believed I could see.

I have memories of various people looking at me from the shadows throughout my childhood. My earliest memories included seeing the white railings of my crib as ghostly figures hovering above me, so I surmised that my ability to see them was something with which I was born.

As I reached the ages of five and six, regular sightings occurred everywhere – at home, at school, and in public. The figures that I saw always stood out a bit from the living people in three particular ways: their style of dress, the fact that they stared at me, too, and the fact that they would often vanish right before my eyes while I was in the process of pondering whether or not these people were real. Besides these visual experiences, there were sometimes strange audio anomalies associated with the sightings – warped voices and, even worse, some of these "entities" would communicate in what sounded like backwards speaking – sort of like one hears if he plays a recording backwards.

In the Big House on Chapala, so much was going on in the spirit dimension that I spent a good deal of time relatively terrified – mostly at night – with all sorts of strange visions and experiences. What's more, there was one visitation that was confirmed by another family member – Casey, who, in my mind, was the biggest skeptic of my experiences, being the one person who was hardest for me to convince.

The event occurred on just a regular night in our former home. Since our bedrooms were on opposite sides of the large landing upstairs, we could see each other if we looked, even while in our own beds. One night, I awakened from a deep sleep, disturbed by some of the warped backward speaking I've described, and I sat up in bed. I could see the top of the staircase, which was particularly close to my brother's bedroom door, and rising up from that final step was a glowing, white figure, just as one might picture in a ghost movie, as though the figure was just completing the long walk up the staircase – it almost appeared to be holding the railing with one hand. I was so astonished by what I was seeing floating there that I blinked my eyes a few times and slowly got out of bed. The fear was taking over, and I was beginning to shake. My thought was to slide along the bookcase that separated the door to my bedroom from my parents' bedroom door and awaken my parents to see. As I got to the threshold of my door, I could see right through the figure, now hovering above the landing, and met my brother's eyes on the other side of the spirit – his eyes were the size of tea saucers – as he was kneeling upright in his bed, also watching this same specter! We gave each other that wide-eyed "uh-oh" glance, and the terror inside both of us was evident. With that, the spirit vanished, and we both opened our mouths in shock. We stared at each other for a moment, and then I returned to my bed, and we eventually found a way to return to sleep. From that night on, I did not doubt the things I could see.

Another example of my clairvoyance happened on a visit a couple of years before to a place in Nevada that had once been a bustling silver mining town called Virginia City. It was one of my mother's favorite places on Earth, for some reason, even as far as she requested to be buried on "Boot Hill," the graveyard to the north of the main downtown area. On one particular afternoon while visiting Virginia City, my parents had taken me for a tour of one of the old mansions that still existed, abandoned once the silver had run out. It was called the Mackay Mansion, named after John Mackay, who purchased the property from George Hearst twelve years after it was built in 1859, five years before Nevada became a state, the same year silver was discovered. John Mackay would become the richest man of the Comstock, so the mansion was lavishly furnished and many of his possessions remained in the home. While on the tour that day, I wandered off into a sitting room, away from the adults, and was delighted to find a room full of actors in period costumes acting out a typical scene from the late nineteenth century – men were drinking, women were playing cards – and I was really excited to be this close to actors! All of the actors simultaneously glanced at me and ceased their activities, which made me feel a bit self-conscious, so I left the room and rejoined my parents and the tour. At the end of the tour, the tour guide asked if anyone had any questions or comments, and I piped up saying that I really enjoyed the actors in the period costumes. The group was very quiet as the tour guide replied, "There are no actors here in period costumes. What do you mean?" The guide said this in a way that made it clear she wasn't toying with me. My mother reached down and covered my mouth – she knew that something was going on with me – and she told everyone that I was just kidding. There were many similar incidences throughout my childhood.

So, suffice to say, at the El Encanto, Casey and I were on high alert for spirits, generally speaking. There was an aura present at the place – not just due to its deteriorating condition – but its age and purpose; a resort whose heyday was during the roaring '20s and bootleg early '30s. Walking the grounds at night, I saw many "people" whose dress and appearance were incongruent with the '70s. Figures would appear, disappear and reappear frequently amidst the overgrowth and maze-like grounds, so I never knew if I was looking at an apparition or a living person; it all depended upon whether or not they looked at me, too, or if they vanished; I had seen too many to mention who fell into these categories.

I was an older child, so I wasn't nearly as afraid as I had been when I was "young." I had never been directly assaulted nor harmed by any of these alleged spirits.

Back to the night of July 4th, after pondering these "ghost studies," I fell into a light sleep. The next thing I remember was being aware of the cool air coming in from the window above my bed in Villa 100 in the early morning, and then it suddenly became much colder. I was also aware, in a somewhat half-sleep, that it was very early indeed – likely three or four o'clock – and as I slowly became more conscious, I could hear my brother softly breathing in his sleep across the room. I was lying on my left side and opened one eye – the moon was now out and was nearly full, flooding our little bedroom with an icy white light. I absolutely loved full moonlight, so my idea was to get out of bed and go take a look outside, and as I rolled over on my back and opened both eyes fully, I could see that the side of Casey's captain's bed was lit with moonlight.

It took a second to register, but something was "wrong" with the moonlight hitting his bed. There was a big section of the cast light that was in darkness – right in the middle – what was causing that? Was there some piece of furniture inside the room casting a shadow? Or perhaps a plant outside? And that's when the creeping terror filled my body and all at once, and the dots connected. That shadow, that outline, was the outline of a person! And, due to the angle of the moon, and my bed, I realized that they were standing right above and behind me – outside, in front of the window directly over my bed, which was open.

I was absolutely unable to turn around – I could not move my body – the fear had me in a tight grip. The fact that whoever this was stood behind me caused me to feel all the more vulnerable. How long had they been standing there?

To get to this position outside my window, one had to leave the brick paths and step down over some low boulders to sort of a gully area beneath that particular outside wall. This meant that the person standing outside my window was not there by accident. It wasn't as if they just happened to be walking by and noticed this window – there was a decision to peer into someone else's room and what could possibly be the motivation for that?

I stared more at the figure's shadow; it was absolutely motionless. So, this person was standing there, unmoving, and looking at what? Down on the top of my head in my bed while I slept? I started thinking the best move would be to scream for help, so I opened my mouth; I couldn't inhale enough to make a real sound, so a low whimper arose from my throat. When I did this, I could see my brother start to toss and turn until he rolled over on his right side and opened his eyes. He sat bolt upright and yelled, "Who is that!!!"

With that, the figure's shadow did a very odd thing – it didn't walk away, it didn't answer – it shot up and to the left – it appeared that it flew away. Casey started yelling, "Who was that? What was that?" and I leapt from my bed, eager to finally get out from under that window.

Awakened by the yelling, our parents came running into the room. For the next several minutes, my brother and I tried to explain what had happened. We were in such an excited state, we were speaking over one another, interrupting and being the youngest, I often found it hardest to get a chance to solo. My dad understood what we were saying, and my mother suggested he go outside and look around. Father wouldn't do it; he tentatively gazed-out the window and said, "Whoever it was, they're gone now."

My father wasn't known to inconvenience himself just because Mother was concerned about something. He flapped his hands in the air over his head and told us he was going back to bed. He thought some wandering guest had become enchanted by the little boy sleeping in the moonlight or maybe it was Andy, arriving after the festival for a visit, realizing we were all asleep, and stopping for a look at her little brother.

I wasn't so convinced. Given my history with spirits, I was aware of the familiar feeling I got when confronted with one, and I had that feeling in that moment. Most people would probably guess that the feeling is something like having the chills, but it isn't. It's a feeling like an electric shock has run through your system and has made all of your nerves, bones and tissues freeze and ache. It is as if the dead could leach something from the living, which powered their ability to appear. As a kid, I never questioned "Why me?" It was just a fact of my life at that point, and unlike adults, I wasn't old enough to be stuck in the belief that everything had a logical reason, nor was able to talk myself out of what my body's intelligence knew; there were supernatural forces at work at the El Encanto, and not all of them were friendly. We would also eventually learn that some of the dark forces at work at the hotel were far from supernatural as well.

In the morning, it seemed that my entire family had already forgotten the incident during the night, but I had not. I stepped out through the side porch of our bedroom and walked around the side of the house to the area below the window over my bed. There in the sand were shoe prints – but not just any shoe prints – these were a lady's shoes – with a distinct heel print and toe. I ran back into the house and retrieved my parents. I took them outside and showed them the prints. My parents looked a little horrified once they briefly discussed and confirmed with one another, eyes locked, that the prints resembled 20's women's brogues, a very distinct style of vintage shoes with a flat toe, and a slight, squarish heel.

I watched them discuss this at length, sussing out the real from the extraordinary – my description of the event, Casey's reaction, the way the peeper vanished, according to me, a kid with what they felt were confirmed abilities to see beyond the veil. Truth is, my parents were a bit overwhelmed by me and each had, separately and together, told me they thought it best that I keep my visions to myself. My mother was also known for her strange clairvoyant powers. She often knew who was calling before answering the phone. On her first date with Father, she had identified an unseen pickpocket who had stolen my father's wallet, after finding the thief much later in a crowded bar, miles away from where the crime had taken place.

She glanced at me in that knowing way, and put her hand on my back, soothing my discomfort. She knew that at least I believed an entity had spent an indeterminate amount of time watching me while I slept, through an open window, over my head and coincidentally the one window of Villa 100 that did not have a functional screen. In some ways I think my mother was hoping it was a spirit, for a real person could have reached in that window and harmed or grabbed me; our family was freaked out by the possibility, each of us with our own version of an unfortunate outcome.

With that, Mother looked at Father and asked that he immediately make sure that my window would get a new screen; although flimsy, it would somehow make her feel safer.

Secrets of a 100 ft. Boy | **131**

Chapter 12 — The Smell

RECORD BOOTH SUGGESTED SONG: "THE AIR THAT I BREATHE,"
THE HOLLIES

"Oh, Arthur, there's no dead body over there in the bushes!" Mother yelled in her nails-on-the-chalkboard strident and impatient voice, once again.

"I'm telling ya, I was in the Navy in the South Pacific and I'm telling ya that I know that smell!" My dad growled so deeply, the effort of hoisting the vowels past his tongue made the carotid arteries bulge under the skin on the side of his neck. His face was turned into a field of red every time this topic arose.

We were all in agreement with my mother and were convinced that it was our sewer line, which we had long since discovered to be leaking before we had moved in. Although Villa 100 was reportedly the best shack in the joint, the odor issue had definitely undercut the fantasy of our "luxury suite," a term used by the front desk.

The exposed iron sewer line to the west of the front door had a six-inch-long, four-inch-wide gash, and it was the main line that transported waste to the public lines under Lasuen Road and was likely the line for several other cottages in addition to ours.

The gash was located right where the line emerged from the ground for a few feet as it made its journey, and not being fully buried is probably how it became damaged in the first place. Around the opening, a stagnant pool of toilet paper and eucalyptus leaves floating in brown water had accumulated about fifteen feet down the slope from our cottage, and it was not a good look. We did not notice the tiny lake of effluence at first since it was mostly obscured by the leaves and fallen bark of the trees. Having lived in Villa 100 long enough now, with a family of four contributing to the flow, the smell had worsened significantly, making the stench intolerable.

Sitting on the screened-in summer porch became something of a "journey," and the porch was my favorite after-swimming-hangout. I would often endure the odor just to sit there, always enjoying the tingle of my freshly burned skin during that long, blowtorch of a summer. The un-heavenly scented still-heated dust-filled air of the afternoon would visibly undulate in the shaft of fading sunlight that passed through the screens of the porch. A flock of little flies danced in the light every afternoon above the filth; it was almost magical to watch these shit faeries from the porch, if it hadn't been so disgusting.

My parents finally complained in a way that got some action - as my mother said in her sly way, "We raised a stink." At last a repair crew appeared early one morning and stood around the refuse pond shaking their heads and covering their mouths with bandanas.

The owner, Mrs. Kinnett, clearly did not like to spend any extra money on maintenance; this was apparent and obvious if one took in the entirety of the hotel, so the repairmen felt sorry for us. Any other repairs around the grounds that were completed were more just bandages than cures, and usually done in a janky handyman style. Conversely, this was a professional repair crew staring at the damage, hired specifically for this task, so they knew how serious an issue an open sewer could be.

My parents could have called the health department, especially since the hotel's restaurant was only about one-hundred feet away. Mother and Father had been asking Mrs. Kinnett repeatedly to fix the sewer, and many of their requests were met with outright denial that there was actually an issue with our sewer. She would tell my parents that it was coming from across the street, that the Montessori school was to blame as a result of its substandard "hippie" teaching methods. Sometimes Mrs. Kinnett would claim that it was a problem with us, the children, not knowing how to properly operate a toilet or perhaps, even, doing our business outside, as she regarded us as being rather feral in nature, due to our long hair and unkempt appearance. That's probably when my mother started to make threats.

Still, the arrival of the crew that morning only happened after several steps: My father first tracked down the gardener, who we all referred to (only within our family) as "Hiya Boy," which was his general greeting for my brother and I, the only long-term resident children – nearly every time one of us crossed his path, he would shoot us a glare with one of his eyes (because of his strabismus) and unemotionally say, "Hiya Boy."

Hiya Boy's real name was John, and he was a smallish hunched-over little person who you could tell had been working outside for a long time. Hiya Boy always wore an old, dirty golfer's bucket hat, a pair of stained and greasy overalls and a worn-out cream and grey windowpane flannel shirt. Usually covered in dirt, his skin had the texture and color of a dried kipper fish and his wrinkles were deeply-etched into his face having spent nearly every day outside for, judging by his weathered look, what appeared to be decades. I thought he looked a lot like a grungy apple doll. He hardly ever said much to us besides "Hiya Boy," and overall, his interpersonal skills were not very good, but that was okay, because none of us wanted to press the issue of further connection. He was probably really tired of transient guests pretending to be his friend only in order to get him to do things.

It was our nature to nickname people, and we meant no disrespect to Hiya Boy and, of course, I doubt he even knew we called him this. We learned to communicate as best we could, and we all found him to be a helpful, harmless and friendly man, who was nearly mute or perhaps he just preferred to communicate mostly in growls, grunts, terse responses and foot stomps. When Hiya Boy saw the ruptured sewer line for himself, he grunted and grimaced, and walked off waving his hands above his head.

Summer was in full swing by this point. In late July, a large number of guests had checked-in for the upcoming 46th show of the Santa Barbara Kennel Club; they were a lively bunch, and for a bit there were a lot of dogs running around the property. As it turned out, the dogs were better behaved than the owners who, as noted by my mother, were practically humping each other on the lawn above the pool, as their dogs looked-on with embarrassment. We were worried that these show dogs would muss their beautiful coats by rolling in the effluence pond, but even they knew better and pretty much avoided it. A couple of the dogs did manage to find some fairly large bones that we figured must have been from a dead deer or something and chewed on them eagerly while their distracted owners *caligulated* on the lawns.

By early August, the El Encanto was at capacity between long-term and weekend guests. Visitors were packing all of the local hotels in anticipation of La Fiesta, a city-wide weeklong travesty ... uh, party ... happening in a couple of weeks and which was first celebrated in 1924, to honor the "founders" of Santa Barbara – the Spanish, Mexican and White East Coast "Pioneers," who all saw the Chumash living quite peacefully and decided that they were irrelevant. I never was nor ever will be a fan of "Fiesta." During Fiesta, one could hear cries of "Viva La Fiesta!" In my family we cried, "Viva La Fiasco!" There were plenty of drinks and stabbings during La Fiasco, so it was a time for us to stay hidden in our hilltop perch.

It was also very hot on the Riviera, and the smell from our breached sewer line was beginning to make the entire northwest corner stink. Other guests began to complain also, and a few guests had left because of the stench; this is the issue that likely pushed Mrs. Kinnett far enough to hire a repair crew to fix it.

The crew began digging right away and we watched from the porch of Villa 100. We were so thrilled to see them remove the old pipe and install a new one, and the embarrassment that other guests might have been thinking the odor was coming from our cottage lifted. We would finally be free from the odor and the disgusting cesspool that had formed. We were all looking forward to and imagining what it would be like to be in Villa 100 without the smell.

Once the repair was completed, we continued to smell something – and my parents were besides themselves trying to figure out what it was. We wondered if the ground had just become so saturated with raw sewage that it needed time to dry out. Although, the post-repair odor was slightly different – more pungent, with new sour notes of decay and pestilence. In a subtle reference to his time in World War II, my father continued to say " … I hate to tell you what that smells like …" – and my mother continued to flap her hand at him, or in the general direction of the large grouping of brush on Mission Ridge Road above our cottage, while saying variations of "Oh, c'mon Arthur, there isn't a body over there in the bushes."

The variations included: "Arthur, stop with the stuff about a body!" or "Oh, please – will you get over this thing about bodies!" and the painfully insensitive response of "Oh, I know, I know, you were in the South Pacific and smelled bodies, blah, blah, blaaaaaah!"

The summer days continued, and depending on the direction of the wind, the odor would come and go, and we thought maybe it was beginning to subside, but it was hard to tell. The fact was, we weren't smelling it all of the time, and that was good. Whenever the odor would return, my parents would begin their back-and-forth about bodies in the bushes, and I continued to leave the cottage to get away from this and other arguments, spending most of my time at the pool.

All of these full days in the sun had really taken a toll on my skin – my shoulders were completely blistered, so my mother was making me wear a thin, blue t-shirt most of the time. I remember marveling at how

I could see the mounds of the blisters on my shoulders underneath the drenched cloth, sort of like a gross dermatological wet t-shirt contest. My mother was greatly concerned about my blistering, so she was finally covering my face with white zinc-oxide, which angered me because it diminished my self-imagined glamorousness.

My brother liked the pool, too, but it was often in need of cleaning and, being four years older than I, he preferred other outdoor activities and there were plenty in Santa Barbara, which is partly why it was also such a magical place – not to mention the glorious Pacific Ocean just a bike's ride away. Casey was into surfing, skateboarding, camping, cycling and a big pull for him was hiking. It was convenient to Villa 100; one only had to walk out one of the many doors and there you were, up in the hills with plenty of opportunities available for exploration. Since this was such a huge pastime for him, our parents, with their limited resources, did what they could to be supportive. With this in mind, he had been gifted new hiking boots for his birthday in mid-July.

When it came to an item such as this, Mother felt it better to give him a card on his actual birthday stating it was good for a new pair of boots; that way, Casey could try several pairs and find some that were of his own choosing. This selection process took a couple of weeks, plus my parents had to save a bit in order to purchase the boots promised with the card; so, sometime after the sewer repair, he finally had his boots. This was a big gift in our family at that time – they were expensive by our standards – so there was quite a lot of excitement about it. As soon as we returned home from the purchase, I put the blue swimming t-shirt over my lumpy shoulders and headed for the pool. My brother stopped in the kitchen for a peanut butter and jelly sandwich before his boots' inaugural hike. I was already down at the pool at this point, likely pretending to be a starlet. Casey laced up the tan leather boots quickly and bounded out the rear kitchen door heading for Mission Ridge Road. Mother watched him from the kitchen window for a moment, feeling pleased that there was some happiness in the cottage for a change, exhaling relief for a moment and inhaling again a bit more slowly due to that odd, lingering smell.

My brother headed west on Mission Ridge, past Lasuen and after a block or so, changed his mind and doubled-back; he wanted to get off of the asphalt and onto any patch of natural earth that he could find. If he continued west, he would have to walk a bit further before getting to that vacant lot. Heading back, he passed behind Villa 100 again, so eager to dig the teeth of his rugged hiking soles into the ground. Casey took a seat for a moment in front of the row of garages to figure out where to go, and stared across the street; that's when he noticed an opening in the shrubbery on the north side of the road across the street from the row of garages, and about five feet before the entrance to a neighbor's driveway, which was about one hundred feet from the northeast corner of our cottage. It looked like a well-worn path, and he couldn't recall noticing it before. Excitedly, he stood and wondered, "What is up that path?"

There was a three-foot high sandstone wall above the asphalt curb, which he easily hopped in his swell, new boots, and he took two more short strides onto the hillside, ducking under some manzanita bushes, and immediately stepped on Stanley A. Greene.

The strangeness of the texture of whatever he was standing on forced Casey to look down and he noticed a few things immediately: First, believing that he was standing on parts of the bush, he expected to see dead manzanita branches under his feet, but as his eyes adjusted to the shadows, he started to notice that these "branches" were jutting out here and there from what looked like an old pair of torn pants.

As his mind grappled with what he was seeing in the somewhat shady spot under the manzanita, his eyes hurried to find any logical reason for why he wasn't seeing what he knew already he was seeing, so he followed the shredded pants and leg bones with his eyes slowly to where there should have been an abdominal cavity, which there was not; he was standing on what looked like a pair of skeletal legs jutting from a pair of twisted, khaki pants, with the rear pockets in the front, which immediately struck him as appearing as though someone other than the leg's owner had pulled them on. No underwear was visible.

Looking a bit further into the shrubbery, Casey was desperately seeking some comforting and rational explanation. There was something else about five feet or so above the lower portion of the body, shoved way up underneath another bush. As Casey's eyes adjusted further, he realized he was looking at a shirt, with a coat still over it, both of which looked ripped and ravaged, with a particularly large hole on the right side which was revealing part of a rib cage. Putting both parts together in one view he could see that there was still no abdomen and instead, just empty space between the hips and legs and the upper torso. As his eyes became even further adjusted to the light, my brother could see the vertebrae of a yellow-tinged spinal column coming out of the bottom of the shirt and jacket.

Casey looked reluctantly at the center of the jacket; he noticed and followed a dirty maroon necktie that was miraculously still in place under the collar of the shirt, which led his eyes eventually to a head, which was turned to one side, and which sported a very mummy-like face. It was completely desiccated, although still covered with the remains of dried skin. Where the eyes had been, there was just big, empty dark sockets, glaring with darkness from either side of a shriveled nose, which had exposed large openings where the nostrils should be. The most horrifying part of all was the large gaping mouth.

The teeth were exposed, and lacking any remains of gums, looked large, and jutting, and vicious, and just plain scary. These yellow teeth were framed with the remaining skin of the lips, stretched to capacity, shredded and flaking.

My brother did the classic horror movie reaction thing and rubbed his eyes because he could not believe what he was seeing; this couldn't be real! His first thought provided a moment of relief when he convinced himself that it was just some old discarded Halloween decoration – the corpse was so dried out and had such a ferociously freakish look on its face, that it must be fake – it was too on-the-nose-for-Halloween to be anything but cheesy, classic, manufactured horror.

He chuckled for a second, feeling so silly that he had fallen for such a cheaply made fake corpse. Then Casey noticed that there were little skeletal hands in a prayer position in an almost angelic sleep pose upon which the head was resting. "How cheesy," he thought again, that the manufacturers of this fake body chose that position! There was even a little, gold ring on one of the bony fingers! Such detail!

That's right when he noticed the familiar smell emanating from the body. A smell my family had noticed shortly after establishing residence at the El Encanto. A smell that had blended in almost completely with the stench of the open sewer. A smell so omnipresent that it had not even registered in his brain when he first leapt onto the dirt above the sandstone. It was the smell that we all had tried to describe for over two months. The smell that permeated our entire lives up until that point, even entering our dreams while we slept. That inescapable smell that had become another family member, living with us in Villa 100, involved in all of our daily tasks, caressing us with its wretched scent. The smell that was so obvious to my father – who had been saying it all along. Casey thought, yes, Mother, that smell was, in fact a "... dead body over there in the bushes."

Casey also realized that the entire time Mother had been flapping her hand in the exact direction of the body as she often repeated this infamous phrase, toward the bushes where there actually was a rotting body. My brother shook his head when he thought how mad Mother would be to have to admit that Father was right (for once).

Casey took his foot and new hiking boot off of one of the legs he'd been inadvertently standing on while he took in the full picture. He was immobilized with shock. He had never, of course, seen a body, and only a rare few would have ever found a body like this in such an advanced state of decay.

The process of discovery and realization had taken about five minutes, but my brother found it within himself to turn around and walk away from the body. He hopped down from the stone wall, taking a moment just standing still and collecting his thoughts, and then he crossed back over Mission Ridge Road in only a few paces. He cut through the area behind Villa 100, passed Tortoisey and the pigeons, and entered Villa 100 through the rear kitchen door.

Mother was speaking to her mother on the yellow wall phone, fiddling with the spiral receiver cord. Mother glanced over and looked at Casey's face – there was something in his eyes that only a mother could recognize. He looked pale and serious. Mother told Grandmother that she would have to call her back. She replaced the receiver on the wall unit and said to Casey, "Oh. My. God. WHAT?"

Casey replied, "Now ... don't get excited." It has been proven time and time that never in the history of anyone uttering the phrase, "Now ... don't get excited," has it ever actually kept someone from getting excited, and this moment was no exception. Mother instantly panicked, thinking immediately that something must have happened to me. Her thoughts, in rapid fire, were: Oh. My. God. Scott was at the pool! Oh. My. God. There must have been an accident! Oh. My. God. Oh, good Lord, not drowning! My brother could see, almost telepathically, all of these possibilities pass through our mother's widening and enlarging brown eyes. "It's not Scott."

Chapter 13 — The Investigation

RECORD BOOTH SUGGESTED SONG: "RIKKI DON'T LOSE THAT NUMBER," *STEELY DAN*

My mother finished guessing all of the possible bad news that Casey was about to report and finally just asked him what had happened.

My brother took a moment and said, "Stop. Just stop. Listen. Mother ... I found a dead body, over there in the bushes." He pointed toward the same bushes at which she'd been rudely flapping her arms when arguing with Father. Mother gasped and put both hands to her mouth.

He described what he had found and that it was just across the street. Mother moved her right hand from over her mouth to her forehead as she realized that her husband had been correct. Mother looked at Casey and said, "Oh, greeeeaaat."

Instead of doing the obvious thing and calling the police, Mother instructed Casey to go fetch Hiya Boy, so my brother exited the kitchen door and jogged a few paces over to the staff apartments that were underneath the guests' parking garage.

Referring to them as "apartments" was another exaggeration regarding the hotel's accommodations. Since these rooms were underneath the garages, they were very dark. What once had been perhaps elegant maid's quarters had devolved over the years to what my mother called the "Dinge Dungeon." One could often smell marijuana emanating from below while retrieving a car from the garage above. We knew that Hiya Boy's room and bath were in the dungeon, and we'd seen some housekeepers coming and going, but we didn't know who else might be down there, so it was surprising that Mother sent Casey to seek Hiya Boy in such a dank, gloomy part of the hotel, especially since he had just discovered a body; she must have been panicking.

There was another fellow we'd seen around only once or twice, and who was a general go-to employee and sub-gardener of the hotel (we'd seen him here and there in different roles), namely a grungy longhaired dude named "Tony." Tony wore a lot of old army clothing during his off hours, so we thought maybe he might be a Vietnam Veteran. With our own father's military background, my parents were very sensitive to the veterans of a war that were treated so poorly by the U.S. Government. When our parents still lived in Los Angeles, they had taken in a couple of these Vietnam veterans, providing temporary housing until they could get on their feet. So even though Tony was somewhat of a scary looking character, we didn't fear him.

Casey entered the long, dim hallway of the cellar apartments. The floor was flooded from a plumbing leak, so he stepped carefully trying not to get his new boots wet. When Casey received no response to his knocks on Hiya Boy's room, he tried the next room over, which was Tony's.

He knocked on Tony's door, and could hear "Ricky Don't Lose that Number" by Steeley Dan at a moderate volume coming from inside. There was a bit of coughing, and then the door swung open, releasing a large cloud of pot smoke into the hallway, and from within the pot fog appeared Tony like a magician making an entrance. He was holding a bong in his hand. "What's up, dude?" asked Tony.

Tony's room was small and dark, with only purple fluorescent blacklights illuminating the interior. Casey could make out the posters of mushrooms glowing all over his walls, along with some promotional posters for rock bands, and a bubbling saltwater fish tank. Tony watched Casey survey the room, and then said, "Look man, what do you want?"

"There's a body over there in the bushes," Casey said rather mundanely, pointing to the general location.

Tony replied, "Sorry, that sounds like your problem – why don't you go find John." Tony shut the door in Casey's face.

Casey returned to Villa 100's kitchen and reported this to Mother.

Mother next instructed Casey to go down to the pool to fetch me. I had been swimming nearly the entire time, and I was still in the pool when my brother walked into the enclosure. I was hanging on the side of the pool by my elbows, so my eyes were at the same level as the pool's patio, and the first thing I noticed were my brother's barely dusty new boots walking toward me. The fact that he wasn't still out on a hike somewhere gave me an instant chill – something was up. Plus, Casey hardly ever came looking for me (unless he was trying to bust me) nor said much to me that wasn't a criticism, so when he leaned over and said in an almost unheard of yet compassionate tone, "Scott, you need to come back home," I didn't argue with him at all. This was the tone of voice everyone in my family used when there was a serious matter. A tone which told each other that all jokes, disagreements and stubbornness needed to be put aside, immediately.

I wrapped a towel around my damp trunks and slipped on my sandals. We walked in silence back to the cottage, myself trailing behind my brother; I didn't even bother to ask what this was all about because I knew something was really up.

We walked the broken brick path that avoided the hotel's main building – the one that went behind the lily pond, through the overgrown trellis. The Wisteria vines were still busy consuming the arbor, which actually seemed to be held in place by the vines themselves. The pond area was dark and shadowy as usual, even more pronounced at the time my brother and I were walking by, as the sun was beginning to dive, making it very hard to see anything as we passed through. Out of the shadows came a voice that said, "Hiya boy," which startled my brother and made him jump; his startlement startled me, so I jumped, too. I was picking-up on my brother's nervous energy. Casey decided not to talk to John, and we scuttled away quickly toward our house and away from the pond.

We entered the cottage through our bedroom and we could hear Mother just finishing up a call to Father. She had called the school where he was teaching that day and had the front office person pull him out of class. Mother said, "Okay, see you soon." She was placing the phone on the receiver when we walked into the kitchen.

Looking at me, she said, "Sweetheart, sit down for a moment – I need to tell you something." I immediately thought she was going to tell me that Grandmother was dead from a demonic cat attack.

The loving compassion in Mother's voice right then was something I longed for, always. In moments such as this, she could be a completely different person; her voice was soft and beautiful, more into the falsetto range, rather that the scratchy and abrasive shrill voice to which she was unfortunately prone. I think her voice was naturally soft, but due to her unbelievably stressful life, her often-mimicked screeching tone was the one we heard most often. So, to hear this calmer voice coming out of her also meant that I needed to remain quiet – this was very serious – and I have to admit, I loved being bathed in her rare, loving dulcet tones anyway.

"Your brother has found a body," she stated in a matter of fact way.

"Oh my god! Is it over there in the bushes?" I said, thinking I was just teasing her.

"Yes, over there in the bushes ... I can't believe it – your father was right this whole time." Mother mimed a slight cough on the "Father was right" part and giggled.

Casey was sitting on a stool in the kitchen looking at her when Father walked in. He had just pulled up in front of our single garage, after a forcibly calm drive since ending his art class early for the Adult

Education program at Santa Barbara City College. He had told his students there was a family emergency. Mother had not provided full details over the phone, only telling Father to come home immediately. All the way home he thought I had drowned in the pool.

As he walked in, Father could see from the looks on our faces that something was really up, in addition to being relieved when he saw me sitting there, too.

Mother had decided my brother should tell the story himself, so Casey told Father about the body and my father shot a glance at my mother, with a sly, knowing grin and the most delicate of affirmative nods. The four of us cracked – only The Addams Family could laugh at a moment like this. It was just so ludicrous that the main argument of the last couple of months had been a debate about the possibility of a corpse in the bushes. It was hilarious to us all, and a relief to know that this debate, one of many, had finally reached a conclusion.

There was a brief discussion as to whether the hotel's front desk or the police should be called first but given the track record with the hotel's service (they had clearly ignored the corpse's calls for tomb service, as Mother pointed out), our parents agreed that a phone call to the Santa Barbara Police Department was first in order.

Mother walked into the sitting room, sat down on one of the colonial loveseats with the kitchen's wall phone curly receiver cord in her hand, stretched to the max from where it attached. When the police department answered, she immediately and calmly began describing the situation to the officer on the other end, which required her to repeat herself a number of times, finally concluding with, "... because, AS I SAID, he was trying out his new hiking boots!" Father was rubbing his chin and shaking his head, making this sound: "Ooo ooo ooo, mmm, mmm, mmm."

My mother explained that we had been smelling the odor for several weeks, but that we thought it was the broken sewer line. My mother paused, listening to the officer for a moment (we couldn't hear what he was saying), but then she shrieked, "I get it! I get it! A body smells a lot different than raw sewage – so I've been told!" Mother shot a glance at Father, who knew better than to gloat at that moment. The officer said that a patrol car was on its way.

Mother stood up and replaced the receiver back on the wall unit with a loud whump and returned to the sitting room. She explained to my brother and I that it was probably going to be a long night and that we would have to answer a lot of questions, mostly directed at Casey.

My father volunteered to go down to the front desk and report the situation to the powers that be for the hotel. He left, and we watched him walk down the long brick path and across the parking area, still holding his chin and shaking his head.

We didn't possess the emotional intelligence at the time, but in the future, I would be able to connect the dots that the body must have been very triggering for our father because of his PTSD. He kept telling us that the odor was something that he had smelled in World War II – but this never really registered for any of us the way that would have prompted us to be more supportive; instead, we all just giggled at him, or denied his knowledge.

Seeing so many rotting corpses in the war must have been hell for any soldier and especially for those carrying other unprocessed, emotional baggage, and an artistic sensibility and extreme visual acuity. It's also for sure that some of the rotting corpses he must have seen and smelled were not all strangers to him but rather, friends and fellow marines in his unit. Our father not only smelled rotting corpses and therefore recognized the odor – but he had also seen rotting corpses, and likely would never be able to unsee them.

Mother had never investigated his assertion enough to discover how he was likely upset by the smell. It was more a point of fact for her that he was just wrong, and she seemed to have lost patience with his old war stories. Mother was no longer sensitive to Father's feelings around the war after so many years of marriage, and I think this was because she related his damage to his inability to generate consistent income, and therefore was to blame for all of their woes. She had also told us that she felt it was her duty to marry someone with "shell shock" and reported that it was the belief at the time that it was the most supportive thing she could do for a soldier returning from war. Providing comfort for these returning men was to support America itself. Therefore, she often behaved as though she were fulfilling some assigned duty rather than enjoying a loving relationship.

It sounds cruel, but Mother didn't have time for his excuses after thirty years, which likely was the fuel behind her passionate arguing about the alleged body in the bushes. It's no doubt that the thought of a body directly across the street from Father's home and family put him on edge, and his PTSD must have prevented him from investigating for himself. We were all too busily caught up in what we thought was the humor of the entire situation – the ongoing debate with my mother – but deep down, I don't think my father really found it all that hilarious. We were all oblivious to the torment he must have been experiencing while inhaling such a triggering smell.

Mother, nor any of us, ever thought to ask Father just how many bodies in bushes had been smelled and seen in the war. The horrible realization that her own petty disdain for his observation, as it related to World War II, caused her to dismiss it as a possibility, which resulted in poor Stanley A. Greene, lying in the bushes, decomposing and abandoned by the world for months. What a sorrowful and lonely ending to an as of yet unknown person. It wasn't just some corpse, some butt of a joke – he was once a man, slowly disappearing in his decaying slumber – in a way mirroring the plight of the El Encanto itself.

While waiting for the police to arrive, I really wanted to go have a look at the body, but Mother refused to let me go; she felt it far too dangerous and risky, plus, she still had that motherly concern that I might be too young to see a real body just yet, especially one in such an advanced state of decomposition. I protested greatly, but to no avail. Casey kept saying that I really didn't want to see it and that he wished he had not.

Night was beginning to extinguish the last shafts of light in our kitchen when we saw the police car pull up and stop on Mission Ridge, near the location of the body. The car switched on its overheads and parking flashers and the officer left the engine idling. We watched from the north kitchen windows as he stepped out of the patrol car with a large flashlight and began shining it in the bushes; he must have also smelled the body, although the corpse was in such a state of decay that it seemed only we had experienced its most ripe and pungent period.

We watched as the officer shined the light here and there in the underbrush, but it didn't appear that he was finding it. We all had that moment of disbelief – had Casey really found a body? Why couldn't the officer find it if it was really there? My brother even began to doubt himself briefly, and this doubt continued to build in him until he could no longer contain himself. In a flash, Casey was out the rear kitchen door and up onto the street – the officer spun around when he heard footsteps and appeared startled. He began to reach for his gun. My brother yelled, "Over there, over THERE!" pointing to the far end of the brush near the entrance to the neighbor's driveway. The officer walked to the east slightly and stepped onto the little sandstone wall. He took one stride and then stood still, shining his flashlight on the ground. In his beam of light, he saw the exposed teeth, practically shrink-wrapped by the desiccated lips in that awful scream-smile that only the long dead will flash. The officer spoke into his transmitter that was fastened to his shoulder. "Officer Ochoa calling for backup."

Within the hour, the police had Mission Ridge Road closed, asking owners of homes beyond the point where the body was to take alternate routes. Obviously, it seemed the entire area had awakened from some long slumber, and there were groups of people walking toward the location from all areas around our cottage. Hotel guests mixed with neighboring homeowners, and there was much discussion going on about it all. By the time the large crowd had finished gathering, the grounds surrounding the northeast corner of Villa 100 were filled with people, some standing, some sitting in folding chairs, all lively and talkative, and cracking open beers even though it was approaching ten o'clock at night. There were now large work lights on stands, and the bushes were lit in their eerie light. There was a forensics team working around the body and the area where it was found. The team was wearing white hazmat-style jumpsuits, which would suddenly cause a glare when they walked in front of the bright lights.

My father had earlier retrieved a few folding chairs for us from the pool. We were sitting out with the rest of the crowd, watching the scene unfold. My mother and father were speaking to people, recounting the tale of the odor and the sewer pipe, and others were finding it weirdly humorous as well. There's nothing my father enjoyed more than a group of people listening to one of his stories, and it brought joy to my brother and I to see our parents working as a team. Whatever hard feelings there may have been about the previous odor debate seemed to be put aside. This was the glue of their relationship – humor and the absurd – and they were perfectly comfortable talking about their disagreement, in the longstanding tradition of poking fun at the ridiculousness of marriage.

There was a new punchline to the story of the odor now. When Father had arrived at the front desk before to inform them of the discovery, Mrs. Kinnett was there in her wheelchair, so Father reported it to her. Her response was, "Oh rubbish. There's no dead body up there in the bushes!"

Now at this morbid block party, our neighbors revealed that they had smelled the odor, too, but also wrote it off, thinking it might be roadkill or something to do with our sewer line. Everyone near us knew about the sewer line, we were assured.

My brother had been questioned by the detectives in charge, and even though he had discovered the body, there was nothing helpful in his retelling nor ours that could assist the police further with figuring out who the poor soul in the bushes was or how he got there. As a matter of fact, the detectives instructed all of us to keep the description of the corpse's location and condition to ourselves. One thing was clear – he had been there for some time. The dry climate of the upper Riviera area had done its job of drying out the body; that's why he looked like a mummy.

At one point, a detective did approach my parents again and informed them, with a hushed voice, that the forensics team had removed the gold ring from the body's finger – only to find that it was engraved on the inside with what was assumed to be the wearer's name – "Stanley A. Greene." We were asked if we recognized his name – we did not.

Due to my brother being linked to the situation through his discovery, we were privy to some of the details as they were discovered, it seemed. Based on their analysis of the scene, it also became clear that much of the corpse's abdomen and innards had been ravaged by animals, an unpleasant thought since Sheila often got out and roamed the grounds and the areas surrounding the hotel as well; and then there were the bones we had seen the show dogs chewing on in July.

Some of the staff of the hotel were also fascinated by the discovery. Cooks, servers and dishwashers were taking turns coming to take a look, since it was after closing time at the restaurant. Gloria, the lead server, came up earlier to take a look while she had tables still, and then returned later when her shift had concluded. She stood with our family for a while, rather silently, as though her mind was elsewhere. Something was eating at Gloria, pardon the expression, and our perceptive mother took note. Later Mother would comment that she believed that Gloria knew something.

Another thing was clear; it was the most grotesque yet exciting thing to happen at the El Encanto for quite some time. As the crime scene investigation continued, the large crowd slowly began to increase, along with the sounds of hushed but wildly excited and increasing mob mutter as everyone discussed the situation.

Now approaching 11:00 p.m., it was still a warm summer evening, so many people were in shorts and tank tops. A few had not only set up beach chairs, but also brought ice chests. All in the large crowd were making jokes and talking, sipping beers and cocktails, so the atmosphere had turned into something like a very macabre neighborhood party. We overheard the neighbor whose driveway was to the immediate right of the body's location exclaim to a group, "Well, I wondered where all of the ants were coming from! I kept having to spray my driveway with the hose – there were so many ants!"

At about quarter past eleven, we could hear the rumbling of what sounded like a big V-8 motor making its way up Lasuen Road and turning right onto Mission Ridge. Sure enough, we turned our heads toward the sound just in time to see Mrs. Kinnett's big, black limousine come around the corner, approaching slowly toward the crime scene. The police department moved the barricades, and all personnel stepped aside to allow the large, lumbering automobile to enter within the shine of the work lights. We could see that the driver had the requisite chauffeur's cap on, and we could make out that there were two or three individuals sitting in the back.

The limo pulled up in front of the little stone wall; the investigation crew had carefully cut back some of the larger, overhanging branches of the manzanita bushes, and it was much easier to see directly into where the body was lying on the ground.

The proverbial hush fell over the crowd as the limousine sat there for a moment with the engine softly rumbling. Next, we all heard the whirring sound of an electric window being lowered, dramatically slow; it was the left rear window of the automobile, directly behind the chauffer, and an officer leaned over, sticking his head into the open window, and then turned and instructed the investigators in the bushes to stand aside. The limo crept a bit more forward closer to the scene, stopping perfectly in front of where the body was located.

We could see the back of Mrs. Kinnett's head as she peered out the window to view the corpse from the comfort of the plush car interior. She gazed for only a moment, then came the whirring again as the window closed. Her limousine started rolling again slowly and disappeared up Mission Ridge Road. There was an outbreak of giggling among the crowd - the Grand Dame of the hotel had her own private viewing, and was now clearly satisfied that there was, indeed, a body in the bushes. The dishwasher from the hotel's kitchen, who was standing next to Father, looked at us and said, "She probably asked them if they would like to take the rest home in a doggy bag."

About twenty minutes after Mrs. Kinnett left, the coroner's van arrived. The forensics team decided it was time to move the body. This was a big moment, and some of the crowd stood from their folding chairs and strained on their tiptoes to get a better look.

The forensics team first tried to lift the upper half of Stanley in one piece, but his head began to fall off. More team members gathered around until there were enough hands to lift the torso, arms, neck and head in one piece, and these were placed into a standard body bag. Next the hips and legs were lifted with care and placed inside as well. Other, smaller parts, some dragged a few feet from the body by "animals" (show dogs) were gathered into smaller bags. The crowd was deathly silent watching this.

After the body was placed in the back of the coroner's van, the mood of the crowd shifted. Perhaps seeing more of the actual corpse as it was compassionately raised from its resting place, illuminated by the unforgiving lights, with its tattered clothing and childlike pose made it all the more real. This was some poor soul, not just a "body." People began to gather their belongings quietly, hugging each other in the reflective glow of the lights, and walking away to return to their dwellings.

Mother had also decided it was time for us to call it a night. We left our chairs in the yard and went back into Villa 100. We were all rather quiet, not just because we were very tired, but because the level of strangeness we had already felt at the El Encanto had just been bumped up a notch, and the reality of this was finally hitting us.

My brother and I crawled onto our beds with hardly a word to one another, and we fell asleep to the low speaking levels of the remaining investigators, combined with the hum of the generator that was being used for the spotlights.

Sometime in the early morning, I was awakened by a cool, morning breeze, the kind that follow a previously warm night. I had been sleeping on top of my covers to due to feeling overheated from the previous warmth. I climbed down from my bed, so I could throw the covers back and slip underneath. It was at this point that I noticed that the door to the little porch off of our room was open – that's why I felt the draft. Then, I noticed that my mother was standing next to my brother's bed staring at him, and even though she was in shadow, I could just make out some details and noticed she was fully dressed. I wondered what Mother was doing awake so early – in her clothing – was she going somewhere?

I whispered, "Mother," and her head turned deliberately toward me. Then, she darted out of the door, her rapid movement causing the hem of her skirt to dance behind her.

Then it became clear – that wasn't my mother.

Chapter 14 — The Waitress

RECORD BOOTH SUGGESTED SONG: "SUNDOWN," *GORDON LIGHTFOOT*

Police Officer: Please state your full name.

Gloria: Gloria Ingram. Do you want my middle name, too? It's Martha. I mean my middle name, so my full name is Gloria Martha Ingram.

Police officer: Are you an employee of the El Encanto Hotel?

Gloria: Yes, I am a waitress in the hotel's restaurant.

Police Officer: Are you aware of the nature of this report?

Gloria: Yes, I know that a body was found up behind Villa 100 by one of the residents and that a full investigation is underway. How long do you think this will take? I'm only on break.

Police Officer: Not long. We were able to identify the body, we think, from a gold ring he was wearing. Did you know the deceased, one Stanley A. Greene?

Gloria: No, I didn't. Maybe I saw him in the restaurant before, but I'm not sure. Do you have a picture of him when he was alive?

Police Offer: No, uh ... no, I don't. Do you think you knew him?

Gloria: Well, I can't be sure unless I see his face.

Police Officer: Understood. Let's shift gears here – can you provide any information regarding the situation? Have you seen anything or heard anything?

Gloria: No, not really.

Police Officer: What do you mean by "not really"?

Gloria: Well, I must tell you there is a member of our staff that I'm afraid of. I've been telling your office about him for months now and nothing has been done about it. I doubt he had anything to do with it, but he does act really strange sometimes and I've called you people about his behavior with me and you've done nothing! It's just terrible – a private citizen being harassed like this and all you can tell me is that you have to see him do it. What idiot is going to exhibit dangerous behavior with police officers around? That's so ridiculous.

Police Officer: I'm sorry, Ma'am, I don't know what you're talking about. Are you saying that you have filed official police reports about someone else that works at the hotel?

Gloria: No, I have not, but that's only because your officers would not take my report. You just told me to avoid him and to let you know if his behavior "got worse." Worse than chasing me with an ice pick?

Police Officer: So, you're saying that another employee has been chasing you with an ice pick?

Gloria: How many times do I have to tell the Santa Barbara Police Department that the groundskeeper here is dangerous before you'll write it down and do something about it! I've had to run for my life from that man!

Police Officer: Okay, Ma'am, I'll take your report now. Please go on.

Gloria: The thing is, I mostly work nights. My ex-husband isn't very into it, but it's the only way we can divide the care of our son between us. Our son lives with me, so I take him to school in the mornings and my ex picks him up after school and our son spends the afternoon usually with him, unless I'm off of work. To make sure I have time for all of this, plus needing to earn a living in expensive Santa Barbara, I usually work the dinner shifts at the restaurant. We close around 10 p.m., so I'm usually able to leave by 11.

Police Officer: Ma'am, what does all of this have to do with the, uh, gardener, did you say?

Gloria: I'm getting there. John, that's his name, John, does more than the gardening. He works very hard around this place – if you haven't noticed, the whole place is pretty much falling apart. Nothing works here. We don't even have all of the bungalows open for guests – some of them on the east side of the property are empty and just used for storage. There aren't as many guests as there used to be, so money is really tight around here. There's not enough staff to keep the place up, the owner is really cheap, but I like the restaurant and our guests are generally pretty cool. There's a family living here – they are charming but seem troubled – they're down in the restaurant all of the time and their kids are constantly at the pool. The parents argue loudly sometimes, so some of us are a bit concerned about the boys. It was one of the kids that found the body, right?

Police Officer: Yes, the oldest boy found the body.

Gloria: Well, I'm not surprised. Those kids are running around all over the place here – they've practically got the hotel and grounds to themselves. But they are sweet kids, in general. Their dog sometimes gets out and is in our restaurant!

Police Officer: Ms. Ingram, could we focus on the gardener and the ice pick?

Gloria: Oh yes, of course. Well, anyway, I've been working here for about six months and I've, of course, noticed him looking at me – well, pretty much leering, while he goes about his business on the grounds. I mean John – he was always sort of staring at me. I arrive at work around 3 p.m. so, about three months ago, I noticed that he was kind of focusing on the area around the main building more and more, almost as if he was waiting for me to arrive. I tried not to be paranoid, chalking it up to coincidence, but then he started waiting outside of the hotel's main entrance after dark. A couple of times we spoke briefly – I said normal, friendly things one would say to any coworker, but I didn't speak enough to him to really have a full-blown conversation – just the standard pleasantries. Somewhere along the line, I think he got the wrong idea.

Police Officer: Well, what do you mean?

Gloria: He began miming at me, from a distance – you know, pretending, like charades – that he was holding someone in his arms and kissing them. Like, he would do this when he saw me – hold his arms in a hugging position in front of himself, and then open his mouth, sticking out his tongue – like he was French-kissing someone, you know? Really weird. The first couple of times I nervously giggled, which I think inadvertently encouraged him somehow. Finally, it became clear to me that I was some object of affection or something, so I told him firmly, no. I just said, "NO!" I shook my head back and forth when I said it and gave him the waving index finger routine. He seems like a regular guy, and well, you know, you can't blame a guy for trying I suppose, or at least that's what I thought at the time, but the way he was going about it was really inappropriate and I was absolutely not interested in him in that way. When he finally realized I wasn't into it, his affectionate attention turned kind of resentful. He started sort of circling around me when I would get off work and was walking to my car. I noticed that he seemed kind of drunk, too, he was rather stumble-y and incoherent at times. He would mumble what sounded like angry things, gibberish really, under his breath and, frankly, it was really already getting quite frightening. This is when I first called the Santa Barbara Police Department to report the activity. Your precinct told me that he would "eventually give up" and that I should "calm down." This is such a "male" way of looking at this. Just ludicrous.

Police Officer: Okay, I get it. Did he continue?

Gloria: Oh yes, his behavior continued to grow more bizarre. The circles around me at night began to grow smaller. Pretty soon he was walking directly behind me, almost making like ... growling sounds. I was really frightened. I asked one of the cooks to start walking me to my car after that. John backed off when he saw that I had an escort, and he disappeared for a while. Then, one truly frightening night, the cook had gone home before me, and it had been several weeks since I'd even seen John, so, without really thinking about it – or maybe I did ... I dismissed it quickly – I left the restaurant. As soon as I stepped-out the door, there was John, and he was holding something in his hand. I looked down, and it was an ice pick! He was standing between me and the way to my car, so I turned around and started running down the path along the top of the pool area – see – over there, that brick path right there. John pursued me, brandishing the ice pick in the air, and making a stabbing motion while laughing hysterically, plus he seemed wasted again, so he was tripping a bit on the loose bricks. I got to Mrs. Kinnett's bungalow ... that's the owner of the place you know – she lives here, too – and I pounded on her door and yelled, "Help!" Her daughter, Mrs. Penner, opened the door and let me in. We peeked through the curtains, but John was nowhere to be seen. Mrs. Kinnett came rolling out of her bedroom in her wheelchair, looking a bit bedraggled, you know, hair in curlers and the day's makeup still on her face, but crunchy. When I told her what had happened, she said that John was a good man and that he was "just kidding" and that I should have "called first before coming over." I couldn't believe it. Mrs. Kinnett then told me to stop bothering them and to go home. Mrs. Penner at least agreed to walk me to my car that night.

Police Officer: And did you report this incident to the precinct?

Gloria: Yes, Officer, I did – and your precinct would not take the report – you told me to avoid John and to let you know if he did it again, also repeating that an officer would have to see him doing it in order to file an official report. Honestly, you have done nothing to protect me and it really stinks. I did warn the rest of the staff about him.

Police Office: Did you ever see John with another person?

Gloria: No, I don't think so ... no, never. The following days after his weird behavior, he was back to his business, mowing, chopping ... you know, grounds keeping and repairing things.

Police Officer: Alright, thank you for your time and I will file this report for you. We'll go talk to John, too.

Chapter 15 — The Tortoise

RECORD BOOTH SUGGESTED SONG: "WISH YOU WERE HERE,"
PINK FLOYD

When we first moved into Villa 100, Father created a small enclosure for our tortoise, Tortoissey, off the rear porch from the kitchen. He swept out the dirt, encircled an area with small sandstones, too high for Tortoissey to climb over, and set up her food and water dishes. I was a little nervous about Tortoissey being so exposed like this, but Father assured us that she was a 'desert' tortoise and would do fine in such a basic enclosure.

I'd grown very attached to Tortoissey as I had with all of our pets. I enjoyed feeding her lettuce and watching her slow, cow-like mastication, while she munched down. Whether it be the motivation of food or affection, Tortoissey would walk up to us when we approached her enclosure.

Up on the little porch above her, my father placed an old Asian-style chest with sliding doors. He turned the side with the doors to the wall of the cottage, and he removed the former back of the cabinet, replacing it with a stapled mesh screen. In this cabinet he placed our two fantail pigeons. The inside was outfitted with perches and food and water dishes. Spreading newspaper on the base of the old chests seemed adequate enough to catch the constant pooping of the birds. To change the paper, you could pull the chest from the wall, open one of the sliding doors, and reach in.

So, this was the solution to part of our pet problems. The Big House had plenty of room for whatever pets we wanted, and it was a big concern for all of us where and how our pets would be housed at the hotel. Father improvised.

For me, having the birds and Tortoissey just outside the kitchen door seemed adequate, because I always wanted to keep my pets close. I would still be able to hear them from my bedroom if anything tried to get them at night.

I had this feeling of always needing to protect them from other people, predators or other unknown forces. I loved pets but was never entirely comfortable having them due to my ceaseless worry about their wellbeing. I had tried and failed with so many over the years (turtles, fish, rabbits and chameleons), so I kept trying to improve my abilities with animals, so they would, hopefully, live longer. Pet deaths could strike me down and cause me to languish for months. Being deeply sensitive, I believed that I could speak to animals, so I was also asking them what they wanted, and either hearing or imagining their responses.

Inevitably, the day came when I stepped out of the kitchen door to feed Tortoissey and she was gone. I looked in her enclosure hoping I was just not seeing her, as she blended in quite well with the color of the soil and the sandstone rocks.

I finally noticed a hole dug into the ground, by the tortoise herself, going under the outside wall of her pen. She had found a way out of the enclosure – not over the sandstones, but under. She must have been tunneling all night. I reached my arm down the burrow but could feel nothing. Tortoises are capable of burrowing thirty feet, or more, and there was no way to get her out. My mother, father and brother all tried to find her, too, and not one of us could see any sign of her, even when shining a flashlight down her burrow. My father concluded that she might eventually come back out, so we tried leaving some of her favorite vegetables at the entrance to her tunnel. Days went by, with vegetables rotting and then being replaced with more by my mother, but Tortoissey never emerged. Finally, I had lost hope and we stopped trying to coax her out. Since the El Encanto gardens were vast, in comparison to the tortoise's size, my father felt that she would be fine. There were cacti, succulents and plenty of plants to eat. There were water supplies and overgrowth – he somehow convinced me that the gardens were, in fact, the ultimate habitat for our desert tortoise, and that she might eventually turn up somewhere on the grounds.

We decided to leave her little enclosure in the event that someday she returned. Tortoissey never came back, leaving me envious of her freedom.

Chapter 16 — The Plague

RECORD BOOTH SUGGESTED SONG: "MIDNIGHT AT THE OASIS,"
MARIA MULDAUR

LOTUS POOL, EL ENCANTO, SANTA BARBARA, CALIFORNIA

Due to the deterioration of things, the El Encanto was existing in a state of inevitability. It was inevitable that shutters would fall from windows, door locks would break, window screens would tear, paint would peel, lights would burn out, metal would rust, and the owner would drink to forget. The hotel felt like a large, squirming organism, settling deeper into its burrow on the Riviera, slumbering and moving, leaking and snoring, cozying up to a large, final dive into an architectural abyss.

We had grown accustomed to the slow simmering and bubbling of the property, its rich odors of the kitchen wafting through the wild abandon of the gardens, with all of the creatures stirring in the shrubs and trees on many sultry summer nights. We watched as Hiya Boy made his rounds every day, doing his best to fight the nearly unstoppable growth of weeds, penetrating through every available opening in the brick pathways and cracked sidewalks. The only advantage he had was the lack of moisture in this arid zone of Santa Barbara, slowing the rot and keeping decay, albeit relentless, at a manageable pace.

At one point, an unexpected rainstorm had suddenly swept through the area, briefly swelling local creeks and soaking the area with a refreshing and lifegiving spray of moisture. The night of the storm, Anthony was with me again, and we enjoyed the coziness of the bedroom as we listened to the rain hitting the roof, while my brother had locked himself inside the Record Booth.

The rain stopped around midnight when we were in bed. Anthony was on our floor in his sleeping bag, while I restlessly snoozed under my covers, excited about the rain that had fallen, and anxious to see how the property looked all shiny and wet. This was the first rain since we moved into the hotel, and I loved how rain could change the look and feel of a place – make it new, and somehow different. It could give everything that extra shine – leaves and paths, lampposts and the old cement flumes would be refreshed. Thinking about all of this, I could not contain my excitement, so I quietly awakened Anthony, as to not disturb my snoring brother, and asked if he felt like taking a look around the gardens.

We were both wearing pajamas and bathrobes, along with furry slippers, as I had also copied Anthony's formal bed attire. We looked like a couple of small Victorian gentlemen, shaken awake at night by some Dickensian ghost.

We slipped out the side door of the bedroom, tiptoeing across the little deck and slowly down the stairs, making exaggerated steps to uptick the possible giggle factor, making our sneak away into the gardens more exciting by adding the possibility that we might awaken my parents or my brother. We goaded and poked each other as we walked away, tempting an all-out fit of the giggles as if we almost wanted to get caught.

My mother had become more concerned about late night excursions since Casey's discovery of the body. She had also become very strict about locking our outside door since I had reported the woman inside of our room during the "Night of the Corpse." We had to leave the door unlocked as we left, so she wouldn't be happy at all about our sneaking out.

I led the way, and we moved south-easterly down the brick path that led to the pond area. As we reached the broader brick pathway in front of the pond, we both looked up, noticing the amazing site of a nearly full moon appearing through the parting clouds, and shining down all around us. Everything was illuminated – the leaves of the shrubs and bushes, shiny from the recent rain, reflecting the moon's light. The brick pathways, moist and releasing their earthly aroma of wet stone, as well as a low-level mist. All of it combined created a magical, eerie backdrop.

The hotel's main building was quiet. The restaurant had ceased operation hours before, and the hotel's lobby doors were closed, although there was likely one person at the front desk in case late night visitors arrived. Occupancy was, at midweek, low, and any guests were asleep, so the gardens were extremely quiet. We were the only two out and about, as far as we could tell. We made our way toward the pool area and when we arrived at the top of the sloping lawn, we had the most miraculous view of downtown Santa Barbara. The rain made everything seem more glisteny, and the street lights and moving cars seemed to sparkle under the remaining clouds, moon and stars. It wasn't until this evening that I understood the name of the place – the El Encanto – it truly looked enchanted that night. As I predicted, the rain had made the place reveal its beauty, like a night flower that had suddenly bloomed, and the darkness hid the damage and the ruin of the place. It looked like paradise to Anthony and me, and we sat on the bench together, in our little evening outfits, soaking in the amazingness that lay before us. For the first time in a long time, I felt lucky.

We sat on the bench in silence for nearly forty-five minutes, but the dampness and cold had begun to penetrate our slightly moist slippers, so we decided it might be time to sneak back. We chose to take the path from the pool to the east of the pond, past the row of attached bungalows. The moon had shifted its position in the sky, and the shadows within the interior of the gardens had grown, and the contrast between the bright moonlight and the shadows became greater – the lights were brighter, and the darks were darker, so as we headed up the path behind tall trees, bushes and buildings, we were having a difficult time seeing.

As we neared the pond, my ears finally tuned-in to the extra loud roar of the frogs. This was their kind of night, and they were singing as loudly as possible. The moisture had also awakened many insects, and as we approached the dark arbor surrounding the pond, we realized we were witnessing an all-out amphibian festival. I never realized that there were so many frogs in the pond, and we could just make-out their shiny backs as a multitude hopped across the overgrown, wet lawn that surrounded the water. Their singing was loud enough that Anthony and I could speak to each other in full voice, so we stopped whispering and stood there, watching this crazy frog party unfold.

Our slippers were quite wet from all the walking around after the rain. My slippers were blue, and due to the fuzziness of the fake fur, had a resemblance to the Cookie Monster from Sesame Street. The fur was becoming quite dirty and matted. Anthony was fidgeting with his bathrobe because he was feeling a little chilled, so we decided to walk back to Villa 100. The first step I took, I heard the crack of a snail shell.

Another step, another crack, and then hearing Anthony's steps also making the distinctive sound of smashing snails. It was hard to see in the darkness of the pond's overgrown arbor, but from what we could make out, it appeared that hundreds of snails were now making their way across the brick path.

I hated smashing snails – not only because I was killing something, but because they were also slimy and gross – and now, I had no choice but to walk as fast as I could, out of the arbor. Every step caused the death of one to three snails, and Anthony and I were completely grossed-out and screaming on the inside, with our hands over our mouths to muffle any sounds, by the time we made it to the pathway that led back to the cottage. The moonlight was intense in this little clearing, and I looked down to see my blue furry slippers matted with crushed snail slime and broken shells, glistening in the moonlight, and then realized that his would be an obvious sign that I had been out at night; Mother would undoubtedly be tasked with washing my slippers. I had no idea how I could do the work myself to get the tiny, mutilated corpses out of my slipper fur, so I was completely full of anxiety.

When we got to the small deck off the side of the bedroom, I took off my slippers and hid them under the stairs, walking up the steps in my bare feet. Anthony didn't want to give up his slippers, so he left them on the porch. We glanced back toward the pond area and were only able to see the dark mound of the wisteria vines on the arbor, and we could still hear the frogs singing in their dank and mysterious enclave.

The next morning, Anthony left rather early, skipping breakfast and saying he was anxious to get home. His slippers were gone from the porch, and I didn't know where he had stashed him. I think he just wanted to get out of there in case it was noticed that we had been out somehow. The screen door on the front porch made a loud slapping sound as it closed behind him, and Mother commented, "Wow, Anthony is in a rush!"

After eating breakfast and getting dressed, I stepped outside to find an amazing sunny day with extra-crisp fresh air – the rain had cleansed everything, and I was elated by the sight of remaining puddles, wet banisters, and the moist bricks. I looked under the side porch stairs to retrieve my slippers and, to my shock, they were gone! I started mulling it over in my head – perhaps a racoon had taken them, given this perfect opportunity to suck snail guts out of the blue fur? That could be the only explanation, I surmised, and I took the worry of my missing slippers and shoved it deep into The Bigger in an effort to forget.

    I made my way back down the side path to the frog pond and once underneath the arbor, I could see smashed snails and broken shells, all pasted to the bricks. I felt a lump in my throat as I reviewed the carnage, but again, I shoved that thought, too, deep down into the recesses of my mind. I stepped across the lawn and peered into the pond to see a lot of very large frogs swimming here and there, resting on the grasses, perched here and there on stones, and perhaps hidden under the dozen or so lily pads that floated on the surface at the far end. They were all quiet now, looking a bit hungover from the previous evening's reveries. I left and headed off to do nothing in particular, which was my favorite kind of day.

    What I didn't realize that morning was that these singing creatures were toads, rather than frogs, and they had been doing more than just croaking at one another. So, it was something of a surprise when a couple of weeks later, large strings of eggs appeared in the pond, attached to the walls, and flowing in long strands almost the length of the pond itself. The water became very choked with these strands of eggs, and many guests and visitors alike stopped to admire the giant biological petri dish that was once a relaxing water feature. The pond's filter and water recycling pumps were becoming clogged with the eggs, so the water became rather swampy, and the entire pond area smelled foul of rotting egg sacks and the amphibian's poop. The heat had returned to the

Riviera, and the warm days cooked the pond and we all bore witness to what the infamous primordial soup must have smelled and looked like.

After about ten days, the explosive hatching began and shortly thereafter, the pond was full of tadpoles. Hiya Boy had done his best to clean around them, removing rotting egg tubes and other detritus, and for a moment there, it was another enchanted scene to view while sitting at the edge of the pond. I took every chance to watch the toads, turtles and tadpoles, and daydream that it was all some sort of fairytale theater to which I had been invited. But, like all fairytales, darkness was just around the corner.

Over time, the polliwogs began to sprout leg stubs, and their tales began to shorten. There was an abundance of food as they almost still pond was a breeding ground for numerous insects, too, so the adult toads had an abundance of food. The adults were quite large in the daylight as they sat and sunned themselves in various locations, also hiding in the overgrowth of plantings that surrounded the arbor they now owned. All guests and everyone else who wandered through and looked into the pond were amazed by all of the activity. Corners of the pond were dark with what appeared to be shadows, but these were, in fact, large clusters of tadpoles. The abundance of life in the pond was astounding and they were almost a sideshow at the hotel – at first.

There was something slightly nauseating to me about the scene. While I was very much into animals, it was almost too much nature going on. Hiya Boy had switched off the recirculating pump completely for fear of clogging the system with the tadpoles, and the summer heat had continued to bake the pond intensely. We all noticed how there were a lot less flies and mosquitoes, as the developing toads were eating every insect in sight. When the young ones were nearing the completion of their development, it became clear that this nature scene was quickly becoming a bit of a problem, but by the time it was realized, a great bloom of toads began spreading out beyond the confines of the pond and arbor and now, one could hardly walk down a brick pathway without coming upon a gang of toads, like a band of local, tough youths, hanging out, just looking for trouble. So, began the Plague of Toads, their shiny bodies constantly moving through the undergrowth, their sounds heard for blocks.

They began to infiltrate the pool area, the rooms, the cottages, and even the hotel's main building. There were toads everywhere and guests were complaining. At night, the sound was deafening, as the toads called to one another across the grounds; a few guests reported that responsive croaks were being heard from the inside of their rooms. There were reports of toads suddenly jumping up on the tables in the bar, hiding out under wet towels at the pool, climbing into parked cars, and appearing without invitation nor decorum, from underneath guests as they sat on the toilets in a few of the cottages. Shrieks were regularly heard throughout the grounds when one of these amphibious hotel-crashers would suddenly leap from a dark corner at a patron. Many of the guests were suggesting the restaurant develop some dishes using the toads.

Next door at the school, the theater and photography offices filed more complaints at the hotel's front desk, and threats were made of legal actions if something wasn't done.

There were smashed toads being found on the walkways, driveways and on Alvarado and Mission Ridge. Having decimated the insect populations, the toads were running out of food, and they began to die. Pretty soon, there were dead, bloating toads everywhere – floating in the pond, the pool, and lying belly-up on the lawns. Hiya Boy could not keep up with the demand, and outside help was finally hired to come in and clean up all of the corpses around the property. Of course, the help wasn't contacted until Mrs. Kinnett herself had trouble. Rolling her wheelchair around the festering toad carcasses was unacceptable.

My family found the whole affair a little funny – just another ridiculous period at the hotel, where one never knew what was around any corner – a toad, a cat, a racoon, a drunk guest, a body, or even a staff member with an ice pick – just like everything else, the place was never short of oddness, style, enchantments, decay and death – anything that could add to the mystique of the hotel, would and could, happen.

Chapter 17 — The Wok

RECORD BOOTH SUGGESTED SONG: "FIRE,"
OHIO PLAYERS

Mother was always working to discover alternative ways to feed our family. There was such limited income and we simply weren't able to be constantly charging food from the hotel's restaurant, which was still putting on airs, and was rather expensive. It was frustrating for me to have a rumbling stomach and be able to smell the alleged fine cuisine being cooked in the hotel's kitchen, knowing that I couldn't have some. The dichotomy of living in a hotel, with so many amenities, and yet not having the resources to enjoy those amenities, was something like a very gentle, subtle torture.

Noticing my dismay, Mother strived even harder to provide delicious meals, even more so than in our other homes. It was almost as if there was a light competition with the restaurant, and she would review their menu and do her best to make some version of their offerings, usually becoming frazzled in the process. Watching my mother cook was a little like seeing an absent-minded mad scientist in a laboratory. She would randomly yell at the ingredients and cookware during the process, misplace things, and search for her reading glasses, which were more often than not on top of her head.

In 1970, a cookbook had been published, simply named "The Chinese Cookbook," which was hugely popular. Mother had purchased the book years before (she kept a stack of cookbooks and recipes in an old picnic basket), yet had never purchased a wok for herself, feeling a bit timid about the system and cooking with such high temperatures and oil; having watched her cook, I worried about these elements, too. In spite of everyone's concerns about her working with hot oil, and due to our situation of secret, marginal starvation, she felt it was time to take the plunge, and she took me along for the drive when she ventured out to purchase her first wok. To her, this was a good investment – according to what Mother had read and heard, it was simple! Easy! Economical! Fun!

There was an Asian grocery and supply store in downtown Santa Barbara, and Mother decided to drive our 1966 Cadillac Fleetwood limousine, which drew some attention when she parked in front of the grocery. When entering, a cheery man behind the counter greeted us with a very heavy accent, and it just made the adventure a bit more authentic and exciting. Mother asked him about woks, and it took him a moment to understand what she was seeking, so she held up the cookbook, and he knew instantly that this was another local, basic, American housewife entranced with the trend; his mood switched from excitement to boredom in a blink.

We found ourselves in an aisle with everything one needed for wok cooking, and Mother was delighted with the interesting utensils; the cooking tools for the wok had an elegance all of their own, and her enthusiasm overtook her fears about cooking with what would be in her hands a potentially lethal weapon. She took all of the wok gear she would need and placed it by the register; the man behind the counter just glared with his arms folded, resting on his large belly. Mother smiled and when he didn't smile back, she refocused and then began looking for ingredients in the food section.

She picked out a number of items by following a recipe in the book and found most everything that she needed right there in the grocery section. Mother selected some frozen carrots, some fresh Bok Choy, some button mushrooms, frozen chicken and celery. There was one item she could not find, and since there was no one else in the store, she called out to the man behind the counter and said, "Excuse me, do you have frozen pea pods?"

The man yelled back, "What?"

Mother restated, in a slightly louder voice, "Frozen pea pods."

The man again yelled, "What?"

Mother cleared her throat, and then loudly overly-enunciated, "Frrrrozen. Pea. Pods." She lengthened each word for a couple of seconds.

The man snorted and scream-replied, "We don't have no frozen tea pots, Crazy!"

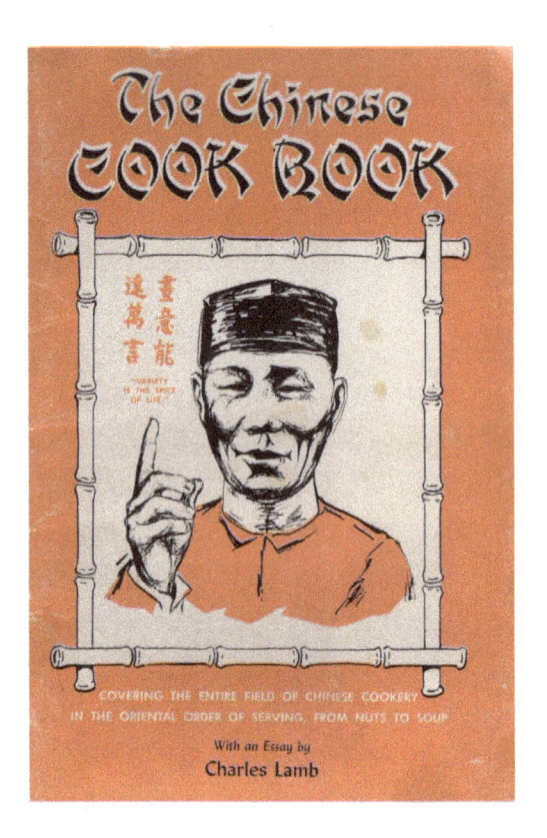

Mother glanced at me and gently shook her head. Then, in her best British posh accent, asked again, "Look here my good man, do you carry Frrrrrozen ... Pea ... Pods? The food, you know, PEA PODS."

The gentlemen smiled, somewhat appreciating Mother's clever accent. He smiled broadly and replied, with an equally cultivated British posh accent, "My dear Madame, nobody has Frrrozen Tea Pots."

Mother just said, "Okay." She completed the purchase of the other items, and as we left the store, she glanced at me and said, "I need to make a quick stop at the supermarket."

It was about four in the afternoon when we returned home, and after putting away groceries, feeding Sheila, and doing some dishes, Mother began working diligently on setting up her wok. She read the cookbook thoroughly to make sure she was doing it all correctly.

When Mother was nervous about something, her hands would shake a bit, and I sat at the kitchen table watching her put on her glasses, read the book, turn to the wok, take off her glasses, then put on her glasses, and read the book again, put the glasses on top of her head, look for the glasses, slide them back on her face, look at the book; the cycle was repeated about five times.

At last, according to the instructions, she seasoned the wok by boiling salt for about twenty minutes, drying it thoroughly, and then pouring in some sesame oil over a medium flame. The sun was beginning to set, the clock was reading a little after six. The kitchen was full of the warm glow of the setting sun, and I could see some of the lights coming on in the neighborhood through the windows of the kitchen. It was a warm, balmy evening. There were the sounds of occasional cars with large V-8 engines, passing by on Mission Ridge with their low rumbles emanating from exhaust pipes, as they accelerated up the slight incline. I could see the various flies and other insects dancing in the rays of sunlight outside, and the green metal original El Encanto streetlight at the corner of Alvarado and Mission Ridge I was sure had popped on. The moment felt magical somehow and I was feeling very cozy in our little kitchen.

The sesame oil was beginning to smoke slightly, and Mother switched on the old wall fan above the stove, which commenced its loud operation.

She began chopping up the vegetables for the wok filling the room with the odor of the bubbling oil; it already smelled exotic and delicious, even though Mother had yet to add the food.

Just slightly audible over the sounds of chopping and the wall fan, I heard a banging noise and after about one minute realized that someone was at the screen door of the front porch. I said loudly to Mother, "Someone is at the door!" and she made an exasperated growl and then asked if I would go answer it and tell whoever it was that she was in the middle of making dinner.

I walked through the sitting room and hallway and when I got to my parents' bedroom, I realized that the knocking was quite loud and forceful, and when I stepped down into the screened porch, I could see Mrs. Kinnett's daughter, Mrs. Penner, standing outside on the stairs with hands on hips.

"I need to speak with your parents."

I replied, "My father isn't home, and my mother is in the middle of cooking dinner."

Mrs. Penner replied, "I don't care, I need to speak with her now."

This woman was giving me anxiety, so I ran back through the house and told my mother who it was and what she said.

Mother slammed down the chopping knife, and said, "Oh gawwwd." Mother really didn't like most people, especially women, and especially females in a place of authority, such as her landlord's daughter.

Mother walked out of the kitchen and I followed for a bit, but because of my anxiety, I made a sharp left turn and went into my bedroom. I climbed on my bed, sitting near my pillows, and pulled my legs up to my chin. I wanted to grow as big as possible. I was figuring that my parents probably had not paid their rent, again, and maybe later that night, we would be moving out. This was the life we led – we never knew when we would be moving, and I had learned it might happen swiftly. I could faintly hear my mother and Mrs. Penner speaking at the front porch – they weren't yelling or anything, but it did sound rather heated. I decided that I probably needed to hear what they were saying – might be important to know what was coming or not, and The Sergeant reminded me that I was officially no longer a child and was on a need to know basis. So, I tiptoed into the little hallway between our bedroom and the sitting room to listen more closely.

Still having a hard time hearing everything, I took the risk and stuck my head around the corner, my body protruding slightly out of the hallway into the sitting room. The room was filled with this amazing, amber, flickering light, caused by the sun's rays filtering through the trees outside. The set of windows on the west wall of the room were reflecting this beautiful orange and amber light – and I felt a bit entranced by it until I realized that the light was coming from the wrong direction, the east, instead of the west, the direction of the sunset.

I turned my head back toward the kitchen, where I also had a pretty good view of the north bank of kitchen windows, and reflected in the windows, I could see flames coming from the stove area on the opposite wall. It took a second for this image to register and it wasn't until I noticed the smoke near the ceiling that I actually began walking toward the kitchen entrance. I stepped in, and to my immediate right was quite a site - the blades of the wall fan were still spinning while on fire! Not only that, the wall around the fan was also on fire, and the oil in the wok was boiling, bubbling, and also … on fire.

It took a few additional seconds for it to sink in that the kitchen was on fire; outside of a fireplace, I had never witnessed such a thing. Time slowed, and I had fantasized that in a situation like this I would be quick on my feet. Instead, I stood for what felt like ten seconds just gasping at the sight. Our kitchen wall burning while the fan made a very strange scraping sound as it spun aflame, over the volcanic column of flames rising from the wok was an oddly captivating site, an artistic presentation of flame and horror. While I was deep within my own fascination with the theme, there was another part of me realizing the consequences of not taking action, and then, The Sergeant yelled at The Bigger me to move, so I found myself running toward the front screen door.

When I arrived, my mother and Mrs. Penner were engaged in a conversation completely unrelated to past-due rent or anything like that. Our visitor was talking about the Montessori school across the street and about that sort of education in general – rather deep in a judgmental, gossipy sort of dialogue, as my mother offered a more sympathetic take on the school. She was leaning against the screen door frame, and Mrs. Penner was holding the screen door open with her body, arms folded, while she leaned on one hip. Both women had shiny, moist skin from the evening's heat, and both had their hair up in buns for the same reason. Then I appeared, leaping down the couple of steps into the screen porch from my parents' bedroom and up to the two women, as they turned to examine me, likely both wondering why I was running and looking so hectic.

My mother had a very strict rule about interrupting, so I stood in a fidgety, consternated way next to her and gently began pulling on her elbow.

"Sweetheart, don't interrupt Mother dear, when she's speaking."

I said, "But, but, I, um, but … "

Both women giggled and continued their conversation while I was reasoning through the conflict of needing to tell them that the cottage was on fire and not wanting to get into trouble for being rude.

"But, Mother, uh," I said.

"I really apologize for him – he knows better than this," Mother said, looking at me at widening her eyes as she did so.

"Oh, that's okay – perhaps he's been listening in on the classes at the Montessori School where children are encouraged to interrupt," Mrs. Penner replied with a judge-y grin.

It felt as if my brain exploded and collapsed into my esophagus – I couldn't breathe for a second, so I bent over and sucked in a huge amount of air. When I stood up, both women were looking at me, confused, and instead of simply exhaling, in my most bloodcurdling scream, the word exploded from my lips, "FIRE!"

Mother's face blanched as she instantly realized she had forgotten about the wok. "Oh my god, oh my god, oh my god …" she repeated as she ran toward the kitchen, with Mrs. Penner behind her, and I, directly behind them.

When we reached the kitchen, the wall was burning quite aggressively and the flames in the wok were about a couple of feet high. My mother spun on her heels and retrieved a large box of baking soda from the refrigerator, dumping it into the flaming grease in the wok; the flames did not complete extinguish. She pointed to a cupboard and looked at Mrs. Penner, who in turn, reached in, and handed another box of baking soda to my mother, who immediately dumped it on the remaining flames in the wok; they weren't completely extinguished, so Mother grabbed a large pot lid from a cupboard and put that on top of the wok – and the flames went out immediately – but the wall was still burning. Mrs. Penner already had a pitcher full of water in her hand, but before she could launch it at the wall, Mother stopped her. "That will spread it! That will spread it!" Mother shrieked.

Mother kept tossing the remaining baking soda at the wall until at last, the fire was out. The kitchen was full of black smoke, and we were all coughing. We all worked together and opened windows and doors. The smoke started to clear, and the two women examined the damage. In one section, directly under the fan, the wall was almost completely burned through to the outside. The wall and ceiling had a dark layer of soot. The stovetop, the wok and all of the chopped vegetables were covered with baking soda and in general, everything was scorched.

It was hard for me to see my mother in distress; the shock, embarrassment and anxiety were all over her face. She said, "Oh my god, I'm so, so sorry." She turned to Mrs. Penner with a look of helpless worry and I think something passed between them – a kind of knowing and understanding between these two mothers. Mrs. Penner shook her head slowly back and forth, and reading the stress on my mother's face, simply said, "We can fix it – we'll get someone to come look tomorrow. Don't worry." She said goodnight and left.

There was a bit of an awkward silence after Mrs. Penner exited. I didn't want to say anything about what had happened because it was obvious that Mother was doing a pretty good job of torturing herself – internally. The line between her eyes was thoroughly creased with worry, and the disappointment with her new "toy" was palpable. I was sad, too, as this was not the evening I pictured. I rarely got time with my mother alone, and the thought of having her first experimental wok dinner with her was something I was actually looking forward to. My father was out teaching an evening art class, and my brother was somewhere in the night, likely getting into some sort of trouble with his friends.

Mother looked close to tears as she began cleaning up what she could of the kitchen. She dumped the remaining oil and baking soda mixture into an old coffee can, tossed the chopped vegetables, wiped-down the stove top and put the dirty bowls and knives from the food preparation into the sink. She turned to me and said, "If we hurry, the hotel's restaurant will still be open – let's go have some good old-fashioned cheeseburgers."

Chapter 18 — The Slapstick Gene

RECORD BOOTH SUGGESTED SONG: "PINEAPPLE RAG/ GLADIOLUS RAG," *THE STING* SOUNDTRACK

For an "old Hollywood family," as my parents referred to us with a drop of sarcasm, the news that the Riviera Theater was going to present a Classic Film Festival was very exciting news indeed. They would be showing films with Charlie Chaplin, Laurel & Hardy, Harold Lloyd, Buster Keaton and our very favorites, The Marx Brothers, among many others.

Having the opportunity to see these films was very special to our parents, especially my father, who had been born in this early period of Hollywood history. Having a father who worked at Paramount Pictures gave my father a special difference from the average audience member. He could tell you where films were shot and by whom, and he could include some lore and gossip too. After all, his father had started in Hollywood's film industry in 1917, just when it was really beginning to boom.

My parents were in the habit of quoting and doing impressions of many of the actors from the silent era to the early "talkies." My father was particularly adept at mimicking Oliver Hardy's "Hmmmph!" at the appropriate times, and my brother and I had already been exposed to many of the films on late night television, so we would act out scenes from the Marx Brothers' bits from their films at any time that called for this. I identified the most with Harpo – the odd, childlike, silent, harp prodigy – with his top hat and trench coat. We had a top hat and old bike horn in our trunk of Halloween costumes, and I would often wear the hat, emulating Harpo, and by communicating with honks. My brother's favorite was Chico, and he could do a perfect impression of him.

There was something else, though, that was vitally important to us as children with all of this. Having these two parents, who mostly argued, come together with humor occasionally was like an elixir of healing, when and if it happened. I remember my parents talking about their favorite movies as they looked over the festival's brochure, while trying to plan-out which days we would be going. I watched them as they identified certain films, which would trigger an exchange of related funny bits. These were rare moments for me – to see my parents bonding and getting along over these films, and I could feel my entire body relax when they were smiling and chuckling. So, aside from being excited about the films themselves, I was also excited about the effect of the films on my parents; we were pretty much guaranteed that they would at least get along as long as the festival lasted. We were about to take a vacation from vitriol, and I couldn't wait.

After going over the brochure, our parents decided that we should attend as many films as possible. They were excited to expose us to some films my brother and I had not seen yet, and also wanted Grandmother to share in the experience.

The first day of the film festival, my father picked up my grandmother and we pulled up at the theater in our limousine, in true movie premier fashion. It was Charlie Chaplin's "Modern Times," a landmark film and a comedic masterpiece. I expected the film to look old and worn, like many old movies I had seen, with visual anomalies – scratches and streaks – but instead, we were treated to an old movie that almost looked like a new film, even though it was in black and white.

There is a scene where in Charlie Chaplin's character, the "Little Tramp" is working in an industrialized setting, and his job involves using to large wrenches to continuously tighten large, and he does this to the point where he can't stop making the motions of tightening bolts. The Little Tramp ends up trying to tighten the buttons on a woman's dress, and at that point, Grandmother laughed so hard that she began to melt and slide out of the theater seat. My mother was in hysterics, not just from the film, but also watching her mother's reaction, which caused us all to lose it, also. The film had wrecked Grandmother; tears were streaming down her face, and she had a wonderful, slightly high-pitched laugh, that made it hard not to join her. She was dressed up for the festival but now her clothes were all rumpled and being pulled in different directions as she slid in her seat.

This is how it progressed through many of the films, and we were able to attend most of the festival. Sometimes are parents attended with us, sometimes not – depending on other obligations – but it was right across the street and very easy for us to go. We were generally high on endorphins when we left the festival from laughing so much, and many evenings were spent afterward with my brother and I doing our impressions of the characters we had seen each day of the festival. For a time being, Villa 100 was filled with its own custom form of slapstick, through which the strengths and gifts of my family were made evident as well. We may have been the "Crazy Camps," but we all shared an excellent sense of humor and were talented performers in our own right.

It was amazing to be part of our family when everyone was getting along – things almost felt, if I dare to say – "normal" – and I remember experiencing great feelings of relief during this period. Perhaps everything would start to get better, and we could thank Groucho, Chico, Harpo and Zeppo (though not as much because he was just too boring), along with Charlie, Oliver, Stanley and many others. These stars of old became like family members to us; we didn't know it at the time, but many of our future pets would be named after these famous actors. The festival ended up being some sort of salve that was rubbed on my family's wounds. While not clearing the injuries completely, this magic salve of classic comedy at least soothed what ailed us - the medicine of laughter heals deeply.

It was also at this time that the family made a personal discovery: So expert were we at integrating the mannerisms and timing of these actors, and then able to perform some of the scenes, we self-diagnosed ourselves with something we dubbed the "Slapstick Gene," which also accounted for the unintentional hilarity of these crazy people I called my own. From then on, whenever we fell, tripped, spilled, dropped, or set fire to something – we blamed the Slapstick Gene.

Chapter 19 — The Owner

RECORD BOOTH SUGGESTED SONG: "LOVE HURTS,"
NAZARETH

Speaking of Hollywood, it was if she was sent over from Central Casting to play the role of an old matriarch; the way she was drawn into the story of the hotel – her clothes, her mannerisms and the wheelchair – all conspired to create the perfect character for the owner of a dilapidated, formerly glamourous retreat, perched above Santa Barbara on a rocky cliff. She would only allow everyone to refer to her as Mrs. Kinnett, and she was the Grand Dame of the El Encanto.

Her wheelchair had a distinctive squeak and creak rhythm as it rolled over the uneven, cracked brick pathways, accompanied by the rattles of the old chair's hardware, all of which at least served the purpose of warning me Mrs. Kinnett was somewhere nearby; there was no need to tie a bell on her, as Mother had suggested.

Mrs. Kinnett generally had some sort of shawl or blanket wrapped around her shoulders, even in hot weather or some putrefying pelt of a long dead creature. It was unsafe for one to assume, based on her appearance, that she wasn't paying attention to all of the goings on around her queendom. It was as if her wheelchair had some sort of radar and alert device, as she generally appeared when I was about to go somewhere that I wasn't supposed to or any other members of my family, and our friends, were doing something of which she just knew she would not approve, even before she saw what it was. In my head, I imagined her appearing in a puff of flame and red smoke like the Wicked Witch of the West from the Wizard of Oz, with her own signature cough-cackle from her lifelong smoking habit. I never saw her laugh but even slightly raising her voice would cause her to erupt in a fit of coughing, so she always spoke in a calm, cool, metered way, generally through clenched teeth, which made everything she said all the more menacing. At the end of nearly every encounter, regardless of her level of hostility, she would add, "I hope you enjoyed your stay," as if suddenly remembering that she was in the hospitality industry and actually running a hotel. The way she said it though, it sounded as if Mrs. Kinnett believed she operated a mental institution which, in fact, she did.

When out on my explorations of the property one day, I discovered an old and worn door behind some overgrown hedges on the lowest ground level of the hotel's main building, unlocked and waiting to be opened.

It was mid-afternoon, and I glanced around the sloping lawn and pool area, as well as the red, cement walkway above me for any signs of the "ghastly Mrs. Kinnett," as Mother called her, near my location. I could see no staff nor anyone else of concern, so I slipped behind the hedges as fast as I could.

As I opened the unlocked door, the knob squeaked (of course), and I was met with a blast of hot, dusty, mildewed air, which seemed to grab and pull me inside this enormous maze of a basement under the main hotel building and restaurant. I resisted its magnetic force, holding onto the doorframe, and carefully looked down a very dim, moldy hallway with many doors. As my eyes adjusted to the light, having just been outside, I could see that the hallway was filled with an odd assortment of items: coatracks, mirrors, kitchen equipment, lamps and even some mannequins, which stood nearly in front of the door. All of the items were covered with black dust and cobwebs, and that was about as far as I could see from where I had entered. There must have been windows in the rooms to my left because there was just enough light emanating from the open doors on the southside of the hallway.

The scene before me was almost too perfectly creepy to be of any actual danger, far too cinematic, I thought to myself. Quoting Huckleberry Finn, what I was looking at gave me the fantods, but ultimately judging the hallway as trite in its almost staged horror movie realness, made me feel better for some reason, and I stepped in quickly, closing the door ever-so-slowly behind me as to not make a slamming sound that might draw attention.

I was now standing fairly close to the group of mannequins, which were all unclothed, but were not like the typical ones I had seen shopping with my mother at Robinson's on upper State Street. These dummies had styling and faces that were vintage in appearance. There was a fair mix of male and female ones, and they weren't bald like modern mannequins, but instead, had carefully modeled hairdos, shaped to appear neatly combed and styled like the movie stars in the golden age of Hollywood. The male's hair was painted black, while the female mannequin's had blond or red hair; regardless, the hair paint on all was chipping and dull.

I gave myself a mental reminder to see if somehow, in the future, I might have one of them in my bedroom because to me, they were more like big dolls than mannequins, and I thought one might look kind of cool standing in the room with some clothes on. At the very least, it would add a spot to hang at least one outfit with our very limited closet space in Villa 100.

I began to slowly step my way down the hallway, around the various objects, looking down at my feet in the little light that there was to make sure I didn't trip on something. I could see what looked like what must have been a Persian rug runner blanketing the floor, but it was completely ruined, worn, dusty, dirty and stained, and of course, mostly obscured by many objects. There was the requisite peeling wall paper hanging in shreds here and there from the walls, and rather ornate sconces hanging on for dear life from the old plaster. For a moment, I wondered if this forgotten part of the hotel had been more opulent than the other areas. As the details of the hallway itself became clearer to me, I could see that the remnants of wallpaper were indeed lavish, felted, and were once very colorful. I could now see about two or three doors ahead of me and the doorknobs on each door I could see were all crystal, the hallway ceiling lights were also ornate, and with my powerful imagination, I could now see it in my mind's eye renewed again. It had a Victorian parlor feel to it, even though the hotel was built in the early twentieth century. I felt a little sad for this level since it was now being used for what seemed to be storage for more forgotten and unneeded items. I sensed that this part of the hotel had not been occupied for decades.

I peered through into an open door to the first room on my left, and this was also filled with old furniture – beds, side tables, and dressers. I stepped into the room and could hear little startled things crawling and moving here and there – probably mice – and I walked over to the window. Through the old dirty and foggy glass, I could see the overgrown vines and plants of the garden outside, mostly blocking the light but allowing enough so that the room was bathed with an eerie, green hue, but still it was quite easy to see the room. It looked as though it had once been a guestroom.

"Wow ... the hotel had guestrooms down here," I said, absent-mindedly speaking aloud to The Sergeant. I stopped for a moment, thinking I heard footsteps but then realized they were coming from above me in the hotel's bar and lounge area. I listened a little more closely and I could hear muffled conversations coming from the bar, as well as the lobby and restaurant above, also somehow comforting to me – if something happened, I could scream, and someone might hear me.

It sounded like a pretty full house up there and then it also occurred to me that someone by the same token might hear me, too, so I reminded myself to keep tiptoeing about carefully, and to keep my thoughts inside.

I took a couple of steps over to an old dresser and pulled open the top drawer, and to my surprise, the drawer was filled with vintage women's undergarments. They were folded neatly, and I was amazed that they had likely remained that way since who knows when. My excitement registered in my increasing heartbeat and tingles, I opened the second drawer, and there were more vintage clothes – really cool stuff, again like I had seen in the old movies; satiny, shimmery ladies' items, but not wanting to disturb them, I only looked at the top layer. More drawers, more clothing, this time some skirts and blouses almost irresistible not to touch, but I knew it was wrong to mess with them, in my continuing efforts to leave no trace of my habitual trespassing into the closed off sections of the property, so I shut each drawer and let the contents be.

I left that first room and continued my journey down the grim hallway, pulling cobwebs from my face and hair all along the way. I wished I had worn long pants instead of swimming trunks for this since my bare legs were brushing against things that I couldn't identify by sensation, as I squeezed by the larger furniture that was crammed in the hallway.

As I stepped in the second room, a new discovery of treasure was made – this one was filled with old bicycles! And even a canoe! Also mingled in were full-length beveled mirrors on wheeled stands, and some gardening implements – shovels and rakes mostly from what I could make out.

The third room didn't have any furniture but was filled instead with boxes of old books and magazines, some dating back to the beginning of the hotel. One box was filled with old El Encanto brochures, and I spent about five minutes thumbing through one with keen interest. Pictured were some of the interiors of rooms still in operation that I hadn't managed to break into yet, so I figured some exploring time, and the risk of possible capture, could be reduced by reviewing the photos carefully. There were no photos of Villa 100, and it seemed that the brochures were aimed at the time the Spanish-style bungalows were built in the '30s. I set down the brochure exactly where I found it and noticed that there were also some old display racks of with old postcards still in them, and a few more pieces of gardening equipment against the far wall. This room was a little darker than the others as the leaves of the plants outside were flattened against the window, almost completely blotting out any light.

Excited to see what was in each room, I repeated a phrase in my head I heard on a television game show and said to myself, "Lets show Steve what's behind door number 4!"

The fourth room was the darkest and creepiest of all; it took a couple of minutes for my eyes to adjust. I stood perfectly still, and it felt very different in Room 4. As my eyes began to dial things in, I immediately noticed that there was a heavily stained, twin bed mattress on a rusty metal frame in the corner, with a fairly deep, concave sleeping dent. This bowl-like area in the bed was very dark brown, and there was a rusty smell. I guessed that perhaps something had leaked from the ceiling above – another busted sewer pipe, perhaps? Against the wall to my right were a couple of classical dressers, with heavily carved designs, which must have been beautiful at one time.

The window in this room was also almost completely blocked with plant life from outside and additionally, there was a dingy curtain still hanging, so the light that was coming in was even more muted than the other rooms, making it hard to see into the corners, and I felt a chill run through my body. Something in this room didn't feel right – I couldn't put my finger on it – there was absolutely no one in the room at the time but I sensed that someone had been in it recently. There was a heavy smell of human dander and body odor, and at that moment, I had the common horror movie feeling of someone watching me.

I glanced at the dresser nearest to myself against the wall, and I took a step up to it. Sitting on top of the dresser was an opened half a bottle of whiskey, also dusty. I pulled open the top drawer fully expecting it to be filled with more women's clothing, but instead there was an assortment of round, sharp objects, that rolled and clanged together with the movement of the drawer. I stopped immediately, hoping no one from upstairs had heard them clang together, but I didn't hear anyone approaching or reacting. After a minute or so, I looked back down at them and I wasn't sure what they were – some sort of kitchen tool – a large, round wooden handle with a sharp steel spike; there were about half a dozen of them in the drawer, and many looked a bit rusty and well-used.

I closed the drawer slowly and opened the second drawer, and there were some almost contemporary clothes – an old pair of jeans and some stained, white cotton tank tops sort of wadded together. I closed the drawer and just as it was fully in, I heard a lot of noise.

I was now directly below the restaurant's kitchen. It sounded like two of the cooks were arguing loudly and that perhaps one of them had dropped a bowl or something, and they were going back and forth I guessed, attempting to clean it up. The voices were muffled through the floor, so I really couldn't understand what they were saying, but I reminded myself to stay quiet. Even with all the unpleasant smells in Room 4, I could now slightly detect the smell of blueberry muffins from upstairs; I smiled and felt safer for a moment.

    I looked back at the dresser and as I moved and pulled open the third drawer, a deep fear gripped me – a restrictive force from within clamped down around my lungs, accompanied by what felt like icy nails being driven into my skin. A huge lump formed in my throat and I couldn't swallow. Chills ran up and down my body and my vision became blurry for a moment. The surroundings seem to appear to me as though looking at negatives I had checked out in Father's photographs. The darkness of the room seemed to coalesce into a swirling cloud, becoming darker, and I couldn't see my hands gripping the handles of the drawer anymore. My heartbeat was pounding in my head, which felt as though it had suddenly become filled with a whirlpool of blood. The sounds of the kitchen sounded further away than they were until I could no longer hear the cooks in the kitchen at all. The heaviness of the room collapsed into me, and then everything went completely black.

    When I came to, I was on my side on the dirty floor. I turned my head to the ceiling and the bottom of the extended third dresser drawer slowly came into focus above me, and I could only guess that I must have fainted. I remembered one other time where I had fainted and that was when I had a searing, high temperature during one of my many bouts with viral pneumonia. This current episode was somehow different – it felt like my consciousness had been squeezed out of my body, and I had a hollow sensation in my stomach.

    There were no sounds coming from upstairs now, and I didn't have any clue how long I had been unconscious. I rolled over into a crab sort of position and pushed myself up into a squat. I was still very dizzy, so I steadied myself with the dresser drawer, using it as leverage as I returned to standing. I looked into the third drawer again – it was almost completely open – but the room was so dark now, I could only see the strips of something that maybe were neckties that were the inside of the drawer.

I looked over at the window and could tell that the sun was nearly completely down, and what little light was coming through the leaves and dingy curtains must have been one of the outdoor pathway lights. I was feeling really uneasy, so I decided to stop my investigation and get out.

I took a few steps and peered into the now very dark hallway. I looked down it in the direction where I had entered and could just barely see the many objects I had passed by, similarly lit by the hotel's outdoor path lights through the various room's windows. I squinted a bit to see more, and I could only just barely identify the silhouettes of the mannequins; their heads nothing more than oblong orbs perched on shoulders now. That's when I noticed one of them moving slightly. I considered this could be due from the fact it was so dark in the hallway and my inability to focus my eyes, so I stared at the one that was moving for about fifteen seconds, attempting to determine if I was just seeing things. It looked like it was rocking back and forth on its feet, and I realized after a few seconds that it was indeed moving, and that it was wearing a dress. The head looked different than the silhouetted heads of the other mannequins, I wasn't sure why, but it looked like someone alive was now there, apparently shifting back and forth on their feet.

It's interesting what panic will do – I wanted to run but I also couldn't move; at the same time, my head exploded with a rapid-fire debate on whether it was better to step back into the room and hope I wasn't noticed or just run for it. There was one thing for sure – I wasn't going back out that way now. I looked away from the mannequins and turned toward the end of the hall nearer to me. The fear had cemented my feet to the floor but, eventually, I did get my feet to move and I took a few giant strides, arriving at the opposite end of the hallway from the group of mannequins.

There was a small landing, one step up, and a door immediately to the left, so I stepped and opened the door and was then looking at a full flight of steps to climb. I couldn't get myself to turn my head and look back to where the mannequins and their new friend were, so I decided that it didn't matter what was going on back there – I was leaving, and all other considerations were irrelevant.

Now, the other task at hand was to get out of the building undetected. With everything that I had been experiencing, I had momentarily lost sight of the fact that I was somewhere I should not be, and I didn't want to get caught. Within two steps, I switched from running-up-the-stairs to creeping-up-the-stairs, and arrived at the top, where there was another door. Just then, there was a sound from below – it was muffled by the closed door at the base of the stairs, and yet unmistakable; it was the familiar sound of the strange, wood and metal pointed kitchen implements rattling around in the top drawer of the dresser as it was being opened in Room 4.

More icy nails seemed to penetrate my skin as the fear and panic washed over me again. I thought to myself, "Don't faint, please don't faint." The sensations were so strong that they caused me to twitch my body from side to side, as if I were being poked. I thought, oh shit, someone had opened that drawer! There was definitely someone else in that room below, and all remaining hopeful thoughts that I had only imagined another figure in the hallway by the mannequins were gone.

I turned the knob on the door in front of me, stepping through and into the darkened kitchen. The restaurant was closed, and the kitchen was clean, which meant it was at least after ten at night – or later – and it dawned on me that my parents must be wondering where the hell I was. As I snuck through the dark kitchen, I was also doing some calculations – if I had entered the downstairs when it was still light, I must have been passed-out on the floor for – what, maybe more than a couple of hours? A darker sensation set into my chest, preemptively feeling my parents' coming anger, but I kept walking until I stepped out of the swinging kitchen doors and into the restaurant. There were still lights on across the lobby, and I could hear guests clinking glasses, talking and the general sounds of adults hanging out; must be some of the staff enjoying an after-work "snoot-full," which was another one of Mother's expressions.

I walked over to the glass doors that separated the dining area from the bar and peering through one of the lower panes, I could see several men sitting at the bar. The lights were coming from above and behind the bar, so the men's backs were in silhouette to me. The bartender was leaning against the shelf of alcohol behind him, arms folded, and he had a large grin on his face. His hair, and the hair of all the men at the bar, was slicked down in some fashion, with some very shiny hair oil or something, which reflected the lights above them. Cigarette smoke swirled from a couple of the men, making the scene look a little hazy.

If I stepped through the doors and turned to my left and walked straight, I would have to go by these men and the front desk to get out. That would likely raise suspicion, or even a phone call to my parents, so I looked to my right, and there was a door on the southwest wall that led out to a set of steps, which was an exit to the outside from a porch area where guests had there morning coffee and pastries.

I stayed close to the edges of the room, making my way slowly to this exit, and was relieved to find it open, so I pressed slowly on the crossbar, trying to be quiet as possible. I exited, and closed the door behind me, which also locked upon closing, and I was now facing the pool from the landing at the top of the steps, and the pool's water was emanating an eerie blue caused by the pool lights. I snuck down the bank of steps, and was very relieved to arrive on the ground, outside.

The entrance to the basement I had used earlier was once again to my immediate left behind the hedges. I was facing the pool and, in the darkness, I felt very incognito, thinking I had at least escaped the basement experience seemingly unscathed. Where I was standing, I was underneath and slightly to the south of the bar's window but could hear no voices from the bar through its window that faced the pool. I was a little curious as to why the bartender and all of the men I just saw would all of a sudden be silent or maybe gone, and I glanced up at the window and noticed that the bar lights were indeed also out. I decided to ignore this, and I started up the sloping, cement pathway, still tiptoeing and sneaking along and when I reached the top of the hill, to my left toward the entrance to the hotel I heard those unforgettable creaks and squeaks, and out of the darkness rolled old Mrs. Kinnett. Mrs. Kinnett lived in one of the largest '30's Spanish revival cottages, near the pool, and was usually pushed around in a wheelchair by her granddaughter, Heidi or Mrs. Penner, but here she was alone – with me.

Mrs. Kinnett's face in shadow made her appearance all the more unnerving as she wheeled her way closer to me, struggling with her gnarled hands to move the chair along the path, with the pace I was most familiar with; it wasn't the roll of someone who was on her way to somewhere else – it was a menacing, slow roll of someone getting closer to examine something. She stopped a few feet from me and asked, "Are you the boy in 47?"

"No – I'm in Villa 100," I replied.

"Oh, you say you're part of that unfortunate family up there. Excuse me, young man, but what are doing out so late? Shouldn't you be home in bed by now?"

"Uh, I, uh, I'm, a, I'm just taking a walk." I looked into her black eyes, which were sparkling in the light of the rather dim pathway light.

"Oh, I highly doubt that. I keep hearing about break-ins happening in some of the areas of my hotel that are off limits to guests … closed for repairs … so children should not be going inside of them. Are you going inside parts of the hotel where you shouldn't even be? Children and other guests are not allowed in closed areas of my property." She leaned back in her wheelchair, folded her arms, and awaited my answer, never moving her eyes away from mine.

"No, I don't know what you're talking about," I said, a little rudely.

"Hmmmph," she snorted, leaning her face forward toward mine, "I think you should come inside with me for a moment."

"No, I don't think I should," I replied.

As I swallowed the painful lump in my throat, embarrassingly audible, I was contemplating an all-out sprint north, back to Villa 100, when Mrs. Penner came walking up behind me.

"Mother, are you ready to go back home now?" Mrs. Penner asked in a tone that was far too chipper for after dark. Her words out of nowhere coming from behind me made me jump, and Mrs. Penner placed her hands on my shoulders.

"No, this boy is sneaking about the hotel - I want to know why," Mrs. Kinnett grunted, flapping a hand in my general direction.

"Are you the boy in 47?" asked Mrs. Penner, in a slightly condescending tone.

"No, I'm not," I said, realizing that I wasn't really afraid of these two. They seemed to occupy some place of superiority and authority in their own minds, as though all of us should quiver in their presence. My family had tolerated their lack of hospitality, and for some time, the stench of an open sewer and a corpse, not to mention the overall lack of maintenance of the property, so I was suddenly not impressed by nor fearful of either of them. This attitude of theirs, instead of intimidating me, made me want to be all the more rebellious and to ignore them. After all, I was one-hundred feet tall, so I rocked impatiently on my feet and decided to just start whistling, the way Bugs Bunny would.

Doubling down the tightness of her folded arms, Mrs. Kinnett said, "Okay, young man, I don't know what you're up to, but you're coming with us to the front desk and we're going to call your room to see if you're really a guest of the hotel."

I loved it – I hope my mother answered the phone when they called Villa 100 – I couldn't wait to hear her snarky reply. I knew my mother couldn't stand these two and saw them as mere characters who should appear in some book in the future, perhaps. Mother would chuckle while describing Mrs. Penner pushing her mother around the broken, brick paths in her antique wheelchair – gave the place "all the charm of an asylum."

"Okay, fine," I replied with a shrug. My denial of their superiority only aggravated them more. Mrs. Kinnett looked at me, motioning with a bony thumb in the direction of the hotel's entrance behind her, and said, "This way."

Mrs. Penner stepped around me to her mother's wheelchair, grabbed the handles, and gently turned it around. We walked and rolled in a somewhat dour precession to the front door of the hotel. I opened the door for them and bowed, and both of them nodded at me with somewhat reluctant thanks and grimacing looks on their faces, surprised by my caustic politeness.

As we stepped into the light of the front desk area, I could see them both better. Mrs. Penner had died blonde hair, which she piled on top of her head, blue eye shadow, thick false eyelashes, and conservative clothing typical of Santa Barbara in the '70s – an innocuous striped top and some faded shorts, in casually crumpled and damp-from-the-humidity cotton.

Mrs. Kinnett was dressed in all black, at least from the waist up, and wearing an old gray felted-wool hat. There was a fetid fox stole around her neck, which had been dead for quite some time, and judging by the look on its face, I surmised that it must have died from fright while being wrapped around her neck when still alive. She had the usual crocheted blanket across her lap. She was figuratively and literally stewing in her own juices, which made me feel a little nauseated. And looking at them both in the harsh light of the lobby, I still had no idea as to why I should view them as authority figures.

I also got a good look finally at myself. I was suspiciously covered in dirt, cobwebs and dust – clearly from all of the nastiness below. I started to brush off my shorts and Mrs. Kinnett yelled, "NOT IN HERE, for god sakes."

At this point, the front desk attendant asked, "Is there a problem, Ma'am," referring the question to Mrs. Kinnett. I instantly recognized him as one of the guys on acid I briefly sat next to at the 4th of July Sale – it was Tony of the pot smoke-filled and blacklight poster room fame, with his longhair tidily pulled-back in a pony tail and looking rather spiffy and different than he usually looked.

"I found this boy wandering around the grounds of the hotel and he's not a guest," Mrs. Kinnett stated flatly.

"I AM a guest," I replied, and continuing, "I'm actually a resident!"

Mrs. Kinnett glared at me and said, "Oh no you're not! I can always tell when a child is from the wrong side of the tracks!"

I wasn't completely sure what she meant by this, but I had the idea that it was some archaic way of saying that I was an undesirable and didn't belong.

"I'm in Villa 100, I've lived here for months, so if I'm from the wrong side of the tracks, then so are you," I shot back.

Mrs. Kinnett looked at me for a second, and then said through clenched teeth to the front desk clerk, "Ring number 100, please."

I happened to glance over into the dark restaurant and bar area and noted that the bar was completely closed. This increased my confusion since there just had been a bunch of men sitting in there when I snuck out, just minutes ago.

Before I thought about possible repercussions, I blurted out "Where is everybody?" pointing to the bar area. Tony had picked up the phone to call our cottage and held it for a moment in the air.

"What do you mean, man? The bar has been closed for hours."

Flabbergasted, I fell silent. I couldn't say anything because that would incriminate me as being inside of the closed main building; and where would I have come from, if I didn't enter through the front and walk passed Tony?

Mrs. Kinnett and her daughter stared at me incredulously while the front desk clerk phoned our Villa. Once the call was answered he said into the receiver, "Good evening, this is the front desk. Do you have a little blonde boy staying with you?" Even through the receiver I could hear my mother's crow-like reply as she yelled, "Well, of course we do!"

Tony just gently returned the receiver and looked at Mrs. Kinnett. "He is a guest." He looked at me and said, under his breath, "You're a cool, little dude." I whispered back, "No, I'm not. I'm possessed by Satan." He tried to hide a smile.

I then turned to the women and asked, "Can I go now?"

Mrs. Penner said, "Well, uh, sure, sure – yes, you're fine."

I turned and walked toward the open front doors and just as I crossed the threshold, I heard Mrs. Kinnett say in her trademark, searing monotone, "I hope you enjoy your stay."

Chapter 20 — The Restaurant

RECORD BOOTH SUGGESTED SONG: "NOTHING FROM NOTHING,"
BILLY PRESTON

The hub, the flight deck of the mothership, for the guests, staff and locals who just loved the hotel, where everyone mixed together and generally had a good time, where it all went down and was discussed, was in the restaurant and bar of the El Encanto.

Temptation was a constant issue for me while living at the hotel. I wanted to order drinks while I was at the pool, or even food, and yet, as always, being on a tight budget or no budget at all made it continue to be a light form of torture. There were times when I did not have the funds to buy lunch but would see visiting children wolfing down burgers by the pool while my stomach growled. Other times, something financially would improve, and Mother or Father would treat us to lunch or dinner – and sometimes, even some ice cream.

Grandmother really did love coming to see us at the hotel and, as Mother put it, the visits fulfilled Grandmother's desire to be waited on. Since Grandmother was the one person in our family who was "holding," yet fairly thrifty with her finances, we were guaranteed some extra treats when Grandmother came to visit. Grandmother also liked being picked up in the limousine and deposited at the hotel's main doors, which gave her the chance to make the grandest of entrances.

Despite her issues with gout, Grandmother was able to walk well enough around the gardens, and of course, get herself to the bar regularly. My grandmother's love of alcohol was notorious; Grandmother was also only about five feet tall, so my mother referred to her sarcastically as "short and to the pint." Mother was careful not to use the word "alcoholic" in her presence, as this was very upsetting to Grandmother, who was in deep denial.

On yet another lovely Santa Barbara weekend afternoon, Grandmother was up for watercress sandwiches and tea at the pool, but before that, was with us in our sitting room just visiting and discussing ongoing family dramas, usually involving the plans for Grandmother's estate when she passed. Very uncomfortable topics for a kid like me, and there was also my Mother's sister, Aunt Benny, to consider, and who clearly had some mental problems. Bored of hearing the same old conversation, I announced that it was time to head down to the pool for some swimming, and my brother said he would go too. Mother said, "Grandmother and I will be down in twenty minutes."

It was the hot midday, so the sun was blazing nearly straight above us. Casey and I had made our little pool nest of lounges and chairs near a table, had grabbed towels, and were spreading them on the seats when we noticed Father approaching, cutting diagonally across the sloping lawn to the pool's west entrance. It was so rare to see Father at the pool, and in his swimming trunks no less. The last and only time he joined us at the pool so far, Mother had burst out laughing when he appeared in his shorts. "Oh, my gawd – your legs are so white - they're signaling aircraft!" she shrieked. I thought it would be funny to repeat this as he approached Casey and I. Father sort of half-smiled and groaned a bit and sat down on one of the chairs. "Your mother and grandmother will be here shortly," he said in a monotone.

"Oh, there they are," I said, pointing toward the hotel.

Teetering down the grassy slope was Grandmother. Mother was engaged at the top of the lawn with another guest. Grandmother continued walking across the lawn as though she had already kicked a couple of drinks back, being a bit unstable on her feet. We three looked at

Grandmother walking slowly down the slope, trying not to trip, while holding her purse. There was just the slightest of breezes, but just enough to cause the floppy oversized brim of her big sun hat to flap up and down slowly with each step she took on the grass. I got the feeling watching her as if I were seeing some sort of circus act because she was wearing a flowery, brightly colored caftan over what was likely a one-piece bathing suit. She must have changed her clothes before coming down, now being perfectly attired for an afternoon tea by the pool.

Grandmother was still wearing her sparkly diamond earrings and tennis bracelet, and the sun was reflecting off of them, causing occasional rays of light to emit from Grandmother's person. She was some sort of vision, not clear what sort, but enough that other guests at the pool were somewhat captivated by her, too, having followed my pointed finger in Grandmother's direction. We could just see her due to the slope being above us, as we looked above the overgrown bushes that surrounded the pool. The other hotel guests at the pool perhaps were also thinking that she might keel over and face plant at any moment, and they didn't want to miss that; Grandmother resembled a Rose Parade float about to crash.

About halfway across the lawn, we all heard the distinctive and recognizable sounds of the lawn sprinkler systems coming on, which was odd because they usually didn't turn on until dark. Just as my mother cried, "Look OUT!", the sprinklers came on full force, spraying Grandmother from nearly every direction. Grandmother started yelling, "Oh! Oh! Oh!" and began feebly trying a few directions to escape, which resulted in her going in wobbly circles. When she could find no escape, Grandmother stopped completely in her tracks, and adopted a stance of relaxed authority; applause erupted from the pool and people cheered her.

Standing there in the middle of the sprinklers, brim of the floppy, wet hat covering her eyes, caftan drenched and sticking to her body, she somehow looked at peace. Above her, there were also a few people at the bar looking out the window, and everyone who happened to be walking by at that moment stopped and just stared; Grandmother had become performance art.

At this point, Mother rushed down the slope to catch up with her, and in her yellow bikini, hurried to her mother through the water, shielding her own face with her hands. When she reached Grandmother, Mother flipped back the wet brim of Grandmother's hat, revealing Grandmother's fogged-over cat eye glasses.

Mother assisted Grandmother the rest of the way to the pool; we could hear them giggling. Grandmother was completely soaked by this point, and her comfy bejeweled slippers were making squishing sounds as she walked around the pool. Other guests patted her back, and one man stated, "Well, I guess you can skip the pool."

Mother and Grandmother made it to the table, and Grandmother set down her purse, removed her hat, and attempted to adjust the table's umbrella, which suddenly snapped closed, enclosing her head and shoulders. We could hear Grandmother's muffled voice expressing her consternation from under the umbrella.

Mother was slightly unglued by the humor of it, but still was able to search for the crank to open the umbrella. At this point, we had the full attention of everyone at the pool. I wasn't sure if I should feel embarrassed or proud of a moment that I knew would live in family infamy forever. It was absolutely clear from whom we had inherited the Slapstick Gene.

Once the umbrella was opened, Grandmother sat down in a chair, and immediately asked for a real drink in lieu of some tea. My mother went to fetch-it for her.

Once the giggles had died down around the pool, the drink was delivered, and the moment passed, my mother and grandmother sat leisurely speaking about all sorts of things and hilarious moments from the past. There were stories of grand shindigs and a party guest who had rolled himself up in a Persian Rug and passed-out on the floor. Endless tales of deep-sea fishing adventures, including tales of strange creatures rising from the open ocean in the middle of the night. I lounged on my chaise listening closely and wondering if other families had such stories. Sitting there by the pool, listening to these two matriarchs of the family talk, I didn't feel so embarrassed anymore by my family. We were just different, and while I wasn't sure how many "different" families were out there in the world, I would be interested in hearing their stories, too.

I had begun to drift-off when we heard some voices shouting from above. There was some sort of commotion up in the bar – sounds of glass breaking, shrieks, and laughter, the voices of the staff yelling things like, "Come here!" and "Get down!" From our vantage point at the pool, we could look up at the restaurant's windows above and just make out the shape of a fluffy dog running amok. Then, the dog disappeared behind a wall and reappeared, as it jumped on top of a cocktail table nearest a window and we all got a clear look at Sheila panting wildly. She had somehow worked her way out of our cottage and was looking for us.

My father ran to the bar, and we all watched from the pool as he tried to get Sheila from atop of the table. The couple who had been sitting at the table were drenched from their spilled drinks, plus, their chairs were overturned, and food was all over the floor. They demanded to know if it was a "lounge act" and told my father that it needed more rehearsals. There was much hilarity coming from patrons in the bar as Father left with Sheila, and they both walked down and joined us in the pool's enclosure. Everybody was petting Sheila. The incident did not ruffle the feathers of the staff; it was still a hotel, after all, and we were still considered guests.

As afternoon slipped into evening, it was decided that Grandmother should stay for dinner – after a few cocktails at the pool she absolutely needed some food – something besides watercress – so we all returned back to Villa 100 to change and get cleaned up. Since Grandmother was with us, there was a clear understanding that we put on our best clothes. Even with all the issues, my family attempted to preserve some modicum of grace, especially when we were in public enjoying a dinner.

Father called and made a reservation at the hotel's restaurant, and once we all assembled to take the walk down the long, uneven brick pathway to the main building, I glanced at everyone in their summertime best; we were quite a crew, I thought. Father had on a shirt, tie and a blazer, and Mother was in a beautiful orange and pink summer dress, with her hair up in a twist. When dressed well, my parents were glamorous to me and I longed to look like them. I was wearing one of my Anthony-esque outfits; a white shirt with a deep blue sweater vest, tan light cotton summer pants and my only pair of brown dress shoes. My brother had reluctantly thrown on his cleanest Hang Ten t-shirt and a pair of new-ish blue jeans. Grandmother had switched back to the clothes in which she had arrived, which included a taupe-colored light silk top and skirt combination, and for extra thrills, she had her silver fox stole wrapped around her shoulders, even though it was a fairly warm evening. Father also made sure that the door was shut behind us and that Sheila was inside.

When we arrived at the hotel's lobby, the front desk person smiled and said, "Welcome," and also commented on what a handsome family we were. He stated that our table was ready and motioned toward the restaurant. We walked in single file in that direction, and as usual, I brought up the rear, which was fine because it provided the opportunity to watch other people as they looked at my family.

In my head I asserted that this moment was dedicated to all the people who thought my family was nothing – watching heads turn as we walked by gave me a sense of accomplishment and was one of the rare moments of sanity that I could savor. Some of the guests who had been at the pool earlier were having to reframe their opinions of us, I believed, as we were not just the poor clowns everyone thought we were. In other words, we "cleaned up nice."

We sat at our round table, which was by the window, and gazed out at Santa Barbara below, its lights just beginning to twinkle. Anytime we had dinner with Grandmother meant she would be buying, and I was very excited to order practically whatever I wanted. I looked around the table as the candle in the middle illuminated the back of everyone's menu as they held them to their faces. Grandmother's diamond ring twinkled on her finger in the candlelight, as she turned the pages of the menu. My father had set down his menu and was watching me watching everyone else – he reached over and patted my shoulder and smiled. I got the sense that Father might know about The Bigger somehow, but The Bigger didn't work if it was talked about – at least that's what I believed; its power was in its secrecy.

The restaurant had a fairly extensive menu, so it took everyone awhile to decide. At Grandmother's command, the first-ordered items were drinks for everyone. Mother and Father ordered beers, my brother wanted a root beer, and Grandmother ordered a vodka gimlet. I asked for a Shirly Temple, wanting to have something that looked like a cocktail, so I could be on the same level as Grandmother. After the drinks were delivered, we all ordered our various meals and after the waitress took the menus away, our family leaned back in a relaxed way into the seats, and Grandmother raised her glass and said, "Here's to a brilliant afternoon tea." We all said, "Cheers!"

Grandmother had a distinctive way of sipping her cocktail, savoring every molecule, like a bee collecting pollen. Her pinky finger was always extended, no matter what sort of drink or container. There was an elegance to her, despite all of her foibles, something that harkened back to her days at the Barnard School for Girls in New York. Sitting there, draped in her fur, jewelry sparkling (and her eyes sparkling as well with the joy of holding a cocktail), it was hard to imagine the cruel woman described by my mother. This evening, Louise Gertrude Craig Fyfe Hopton, was the essence of joviality, and her wit and intellect were truly entertaining. It was on this occasion that I decided to always extend my pinky while sipping beverages. "Sip and extend, sip and extend, sip and extend" I repeated within The Bigger, and instructed The Sergeant to remind me in the future so it would become a habit.

Just then, a rather ravishing woman walked by our table, who was followed by her much older date as they were being led to their table by the host. The woman was a statuesque brunette with a copious bosom and tight waist. She was dripping in silver and jade jewelry, which was offset nicely by her overly-tanned skin. Her eyeshadow was a smoke-y silver, which was an interesting contrast behind her lengthy and dark black false eyelashes. I wasn't used to seeing someone quite this done-up, so I stared a bit as she passed and then also noted that everyone in the restaurant was staring, too.

I looked at Mother, who was the only other person no longer looking at this woman. Mother was nearly finished with her beer already and was in the process of rolling her eyes when I asked, "Why is everyone staring at that woman?" I thought maybe this person was some sort of movie star or something, but my mother replied with an exceedingly droll tone, "Boobs." Grandmother overheard this comment and let out a high-pitched giggle, just as the ravishing woman was taking her seat at a table underneath one of the larger windows. Hearing Grandmother's giggle, the woman glanced at our table with her nose in the air as if she were trying to smell our insolence from across the room. Father turned back to the table, shaking his head, and let out a "Mmmm mmmm mmmm." Mother said, "Oh brother."

Grandmother was still giggling and was now holding a handkerchief over her mouth, which was the Barnard thing to do. I glanced again over at the ravishing woman's table, and her date also took a seat, so the woman moved her gaze to him and smiled widely with huge, white teeth. Mother saw me looking and looked again over her own shoulder, turned back and uttered, "She's all teeth." This time, though, we knew that Mother was trying to egg us on a bit, and as so often happened, the jokes were no longer about the person per se, but the target person had just become an inspiration to show off the family's humorous creativity when it came to ridicule.

Father, Brother, Grandmother and Mother were sharing quips, just slightly not under their breath enough, and I was feeling a bit awkward, so I kept watching the woman, wondering if she would know that the family snickering over here was talking about her.

Luckily, our waitress arrived with our dinners, and I felt some relief that the family would be focused on their dinners and not the woman. We all settled into our seats and had just begun eating when there was a strange rattling sound, followed by a shriek and then the sound of breaking glasses and gasps from other tables. My entire family turned our heads together in the direction of the sounds. We were surprised to see a large window screen, with one end on top of the ravishing woman, and the other end resting on their table. Apparently, she had attempted to adjust the drapes, which were now enveloping her, and the window screen had fallen from the window as well in the process. Drinks had been spilled and her older date was leaning back in shock, while the woman herself looked as though she was wearing the drapes, as well as being pinned under the heavy, wooden-framed screen; she was also trying to lift it all off of her, and we could see the white palms of her hands pushing on the underside of the wire mesh.

None of us gasped. None of us uttered a sound. We all turned slowly back to face one another in absolute terror that one single inkling of a smile on anyone's face would cause the entire family to cave into a pit of hysteria. We knew this would be a terrible thing to do, so with all of our might, we sat on own personal volcanoes of potential cackling, trying to resist the building pressure by acting as mundane as possible on the outside, as if what we just saw was the most normal thing ever.

Members of the hotel's staff were trying to lift the screen off of the woman, and no longer able to contain the Slapstick Gene, Grandmother said with the most perfect delivery, "Someone should have screened her before she came in."

Kaboom.

And now ...

From a handwritten note jotted by Mother about the incident with the sprinkler, transcribed for your pleasure, dated February 19, 2004:

"When Mother [Grandmother] was invited to the El Encanto for watercress sandwiches and tea (she was a reverse teetotaler – always a little too totaled for tea) by the pool, she was strolling across the lawn to the pool area when the sprinklers came on causing an MTV dance on her part, which would have impressed Michael Jackson. I caught up with her (reassuring the worst was over) and escorted her the rest of the way to a quiet corner in the pool area – a table with an umbrella for shade. Mother reached for the umbrella to adjust it and it suddenly clamped over her like an upside-down giant clam – I could hear her mumbling – kicking her exposed extremities in an attempt to free herself. When I managed to extricate her, she said, "Forget the tea – get me a DRINK!"

I immediately availed myself of the use of the handy poolside phone (I knew better) to call and order THE DRINK; no response – of course. Mother said, "Well, go to the dining room and order it there!" I responded to her now immediate need for said libation and entered the lobby, where Mrs. Kinnett (the owner of the hotel) was seated.

I explained what had happened. "Well," she said, "go find somebody and order it yourself and take it to the pool." Then she added, "And don't wear your bathing suit in here next time – it's against the rules!"

Chapter 21 — The Capture

RECORD BOOTH SUGGESTED SONG: "BILLY, DON'T BE A HERO,"
BO DONALDSON AND THE HEYWOODS

The old adage, "They always return to the scene of the crime," was true, according to the detectives who were still working on the case of Stanley A. Greene, erstwhile Halloween decoration and infamous body ". . . over there in the bushes." Clearly, the police suspected foul play, and not natural causes, or else they wouldn't still be present at all.

It stood out that we had not really heard about the continuing investigation since the discovery of the body and the El Encanto had returned, since my brother's discovery, to its regular story of debauchery, languish and neglect, already in progress.

We had been enjoying ourselves on the grounds, while fights between the parents continued almost on a daily basis, with a break only during the film festival and when Grandmother visited. We had been spending time in the Record Booth, at school, or playing with friends. Of course, we all talked about the body occasionally, mostly because it was an interesting story, and every telling required the recitation of Mother's ill-fated and wildly incorrect admonishment.

One of my mother's attributes was her ability to laugh at herself, so she also included her statement every time she retold the story. For all of us, the telling of the story usually ended with the inevitable question from the listener, which generally was, "Did they catch who did it?"

The truth was, they had not. It's not as if the investigation had stalled. Every once in a while, one of us would see a detective going in and out of various buildings or talking to a member of the staff with the requisite notepad and pen in their hands; the Santa Barbara Police Department was still on the case, but their investigation had an air of secrecy and subtlety. Whenever one of us would approach a detective to ask how it was going, they would simply smile and say, "We're working on it."

For them, too, the overgrown gardens provided multiple hiding places and stake out spots, so for all we knew, we were all being watched. No one ever saw the detectives in their actual spots, but you would occasionally see them walking to their cars, which they parked below Orpet Park, after finishing whatever they'd been doing on the property.

Underlying all of our experiences for those months was the sense that we were all living in a true crime novel. As if there weren't enough intrigue due to the general vibe of the place, we also had this little story secretly unfolding and everyone at the El Encanto was quietly aware that the police had not given up. Under-the-breath conversations among the long-term guests and staff were held in shadowy corners, everyone also tracking each other for any new information.

It might have seemed to the weekend guests that the staff and the live-ins, as we were called, were gossiping by the way the conversations sounded and appeared. The El Encanto was not advertising to new arrivals that there had been a murder victim discovered across the street from the premises because they knew, along with the appearance of the place, that this sort of publicity would likely be the financial death knell.

The official word from the front desk to us was to allow the detectives to continue their work and to basically keep our mouths shut when speaking to new guests or visitors. This word came directly from the detectives themselves, via the conduit of the hotel's front desk, and Father, being an amateur Sherlock Holmes, surmised that they were indeed on the trail of the killer, and they wanted the killer to think the investigation had stopped.

We all agreed that his reasoning made sense, so there was a feeling of comradery among all residents and staff to keep things on the hush-hush to help them catch the perpetrator. This caused a moldering tension at the El Encanto; since the detectives seemed mostly focused on being on the grounds, in street clothing, they must have believed that the killer was at the hotel, too. Put simply, it turned out that we were all living with a murderer and had to pretend we were not.

This fact made walking the gardens at night quite a bit more of an adventure, and what had already been a fractured fairytale experience before the discovery of the body had become an actual place of death and true fear, where I was always looking over my shoulder.

My routes to here and there on the property became even more secret, and I often chose the brick paths less traveled. I snuck around the place like a shadow, and if I heard foot falls approaching me, I would leap into the overgrowth or hide behind a bush, observing in silence.

On one particular evening, I was making my way at night down the path to the east of the pool area, which also happened to be in front of Mrs. Kinnett's own cottage.

It was certainly a Villa fit for a queen – well, a queen of a derelict country – and was a bit more stylish as all of the '30's Spanish-style were. I was always intrigued by those units and curious about the splendor that was likely revealed within. I glanced over at her front door and it was slightly ajar. The door was flanked by two dog statues, which were custom made in the images of Mrs. Kinnett's two Pekingese dogs, Brandy and Cognac.

Given the fact that there was a murderer on the loose, I was a bit nervous. I was debating whether or not to approach the door and maybe just shut it for her when I heard some footsteps approaching from the path that led from the front of the hotel all the way to the east side of the property, one of the darkest corners. The foots were shuffling along and I heard a grave cough. That's all I needed, so I leaped with the quiet skill of a hired assassin onto Mrs. Kinnett's front porch, stepped through her door, and closed it behind me.

I was now inside what I considered to be a small palace. Once I entered, I found myself on a landing with a banister looking over a large living room one level down, with a big fireplace and full of antiques, including a piano. I immediately realized that this unit, unlike every other one, was not in disrepair or dated. It was clean and beautiful. I quickly felt a little angry, realizing that our Grande Dame was using whatever funds she had to make herself the most comfortable. In my mind, this was not the spirit of hospitality, so I felt justified in trespassing into her home to seek the truth.

I checked out her entire residence – the bedroom was particularly lavish – and each piece of finery I found, the more resentful I became. There was a huge vase of flowers on her dresser and I wondered if she was buying flowers while we suffered with an open sewer during those early months?

How had such a person come by ownership of such a hotel? It seemed to me that the wrong people were the ones in control, generally everywhere, including within my household. I wished I had the ability to fire them all, hand Mrs. Kinnett and my parents their pink slips, and send them packing. Something about seeing all of this luxury in her Villa just exaggerated the disparities in my life, and I felt more and more aggravated the longer I stood in her home.

I walked up to the piano and noticed a large picture of a man in uniform; there was a small, oval plaque at the bottom of the frame, which read "Our son - RIP." The picture also had a black ribbon draped across one corner.

Apparently, being in her Villa wasn't going to last long because while I was standing in her living room below, I heard the front door open. Like a hare, I jumped behind her sofa and heard the familiar wheels as they entered the top floor landing, bouncing across the grout between the tiles on the floor. Pushing behind her was Mrs. Penner, and they were in conversation about a broken sprinkler and flooding in the "northeast corner." I shrunk down as most I could – this was no time for The Bigger – and listened as they continued down the landing to the top floor master bedroom.

It occurred to me that Mrs. Kinnett must never be in the lower level room that I was in, unless there was some way to wheel in from the outside. I nervously glanced around for a door and finally spied one in the southwest corner. Hearing their voices from upstairs (it sounded as though Mrs. Penner was helping her highness into her bed,) I tiptoed over to the door. It was deadbolted with no way to open it from the inside without a key. I was going to have to go back upstairs to the landing and make my way somehow silently to the front door.

As I crept slowly to the stairs, I heard Mrs. Penner's voice getting louder. She appeared at the top of the landing and began walking as though heading for the stairs to walk down to the lower level. I dove behind the sofa again and heard her feet come down the stairs. She yelled upstairs to her mother, "Oh, I just thought I heard something down here."

Mrs. Kinnett replied, "It's probably one of those obnoxious, creepy little boys." My heart turned to cement within my chest. Did she mean my brother and me? We were the "creepy" ones? It was all I could do to keep myself from standing up and yelling, "Creepy? You are the Mayor of Creepy-ville!" Instead, I coiled a bit lower on the floor.

Mrs. Penner had stopped on the second to the lowest stair and was quietly standing there, straining to listen closely to hear the tiniest of noises. I stayed perfectly still, my face pressed against the floor to make my breathing quieter, something that I had seen in a movie.

After standing there for about three minutes, Mrs. Penner turned and began walking back up the stairs. She walked back into the master bedroom and Mrs. Kinnett said, "Maybe we have mice again."

Hearing the continuing sounds of Mrs. Kinnett getting comfortable in her bed, while she delivered a series of "May I have my ..." requests to her daughter, I stood up slowly and began to make my way to the stairs when out of the corner of my eye, I saw a shadow standing in the northwest corner of the room. I couldn't see who it was but I heard a hushed, gravelly voice say, "Hiya Boy."

I instantly darted up the stairs like lightning and was at and through the front door in a flash. I didn't care if Mrs. Penner heard me, and I didn't care if Mrs. Kinnett heard me. I was startled to the point that nothing else mattered but getting out of that Villa. I moved so quickly that I left the front door open behind me and as I ran up the path, I heard Mrs. Penner faintly say, "Oh John, it's you."

As I made my way quickly past the lily pond and arbor, my mind was burning with realizations and questions. How come Mrs. Penner and her mother weren't surprised to see John in the villa? Was he there the entire time I was – I can't imagine how I didn't notice him standing there before. Was he going to tell them I was in her house? What would happen now and how would I explain the intrusion? The fear and anxiety only pushed me harder to run as fast as I could, and I blew by two men standing in the shadows just below our place.

Into my bedroom's side door and under my covers I went directly. I could hear the family out in the sitting room and my mother yelled, "Good – now stay in!" in my general direction.

I drifted off into an uneasy sleep until we were all awakened at about two in the morning by the flashing lights of many police cars. We all wearily emerged from our rooms, coming together in the sitting room and my mother said, "Uh oh, I wonder what's going on." We all followed her through the kitchen to the back door. She pulled aside the yellow drapery and peaked outside.

"Oh ... there are three or four police cars stopped on Mission Ridge and they have their big search lights on." Their presence was all the more eerie since no sirens were blaring – only their lights on and their motors off.

Father asked Mother to step aside, and he opened the back door and stepped onto the porch next to the pigeon hutch. He bobbed and weaved a bit to get a good look at the scene and said, "They've got someone in the rear seat of one of their cars."

It felt strangely like a replay of the night the body was taken away, but being so late, we couldn't be sure if other neighbors were aware of the happenings at all. We were only up because the lights were so close to Villa 100 that they awakened us. Father couldn't see anyone else but about six officers standing in the center of the stopped cars speaking quietly to one another.

Father stepped back into the kitchen, shut the door and looked at all of us. "We better just leave them alone and let them do their job. I don't know what's happening, but it seems as though they've arrested somebody."

After a few minutes, one of the police cars motors started, and the car began to slowly move up Mission Ridge. Through our kitchen door's window, I could just barely see the silhouette of a small person sitting in the back seat – the bright search lights of the other police cars created the perfect contrast. As the moving car became visible for only a moment between the spikes of two large century plants, I could see the outline of a golfer's cap on the passenger's head.

Chapter 22 — The Murder

RECORD BOOTH SUGGESTED SONG: "EARACHE MY EYE,"
CHEECH & CHONG

In retrospect, it was obvious who had murdered Stanley A. Greene – that's what the detective was saying as he stood in the screened front porch of Villa 100. Apparently, the police knew all along but needed the killer to incriminate himself, so they could make the arrest and prosecute, without a shadow of doubt.

Even for 1975, the detective was strangely forthcoming with all of the information – I suppose it was a watertight case, and they weren't worried about letting out the details of the crime or perhaps he felt that our family, more than any other, needed to know the truth, since my brother had found Mr. Greene's body and we were, therefore, directly impacted.

Listening to this sitting on my parents' bedroom floor, it occurred to me that there wasn't a dark corner of the El Encanto that didn't contain a shadow of doubt – it was all shadows, the gardens full of overgrown anxieties, the abandoned bungalows filled with forgotten regrets. The walls and corners everywhere were stuffed with the highs and lows of human existence. The El Encanto's foundations crumbled under the weight of many indiscretions. How heavy a burden the property carried, least of which was harboring a murderer.

But harbor a murderer it did, and as I listened to the story as it was told to my parents, I became more and more aware of what actual danger I was in when I had been sneaking my way around the property at all hours, turning over and examining every stone, creeping behind every shrubbery, and opening every drawer in the strange basement rooms under the hotel's main building.

Stanley A. Greene and Hiya Boy John were apparently friends for some time. When Stanley was asked to leave the rundown, pay-by-the-week room at downtown's dive hotel, Hotel Santa Barbara (another place that had shoved its glory days untidily in its rear pocket), it was due to his drinking and extensive gambling debts, which easily led to him constantly being behind on his rent. Stanley and Hiya boy had been poker buddies, both playing in secretive money games around town since after World War II. Their fortunes and debts were intertwined, and they were forced to support one another whenever they could, because frankly, it seemed that no one else would have them.

The detective was typically insensitive to the plight of the two men, but Mother and Father could immediately access their compassion, as they heard the significant points to the story, my mother would let out "Oh boy," or "Oh, how sad." Father would just grunt and even though I couldn't see him, I knew he was doing his sympathetic head shaking as he heard the story. Both of them were uniquely compassionate when it came to veterans, and both Stanley and Hiya Boy were veterans who were clearly traumatized by their service and drinking to medicate themselves. Thus, a downward spiral began that took decades to develop, culminating in one fateful evening at the El Encanto.

After his eviction, Stanley and Hiya Boy concocted a plan so Stanley could live rent free in the basement of the main building. When I heard this, a shiver ran through my body when I realize I had been in his room – that was the place with the old, saggy mattress and the dresser full of sharp objects and clothing. Was that strange sensation that came over me, the one that made me faint – was that Stanley's ghost trying to contact me? Contemplating this, I felt nauseated and worried how my presence in the murder victim's room could be misunderstood.

The detective continued that one evening, Stanley and Hiya Boy had been playing poker in Hiya Boy's room under the row of single garages that were near Villa 100. They had been drinking quite a bit, and Stanley was losing. A disagreement began between the two old friends, which caused Stanley to exit the room and stagger down, as quietly as he could, to his basement hide away.

One of the oddest facts to arise from the investigation was the discovery that Stanley actually had a home, on Mission Ridge, just up from where his body was discovered. Furthermore, he had a wife.

A baffling fact for the police department to consider – and we too were taken by surprise by this news. The police were unable to share information about his wife or the reasons why Stanley had chosen to shack up at the hotel with Hiya Boy; their discussions with Stanley's wife were private and would continue.

Evidence showed that the two men were indeed, at least part-time for Stanley, living rather feral existences and furnishing their separate El Encanto rooms like pack rats, gathering the forgotten things of the hotel around them, feathering their nests from what was essentially a free secondhand store. Hiya Boy's room and the hallway outside of it were also filled with old hotel items. The odd thing was that both men had also collected women's garments and based on some uncovered evidence, they knew that the men weren't opposed to wearing the women's clothing, as there were old photographs found in Hiya Boy's room of them both dressed in feminine garb. The detective stated, "We don't know if they were 'boyfriends' or what, but there was definitely something unusual going on between the two men. There was evidence that the victim's clothing was placed on his body post-mortem"

Again, a shiver seized my body – the brogues! I could only conclude that it had been Hiya Boy gazing at me that night through the open window on the 4th of July. Mother must have had the same thought because she gasped when she heard this. Thinking about some drunk, old man, staggering around in women's clothes and shoes, and then stopping to stare at me in the moonlight absolutely freaked me out some more. Perhaps not just any old man – the murderer himself – late in the evening, looking down on me. Or worse – had it been Stanley's ghost looking at me? Was he forever doomed to walk the grounds of the hotel for eternity wearing a dress?

From Hiya Boy's confession and statement, on the night of the murder, whenever it was, Stanley had staggered home after the disagreement and Hiya Boy remained in his own room drinking. But he was upset. Here he was, providing room and board – and stealing food from the kitchen – and Stanley owed a lot of money to Hiya Boy, lost throughout a multitude of poker games; Hiya Boy decided to go down to Stanley's basement hovel, get his money, and throw Stanley out of the hotel. He felt that Stanley was taking advantage of him by remaining at the "nice" hotel longer than Hiya Boy had intended. The cooks were beginning to notice the missing food, more than the stuff that Hiya Boy himself was taking, and so he was worried that the "Lady" (meaning Mrs. Kinnett) would find out about the squatter living in the basement and remove them both. There would be no place for either of them to go, except perhaps joining the legions of "bums" living down in the extensive trees and shrubbery that grew out of the gully between the railroad tracks and Cabrillo Boulevard across from East Beach. For some reason, Stanley did not want to go home to his wife.

On the night in question, Hiya Boy entered the abandoned basement guest rooms in the hotel's main building, through the same door I did, walked down the hall, past the other rooms, and then entered Stanley's room to find him passed out, drunk. Hiya Boy began to dig through Stanley's belongings and upon opening the top drawer of his dresser, found a collection of ice picks from the kitchen. In his obliterated drunkenness, Hiya Boy gathered that Stanley was secretly plotting to murder him to get out of his debts. In a flash, Hiya Boy had grabbed an ice pick, turned around, and plunged it into Stanley's abdomen (likely aiming for his chest) while he was still passed-out. This coincided with the position of Stanley's body as described by my brother – Stanley was in the classic sleeping pose – on his side, resting his head on his hands, which were in the prayer position.

No one knows if Stanley died instantly or not, but another stunning fact was that Stanley's body was not immediately moved from the bed where he was killed. A lot of the objects in the hallway – the mannequins, the furniture, the old equipment, were moved from the various rooms in the basement into the hallway as to make exploring almost impossible. The only reason that Stanley was eventually moved was when the kitchen staff had complained to Hiya Boy that they could smell "dead rats or something" emanating from the basement underneath the kitchen, and Hiya Boy realized he had to do something else with the body. Stanley's body was moved via a wheelbarrow, which was found in one of the abandoned cottages, and the wheelbarrow had just enough dried flakes of blood, buried under leaves and dirt, to tie the samples taken to Stanley. Of course, I thought for sure I knew which of the abandoned cottages had harbored the wheelbarrow.

Still, the detectives didn't feel as though they had enough evidence to arrest Hiya Boy, so they waited. This was planned from the beginning – that's why the small article in the Santa Barbara News Press was so minimal and vague – the police department didn't want anyone to know that they had any clues as to the perpetrator. What was also tricky was the fact that Stanley's torso had been fairly ripped apart by neighborhood dogs – and perhaps visiting show dogs – coyotes, raccoons and who knew what else, so they really had very little physical evidence that Stanley had been murdered at all. There was also no physical evidence that Stanley had crawled into the bushes himself and simply died there. The investigators determined after reviewing the discovery site that the body had been placed there, which meant the man had died somewhere else. Pretending the investigation had quieted down, they secretly staked-out the bushes where Stanley was discovered based on an interesting psychological fact – the well-known assumption that the guilty will always return to the scene of the crime, and this time, it worked.

Hiya Boy must have thought that the investigation was over and that he had gotten away with it somehow because, on the night of his arrest, he was apprehended while trying to place a box of Stanley's belongings, which included dishes, a couple of books, some shoes, some underwear, in the exact same spot in the bushes where he had dumped the body. The police were lying in wait for him and they had the evidence they needed to make the arrest. Hiya Boy had been cooperative and had filled-in the blanks for the detectives and in their minds, the case was closed.

My head was spinning with all of the times I had seen Hiya Boy around the property. It seemed like he had hidden passageways because he could practically appear out of nowhere at any time. He had gained his nickname for this very reason. Around almost every corner I turned, there he was, glancing up from whatever he was working on and saying, "Hiya Boy." The truth became clear to me that while the detectives may have been watching all of us, Hiya Boy was watching me, knowing my habit of exploring everything on the hotel's grounds. That must have been his figure that appeared on the at the end of the hallway the night I passed-out in Stanley's old room. I was also concerned about how much the detectives knew about me – they must have seen me coming and going from the side bedroom door, watching me as I made my excursions day and night. I was gritting my teeth in anticipation of the detective saying something related to me, but he never did. After finishing filling-in Mother and Father, he simply asked that they keep the details to themselves and let the Santa Barbara Police Department finish up; my parents agreed.

I heard the screen door swing shut, so I jumped up and made my way back to my bedroom. I heard my parents discussing things quietly in their room, and then Father left Villa 100 and I saw Mother walk by my bedroom door, heading to the kitchen to start dinner.

Lying down on my bed and staring at the stained ceiling, all I could think to myself was that this was just another typical evening in little Villa 100, the wee cottage hidden behind overgrown oleanders and slumbering under the canopies of tall eucalyptus trees. There was a shift in the energy of the grounds, and even though very few people knew it, we were in a much safer place. I looked around my room at the old wall paper, the chipping paint on the window frames, listened to the sounds of the creaking floorboards and water rushing through the loud plumbing as my mother prepared dinner in the kitchen on the other side of our excruciatingly thin bathroom wall, and I truly fell deeper in love with the El Encanto, every bit of its overgrown, moldy, murderous, forgotten-ess was indeed my true home.

Chapter 23 — The Showing of Hers

RECORD BOOTH SUGGESTED SONG: "CROCODILE ROCK,"
ELTON JOHN

After Hiya Boy's arrest, the El Encanto seemed more peaceful. It's interesting how a place, whether it be a room, a house, a cottage or even a hotel and gardens can absorb the anxieties of those who dwell within. Now it seemed the property itself was more at peace with the absence of the strange energy of its deadly maintenance man and gardener.

It had been months since the body was first discovered, and with only a few long-term residents and staff mixed with a transient population of guests, the memories and talk of the body, the murder and the subsequent arrest were tucked away, shoved into the deepest recesses of the gardens, filed in some musty old dresser in the abandoned cottages, folded into the ever-increasing lore of Storke's Folly, and effectively archived with everything else the hotel had seen, adding to the collection of the forgotten episodes - and everyone moved on. We were heading into fall, which in Southern California could be one of the hottest periods of the year, so it still felt like summer at the El Encanto. We continued to invite friends up for a swim in the pool, and with school in session, fewer took us up on our offer.

My brother had progressed further into his fifteenth year of life, and he was more interested in surfing at The Pit (the local nickname for Hendry's Beach) and spending time with his friends, likely smoking pot and sneaking beers. His hair had grown long and was streaked with blond from his dumping of hydrogen peroxide on it and baking in the sun. Mother nicknamed him "The Man Who Isn't There," due to his long absences from home. He often spent the nights with friends, which was fine with me because I got the bedroom to myself. We were no longer particularly cordial to one another - he saw me as a child and saw himself as a grownup.

In addition to his deep-seated issues with my very existence, something in the way I conducted myself really seemed to bother him – perhaps it was my inaccessibility or the fact that I simply wasn't really interested in the same things. Other kids my age were just beginning to get pulled into the scene at The Pit, but I found the scene not very enticing. They were a bit rowdy and tough down there, with a lot of emphasis on the sort of male fronting that young men do, showing off with daring stunts on skateboards, bikes and surfboards, talking about the huge waves and wipe-outs. Long hair was a serious trend and most teenagers looked rather frightening to me.

I was clearly going to be late for puberty and was still very small physically, with no sign of the tiniest bit of adolescence. When it came to grandiose displays of physical prowess, I avoided these practices at all costs. I was afraid of hurting myself, I didn't like doing crazy stunts, and also didn't like being teased or being called a "chicken." I just avoided the situation by hanging out with Anthony, when he could, or by myself, lost in my daydreams and seeing my visions, and keeping it all to myself, and processing it in The Bigger. The irony was that my reality would be a fantasy world to others, so I never shared what I saw or what I knew. Mother would often comment that I kept my cards close to my chest.

I was noticing some other things, too, though, while observing the other kids who were visiting the hotel and in particular, the boys. I had a fascination with other boy's leg hair – their blond wisps shining against their tanned skin, which caused me to have a funny feeling inside. I wasn't sure what it was, but I knew somehow that this was something to also keep to myself. I would find myself staring at boys my age, and older men, from behind my sunglasses – and experiencing feelings of relaxation and pleasure in some new, subtle ways.

One day at the pool, I hit the jackpot in my voyeuristic lottery; one of the guest boy's fathers at the pool. He was a handsome, muscular, hairy man – probably in his mid-thirties, and I waited in great anticipation for the removal of his shirt. When he took it off, I couldn't swallow – he had a thick pelt of fur running all the way past his navel, and I didn't know what to do with the feelings I was having. There was a stirring in my shorts, and I covered my lap with a towel.

This manly man dove into the pool, and I watched as he climbed out the other end, the water plastering his thick leg hair to his skin. I didn't know it at the time, but I was having my first truly erotic feeling and unfortunately, had no context for it and didn't know what it was. I just immediately felt ashamed and I had no idea why.

Of course, I had heard and had been subject to name calling like any other boy – I was called "sissy" or "faggot" or "fag" for the slightest signs of weakness, like missing a thrown Frisbee or ball – but we all called each other that, so I associated these words with weakness rather than sexuality. We used to even play a game called "Smear the Queer," which involved a Hippity-Hop and a football.

Despite the lingo of gayness being in our childhood vernacular, I had not been exposed in any way to the concept of men having sex with other men – I wasn't thinking of sex at all yet, truth be told, perhaps due to my stunted development. I was curious like most young children were, but I still didn't equate this behavior with sexuality, and certainly not homosexuality, a word that was never uttered in our home.

Mother and Father had friends in Hollywood back in their past who apparently had been gay couples. They never used the word "gay" or said, "gay couple" rather referring only to these couples by their names, like their friends "Roy and George," who I just knew were always together

– lived together, traveled together – and visited my parents together, but there was no mention of them as a "couple."

So, there I was at the pool, having a rapid heartbeat and the smallest of erections, looking at this boy's father with utter fascination. He walked from exiting the pool over to a chair next to a table and sat down. Out popped his penis, slipping from the confines of his very short swimming trunks and I was confronted with my first view of an adult man's cock.

I was captivated. It hung down from the chair, a bit darker than the rest of his skin. His balls were covered with hair and I could just make-out the dark mat of his pubic hair above. I didn't even know at that point about all the hair, so I was equally sexually excited and just plain amazed by it. Then, realizing he was exposing himself, he quickly stood up, reached into his shorts and readjusted himself, but the sight I had just witnessed was emblazoned into my memory and when I shut my eyes, I could still see it. With my eyes closed, I tilted my head back, in sort of a Stevie Wonder-esque headshake, picturing his amazing penis, and when I returned to center, I opened my eyes and the man was looking at me with a very inquisitive expression.

I turned my head quickly, feeling busted for a moment, and acted casually as if I were just observing the surrounding flora and fauna. When I looked back, the man was gathering his belongings and calling to his son to get out of the pool. I tried my hardest not to watch as his wet, muscular legs walked away from me. I had a longing for him I didn't understand – I wanted to go with him.

Feeling embarrassed, discouraged and distracted, I stood up from my chaise and realized immediately that my penis was erect – was it because of the man, I wondered? But boys are only supposed to like girls, right? At this point in my life, I wouldn't even know what to do with my penis if I were confronted by a willing girl – I knew nothing of intercourse, my parents avoiding the subject without fail. All I knew was that my penis felt good when I rubbed it but that was about as far as I understood anything.

I folded my towel in my arms in such a way that it hung down and provided covering over my crotch, and I walked out the pool's exit to the east because it was closer. All the way back home, my flip-flops smacking my feet as I strolled along the now familiar brick pathways, I mulled over what had occurred. I had never felt anything like that before, but I was equally scared of experiencing it again at the same time hoping it would happen again.

I was very conflicted when I entered my bedroom and relieved to find that I was home alone. I walked into the bathroom and draped my towel over the edge of the clawfoot tub, so it could dry off. I had the funniest feeling – a kind of loneliness suddenly, like someone who has a crush on somebody and it's pointless, as I had seen so often in movies. There was a deep sense of isolation. My feelings were so out of context with what limited information I had about the world of love and sex, my mind was almost blank except, I could not stop thinking about that hairy man and I had the feeling that somehow what I was feeling was just plain wrong. These feelings were big, bigger than The Bigger, and on an entirely new level. I wanted to know where that man was – which cottage – I contemplated how I could see him in the shower – could I look through a window? I started imagining what he looked like completely naked and my fading erection stood at attention once again.

I started to make the connection that with my imagination, I could picture things that would actually make my penis feel really good, so with that in mind, I wandered over to my bed, and fell on my back, appreciating the cool covers in the warm air. I reached down with my hand to see if my penis was as hard as I thought it was, and the more I touched it, the better it felt. So, I pictured the man naked, and kept touching and rubbing my penis. It was my first feelings of this sort of pleasure, and I believed I was the only one to have possibly discovered it! This was available all of this time? This experience, and these feelings I had about this man, I decided I must keep them all well inside of The Bigger; nobody had to know, and with that thought, I stopped worrying about what the world might think, and really got into thinking about the man and touching myself.

The deeper I thought about him, rubbing and rubbing myself, picturing his legs, his arms, his penis, his face, all the hair and his eyes, the more pleasure was mine. I lost track of time, and after a while, I felt exhausted, then fell asleep with my right hand inserted into my swimming trunks.

I awakened to my brother saying, "What are you doing?" I quickly jerked my hand out of my swimming trunks and said, "Nothing." My brother just rolled his eyes.

Combined with my own realization that I was experiencing these new, strange feelings, and the fact that Casey had perhaps noticed my hand down my trunks (I couldn't be really sure if he had, I wasn't going to ask) created a deep feeling of shame and embarrassment, and I wanted to cleanse myself of the incident. I decided then and there, I was going to only focus on the feelings I had been having about girls – and I did have those feelings. I was very curious about girls – I admired their beauty and flowing hair, the way their faces were so often much prettier than boys.

I had been, off and on, hanging out with Mrs. Penner's daughter, Heidi, who was around two years older than I and was often visiting the hotel. She swam in the pool a lot, and whenever she was at the hotel, we'd sit and talk on one of the many benches.

I had something of a slight crush on this older girl. Her blonde hair had been made a radiant gold by repeated exposure to the sun and swimming pools. Her skin was a dark tan, and her eyes, a bright blue. We looked a little like siblings, and very often, other guests of the hotel would make the comment that we were a cute brother and sister as they strolled by.

Heidi had another gift to bestow upon me in addition to her

intermittent friendship – a dictionary of words and phrases Mother had told me never to say. I learned the words, "shit" and "fuck" from Heidi Penner, and I knew what "shit" was, but I didn't understand "fuck."

So, early one particularly warm evening, we sat on the bench overlooking the pool from atop the grassy hill, enjoying the twinkling lights of Santa Barbara below, while we ate some ice cream out of cups provided by one of our "contacts" in the kitchen. So, I asked her, "What does "fuck" mean, anyway?"

She exploded with the giggles, the ice cream in her mouth bubbling on her lips. "You don't know what "fuck" is?" Heidi said, eyebrows raised with condescension and amazement.

"No, not really ... I mean, I think I know, but I'm not sure," I responded so meekly that it made it obvious that I didn't know.

"It's when a man sticks his dick inside of a woman, you know, in her pussy," she said casually taking another bite of her ice cream.

"Pussy?" I said, wanted to grab the word and put it back in my mouth as soon as I said it.

"Oh my god, no way – do you even know what a "pussy" is?" she quickly replied, almost speaking over me. She was beginning to grow impatient with my naivete.

"Boys have dicks and girls have pussies – it's like a hole where you have your dick, but instead, girls have a hole," pointing at her crotch while she said this.

As soon as the realization came to me – that when a guy's dick is hard, he can actually slide it inside of some hole on a girl – I shuddered. All I could think about it how close you'd have to be to a girl in order to do this and it was a level of closeness that made me really uncomfortable, even to think about it.

We sat there in silence for a few minutes, just eating our ice cream. I was having to rewrite the story in my head about men and women, marriage and children. I'd been operating under the belief that women became pregnant when they kissed their husband at their wedding – I thought that's what the "you may kiss the bride" line was all about – now that they were married, the man was allowed to kiss his bride in a way that created a child inside of her.

Now, suddenly, we were talking about men taking their private parts and literally inserting them inside of some woman, and the thought made me feel a little ill.

I stood up and said, "I … I … uh … I think I want to go home now. Bye." As I walked away from Heidi she said, "Hey – by the way – Fuck You!" and cackled like a witch.

That would be the last time I ever hung out with Heidi Penner alone. Our discussion was so adult that it almost seemed mean to me. I placed her in my mental file of kids that were under suspicion – she now frightened me a little, and I just wanted to get as far away from her as I could.

I was curious – what did this alleged "hole" look like? I certainly didn't want to see Heidi's hole now, so I began pondering how I could get a look at one of those things in some easy, undetectable and private way. It was more blank curiosity than anything sexually exciting for me – I was on another scientific expedition of discovery – and I knew some girls that I trusted, and one of those was my friend for the last three years, Mary.

Mary and I had met on Butterfly beach when we were seven. I had an extensive collection of these small, rubber animals that I played with frequently, always taking a couple to the beach whenever we went. I did dangerous things with them, like burying them in the sand or even worse, taking them into the surf, where many were pulled from fingers by the waves. One of my favorites, a tiny elephant, was yanked from my hand by the whitewater, and I was running around on the moving, tidal sand looking for it when I heard a nice voice say, "Here it is." There was Mary, holding my elephant, wet sand splashed on her legs and her pink, one-piece bathing suit. She collected the same animals, so understood the obsession, and we stood for a moment in the crashing surf discussing our collections and which animals we each had back home.

Mary asked why I had chosen to take the elephant to the beach that day, and my response was that I heard elephants never forget, so I didn't want the elephant to be mad at me for leaving him at home. This made perfect sense to Mary and we became friends instantly.

We introduced our mothers to each other, and they also formed a friendship that would last decades and include international travel together, but we couldn't know all of what was to come while clutching our animals in the waves that day.

Fast forward a few years later, and Mary was one of my closest friends and as it goes, she was often at the El Encanto pool enjoying herself while our mothers chatted on their chaise lounges.

I made a plan that the next time Mary and her mother came over from Montecito to spend an afternoon with us at the pool, I would ask Mary if I could have a look. Mary and I had never gone there before, so it might take her a little aback if I asked, but I knew that we were good friends and much older now, so we could have an adult discussion about exactly what it would mean and not mean, too.

After several days, I heard from Mother that Mary and her mother, Aileen, were indeed coming over that day to hangout by the pool. I was really excited to see Mary, in spite of the fact that I felt a little shameful that I had an agenda this time.

Mother and I met them at the pool, and Mary and I immediately jumped-in, playing games like Tea Party at the bottom, showing each other our prowess with safe stunts such as underwater handstands, racing dives, cannonballs, swimming styles and submerged somersaults where the ultimate contest was to not have to plug your nose with your fingers but rather, being able to complete the maneuver without water entering your nasal cavities.

The sun was shining brightly overhead, and Mary's shiny blonde hair looked like spun gold, being wet and extra sun bleached, revealing to me that she was spending a lot of time at Butterfly Beach. Watching the sun's reflection off of the pool water into her giggling face caused feelings of happiness for me.

Remembering that I had a project to complete, I asked if Mary wanted to walk with me back to Villa 100 and grab some snacks, which was only partially a ruse because I really wanted the snacks, too. Mother had informed earlier that ordering food from the restaurant via the pool phone was off-limits today, due to money concerns, so she had purchased tortilla chips and sodas at the market, and they were waiting for Mary and me back at the cottage.

We told our mothers that we would be right back, and I'm not even sure that they heard us because they were so deep in conversation; it made Mary and I happy to see that our mothers were such good friends, too, a fact for which we took full credit.

We walked my favorite pathway to the east of the lily pond, barefoot this time, feeling the coarseness of the bricks under our feet and enjoying every minute of it. Realizing that my brother might be home, I took a detour to a particularly overgrown part of the garden and as soon as we were deep in the vines, I turned to Mary and said, "I wanted … to … umm … ask you … can I, umm, see it?"

Mary replied, "See what?"

I sheepishly pointed to her crotch; I could see two vertical humps underneath her tight, wet bathing suit, which made me even more curious. Girls don't even have balls I bet, I exclaimed loudly within The Bigger.

Mary looked at where my finger was pointing, and she asked, "Why?" She seemed a little stressed-out.

"I've just never seen a girl's before, so I'm just curious – I don't have anyone else to ask."

Mary thought about it for a moment and was unperturbed. "No biggie. Sure, why not?" she said casually, and pulled the crotch of her bathing suit to the side. What I saw amazed me – it sort of looked like a mouth but going up and down. Mary looked at me and covered herself up.

"Okay you pervert, let me see yours then," she said with a grin that told me that everything was fine, and this was all in fun.

I pulled down the waistband of my swimming trunks, and she looked and shrugged, giggling a little more. "Can we go get the chips and sodas now?"

Years later ...

It was decades before we would ever speak of the peeks-at-each-other's-junk moment again. It happened about thirty years later, at Mary's fortieth birthday party. Her mother Aileen had long since passed away, but her father was still alive and was in attendance with his wife. John was a rather good father, albeit a bit uptight and conservative. He was always dressed impeccably and had an elegant air in all he did. An attorney in San Francisco, he had built quite an estate for himself, so we all behaved ourselves around him. He knew that I was gay because I had come-out several years before, but I never spoke to him directly about this because I wasn't sure how he would react.

At Mary's party, the champagne was flowing in the little restaurant in North Beach where we all had gathered. The time of the evening came when toasts to Mary were being made, and fueled by at least three flutes of bubbly, I stood and proposed a toast, forgetting that Mary's proper father was in attendance.

I said, "Here's to you Mary, my oldest, dearest friend and the girl who showed me hers!" Everyone laughed uncomfortably, except John, who kept blinking his eyes as he slowly processed what this meant exactly.

Mary stood up, too, and replied, "And, look what happened!"

Chapter 24 — The Winter (of our discontent)

RECORD BOOTH SUGGESTED SONG: "SUNSHINE ON MY SHOULDERS,"
JOHN DENVER

As summer will, the Summer of '74 ended, the extended warm weather into fall was over, and the inherent vibes left without saying goodbye properly. Afterward, I was just back in school, in fifth grade, and counting the days until the winter break.

An odd thing had happened over the summer – we were all surprised to see that I had actually had a growth spurt! I was a bit taller and for the first time in my life, I was not the shortest kid in my class.

I think the time at the hotel had taken its toll – the frights, the ghosts, the murder, the investigation, the kitten, and my burgeoning feelings toward men – it all added up in my head and the sum of the total was "all too much." I could feel myself bursting a bit at the seams and being in school I felt very far advanced in comparison to my classmates. I didn't notice it was happening, but all of the emotional and intellectual requirements of dealing with our strange life at the hotel had propelled me even a few extra miles into adulthood, and the other children seemed rather simple to me.

These big topics of murder investigations, and the dynamics between Mother and Father that I had no choice but to witness in such tight quarters, had an impact on me that I didn't notice until I was with other children to provide the needed contrast. All of that stretching into The Bigger, and all of those times that I had grown to my one-hundred-foot size, had caused me to grow in ways here in this physical plane of reality.

Plus, I had a sickness inside of me. The decay of my childhood was more than well underway, and I started to see the world for what it was. I was no longer able to really separate myself, at least energetically, from the adults who were my teachers. I saw them as the bedraggled, underpaid grown-ups that they were, struggling to make ends meet in this expensive town, just like my family. I knew that they were likely going home to their own fights with their husbands or wives, because the separation of the poor from the rich in Santa Barbara was vast. To be "middleclass" in Santa Barbara, would be to be considered "rich" in any other town.

For months I had been watching the Santa Barbara elite come and go from the El Encanto's gardens, restaurant, and hotel, treating it as rather a novelty to stay there, I suppose, and this opened up my mind and provided a bigger picture that no fifth grader should ever be concerned about.

The cramped Villa 100, and the Mercedes bus to school, and my fantasy of being one of the "elite" or at least pretending to be, was unsustainable when faced with my new, larger, adult view. I couldn't kid the kid in me any longer, so I recognized that I was a poor one, going to an elementary school, right next to the freeway, in Santa Barbara, and living temporarily in a rundown cottage at a hotel because my parents had been unable to find a better solution. Feigning glamor had become a false antidote to impoverished obscurity, and that fall was the birth of my search for real answers rather than false ones.

Because of our financial situation, we had been subjected to all sorts of unpleasantries at the hotel, including the bad plumbing, dangerous electrical and unsafe conditions in an overgrown garden often full of weekend strangers. Plus, there were the dangers to us as individuals within a family unit – the rooms were too close to each other, so the soups of each of our own psyches kept spilling into one another's bowls. We were all suffering from "Villa Fever."

As the first few weeks of school progressed, I felt my bitterness growing with regard to my home life and situation. At recess, I would look wistfully at the freeway through the chain link fence of the playground, remembering all of the much better schools in Santa Barbara that I was not attending. I couldn't know then that a different school may not have made a difference, since I would be packing my own personal pain into my lunchbox regardless of what school I was bused to.

There were numerous private schools available – including a Christian Day School - where my brother and I had only lasted two and three weeks respectively, which was another story onto itself, an experiment gone wrong that happened a couple years before we moved to the El Encanto. The point was that we had tried a nicer private school, only to fail miserably; because of our family environment, we were both too "feral" for most places, which relegated us to the lowest rung of the public-school system.

Filled with all of this angst and feeling more like an adult than a fifth grader, I began to show uncharacteristic bad behavior around the school yard, breaking through the perimeter fortifications of The Bigger of my own volition.

In class, I was the model student. I had been accelerated into an experimental type of teaching, which included a room devoid of the standard desks and chairs, instead replaced with elevated bunk bed-style lofts, sofas, couches and reclining chairs. I was given the opportunity for independent study, which essentially meant that I could choose various subjects myself and complete assignments and tests at my own pace. I was also given leave to choose my own books for recreational reading. This style of classwork and the environment were perfectly suited to me, and I immediately dove into my learning with a voracious appetite. The idea of not having to follow along, or complete any studies in a particular order, and especially, not needing to be in synch with other students fit my personality well.

Outside during the recesses were an entirely different subject. I began taking risks. For example, there was an afternoon where I knew all of the teachers were gathered together for a meeting in a room with open windows, so I accepted the dare of another kid to stomp on an empty milk carton right outside of the teacher's meeting to hopefully cause enough of a POP, that all inside would jump. As soon as my foot met the top of the carton, I realized that the carton was not empty, but in fact was full, so a spray of milk shot through the windows, hitting several of the teachers. Afterward, at the principal's office, I was met with confused looks because I had never done such a thing before – there was general concern for me, and my tangential and harried explanation to them resulted in my being escorted to the nurse's office for a bit of a lie down until I was making sense.

Next, there was an afternoon where Anthony and I had decided that it was a fun idea to hurtle rocks over the fence at the oncoming traffic of the freeway, which quickly resulted in the sound of shattered glass. Apparently, the driver was okay, but had decided to take the next off-ramp and visit the school from where the stones had been thrown. He described to the Principal that the perpetrators were "a little boy with blonde hair and a little boy with black hair." The principal knew exactly who he was describing, and before long, we were pulled out of our respective classes and into the principal's office to explain and apologize to the driver. Whatever we said must have been rather convincing, because the driver was willing to take care of the repairs himself and our parents were not notified. Still, there were curious looks on the faces of the school's administration, straining to understand why historically good students were suddenly turning into vandals.

The final straw came when I saw a televangelist one Sunday morning and got the creative idea of playing preacher at school. I gathered a group of kids to portray my "followers," and I spent the better part of an afternoon recess combing the playground for sinners to be saved and healed. We zeroed in on the unsuspecting victims, who were then held down by my followers, while I gripped a Bible and placed my hands on their foreheads, exclaiming loudly, "Rise and be healed!" The teachers assigned to yard duty finally noticed what I was doing, and I found myself back at the principal's office.

The Principal tried to understand my explanation that it was all just a big joke, but he pointed out that many of the children I had "saved" were already from religious families and that my behavior had frightened them greatly. He had no choice but to call my parents, and before I knew it, my mother arrived in our big, black limousine to escort me home.

As I climbed into the car and sat at the end of long bench-style front seat, Mother looked at me very calmly and asked, "Now, why were you saving people?" I couldn't explain it to her in any way that justified my actions, so she simply said, "Well, whatever you say, but just don't do it again!"

Back at the hotel, my discontent grew and continued through the fall as we entered November. Without Hiya Boy's presence, the hotel really began to decline, and we all began to realize how much he actually did, when he wasn't busy crossdressing and murdering his poker buddies.

The pool had turned a deep green from the unmitigated growth of algae, but no one at the hotel posted signs warning us of this. The decent folk of the world knew better than to use the pool while it was in this condition, but I was a kid who regularly swam in the many creeks running through the Mission Canyon area, so a little moss didn't frighten me. What it did guarantee was that I would be the only person at the pool, so I swam in it frequently despite the fact it was turning greener and murkier with each passing day.

The water became so choked with algae and moss that my light blond hair began to turn green, too. That was when Mother caught on what I had been up to and forbid me to use the pool again. She must have also complained to the management because soon after my personal ban, a sign was posted at the pool stating it was closed until further notice.

As November progressed, I was closely watched at school, and I was closely watched at home. Even The Bigger provided no refuge in which I could hide. It was as if all of the adults had suddenly caught on to me, and I lamented in the fact that I had broken one of my biggest steadfast rules, which was to do nothing that would draw too much attention to myself. The pranks at school had only served to guarantee that I was now being pointedly monitored, so I felt the oppression of this extra attention, which further fueled my feelings of discontent.

Villa 100 began to feel extra stifling. Without the escape of the pool, I spent endless afternoons wandering around the hotel grounds and bored with that, I began to expand my wanderings to the buildings across the street, which housed the photography school, the movie theater and the Montessori. I would roller skate through the campus, the loud clacking of my wheels on the tiled pathways echoing in the little tunnels and passageways. Occasionally, a student or a professor would come out of a classroom, annoyed by the clatter, asked me to stop, which added to my feelings of having "nowhere to go."

The distance and isolation of the Riviera area from downtown was becoming more profound for me, and I was slightly envious of my friends who lived downtown – easy access to all of the stores and movie theaters. I began to call my friends' homes, "Real Houses," feeling like an oddball when speaking about my life in a hotel. My disenchantment with the El Encanto loomed large for me.

My brother had become an intolerable fiend, capable of terrible insults and attacks on my fragile self-esteem, along with displays of hormone-driven physical prowess that turned him into something to really fear. He was continuing to grow bigger, smellier and meaner than before. There was an additional odd smell associated with him now – the musty, sweaty odor of a pot smoker. The only upside was that he was spending more and more time away from home, mainly skateboarding up at the ruins of the Chinese Gardens in Montecito.

My brother had become quite the daredevil, skateboarding in the Garden's abandoned pool, which featured a pile of rusty metal and dangerous, thorny and dead shrubbery piled high in the bottom of the pool, which he and his friends would skate around. As a result of his hardcore attitude about his risk taking, my nervousness about such things made me seem weak and strange to him, so he began to openly make fun of me as a "little chicken shit."

When he was home, it was usually because he had injured himself and Mother was tending to him. He was constantly bleeding from some part of his body, due to this accident or that one, and it happened with such frequency that I stopped reacting to his display of physical damage; I just thought his injuries were the result of his own stupidity and easily avoidable, and I couldn't figure out where the thrill was in hurtling one's body toward an inevitable injury just to impress your friends.

This made it clear to me that in yet another way, I was different than other boys. I did enjoy riding my bike and roller skating, but I never attempted wheelies or jumps, or daring maneuvers. I did my best to keep things under control, and it wasn't completely out of fear; again, within The Bigger, I had analyzed the risk-taking behavior of other boys my age, or older, and had deemed stitches and bandages the result of "illogical" behavior.

In my free time, I preferred to read, or draw, or just to take a walk, rather than hanging out with a group of kids and doing "stupid stuff." Apparently to many, this attitude of mine made me seem snobbish and aloof, and I was often accused of believing I was "better than everyone." I did believe that it was a better choice to avoid injury, whenever possible, and I did think the behavior of what the typical male teenager felt was "cool" was rather stupid and a waste of time. I didn't want to be "cool" if "cool" meant acting like an idiot.

It was easy for me to come to the conclusion that my acting-out as a minister at school, or throwing rocks, had temporarily placed myself in the same zone as other boys and that, more than anything, made me stop. I didn't want to be like everyone else, and it was a personal badge of pride that I realized that I had a choice in the matter. So, from then on, I became a "good kid" and the brief days of being a bully or a vandal were behind me.

During the rainy days of November and December, I spent a lot of time in the Record Booth, or at the matinees downtown, or just enjoying the alone time in the room when my brother was absent. Being home most of the time, I was privy to my parents' arguments more than ever, and it was obvious that they were having misgivings about living at the hotel as well. After all, there had been nothing less than a murder, and that combined with the closed pool and the increase in the speed of the dilapidation process since Hiya Boy was taken away, really began to erode the feelings of charm we all first felt when we moved in.

We spent a simple and toned-down Christmas in Villa 100, with a small tree and very little presents. New Year's Eve was a bust, too, because my mother refused to let me outside due to the rampant partying heard around the hotel. She was concerned about the drunk guests, so I slept through midnight and awoke to 1975.

As winter turned to spring, I began to notice that my parents were circling rentals in the real estate listing section of the Santa Barbara News Press again. There were discussions and concerns over the eviction from the Big House, so they were having difficulty getting any landlord to rent to them. The search went on for a couple of months, with many rejections of them by landlords due to the eviction, but finally Father located a pretty nice house on upper State owned by possibly the oldest man in the world, Mr. Wallace Hibbard.

The house at 2219 State Street was a very elegant Tudor-style home, u-shaped, with a central front courtyard with a small patio. The front yard was adequate, although loud because of the constant traffic on State Street, one of the main streets through town. Still, the property was in a desirable section of State Street, and the street dividers were landscaped islands full of pretty trees and flowers. This stretch of the street was also constructed over the foothills of the Mission area, so it had little ups and downs, which made driving on it more enjoyable than elsewhere on "lower State." It turned out that 2219 was at the summit of one of the highest little hills, which provided a little bit of a view from the rear of the house.

Since I was not out "hanging with the boys," I was with my parents the day they went to meet Mr. Hibbard at 2219 State. We arrived in the late afternoon, after my parents picked me up at school. Both my father and mother were dressed well – my father in a navy suit, white shirt and a red neck tie, my mother in the beautiful orange and pink dress, with her red hair pulled up and back into a stylish swirl of a bun.

Earlier in the spring, my father had finally sold the limousine, opting instead for a Jeep Cherokee, a big rumbling 4 X 4. My father pulled into the driveway in our new Jeep and parked just enough to be off of the sidewalk, as the driveway sloped down, and Father was not sure yet how he would turn the enormous car around below.

My parents stepped out of the car first, and I climbed out of the deep back seat. The air was cool and crisp, since it had just rained the night before, and in the afternoon sunlight, my parents looked like models from a magazine to me, I lamented within The Bigger again my sad belief that I would never be as good looking as they were.

We glanced around looking for the owner, but he was nowhere in sight. The main entrance to the house was on the north side, where we were parked, so we walked down the red-tiled walkway to the elegant front door and Father rang the bell. We waited a moment, and there was no answer. We then heard the rumble of a large vehicle behind us, and turned toward the street to see a looming, black car slowing and parking on the street out front. As we walked toward the street, we saw a very small, very old man, struggling to open the large door of his car. As we grew closer, there was a move among my parents to go help the man in the car, but by the time we reached the sidewalk he had managed to climb out and stand up in the street. This was very anxiety producing, as cars were whizzing past on the busy street and the old man was moving very slowly. He stumbled and slid along the exterior of his car, and the heavy driver's door slammed shut behind him in almost an afterthought. He clung to the side of the car as cars continued to fly by on the street, and he ambled toward the back of his vehicle looking as though he was hanging on for dear life, gripping whatever design features of the automobile that he could to steady himself.

When he reached the rear of the car, he slid along the trunk to the curb, then gripping a small branch that was protruding from the tree, he pulled himself up, tripping a bit on the tree roots before landing firmly on the sidewalk. He carefully brushed-off his black suit and straightened his hat. He pulled a handkerchief from the inside pocket of his coat and wiped his brow and upper lip. He did all of this without realizing that my parents and I were standing just at the edge of the entrance path to the property watching him.

The elderly man glanced up at us, and sort of jumped a bit, quickly covering his startle with a broad, yellow-toothed smile and began walking very slowly toward us with his right hand outstretched in front of him.

"Hello, I'm Wallace Hibbard – and you must be the Camp Family?"

My father reached out and shook Mr. Hibbard's hand. "Yes, that's correct sir. I'm Arthur Camp and this is my wife and one of our sons."

"I'm very pleased to meet you all. Here, let's go take a look at the house." We stepped aside so Mr. Hibbard could pass. We followed behind him back down the path to the front door, walking extremely slowly in order not to overtake him. Each step Mr. Hibbard took was a stride smaller than seemed humanly possible. As Mr. Hibbard passed through a ray of sunlight, Mother and I both saw the same thing; a spider web was attached from Mr. Hibbard's right ear to his right shoulder, with a tiny spider in the middle. Mother and I telepathically agreed not to make each other's eye contact, as we knew this would cause us to lose it. It was just that Mr. Hibbard was so very old and slow, a spider had been able to build a web on him. To us, this was excruciatingly funny.

After what seemed like an eternity, we reached the front door, which was gothic in style and painted park bench green.

Mr. Hibbard put the key in the door, and it turned and unlocked with the clang that only a very old lock can make. We stepped into a small but stylish entry hall. To the right through a swinging door was the kitchen, to the left was a room Mr. Hibbard referred to as the "Library." Even this far into the home I was already in love.

It was quite a place. Not only would Casey and I have our own bedrooms again, but there was an additional large living room in the middle, and a room behind that one, separated with French doors. The home was large, vintage and sunny; in other words, perfect.

The only issues we could see were the unfortunate paint job on what must have been original would beams in the ceiling; someone had painted them a strange light blue color. To match this, the middle rooms had been carpeted with royal blue carpeting. Despite both colors being in the blue family, they were decidedly uncomplimentary.

Mother nervously said, "Well, this is an unusual palette."

Mr. Hibbard responded, "Yes, well, you see, the last tenants were something of a religious sort – there were many of them living here, more than I had agreed to. They painted the beams and replaced the carpet without telling me, and when I discovered these changes, they explained they were part of their religious beliefs. Something to do with Jesus

Christ, or something of that sort of thing." Another telepathic message passed, this time between my father, Mother and I – the word "cult."

So, the property had been occupied by a cult – so what? Just look at those Tudor-style, lead-paned windows!

After a tour of the rest of the house, my parents and I stood pondering the place and feeling the vibes of the cult. Mr. Hibbard said, "So, you are the family that is interested in buying the place, yes?" My heart sank.

To my mother and my astonishment, Father replied, "Oh, yes, yes we are."

What in the hell was he talking about?

I felt angry that here I was, in love with another house, and we were probably not going to be living in it.

"Well, let's discuss that, now, shall we?" Mr. Hibbard queried, directing it to Father.

"Okay, sure," Father responded. Mother looked at me and rolled her eyes.

"We're going to step outside for a moment," Mother said as she put her arm across my shoulder and led me to the entry hall. As we stepped out, we heard Father start with, "So, here's my idea … "

Mother and I stood in the front yard, and while it was a nice front yard, surrounded by hedges, the sounds of traffic from busy State Street were hard to ignore. We began to discuss reasons why the property wasn't so great – mainly, the noise from the street. After living for nearly a year up on the quiet Riviera, away from town, the ambient sound coming from the seemingly never-ending flow of cars was nearly deafening to us. The front yard, in our minds, was almost rendered useless because of the noise. Because 2219 was at the tip top of one of the hills, cars were gunning their engines and squeaking their breaks on both sides, all the time. The large 1970's cars were mostly equipped with loud, V-8 engines, and breaks that strained to control their weight.

I knew what Mother and I were really engaged in - we were both disappointed, and following a family tradition, were trying to mask our disappointment with criticism.

Eventually, Mr. Hibbard and my father emerged from the front door. Mr. Hibbard seemed to slide toward us with Father making funny "big-eyed" faces at us from behind him.

"Well, it's all settled then – congratulations," said Mr. Hibbard, extending out his hand to my mother, who shook her head with a somewhat bewildered look on her face.

My father looked at us and mouthed the words "Lease to Own," with a very excited look in his eyes.

"Thank you, Mr. Hibbard!" exclaimed Mother. Mr. Hibbard who was already making his way back to his car. Turning his head or entire body might have proven to be too much effort, so Mr. Hibbard just waved a hand above his head, knocking off the spider and web attached to him in the process.

We were overjoyed riding back to the El Encanto. We believed we were actually going to own a home previously occupied by some unknown religious cult, which was of great entertainment value.

Chapter 25 — The Check Out

RECORD BOOTH SUGGESTED SONG: "SEASONS IN THE SUN,"
TERRY JACKS

Months after Hiya Boy's arrest, Mrs. Kinnett had still not found a willing replacement. Also, she did not want to pay the realistic salary someone should receive for taking on such a project; she was offering the same amount she was used to paying, and not one qualified fish would bite the rusty hook.

In addition to killing his friend and poker buddy, Hiya Boy had done more than any of us had ever noticed, scuttling about the property as he did, always in the shadows, from task to task. It was a big place and a large garden for one person to care for, and with his arrest and absence, it felt as though the Santa Barbara Riviera was finally shrugging and trying to shake the hotel off.

As maintenance issues will do, they arrived in swarms, and everything seemed to be going wrong. The pool was still dark green and full of algae. Tadpoles could be seen darting around just under the surface. The "closed" sign had been hanging on the entrance to the pool so long that it was covered with spider webs.

The gardens were becoming unspeakably overgrown. Winter had arrived and left, leaving leaves down on the ground, covering the pathways and hiding dangerous and dislodged bricks protruding at just the right places to provide ample trip opportunities. It had been a very wet spring, so the plants were growing at an alarming pace. What had once been somewhat of a lovely and slightly threatening jungle in which to stroll was becoming a place where a machete is required to forge a path. There was a pervasive smell of moss, mold and mildew everywhere one walked in the gardens.

Large piles of eucalyptus bark and seed pods covered the hotel's circular entrance driveway, and from Villa 100 we could hear the pod nuggets echoing inside the tires of the large '70s vehicles pulling in as they were crushed under big, rubber tires.

In spite of the fact that Hiya Boy was technically a killer, conversely, he had been a caregiver and nurturer of life, and the gardens were in dire need of his services. He had the place so memorized and customized to his own style of care, that the other staff members enlisted to take up the slack couldn't crack the code of the El Encanto Hotel and gardens left behind by our infamous gardener.

Yes, guests were still coming to the hotel, mainly on the weekends, but it seemed that their stays were much shorter. The entire operation was clearly understaffed, and even my hot blueberry muffin connection with kitchen had faded into a happy memory.

More things were going wrong with Villa 100, and there was little to no responses to my parents demands for assistance. None of us wanted to say it aloud but staying at the El Encanto hotel just wasn't that much fun anymore, and it had been the sort of "fun" we had to work hard to access to begin with. The arrest of Hiya Boy had hastened the end of an era, as though that particular episode broke the crawling pace of the property enough where it was now at a full stand still.

I believed there was more to the connection between Mrs. Kinnett and Hiya Boy than anyone else understood. I kept remembering the night that I had snuck into her Villa, and he was there – arriving from where – some secret passage? I couldn't express any of this because only I knew of my trespassing, and I wanted to keep it that way. Not that I had more room for additional stuff to hide - The Bigger was becoming cramped, and I could feel the weight of my secrets beginning to crush me as though I were a eucalyptus seed pod, perhaps releasing the echoes of my confidences out into the world.

Despite our Addams Family-esque enjoyment of the story of this true-life murder mystery, it did cause my parents to really question if the surroundings of the hotel were indeed a safe place for their children, or themselves. We never heard what had happened to John, our Hiya Boy jungle whacking, ice pick-carrying poker player. We didn't know if he had a trial, or what had become of him. After my parents were told the confidential story, John was simply gone and that was that. An article never appeared in the paper, and we never saw the detectives again.

I think Mother had some fear that Hiya Boy could be back somehow, hiding somewhere in the shadows – or perhaps, may have blamed us somehow for his arrest, since Casey had found Stanley's body.

Whatever charms we had felt when we moved in the year before - and it had been a most unusual year, even for us - and while it had been entertaining at times, the murder-mystery honeymoon of our stay at the hotel was over, at least in our hearts, and we grew anxious to return to our own private family circus rather than be in a carnival of someone else's design.

When the call came from Mr. Hibbard confirming again that the house at 2219 State was ours if we wanted it, there were mixed feelings of elation and sadness. While being in a hotel was just such an interesting story, it was abundantly clear that it wasn't sustainable, and we were weary from the adventure and looking forward to getting back to a true home living situation. So, Father went downtown to Mr. Hibbard's office and signed the documents.

Because Father had negotiated a lease-option situation with Mr. Hibbard, it was understood that we were moving into a home that we would be buying, and whatever feelings of grief we had leaving the hotel were overshadowed by what seemed to be a true opportunity to own a home – this time in writing. My parents had not really ever recovered from the foreclosure of the home in Los Angeles during my mother's pregnancy with me; what followed the loss of that home amounted to a series of rental properties that never really seemed to work out, except for the Big House, which had been lost under very painful circumstances. The foreclosure in L.A. and the eviction from the Big House were psychologically linked for my parents, particularly since there had only been one rental home in between, so the prospect of privately working out a purchase with Mr. Hibbard for 2219 State Street was hailed as the true beginning of the financial and recovery of stability for the family.

Also, we knew from the beginning that living at the El Encanto was somewhat temporary – we just didn't know for how long – so now, it was strange to us that we had considered Villa 100 as anything other than it was – a hotel "room." Hotels, by their nature, are designed for transient occupancies.

I was now approaching 11-years-old, and Casey was a continuing nightmare of hormones, pimples and anger twisted into the shape of a human, so knowing that, I was ecstatic that I would have my own room again. No one had to convince me that moving to a home where I would have my own room again was a good idea. Whatever little was left of my older brother who was my protector and friend was gone. From my standpoint, the problems with the family had turned him into something like an ogre.

Rather than being a big finish with a bang, our stay at the El Encanto wrapped up as we quietly packed our things, and carload after carload were moved slowly into the house on State Street. When the day came to leave the hotel for good, there was some melancholy feelings for me, but also relief as I walked around the gardens for the last time, and witnessed again its overgrown ivy vines tumbling into stagnant pools of water, drunken hotel guest staggering through the thicket, and the sights and sounds of so many people in the little bungalows on their weekend getaways making so much noise. I stood for a moment, releasing a large exhale, very content that we were making our exit.

I felt I needed to say goodbye to one of my most favorite places, especially, so weaving through the overgrowth, I made my way to the pool, which had yet to be cleaned. The water was a deep, mossy green color. All of the chaise lounges were folded and leaning in a corner. I could see a few bags of tools poolside, so there was clearly some major problem with the inner-workings of the pump system. I glanced over the pool for the last time, taking in the view of Santa Barbara below, trying to wrap my mind around the reality that I would no longer be a guest of the hotel, nor would there be any clear reason to visit any time soon.

I turned and began walking back to Villa 100, where Mother and Father were likely putting the last remaining items into the Jeep. I stopped for another moment at the lily pond. The overgrowth was stunning to the point it was passing the normal into the truly supernatural. Curls and twists of vines and leaves, gorgeous depths of colors and textures, mixed with the bricks and arbor structure in a dance that was a step beyond reality. I gazed at what was before me in detail as to imprint it on my memory – I never wanted to forget this. This place of darkness, where good and bad embraced. Without regular trimming, the pond and area around it had become a truly enchanted and mysterious space.

"Hiya boy ... " – a voice came from some deep corner. I fought with the moment – did I really just hear that? Or did I imagine it? I didn't care – no more, I just wanted to move on. So, rather than determine for sure, I turned sharply on my feet, and bolted away from lily pond with fear and excitement for the very last time.

When I entered Villa 100, Mother was furiously cleaning the bathroom, even though she knew a maid would be coming to the cottage after we left to do the same thing. I helped Father load the last few boxes.

When all was finished, Father shut-off all of the lights in now empty cottage. I'm climbed into the back seat, and as my father backed out of the driveway for the last time, stopping directly next to the infamous bushes above the sandstone wall; at least we had the opportunity to at last check out of the El Encanto Hotel, something that Stanley A. Greene would never be able to do.

As our car headed down APS and away from the hotel, I fantasized that someday Mrs. Kinnett would be finally removed from the grounds, deemed criminally insane due to her management of the property, at last whisked away to a prison for errant hotel owners. I was a little sad that I would not be there to say to her, "I hope you enjoyed your stay."

CALENDAR MONTH	PAY DATE	RENT CHECK #	RENT MONTH FROM	PAID TO	HOW PAID	DATE PAID
MAY	31	1	6-1	July 1 '74		
JUNE	14					
	28	2	7-1	AUG 1		
JULY	12					
	26	3	8-1	SEPT 1		
AUGUST	9					
	23	4	9-1	OCT 1		
SEPT	6					
	20	5	10-1	NOV 1		
OCT	4					
	18					
NOV	1	6	11-1	DEC 1		
	15					
	29	7	12-1	JAN 1 '75		
DEC	13					
	27	8	1-1	FEB 1		
JAN	10					
	24	9	2-1	MAR 1		
FEB	7					
	21	10	3-1	APRIL 1		
MAR	7					
	21	11	4-1	MAY 1		
APRIL	4					
	18	12	5-1	JUNE 1		
MAY	2					
	16					
	30	13	6-1	July 1		
JUNE	13					
	27	14	7-1	AUG 1		

Footnote — The Guests

It was the early 1990's, and Gil and Stephanie, or Steph to her friends, had heard that one of their favorite spots in the world, the old El Encanto Hotel, was going to be purchased and remodeled, so they decided to drive from their place in Malibu and spend the weekend in Santa Barbara before it was too late to enjoy the place as it was.

When they arrived, they could see that there had been many improvements and repairs, but the place, in general, was relatively the same as when they stayed there in the mid-'80's. The brick pathways were still uneven and dangerous, the landscaping around the grounds was still wild and overgrown in places, and the cottages were relatively the same.

They could even recall a time when they stayed at the El Encanto in the mid-70's, when a body had been found by some little boy, and it was quite a circus. For them, the discovery of a body only added to the mystique of the place, and they vowed to return many times again in the future.

Gil and Steph stayed in one of the bungalows near the pool, and spent the weekend eating, swimming and making love – and, taking strolls through the gardens.

On their last night, after eating dinner in the hotel's restaurant, they decided to take one last stroll through the gardens – they would be leaving early in the morning.

The moon was full, so the gardens were absolutely magical. Dappled moonlight trickled to the brick paths below through the overgrowth. The lily pond was still there, and they found one of the repaired benches between the brick columns and under and area where the wisteria had been trimmed back a little. They sat in the moonlight and remarked to one another how incredibly romantic and magical the El Encanto still was.

Gil slid his hand under Steph's hair, gently grasping the nape of her neck, and pulled her face close to his own. He gave her a deep, passionate kiss and then pulled away, opening his eyes to look at her face in the moonlight. Then, something in the distance over her left shoulder immediately caught his eye; there was a large, boulder-like object that seemed to be moving slowly across the brick pathway, heading into some deep overgrowth. Gil gasped and said, "What is that?"

Steph turned her head and stared in the direction that Gil was pointing. She said, "Is that a moving rock?" They stood slowly and walked toward the object, clasping each other's hands tightly. They reached the moving object just as it was entering the bushes.

Looking down at the round shape, which was bathed in moonlight, they could clearly see the rear end of a very large tortoise, disappearing into the bushes.

The End

Epilogue 1 — That Pic by the Pool

On top of everything else I have described, up until the time we moved into the El Encanto and afterward, I was also somewhat of a sickly child, the classic Dickensian Tiny Tim, but with far more of a myriad of health challenges.

I had suffered viral pneumonia a number of times and had been given some fairly heavy-duty antibiotics as well, and the neighbors had often expressed their concern about my skin tone – which during the winter especially, bordered between a sickly pale colorless flesh tone to a downright blueish color. Meddlers would give my mother unsolicited advice, such as that I needed to be outside in the sun more, like a "normal" boy, and voice their additional concern that I was generally inside too much.

After many doctor's visits, it became clear with testing that I was truly anemic. I often complained of lights being "too bright," and this was chalked-up to a somewhat imagined link between my anemia and damage to my retinas. Within a couple of years, it would be discovered that I was suffering from some rare blood disease, which made it difficult for my body to absorb enough iron and proteins from my blood stream, which may have accounted for my light sensitivity, but we didn't know that yet.

One of my favorite characters when I was a kid was Snoopy, a central part of Charles Schultz' "Peanuts" comic and cartoon series – but not just Snoopy, but especially when Snoopy became "Joe Cool" by sporting a pair of sunglasses and generally acting hip to the jive.

With Joe Cool I had found a relatable figure, so I too began wearing dark glasses whenever possible – not only did this ease the effects of bright lights on me, but it also provided a sense of safety and detachment, two things I deeply craved as a child who felt very unsafe.

Of course, this meant that anytime I was down at the El Encanto's pool, I would quite often be sporting some sunglasses, usually borrowed from an adult, and it was on just such a day at the pool that my father arrived with his camera and instructed me to pose.

My father handed me his sunglasses and his hat, and told me to sit down, and there you have the cover photo of this book.

When I look at the photo myself now, I do find it a bit hard to believe that this blonde-haired little person, this wannabe Joe Cool, was ever really me. I appear healthier and more relaxed than I remember. I even have a hint of a tan. Considering my appearance in this picture, then imaginimg myself in the activities described in this book, creates a bit of a cognitive dissonance for me, the conflict arising from all that was going inside then, while on the exterior, I just looked like a typical Southern California Kid. And I also think about all the things that had led up to that moment, and I ponder how every one of the millions and millions of photos out there, dropping like leaves in the fall of humanity, also have their own backstories.

So, there I sit, next to the pool, posing for my father, forever trapped in a moment of time, a small body holding some very big issues.

Epilogue 2 — Murder – A Family Affair

Aunt Benny murdered our grandmother in her townhome a week before my fifteenth birthday on May 23, 1979.

At that point, we had moved an additional three times since we left the El Encanto – a couple of homes in Santa Barbara, and then a third move to a place called Incline Village, on the Nevada side of Lake Tahoe. It was a much different reality than Santa Barbara, and we'd only been there about a year and a half when Mother received the call from her sister with the news that their mother had an accident. What Benny told Mother was that Grandmother had fallen down the stairs in her townhome because she was "drunk again" - the fall had snapped Grandmother's neck; a very unceremonious end for the "Eternal Coquette."

Since we had moved to Lake Tahoe, Benny had overtaken the duty of driving Grandmother to her hair and doctor's appointments. On the tragic day, Benny had arrived at Grandmother's home, rang the doorbell, and there was no answer. Using her own key to the place, Benny was unable to open the front door as something was blocking it. The front door to the townhome was directly in front of the bottom step of the interior staircase, which led to the second floor. What was blocking the door later turned-out to be Grandmother's body. Benny continued with her story saying that she called the police, who were able to force/shove their way into the townhome, where Grandmother's body was discovered, and of course, the coroner arrived, and she was taken away in due course.

My mother was absolutely in deep pain by the end of the call. She blamed herself for the death – she believed that because we had moved so far away, Grandmother was lonely for us, which increased her drinking. My mother made the entire incident her own fault and fell almost immediately into a deep depression. Arrangements were made for a trip back to Santa Barbara; my father would stay in Lake Tahoe, and since it would be my summer break from high school soon, I would be going with Mother.

In the interim, Mother came to learn about a few strange things. After nearly a decade of being named the Executrix of Grandmother's estate, Grandmother had revised her will only three weeks before her death, naming Benny the Executrix. Grandmother had failed to mention this prior, recent change to Mother during a conversation where the last and final revision was discussed, and Grandmother had stated that Mother was still Executrix and only discussed other minor changes. So, in reality, there had been two revisions, one making Benny the Executrix, and then another, switch the position back to Mother. As Mother put it, Benny had attempted to give Grandmother's estate a bad "heir-cut."

Mother and Benny had never been loving sisters – rather, they were often at each other's throats throughout their lives, Mother painting Benny as the ultimate narcissist and a sociopathic individual. On numerous occasions during their childhood together, Aunt Benny had reportedly attacked Mother, at one point pinning her down and pounding Mother's breasts while screaming, "You're the reason I'm flat!" Apparently, Benny was unhappy with the size of her own bosom. Mother reported other stories about Benny, including accounts of avarice where she was able to get hold of pieces from Grandmother's extensive jewelry collection.

Grandmother had confided in Mother that she was afraid of Benny – that Benny had become enraged on several occasions when her wheedling didn't work, and Grandmother had refused to give her some specific piece. The most important and costly jewels were held in a safe deposit box at a bank nearby in Santa Barbara, and were there at the time of Grandmother's death, safe from Benny's reach.

The townhome was filled with numerous valuable items, including the silver fishing trophies, sterling silver flatware and tea sets, rare collectible porcelain items, Persian rugs, and an amazing array of antique furniture and art works – some of which Benny had been trying to convince her mother to give to her, without success.

By the time we arrived at Grandmother's townhome, it was early June, about two weeks after Benny's call. Grandmother was already autopsied and cremated, and her ashes were in an urn sitting inside. We opened the front door and were immediately confronted with a large bloodstain on the gold carpet at the base of the staircase. This was the final blow to what little shred of my childhood innocence was left – seeing Grandmother's blood like that – it was the last straw; all of the enchantments of my childhood were completely dead now – murdered by this moment.

Benny and Mother detested one another so thoroughly that Benny was not present even to greet us at such a somber and depressing arrival. It was one of those experiences that form an indestructible trauma bond, and from then on, Mother and I knew we had a true friend in one another.

After getting over the initial shock of seeing the bloodstain, Mother and I entered the townhome and, of course, Mother noticed immediately that some of the more valuable items were already missing. Her mood quickly changed from grieving to irate, and she suspected something rotten was going on. Along with the urn, Grandmother's autopsy report and the police report were sitting on the coffee table.

Mother set down her bags, pulled out a pen and paper, and began writing down which of Grandmother's belongings were missing. I trailed behind her sheepishly, feeling very overwhelmed by the situation. There was no moment of a heart-to-heart – no checking in on my feelings from seeing my grandmother's bloodstain on the floor. Not a moment to process the strangeness of being in her home again, imagining the horror of Grandmother's last moments. Other than the missing items and some washed dishes, the place was pretty much exactly how Grandmother had left it and it was eerie being in her time capsule.

I needed to use the restroom, and stepped into it, remembering Samantha's imprisonment there, and thinking she might still be outside somewhere. I could still smell my grandmother's perfume, and suddenly my body erupted with chills and goosebumps; the bathroom was suddenly freezing cold, and I couldn't wait to get out of it.

Stepping back out into the living room area, my mother was making her way to the stairs to continue the inventory on the second floor. Neither of us could face stepping directly on the bloodstain, so we each grabbed the stair's railing to hoist ourselves over it, noticing right away that the railing was very loose. We made our way up the stairs to the top where we could see that the railing had been completely pulled from the wall. The plates that once held the railing in place were dangling from the wooden rail itself, woodscrews extended from the holes in the plates, loosely jiggling in the air, with bits of plaster stuck in the metal spirals.

I didn't say anything out loud, but the feeling at the top of the stairs was like a leftover, hovering mist from some violence that had taken place – I couldn't explain the sensation, not even to myself. I felt helpless and scared. I kept looking at the railing pulled out from the wall, and imagined Grandmother – what, hanging onto it? Trying to balance herself with it? How could she pull it from the wall? Mother was staring at it too with her mouth agape, and I wondered if all the same feelings and thoughts were filling her. We both felt the need to cut wide around the protruding railing as we stepped up the last stairs, also carpeted, and onto the landing of the second floor.

We turned slowly, and both looked down the stairs, practically hearing the tumbling sound of Grandmother as she fell. My mother visibly shuddered, and tears were filling her eyes. I could see that now, despite all of the complaints about Grandmother, that there had been love there too. It was beyond unnerving to see the bottom landing too, from this vantage point, with its darkness and bloodstain. "Just horrible," Mother said with a hollow tone.

Stepping into the guest bedroom, which was adjacent to the top floor landing, Mother noticed immediately that all of the silver fishing trophies had been removed from the bookcase Grandfather had built to house them. She gritted her teeth and growled, "That goddamn thief!"

We turned and continued to Grandmother's bedroom opposite the guest room. The room was small to begin with but made even smaller by the fact that Grandmother insisted on keeping her huge four-poster bed inside. Despite feeling cramped, Grandmother's bedroom was splendid, with beautiful furniture, mirrors and artwork. Of course, all of the jewelry cases were gone, but strangely, Grandmother's furs were all in her closet, with numerous suitcases that Mother knew were filled with family photographs and other treasures. Mother said, "Aunt Benny must have missed these."

There was an inaudible yet heavy psychic din in Grandmother's bedroom. The framework of her reality had been sucked out by some enormous release of pressure, and the remaining silence still contained something, the room perhaps still occupied by tremendous grief from the loss of unfinished tasks and plans. The sudden interruption of Grandmother's life had our ears ringing in the black hole of her absence, yet it was not an empty vacuum.

My mother walked like zombies to the little mahogany stairs at the edge of the bed, and she took them slowly and then turned and sat on the bed coverings. Her feet were dangling off the side, and for a moment, she looked like a little girl to me. Mother began to cry in a way I had never witnessed. All the lack of resolution with her mother fell down her cheeks, in increasingly heavy streams, until she was folded over, weeping into her hands. I wasn't sure what to do – I hadn't really learned the emotional skills needed for this moment, so I just stood watching her, my feet glued to the ornate rug below.

I couldn't bear to watch my mother becoming completely unraveled, so I stared at my feet and noticed all of Grandmother's little bejeweled slippers' toes jutting out from just underneath the bed's dust skirt. They were the only shoes she could wear with her gout, and the image of the swollen tops of her feet, which were often nearly purple and covered with dry, flaky skin, appeared on my psychic television. I shuddered a bit thinking about those same feet twisting through the air and then, alternatively, folding beneath her as she crashed down the stairs to her death.

Mother began to pull herself together and looked me and said, "I'm sorry." I was unable to say anything, so I just stared back. She climbed down from the bed and stood next me. She put her hands on my shoulders and said, "It's going to be alright." I felt guilty that I hadn't been able to comfort her, and now I was being comforted. Mother said, "We're going to have to sleep here – this is the only bed – are you okay with that?" I managed to squeeze out a quiet, "Yah," and then I began to realize how much I was going to miss my grandmother and the shuffling of her little feet.

A death like hers is all rather abstract due to its incomprehensibility. "Grandmother fell down her stairs and died" was like some fantastical tale I had only heard, until I was standing in her room after seeing the loose banister and the bloodstain below. It was no longer conceptual; it was real. This violent death had happened to an imperfect yet still very loveable person. I felt bad for Grandmother that her last moments on earth were spent in such a horrific way. She didn't deserve it, not that anyone would.

With all of these hard feelings swirling about, mental images of her tumble, the shock and horror we were both feeling yet unable to express, Mother and I decided it was better to just get settled rather than remain in her room trying to process these nearly unimaginable sensations.

I left the bedroom and casually strolled into the opposite other bedroom, that was being used essentially as an office. It contained that large bookcase that my grandfather had constructed for the fishing trophies, which were all missing – I could see their silhouettes left behind in the dust on the shelves. One trophy remained – the mounted sword from a Marlin. The bone was a somewhat yellow color, not white, and at the base was a little bid of the leftover hide of the Marlin's nose, which had been treated with something to keep it from rotting. It remained perpetually moist, and still had a gross and sticky feeling to it. I was hoping already that we weren't taking it back home.

I left the room and returned downstairs, having to pass again by the perturbing railing and bloodstain. I grabbed my bags and carried Mother's upstairs for her as well.

J.K. FRIMPLE'S RESTAURANT Santa Barbara, California

We opened up our suitcases in Grandmother's bedroom and pulled out fresh clothing. Mother decided to take a shower, but I just slipped on different clothes as we had decided to go out for some food.

Mother thought we should go to one of Grandmother's hangouts, J.K. Frimple's on the corner of State and Valerio Streets, just around the corner. We ate there a lot with Grandmother when we lived at the Big House, so I liked the idea. I could see that Mother was doing her best, realizing the grief her young son must be feeling, so she was beginning to formulate plans that would comfort me and help me get over the loss. Within The Bigger I knew what she was up to – it was "Rather obvious, don't you think?" I said to myself – but it felt good, so I controlled my impulse to say something and expose her attempts at cheering me up. Besides, I had fond memories of Frimple's, so we walked the familiar sidewalks to the restaurant.

J.K. Frimple's was known before as The Blue Onion, which was a popular drive-in in the '50s and '60s. Before J.K. Frimple's, the restaurant was named "The Fig Tree," in reference to the enormous fig tree the restaurant surrounded.

When we frequented the restaurant with Grandmother in the days of The Fig Tree and the Big House, the coveted tables were the ones next to the large pane windows in the center of the restaurant where you could view the trunk of the enormous fig, so I usually made a fuss unless we got one of those special tables. The Fig Tree's management must have noted the demand for seating at the tables around the tree and saw an opportunity to increase business. What they decided would be a good idea was to import a wallaby couple from Australia, and install them as mascots underneath the fig, making the surrounding glass their cage. You see, they figured the wallabies would feel at home because the fig tree was native to Australia as well. There was some clear misstep in their thinking – the wallabies were living animals, requiring a much larger enclosure then the glass box under the tree, which had very little flat ground because of the tree's large roots.

For a while, the wallabies were a big hit, and every kid in town wanted to sit at one of those "habitat" adjacent tables to watch them. Over time, the wallabies began to have "issues."

As I sat there with Mother reminiscing about all of this, we began to chuckle together. It was one of the first times I saw my mother smile since receiving news of the accident. We were both thinking the same thing. An event that had occurred during one of our last dinners with Grandmother at the restaurant.

Of course, we were sitting at one of the ringside seats with Grandmother. That day, we were there for lunch, and it was just me and Mother joining her. We'd heard through the grapevine about the wallabies lascivious behavior but had never witnessed it. When the server arrived to take our order, Grandmother began to speak and just then, the wallabies emerged from a little doghouse-style structure wedged at a slight angle between the tree roots, hopped over until they were directly through the glass where we were sitting, and began to mate ferociously. Without saying a single word about it, Grandmother simply held her menu with one hand against the glass, blocking the wallabies live sex act in progress, and continued to calmly order her lunch. It always felt good to me to be there for the had-to-be-there moments, and three of us talked about the event quite a lot afterward.

Sadly, the wallabies did not fare well in their new home. Due to lack of informed care, they both became visibly ill, and the sickly pair behind the glass began to upset diners. Their enclosure had not been kept very clean, and the unlucky pair had wiped a lot of poo on the inside of the glass. At long last, they were rescued, treated and given a proper enclosure at the Santa Barbara Zoo, located on the land that was formerly the Child's Estate. It's a beautiful part of the city, right near the sea. From a glass box to a seaside habitat. I was relieved for them.

After sharing this fond memory of Grandmother, both of our mood's improved, and we returned to Grandmother's townhome, with our strength renewed, confident we could settle things and return home to Tahoe in a couple of weeks.

With the initial shock behind us, and feeling more empowered, we were able to climb into Grandmother's bed, after Mother had put on fresh sheets of course, and settle in for the night; it was around midnight.

Grandmother's bed felt luxurious to me, having spent most of my life in a twin bed. Her sheets were of a fine quality, her pillows plump and sumptuous, the bed coverings soft and comfy. Neither myself nor my mother were very large people, so there was plenty of room for both of us, and we fell asleep quickly in our own separate sides of the bed.

I'm not sure who heard the sound first; all I know is that we were both very suddenly wide awake and sitting bolt upright next to each other in the bed. There was a bizarre, electric feeling in the air - it was just like the sensation my brother and I felt when we witnessed the apparition in the Big House.

Invisible tendrils seemed to brush our faces, and it was very still inside the townhome. I looked at the digital clock on the nightstand on Mother's side; it was 3:00 a.m.

We couldn't hear any traffic outside, or any other sounds ... other than ... a soft "shuffle ... shuffle ... shuffle" across the rug downstairs. The sounds traveled close to the bottom of the stairs, and then seemed to turn around and head back toward the kitchen. The soft, sliding sounds also seemed to be stopping and then going in circles. As we listened more and more closely, the sounds increased in volume, until we were able to unmistakably determine the sound of Grandmother shuffling in her slippers.

Our eyes widened, and we turned and looked at one another. Even though it was early in the morning, the room was lit from a courtyard lamp outside, so we could see each other fairly well. We stared into each other's eyes and listened as the shuffles continued. Without saying a word, we both knew who and what was downstairs.

After what seemed like at least fifteen minutes, Mother held her finger up to her mouth to indicate that I should remain quiet. She slipped out of bed and walked to the small landing at the top of the stairs. Then, she said aloud, "Mother, if that's you downstairs, please don't come upstairs. We're frightened. We're here to help you. Please tell us how we can help you." Once the sound of my mother's voice stopped, so did the shuffles.

Mother didn't receive an answer. She stood for quite some time waiting, but nothing more was heard. She climbed back into bed and said to me, "I think she just wanted us to know that she is here."

We both fell back to a classic, uneasy sleep – our eyes were closed but our ears remained wide awake. I was aware of all the ambient sounds around me, even though I was dreaming also. It was Grandmother in my dreams throughout the night. Sometimes sitting on her lounge downstairs. Sometimes at her huge dining room table. Sometimes standing at the base of the stairs, staring at the top.

I awakened to a chill in the room. My mother was already standing next to the bed. "Geez, it's cold in here," she complained in my general direction. She had her flannel nightgown on – the one she like for the cold Tahoe nights – but she was still shivering. "Well, we might as well get up," she snorted.

The processing of my grandmother's "estate" began in earnest that morning and continued for a week. This included deciding what was to be kept, and what was to be sold. Personal effects were packed into boxes we obtained from cruising the loading docks behind several grocery stores. We were mostly left alone – not even a word from Aunt Benny – nor any well-wishes from friends of my grandmother at the Senior Center.

After so many days of silence and constant reminiscing as objects were packed in boxes, the doorbell rang.

I opened the door and there stood a small, very old woman. "Is your mother at home?" she asked. Mother emerged from behind me and said, rather curtly, "Yes."

"I am so sorry for your loss my dear. So terrible. We were all worried about your mother. She felt very lonely after your family moved away," the woman said blankly while staring at me and not my mother.

My mother lost it and started to cry. The guilt she felt from leaving Grandmother alone in Santa Barbara gripped her again. I really didn't understand what turmoil she was going through inside, but she seemed tortured.

Mother invited the woman into the townhome and offered her tea. They talked for about half an hour. Listening to the woman, I decided I didn't like her. There was something in her approach that felt … untrue. She talked about this great friendship she had with Grandmother, yet, none of us had ever heard of her before. This visitor was offering much needed comfort to my mother, to the point it clouded Mother's perception, and I think she wasn't aware that she may be being emotionally manipulated.

After a thirty second or so crying jag, the visitor offered my mother a tissue from Grandmother's silver tissue box and said, "So, I wanted to ask you something. Your grandmother promised me that glass display cabinet there, and my son is here, and we could move it out right now if that would make it easier for you." The visitor pointed to an exquisite antique curved glass cabinet with inlaid wood and other embellishments. To my shock, Mother said, "Oh, ya, sure, okay, I'm sure she would want you to have it."

With that, the old woman arose, walked to the door, and gestured in the direction of the back of the complex and called loudly to persons unseen, "Okay!"

I stopped what I was doing and said to Mother, "Don't. Don't give it to her." But it was too late – a large man with a smaller teenage boy were in the townhome, had both hands on the cabinet, and carried it out in a blink of an eye. The old woman stopped at the door and said, "I am truly sorry for your loss," and quickly closed the door behind her.

A fight erupted between Mother and me. I couldn't believe that she had let herself be tricked by this woman. Who was she? Why had we never heard of her? She had nothing in writing declaring that she should get the cabinet? "What are you doing?" I shrieked at Mother. "You'll understand when you're older," she replied.

But the floodgates were opened. Over the next week, there were numerous doorbell rings and complete strangers at the threshold, there to claim furniture, art and other belongings that Grandmother had allegedly "promised" them. Even though The Sergeant was screaming in my ear to do something, my mother was giving Grandmother's stuff away to anyone who showed up claiming it.

After watching many very nice pieces leave the premises, including an exquisite Persian rug, I had enough.

I may have still resembled a child, but once again, inside I grew yet another level. I felt older than my mother. I placed my hands on her shoulders and said firmly, "You have to stop. You are going to regret this. These people are ripping us off." It must have been the tone of my voice, because it worked. Mother said, "You're right. Thank you."

Luckily, there was quite a bit left after the pillaging by my grandmother's self-proclaimed friends. The next time the doorbell ring, I answered it and told them we were busy settling the will and they would be notified if there was anything for them. Word must have spread because the visits ceased. It was another hard lesson for me regarding how low human beings could sink.

This unfortunate activity triggered my mother and she decided to read the will. It had been sitting on the coffee table since we arrived, with the autopsy report and the urn, still untouched. Mother began flipping through the pages, becoming more and more enraged as she read what seemed to be the final version. Apparently, not only had

Benny been named Executrix just weeks before Grandmother's death, but she also had made Grandmother change the distribution of the estate in Benny's favor. Mother and her family were to receive only a small portion of the entire estate. Luckily, there was another astonishing find of another will underneath the first; this was an even more recent version than Mother had believed – in this one, Mother was returned to her position as Executrix. A safe deposit box was also mentioned, so we realized we needed to go to the bank as well. After reading the will, Mother snapped out of her weeklong grief-induced hypnotic state and realized she needed to get a lawyer.

It became clear then that she had better review the autopsy report as well, which turned out was full of surprising conclusions. The coroner felt that some of Grandmother's injuries (contusions) were inconsistent with a fall down a flight of stairs. He stated that Grandmother had strange bruising around her neck, as well as some blunt force trauma to her head as though she had been struck prior to falling.

Next, Mother read the police report, which stated that they were called approximately forty-five minutes after the time of death, and as she compared this document to the coroner's report, Mother's face lost all color.

According to the police report, there were also signs of a forced entry into the dining area window at the rear of the townhome; the window screen was bent, and there were scratch marks indicating that it had been pried-off from the outside, probably with a screwdriver.

Mother stood, grabbed her purse, looked at me and said, "We're going to the bank to get the safe deposit box." She had a look on her face as if she had suddenly found a long-missing piece to a thousand-piece jigsaw puzzle. Something had come together in her head. The grief in her eyes was replaced again with sheer rage. Her brown eyes turned solid black.

We had a tense drive over to the bank, which luckily wasn't very far away. Grandmother had authorized Mother to access the box years before, and the authorization was still valid. Once inside the vault, Mother opened the box, finding it completely empty.

As soon as we returned back to the townhome, Mother called the police to report the theft. Mother also hired an attorney.

With the authorities involved, Mother continued with the task at hand, but she was visibly shaken. With still no word from her sister, Mother's suspicions grew hourly, reaching a fever pitch the day before we left to return home. Mother looked at me blankly and said, "I think Aunt Benny murdered your grandmother."

Our last week we continued with the process of sorting through Grandmother's belongings, most of which ended up being moved into a storage unit nearby, as there wasn't room for everything in our house in Tahoe. As we wrapped and packed, the words that Mother had said to me were running on the treadmill in my head, intruding on my focus.

I had heard over my childhood about Aunt Benny, and her propensity toward physical assaults. My mother also constantly described her as devious, malicious and just flat out nuts. I had only had one odd experience with my aunt over the years, which was the one and only time my mother had left me with Benny for an afternoon.

In the first several years following my birth, my aunt was part of our lives, despite what had happened in my mother's childhood with her. We took road trips with Aunt Benny and her husband, who we called Uncle Young, a contraction of his last name, Youngberg. I absolutely adored Uncle Young – he was the kind of man a little boy like me really looked up to; tall and strong, capable, and well equipped to handle situations. Of course, there were no sexual feelings towards him, but I would say I had a bit of a crush on Uncle Young, so he was the main reason I didn't mind visiting my aunt in those early days; I felt safe around Uncle Young.

They had a home at one point out in Death Valley, and our parents left one day with Uncle Young for some sightseeing, leaving Casey and I in the care of Aunt Benny. As soon as the rest of the adults were gone,

Aunt Benny locked us in an entry hall closet, and only releasing us, a few hours later, when the other adults returned. She threatened us with some imagined punishment if we told the others that we had spent the entire time in a dark closet. From then on, I wasn't much of a fan of Aunt Benny.

The news came of Uncle Young's death while we were still living at the Big House, and I sobbed so hard that it concerned my mother. As she described it to me later, I had a breakdown and was inconsolable. All I remember her saying to me at the time was the it was wonderful how much I loved Uncle Young, and that he would know in the afterlife that I cared so deeply.

Over the next years, without the gentle and firm guidance of Uncle Young, the relationship between my mother and her sister deteriorated. They became full adversaries, smiling at each other through their clenched teeth whenever they were together with their mother. There was a constant battle of who would be Executrix of Grandmother's estate, and the role passed back and forth, my mother claiming that Aunt Benny was coercing Grandmother. Grandmother also complained to Mother that Benny was taking things from the townhome.

There must have been some truth to it all, because Grandmother preferred to have our mother do most of the caretaking and helping, while trying to leave Benny out of it. This changed with our move to Tahoe.

The last week of packing, the conjecture that Benny had potentially murdered Grandmother was a festering wound in my mother's side; she couldn't stop thinking about it. This was the time she confessed to me that she thought Aunty Benny had murdered Uncle Young as well. For fifteen-year-old me, this was a lot to take in; I still grieved quietly about Young, and I was now hearing that Benny had murdered him too.

My mother had many unfortunate qualities for sure, but one quality she did not possess was the ability to lie. My mother always told the truth, even if it was painful to do, and she detested liars, and her assessment of Benny was that she was a pathological liar. The rage was real.

By the time we were ready to go, Mother was drained by her own thoughts – including her guilt over leaving Grandmother alone with my aunt in Santa Barbara, when she knew better. Mother continued to blame herself for the death.

While we were packing the last small pieces of my grandmother's belongings that we were taking home into the small trunk of our 1975 red Mazda Cosmo, Mother inadvertently set the car keys down inside and closed the trunk. We were now locked out of the car and the townhome. My mother stood still for a moment, with the hot early summer sun of Santa Barbara beating down on us in the complex's rear parking lot and said nothing. She looked as though she were going to erupt with rage, but instead, she began to cry ... which turned into weeping ... which turned into wailing. Mother finally let go fully, and she crumpled down to the asphalt, cradling her face in her hands. I looked at the back of the apartment section of the complex, which was facing us, and could see curtains being pushed aside as neighbors looked to see what was going on. My mother's grief was on display for all. This triggered a sense of protection within me, and I squatted down next to Mother and suggested she take a seat on one of the patio chairs in the corner of the lot. She didn't argue.

We sat there for about five minutes, and finally an older man approached through the breezeway into the lot and asked if we needed assistance. Through her tears, Mother said, "Yes – would you call a locksmith please."

On the drive home, we didn't speak much – it was as though Mother was worried about crying in front of me; the only thing she said about it was, "I'm sorry Scott." I didn't have the emotional maturity yet to tell her it was okay; all I could offer was a classic teenage shrug and the words, "It's no biggie."

After that, a lengthy battle ensued between my mother and Aunt Benny over the estate – through their lawyers. Many startling things were revealed in the process, including a safe deposit teller at the bank who confessed, during her deposition, that she had accepted a bribe from Aunt Benny to let her into the box, even though she wasn't on the signatory card.

The Santa Barbara Police Department were slow to get involved, considering it to be some weird dispute between two crazy sisters over a will. They ignored the suspicious time sequence of Grandmother's death, when Benny had entered the vault at the bank, and when she later called the police saying she couldn't get into Grandmother's townhome, even when Mother pointed-out that the keys to the safe deposit box had been in Grandmother's desk drawer.

Eventually, Mother was able to retrieve from Aunt Benny several items of jewelry that were clearly left to my mother in the will, and this was achieved because of the lawyers. To this day my cousins in Louisiana, the two doctors, likely have family belongings that rightfully belong to my brother and I, including a diamond-studded pocket watch meant for me. I've accepted this will never be rectified. Mother had broached the subject often over the following years with Benny's two boys, Rush and John, multiple times, but they simply didn't want to discuss their mother or what happened.

At the end of the legal battle, Mother had to drop the case – it was eating away at her meager resources, and she needed to settle so she could receive the liquid funds due to her, which had been on hold during the negotiation.

By the end, my mother was with a different attorney because her first attorney, Ted Keaney, had been arrested naked and running down the tarmac at the Honolulu Airport and subsequently disbarred – just when we thought the drama couldn't get any more bizarre.

Once the case was over, my mother was deeply depressed. Father had a scary moment where he witnessed Grandmother's ghost walking through our house in Tahoe from a bathroom to the opposite end of the hallway, which led to the master bedroom; we saw his face right after the episode – he was pale, shaking and crying. We believed him because we believed that Grandmother was not at rest.

It was in this same bathroom that I would find Mother months later, unconscious on the floor, having attempted suicide by taking a handful of pills. I have no idea where she got them, but needless to say, it was tough being the boy who found his mother like this, particularly after everything we'd been through.

Mother survived.

Epilogue 3 — A Return To The El Encanto

About a month before my 58th birthday, and I found myself once again at the El Encanto.

My husband and I decided to drive from Northern California, where we were living at the time, to Santa Barbara for my birthday and to visit Casey and his wife, Clara.

We picked what looked like a fairly decent hotel down by Fisherman's Wharf, which turned out to be a complete shithole. We had prepaid and booked the room for a week, but after suffering what seemed to be a methamphetamine-fueled argument between two long term residents, just outside our window, we decided to leave, forfeiting over two-thousand dollars as the place would not offer a refund to us. Welcome to Santa Barbara, and, what a perfect coincidence that we were driven from a hotel by arguing guests? Sound familiar?

Perhaps this is what triggered me to book a room at the El Encanto, the familiarity of the situation pouring lemon juice in this old wound. One thing though – the El Encanto was then a five-star hotel, and quite pricey.

We agreed, though, that since I was already underway with the process of writing this book, we could look at it like "research," and perhaps being on the hotel's grounds again would help my memories rise to the surface, like a bloated toad in the lily pond. So, we booked a room and headed to the Riviera.

Pulling into the hotel's circular driveway in what, for me, was my fancy new paid-for car, I have to admit, felt like a quiet triumph. I was immediately involved in my thoughts, imagining the ten-year-old me seeing into the future, and how this would have looked to him. He would have thought that he and I had "made it," arriving as a guest in what would essentially look like a spaceship to someone from 1975.

And, this feeling of success washed over me. Over my life, "success" has been very ephemeral, as my fortunes have risen and fallen. I haven't reached the kind of success, financially, that has been sustainable, but I'll never give up on this front. Of course, I have experienced more meaningful and profound successes, which I treasure more than anything. But the moment I was pulling into the El Encanto, I was financially flush, so I gave the little ghost-me lurking in the bushes a wink of reassurance.

It was also pretty cool that a handsome valet approached the vehicle and opened the door for me, and said, "Welcome to the El Encanto, Sir." I liked the sound of this. I looked at him, losing control of myself momentarily, and replied, "I used to live here!" I then continued in a rapid-fire, forty-five second list of the bullet points of my residency, ending with "... and my brother found the body!" The valet looked amused and slightly bewildered. I have the tendency to information-dump on strangers, which I hope is part of my charm.

As I stepped out of my car, I immediately turned and glanced in the direction where Villa 100 once stood, pointing it out to the poor valet, of course. Sadly, our beloved, or at least beliked or betolerated, villa had been torn down in the early '90's renovation and replaced with a building that functions as the current staff's offices and changing rooms. Our long brick catwalk is also gone and replaced with a large, gaping entrance to an underground parking garage.

At that moment, I felt as if I was on my own "Trip to Bountiful," and was experiencing a mix of elation realizing that I had survived this part of my childhood. There were also feelings of melancholy and grief, as the red-hot brand of how much time had passed burned into my psychic flesh.

Conversely, I had never stayed at a five-star hotel before, so I knew we were in for a treat. In what to me was a nod to the hotel's somewhat relaxed history, dogs were welcome, so our beloved canine ward, Upton O'Goode was with us, too, for what would turn out to be his last adventure with us.

This time moving into the hotel, instead of some middle-of-the-night panic-moving, I was treated to relaxed valet service, as my luggage was removed from the car, so we could check-in. Another valet parked our car in the garage and I witnessed, firsthand, how time could heal wounds. Another small quiet victory was quietly celebrated in my heart.

Here we were at the front desk, which was relatively in the same location as the original, yet the main building of the hotel was now a grand spectacle of charm and beauty. I was happy for the hotel, seeing it receive the care and honoring it always deserved. Another tide of warm feeling washed through me, and despite the expense, I knew right then we had made the correct choice. I was already feeling more inspired to write my book.

It goes without saying that the entire front desk also received my bullet point story of how my family had lived there. They were all quite interested, it seemed. The concierge said, "Yes, I did actually hear once that there was a murder and a body here, but I thought it was just a rumor! This is so amazing! So happy you've returned, Mr. Camp – welcome home." If my parents and grandmother could see me now.

Our room was exquisite, with a giant bed, a fireplace, a huge bathroom and lovely porch. It was located in the same area where the abandoned cottages had been, and was entirely new, constructed to meet the Santa Barbara architectural guidelines – mission-style. Included were a plush dog bed and treats for Upton as well. Perhaps the spirit of Sheila was receiving some healing too.

It was a warm early May day on the Riviera, but not too hot – just perfect. We took the opportunity to take a stroll around the grounds, on the now very even and stable brick pathways. I made a beeline first to the lily pond and arbor, which still existed and had been restored. It is a beautiful spot now that can be reserved for weddings. I giggled to myself while looking at the now pristine pond, seeing the multitude of toads in my mind's eye. I was in a secret discussion with the hotel now, the two of us being the only ones present who would remember those days. It felt like the grounds recognized me, and a broad smile covered my face. I was almost euphoric.

We walked down to the pool area, which now had a very large, infinity pool, facing the direction of the view, as opposed to the old pool. There was no enclosure blocking the view to the Channel Islands, and I was in some sort of private celebration with every cell of my body reacting with pleasant chills and tingles. Going back can be a good thing, given the proper circumstances.

Looking to my right from the pool, I could see that the horrifying basement that I had once crawled through had been replaced with an elaborate ground floor, including a world class health spa. I thought to myself, "If they only knew."

My patient husband was politely enduring my repeated outbursts as I pointed and showed him where events in my upcoming book had occurred, explaining the prior layout of the property to him, showing him which buildings had been preserved. Several of the craftsman cottages and many of the Spanish bungalows had been restored and remained, including Mrs. Kinnett's.

Being a fully grown adult on the grounds made everything seem so much smaller, and the grand dame's former home wasn't as fancy as I had once believed. In fact, the entire property seemed to have shrunk as much as I had grown. In some ways, I had finally obtained my one-hundred-foot stature.

It was good to be there, without any need for The Sergeant, or any other childhood coping strategies. There was no way to adequately express the multitude of feelings I was processing, so I was quiet for long periods as well. As soon as a painful memory awakened, a healing would rush from my much better present, like a white blood cell attacking an infection. I realized that the part of my childhood spent at the El Encanto was being restored, just as the hotel had been.

I took a deep breath and suggested we stroll down the hill and pay a visit to my brother. It was then that I realized what he and I both needed – a swim in the pool.

We visited with Casey for a while and then, headed over to State Street. Locations tied to different eras in our family were everywhere, and as anyone who returns "home" after an absence experiences, my brother and I continued to look at places and shake our heads together in disbelief that it all had happened in the first place.

Santa Barbara remains a beautiful place. Unfortunately, the classism and snobbery have increased along with the home values and the population. As evidenced by a quick experience we had on our walk downtown.

We stopped for lunch at a little spot, and again, I was secretly relishing the fact that I could afford anything I wanted on the menu; more positive contrast to all the years before in Santa Barbara. While sitting at the table, my brother expressed a wish for a large-brimmed black hat, so he could block the sun, and noticed one for sale in a small boutique a few doors down from the restaurant.

I like my brother's style. He believes in spending very little on clothing, is partial to wearing all black (a self-described "Goth"), and wisely purchases most of what he wears in secondhand stores. These are admirable qualities in a person, yet, when he stepped into the small store displaying the hat he was interested in, the salesperson behind the counter did not even acknowledge his presence, let alone ask him if he had any questions. He walked back to the restaurant and said, "She pretended not to notice me; must be how I'm dressed. Why don't you go try?" He gestured at me.

I'm a bit of a fastidious dresser. I'm fond of nice clothing, I admit. It's all about the fabric for me. Today, I was wearing one of my summer ensembles. It was a bit dressy (as usual) I suppose, but to me it felt casual. This is what Casey meant. So, I got up and walked over to the small shop. When I walked in, the salesperson came immediately from behind the counter and asked if I needed any help. Ah, Santa Barbara, you have not changed a bit.

When I exited, Casey and my husband were standing outside. Casey said, "See, she wouldn't even talk to me," and made an up-and-down gesture toward my clothing. Turned out the hat was too large for him anyway.

Later on, my husband and I returned to our room at the El Encanto and decided to nap before having dinner. Upton was tired, too, from all of the walking. As I drifted off, I realized that, so far, I was being treated better by everyone I encountered so far in Santa Barbara than I ever had been before. Was it my clothes? Was it my greying beard? What was it? I was enjoying the change, while at the same time, feeling less-than-triumphant now being accepted for such shallow criteria.

We had an amazing meal down at the hotel's dining room, and I was getting used to this new story for me and the hotel. I was an honored guest – the rumor had spread around the staff about my previous residency, and a few other employees of the hotel asked for details. I told them I was going to write a book about it, and they all hoped to read it someday. Everyone was calling me "Mr. Camp," and every time I heard this, I giggled to myself. Little did they know the feral and secretive child I had once been; sneaking out of broken-down cottages, and sometimes so broke that I was going hungry. I had a slight feeling of "Imposter Syndrome," but kept working on myself so I could open up and let in the joy of this new experience in a place where I was once so troubled.

As we walked by the valets, the handsome one who had opened the car door for me earlier asked what our plans were for the rest of the evening. I mentioned we were here celebrating my upcoming birthday in June, sort of, but would probably be taking it easy tonight. He responded by asking if I would enjoy it if he came up to the room and did a birthday striptease for me. I just laughed awkwardly and didn't really respond. I couldn't tell if he was serious or not, which is an ongoing dilemma for me when others are flirting. Flattering I suppose, but I'm a monogamous married man, so I decided to stuff the exchange into my Who Knows? File.

After this long, first day in Santa Barbara, and a stroll once again past the lily pond, we at last climbed under our extravagant bedding, and we fell to sleep quickly – including Upton, curled at our feet.

Next thing I knew, I was in a very large room at an extraordinarily fancy party. There were people all around me, most in vintage dress from the '20's and '30's. The floors of the space were multilevel, furnished with the most exquisite antique furniture. There were ladies with long cigarette holders in their hands speaking with gentlemen in shiny top hats. I became concerned I was underdressed, so I glanced into a very ornate gold-framed mirror and was surprised to see the elaborate attire I was wearing; I fit right in.

A rather fabulous looking flapper-type woman approached me and told me the party was in my honor to celebrate my upcoming book; the thing that stuck out for me about her outfit were the beautiful bejeweled brogue-style shoes on her feet. And then, I was walking, and party guest after party guest approached me as I circled through the venue, each telling me how excited they were for me, and how much they supported my efforts. The flapper had her arm in mine, and whispered into my ear, "They are all former guests of the El Encanto, and they're so pleased to see you again."

It seemed like the party went on forever, as the champagne flowed well into the wee hours. I felt tired and told everyone that I just had to sit down for a moment. I found a beautiful soft, rose-colored velvet chair, with an interesting back shaped like a single angel wing. I leaned back and closed my eyes.

When I opened them again, I was back in our room, and it was morning. I actually felt as though I had been partying all night. I felt as though I had a ghost-hangover; sometimes when I dream about drinking, I will awake with that horrible feeling of over indulgence.

I texted Casey and invited him and Clara up for a swim in the pool later in the day. We sat the rest of the morning on the veranda and sipping coffee, listening to the sights and sounds of the El Encanto grounds as they awakened too, and I truly felt like a guest for the first time. Fairly eerie to be sitting almost exactly where there once stood an abandoned cottage full of mattresses.

I looked out and pondered all of the renovations undertaken over the many years, and how they had changed the energy of the place quite a bit. It felt far removed from the its past as though the modifications had inadvertently functioned as an exorcism.

Down at the pool later, we arrived just in time to have free ice cream and popcorn. The pool is large and glorious now, and yet familiar, because one still gets to stare at the amazing view, which unless looked at very closely, is very similar to what I recall from our tenure at the hotel.

Layers upon layers of deep unnamed traumas were washed away as I swam. The air was warm, the sunlight a beautiful golden hue. In keeping with my habit of telling everyone who worked there (who would listen), I provided the pool attendant with a brief synopsis of the "body in the bushes" story; he was amazed. Next, Casey and Clara appeared, and before I knew it, there was Casey and I back in the pool at the El Encanto. We just looked at each other and shook our heads in disbelief. Had it all really happened? We tried to review our co-memories as we bobbed in the water, but if felt as though we were seeing everything reflected in a funhouse mirror – it was distorted and surreal, and we worked together to help each other remember key points and extra funny parts about our stay so long ago.

The pool attendant reappeared, and I gestured to my brother and said, "This is the guy who found the body." The attendant looked at my brother and said, "You, Sir, are a legend," and he handed Casey a free cup of ice cream.

I found myself walking back to the room experiencing the nostalgic sensation of my bare feet on the warm bricks of the pathways, leading us through several areas still filled with the original craftsman bungalows. I was very excited to note that much of the original distorted glass remains in their windows, but these accommodations are very nice now, with all surrounding vegetation neat and trimmed.

Further up, there are several large, stucco buildings that house many rooms, including ours, and this area looks more like a small Spanish village rather than a hotel. I couldn't deny that it is beautiful now. So, with my classic shrug, I tipped my invisible hat to progress, and let go. I was having a fresh experience at this former home, and I metaphorically booked that feeling into one of these fresh new rooms; I hope it enjoys its stay.

The rest of our vacation at the El Encanto continued for a few more days. I explored the grounds as I had nearly fifty years before, but it wasn't the same – well, of course it wasn't. While it is now a beautiful and remarkable place, the restoration having gained the hotel's rank among the five-star establishments of the world, it has lost all of the funky and dark mystique it once had, and I would doubt anyone else would want that returned – except for me.

There is something beautiful about imperfections. There is something magical about the wretched. I felt a bit melancholy as our stay neared its end, knowing that the indescribable edge-of-disaster allure of the El Encanto was gone; the dreams of the flappers are now lost to time, and their hangovers have ended.

I'll leave you with one small item; the shower in our room wasn't working. We called the front desk, but they never fixed it. I pictured Mrs. Kinnett in a hidden chamber somewhere, still in charge, her head alive and preserved in a glass jar (backlit for dramatic effect, with many wires, tubes, fluids and pumps all around), saying, "Well they have a tub, don't they?"

While the unfixed shower irritated my husband, I took secret joy in the fact that some things never change.

Epilogue 4 — How Scott Camp Became Julien Charles Leigh Löwenfels

If you could hear the way my mother's somewhat high-pitched and often shrill (especially when excited) crow-murder voice yelling "SCAAWWWTTT!" repeatedly throughout the days and nights of my childhood, then you would likely pin this as the reason that I decided to change my name; but it wasn't just that.

Apparently, while pregnant with me, the plan all along was to name me "Julien," whereas the name "Scott" came to her during the panic of being taken to the delivery room; she suffered an existential crisis while trying to wrap her head around the spelling of the family name "Julien," which was taken from some ancestors on Grandmother's French side, namely the Jacoutót Family. Mother's painkiller-induced fear was that the other kids in school would think it was a girl's name, most people being more familiar with the "Julian" spelling. Worried that I would be picked on later when I entered the school system for this reason, she chose the name "Scott" at the last minute (while she was high,) instead, basically because we have Scottish ancestry as well.

Funny thing was that I never related to the name "Scott," and I didn't know why. As mentioned before, in my childhood, I simply hated the way it sounded coming out of my mother's mouth. Then there was the somewhat cosmic irony that changing my name didn't spare me teasing at school at all, as children are most clever in this way, and I was delightfully known as "Scotty Wotty Tissue" throughout my elementary school career; I will always wonder what they would have come up with for "Julien," a name that doesn't present any readily available demeaning rhymes.

Another curious thing was that, besides the teasing and my mother's way of saying the name, "Scott" simply did not resonate with me. I didn't have this concept of resonance in my thought processes at the time, but I knew on some visceral level that something was off; I literally cringed when anybody said the name. Also adding to the mix was another unintentional habit of mine, which was often failing to respond to the name "Scott" at all, particularly coming from teachers and other adults – they would have to call my name three, maybe four, times before I would react; this is likely why my mother was prone to repeating my name several times when she yelled for me.

Perhaps it was just all of the trauma static around the name for me but, looking back, it seems to me that something deeper was going on; it was as if my soul knew that "Scott" was not my "real" name.

As I grew older, I tried different things in an attempt to address these feelings. For a short while, when I was around twenty-three years old, I enrolled in fashion school under the name "Charles Camp," utilizing one my middle names, but quickly grew agitated at the sound of my placement counselor at the school calling me "Charles." Nope, I didn't like it. Not a problem, though, because I dropped-out of fashion school within six weeks due to what I deemed at the time to be an unsatisfactory curriculum and the fact that for many of my classes no professor ever materialized, so to speak.

By 1990, and by complete happenstance, I ended up working at the television show "America's Funniest Home Videos (AFHV)" at the ABC Studios on Prospect Ave. in Los Feliz, during a four-year stint of living in Los Angeles, a particularly terrible time for the city, which included the Rodney King verdict riots. One can still watch old reruns of AFHV from that period, when the show reached Number 1 in the nation, and see my name, "Scott Camp," roll by on the credits. As amazed and proud as my parents were at the time, I secretly bubbled inside; when I should have been excited to see my name "up in lights," instead I was feeling a sense of embarrassment; what the hell was the issue with my name? I continued to stew upon it.

After a little over a year with Vin Di Bona Productions, I fell out of favor with my employers and by 1991, I was back in the job market in Los Angeles, at a time that was essentially an economic recession due to the Gulf War. I hopped, skipped and jumped between twenty-two temp jobs that year, driving across the vast expanses of the city in my non-air conditioned 1973 Super Beetle, feeling stressed and discouraged. Over and over again, I completed applications for jobs with the name "Scott Charles Leigh Camp," feeling a sense of insecurity and unhappiness every single time I wrote down the name.

Early in 1992, my old friend Jennifer Prietto and I ran into each other on Bunker Hill while I was working at a brief temporary gig I had obtained at a law firm there, reorganizing a huge system of files. Standing in front of a high rise on a windy, downtown day, I told Jennifer of my plight of only being able to land temp jobs, and she replied that she knew somebody at a law firm just across the street, namely Richards, Watson & Gershon, LLP, and they had told her they were looking for someone to work at the message desk in the bowels of their lowest floor. I absolutely jumped at the chance to get off of the temp job unmerry-go-round, and she facilitated an interview for me.

It can be hard to explain the excitement of landing a job to anyone who hasn't had to really struggle in life, but when a job is all that is keeping life on the street at bay, one is very excited to find viable employment, so I was very happy and relieved to have won a "permanent" job. Full-time benefits and vacation pay were included, which were also a boon to me. ABC television had not offered these benefits during my time working at AFHV, and I was ordered to work many overtime powers without overtime pay; hooray for Hollywood.

Within a year at the law firm, I had worked my way up from the message desk to "Docket Clerk," a position where I was responsible for setting all court dates for the attorneys. It was a big responsibility for me at the time, I had my own desk in the file room, with two great people, India and Phillip, with whom I felt a strong comradery. We were a little family in the windowless room and with our door closed, there was a lot of joking around and sharing of vulnerabilities; we all became very close.

During one of closed-door deep chats, I told India and Phillip about how much I detested the name "Scott," and while India thought the name was a fine one, she simply stated, "Well, then I think you should change it!" We all discussed the importance of a thing like this – one's name is likely one of the words we hear the most in our lives, and if it is unhappy and painful to hear, why keep it? What a concept – I could legally change my first name and move on – but to what?

I started trying out different names in my head, but none of them seemed right. India and I agreed that the name would come to me eventually, and to just sit tight. Somehow just knowing that I was going to change it made hearing "Scott" a little less irritating.

It was during this time that my parents had moved to Ojai, so I would visit them on the weekends – Ojai was about an hour north of Los Angeles. My brother, Casey, and my sister, Andrea, also lived with my parents at the time, which was somewhat acrimonious, but again I'll say, that's another story.

It was on one of these visits that, without even knowing that a name change was on my mind, my mother suddenly piped-up and asked, "So when are you going to change your name back to your real name?" I was silent with shock for a moment; the shock that there was some other name that she thought of as my "real name," this coming from the person who gave me the accursed "Scott" name, and the other shock that somehow, she knew I had reached some sort of apex in my struggle with it. "What do you mean, my real name?" I asked. She responded my telling me about her last-minute switch during my birth, and this was the very first time I had ever heard that I was originally to be named "Julien." As soon as I heard the name, my complete system relaxed – it was a profound feeling – like a lion having a thorn pulled from its paw. I knew immediately that this had been the issue all along; "Scott" was never supposed to be my name in the first place. I made the decision right then and there to change my first name to "Julien" immediately, which was the first of a few best decisions for myself I have made, even though my family, namely my brother and sister and some peripheral friends, who I believed would be supportive, would turn out to be absolutely the opposite, thinking the change a "stupid thing to do" and refusing to use my new name.

Since I still didn't have a lot of money, changing my name through the court system wasn't possible. Doing a little research, I found an easy way that was available at that time in the country – I could simply apply for a new Social Security Card with "Julien" and legally change my name that way. So, on an oddly cold and overcast downtown L.A. day, I walked over to the Social Security Administration offices and applied for a replacement card under the name, "Julien Charles Leigh Camp." It was done.

Of course, India and Phillip were very supportive and transitioned immediately to calling me "Julien." In an effort to help the other people understand, I wrote a short story about the name change it handed it out. Outside of the law firm, there was absolutely no support.

Longtime friends would say things like, "Oh, but I still get to call you 'Scott,' right?" This is something my sister asked as well, and she passed on her disdain for my name change to her children as well, and my doing this became something of a joke within the family. I had to watch as old friend's side-giggled to one another, while they uttered the words "pretentious." Casey mentioned it to his girlfriend at the time, Ariel, and her response was "Oh, they all change their name to 'Julian'"

[Julien]," "they," meaning gay men, so not only was her response unsupportive, it was also homophobic.

The worst came from my partner at the time, Tony (same name as the front desk clerk at the El Encanto), who also thought the change was just some pretention of mine, and need to glorify myself, and he literally rolled his eyes and refused to use my new name. Many arguments ensued, and it began to tear a hole in the fabric of our connection. What he finally did in response was to begin going by the name "Anthony," to "teach me a lesson." "Tony" was his full birthname and was not a shortened version of "Anthony," so his decision to do this was literally only to passive-aggressively cause harm and an attempt to shame me.

Something interesting happened for me, though; like all truth, my name change, revealed the unhealthy dynamics that surrounded me – it became the ultimate filter, determining who really had my back, loved and supported me, and who, driven by their own insecurities, were not in my life to enrich it. I was so grateful that I had changed my name – it showed me clearly who the players were in my life, and who truly supported me; very revealing, indeed.

As I moved forward with the name "Julien," I can report that everything began to change for the better. People who were meeting me for the first time would say, "Oh, you look like a "Julien." I kept receiving these little positive nods randomly and from unrelated sources that let me know that I had done the right thing.

My parents were fully-supportive – not surprising, coming from my mother, who's big, fat idea it was in the first place. Also, my father, who instantly switched to "Julien" and never said a thing about it. For him, it was almost as if I had always been Julien, and he was very respectful. My mother, as well, was able to make the switch immediately, with hardly ever referring to me as "Scott," again.

As they years continued to roll by, I moved a bit, switched careers (and partners,) and by the time I was in San Francisco, single, and living in the city's Castro District, "Scott" was such a distant memory that I even forgot that I was ever named it. The only time I thought about it was when I first met my friend, Scott Campbell, and I secretly giggled at the coincidence, though I never mentioned it to Scott.

I found myself traveling deeper and deeper into the better pastures of the Land of Julien, and after ten years, in the early two-thousands, I found myself surrounded by a community of artistic self-proclaimed freaks and weirdos, connected to Burning Man. My partner in that era had even written a song named "Julien," which he had once used to serenade me for Valentine's Day, and it made me think of all of the wonderful blessings the name had bestowed upon me.

Back in the simmering cauldron of my Camp Family siblings, there was still remaining consternation over my name change, now approaching fifteen years on the road, and I began to really wonder what the issue was about for my siblings – why was it such a no-no for me to make this change?

Eventually, my sister caved first, and began to call me by what I considered my name: Julien. The last time she mentioned Scott, she said something unconvincingly sweet like, "… but you'll always be Scott to me." In my opinion, this is still a passive-aggressive way to show disdain and I don't have time for it.

My brother and I were estranged at that point, over something else entirely, which lasted about ten years. After our mother moved in and I began caring for her in 2006, it began to shift a bit for my brother. I had sent an email reminding him that for most of his life, he had been going by a name that was nearly a nickname for him, "Casey," as his legal birth name was "Craig." I also pointed out that our mother, born Dorothy Elise Fyfe Hopton, had chosen to go by her middle name, "Elise," because she hated the sound of her mother saying "Dorothy." In a way, I was merely keeping with a family tradition. His response to this email was simply to reply, "Geeezsh." He never mentioned it again, and began to call me Julien, with only a modicum of hesitation.

My mother lived with me, in my guest house, for the remaining thirteen years of her life, and I was her sole caregiver, with a little help from nearly daily phone calls from Casey and Clara. For the most part, the discussions were open and healthy, and we had much more important things to discuss than the changing of my name.

In the last year of Elise's life, I met my (now) husband David Löwenfels, so it's fairly easy to guess how my present last name came about. I would say briefly that during this unprecedented time in history, a time, as far as we know it, where it is at long last possible for one man to take another's name in wedlock, I feel it is important to get this fact into the historic record for posterity. I'm rarely political, but I want our family descendants to know who I was and who I loved, for all of those "colorful" uncles out there whose partners were never acknowledged, or worse, ignored during life and discarded from the family records, to disappear into obscurity. I'm proud to take my husband's last name, and for me, the decision not to adopt a hyphenated version of our two last names is even the further step I want to take to honor the love I have for this man.

So, this is how Scott Camp became Julien Löwenfels.

I often heard from the community that many families have trouble with a member who comes out as gay, or queer, or trans, or non-binary – whatever the case may be – because it feels as though the person, they thought they knew, "dies." Looking at my siblings (and unsupportive friends) through this lens, my speculation is that Scott had been a person who they felt they knew, who first came out as gay, and the person they thought they knew died metaphorically at that point. Perhaps "coming out" again by changing my first name made it feel like a double homicide of "Scott." Or, they just thought it was plain stupid for me to change my name. I don't know, and I never will, and at this age, I'm completely out of fucks to give.

I finally realized that "Julien" was actually the true name of The Bigger. What I understand now is that the adult "Julien" me was watching over the proceedings in my "Scott" childhood, sort of a self-guiding guardian angel. I think this was a result of the massive amount of therapy I embarked upon to heal myself from my childhood, including some exercises where, in nearly hypnogogic states, I have returned in my imagination to times of abuse or trauma in my childhood to "rescue" my former child self. I've imagined that Scott, the child, somehow felt this presence from the future – some sort of cosmic healing time loop – and called it "The Bigger," without realizing it was just himself, a safe adult in the future, with our true name "Julien," coming to protect him in the most important and controversial moments of our childhood. It's quite something to imagine that we all may have this power.

To this day, I'll still do this exercise during meditation, to connect past, present – and even future me's – in a three-way communication, letting each other know that I am here, The Bigger Julien, for all of us, continually working on healing, as we move forward through the rest of our life, the ultimate goal perhaps being the realization that there is no self, no older nor younger selves, nor separate times, but that we are one with the ultimate "Bigger" that is available to us all.

Milton Keynes UK
Ingram Content Group UK Ltd.
UKHW020250071024
449186UK00015B/59/J